Books by F. L

The Pathways T₁

The Fairy's
The Acadeₗ
The Princess And '₁.. ⌣.. ⌣. ⌣
The Cascade

Novels

In The Slip

Praise for The Pathways Tree Series

"The world is Neil Gaiman, jokes are Terry Pratchett, and the politics are George Orwell, all originally made and sewn together by a brilliant wordsmith and storyteller who would please any fans of such authors." Miranda Kane, comedian.

"This is a complex, often dark but still comedic world. It manages to avoid both post-modern tweeness and intellectual abstraction with its earthy characters and F.D. Lee's humour." Andrew Wallace, author.

"If you like Terry Pratchett, or the Artemis Fowl books, you'll like this." Rhonda Baxter, author.

"F D Lee has crafted a wonderful world with a very interesting and wholly loveable protagonist, whose strength of character and self effacing determination to do the right thing made this book, for me, unputdownable." Reader review.

"Lee's imagined world of fairy godmothers, trolls, gnomes, ogres, witches, elves and much more besides living out a troubled existence in an Orwellian dystopia is impressively expansive and detailed." Reader review.

"Lee's witty, satirical storytelling carries the reader with a light touch through unexpectedly dark and twisty territory." Reader review

The Academy

Cover designed by Jane Dixon-Smith
http://www.jdsmith-design.com/

ISBN-13: 978-1537767314
ISBN-10: 1537767313

About the Author

Faith is an avid reader, and lives in London with her husband and cats. The cats are engaged in a long running battle for the rights to the window sills. Faith glumly suspects it will end in tears, and she will be the one buying the kitty treats to make it all better.

Here is a picture of one of the cats. Faith is underneath.

This book is dedicated to my very own ghostbusters, whom I know I can always call, and to Esmerelda Weatherwax, who, like Bea, wouldn't have stood for it.

The Academy

The Pathways Tree, Book Two

The General
Administration

The First Department: the Contents Department

Run by the brown suits, the Contents Department is the administrative arm of the GenAm. The Contents Department deals with infrastructure, insofar as Ænathlin has anything so organised. All propaganda materials are produced by the brown suits, as well as organising communication between the various departments, maintaining order on the streets, checking Fiction Management Executives (FMEs) and other permitted fae through the Mirrors, distributing the ration tokens for those who work for the GenAm… A hundred little thankless jobs, but without which the great machinery of the GenAm would surely falter.

The Second Department: the Indexical Department

Unlike the other three Departments, the Index is kept below ground, underneath the main GenAm buildings in the centre of the city. The index is where all the completed Books are kept safe. The grey suits, as the Indexers are known, are an odd bunch, even by the seemingly generous scope of a city that includes amongst its inhabitants trolls, imps and gnomes. Indexers spend the vast majority of their lives underground, surrounded only by the Books—not a vocation for those who value the company of others.

The Third Department: the Plot Department

The blue-suited Plotters control the Plots, deciding which are run and which FMEs get to run them. As such, they enjoy an extremely high status, one matched only by the Redactionists.

Working beneath the Plotters are the FMEs themselves. The title Fiction Management Executive is a loose one, and really means anyone involved in generating belief via story telling. The highest level FMEs are the villains (usually witches) and the mentors (usually godmothers), as these are positions that always involve direct involvement with the characters.

Thus although technically a tooth fairy, for example, could claim to be an FME, it would be a brave one to try it. As a result, there have evolved two sub-groups of FME, the morals and the misks. Morals deal with shorter stories, while misks perform those little acts that bring in small amounts of belief, usually from children.

The Fourth Department: the Redaction Department

Very little is known about how the Redaction Department is run, something which the Redactionists are at pains to maintain. Or, at least, they make sure *someone* is.

What is known is that the Redactionists work in the shadows, that they employ spies and informers, and that it is the so-called 'white suits' who carry out the Redactions. Redaction is the Teller's ultimate weapon. A small white stone, known as an Eraser, is placed on the forehead and, once the stone touches skin, the mind of the fae who is being Redacted is emptied. The dead-heads, as Redacted fae are called, usually end up working in the Contents Department, little more than drones.

The Cerberus (the Beast) works, if not for, then with the Redaction Department. It is the Beast that hunts out any fae thought to be a threat to the General Administration, delivering them to the Redactionists to be dealt with as they see fit.

Prologue

Here the snow did not fall. To fall implies a lack of purpose, of agency, of will. The snow knew exactly what it wanted, and that was complete domination. Here the snow bombarded the land.

And yet, faintly visible through the microframes that existed between each kamikaze snowflake, was a light.

The building was made of thick stone, all but hidden from view by the storm and the trees. It had once been home to the grounds-keeper, but it was a home no longer. Like the frozen world outside, nothing of its original nature remained. No pictures adorned the walls, no old pieces of furniture, well-loved and long-used, cluttered the floors. Instead, it was now a space of utility, each of its rooms filled with tools and purpose.

Trapped in darkness behind a blindfold, Isabella stumbled down the staircase, the incessant pull of the chain at her wrists giving her no choice but to descend. The air shifted as she was led down. It was warmer here than in the cell, and her skin felt tacky with sweat after the cold. Her dress caught on something, holding her in place. Another sharp tug on the chain, the dress ripped, and she was on flat ground again.

Closing her eyes behind her blindfold, she concentrated: The floor was stone, cold and unforgiving, pressing against the soles of her feet. She couldn't hear the storm clearly anymore, just the faint wail of the wind, screaming in the distance. What she *could* hear was the creature standing next to her, breathing heavily, and, beneath that, the chime of glass touching glass.

Her thoughts were interrupted by a heavy shove to her shoulders. She fell forwards, instinctively placing her chained hands in front of her to break her fall. She felt leather, smooth and cool.

Large, calloused hands grabbed her and spun her around, pushing her backwards onto a chair. The creature. It lifted her arms, removing the chain from her wrists in quick, well-practised movements.

Instantly, Isabella brought the flat of her hand up, hard and fast. She ignored the pain in her wrist as her hand connected with something hard and fleshy, hopefully, the creature's nose.

A yowl of pain.

Isabella dived forward, away from the sound. She hit the floor on her knees, a sharp jolt shooting up her thighs. Scrambling to her feet, her legs stiff from days of sitting, she launched herself forward, reaching up with one hand to pull the blindfold from her eyes.

Bright light filled her vision, causing her eyes to snap shut. Tears trickled through her eyelashes and down her cheeks. She ignored them, her only thought to *get away*.

The back of her head exploded in pain as the creature grabbed her hair. Kicking and screaming, she was dragged backwards, towards the leather chair.

"Be careful! Don't hurt her!"

Suddenly thick arms encased her body, the creature's rough hands grabbing her and picking her up. Isabella kicked her legs, trying to land a blow that would force it to drop her.

Useless—wherever her feet or knees landed, they just hit against solid flesh.

It was over in seconds. She was back in the chair, her vision blurred by tears and white spots of pain. Adrenaline coursed through her veins, flooding her stomach with burning nausea. Her wrists were tied to the arms of the chair with padded straps, her chest and legs bound in the same way.

Squinting through her tears, Isabella could make out two indistinct shapes. The first she recognised as the creature, tall and wide, much bigger than any man. But the other one was smaller, a dark shape, dressed in black. A woman.

"Please, please, let me go," Isabella begged, hoping that this new woman would have more sympathy than the creature. "I have a family—a daughter. Her name's Irene, and she's five years old. Please, I can pay, we have money—"

"She's feisty," said the woman, ignoring her. She had a deep, pleasant voice, with an accent Isabella didn't know. "Replace the blindfold."

Isabella's world went dark, and she again heard glass being moved, clean and sharp, cutting through the sickness her panic and pain had caused. It was almost a friendly sound, reminding her of evenings with her husband and their friends, drinking sweet fortified wine while the children played; of somewhere far removed from this cold place she'd been brought to.

It occurred to her then, in a way it hadn't before, that she was never going to leave this room. She would never see her husband or her daughter again.

Isabella screamed, struggling against her bonds. But she was exhausted, the debt of her frantic flight demanding immediate repayment, and the straps holding her down were strong, much stronger than she was. Her screams turned to sobs, and finally to whimpers.

"See? Feisty," said woman, once she'd quieted. "This is the one, the one, the one."

There was a pause, and then a muttered conversation between the creature and woman.

Silence again, except for the sound of glass.

Cool breath brushed against Isabella's face.

"You won't believe me, but I've been waiting for you," whispered the woman. She was speaking gently, calmly, like a mother to an upset child. "Don't be afraid. You're going to help me, and in return, I'm going to take all your troubles away. All those worries about what you might have said to upset someone, all that anxiety over how you're going to pay the bills, about what your life *actually* amounts to. Who will remember you when you die... Who loves you while you're alive... All the things that keep you awake at night, spinning around in your head. Soon, they'll all be gone."

Isabella felt cold glass against her lips, and then nothing.

I

At a dusty table, in the corner of a dustier pub, a deal was struck.

The customer pulled four GenAm ration tokens out of his satchel and placed them on the wooden surface. The Raconteur eyed them greedily, already imagining all the things he could purchase.

"What d'you wanna hear? I know all the greats," he said, taking the view that the best way to keep the tokens where they belonged, i.e. in his possession, was to give the customer exactly what he wanted.

The customer leaned back in his seat, stretching his long legs out in front of him. "Tell me the one about the cabbage fairy."

The Raconteur hesitated.

Everyone who lived in the city—even the ones who actually lived under rocks—must have heard the story about the cabbage fairy by now. It was all anyone could talk about, especially here, by the wall. She was a *local* girl, after all.

But the four ration tokens being offered were the closest he'd come to payment in weeks. He managed to scrape a living telling anecdotes and yarns in exchange for old clothes, a loft to sleep in or bread and beer in one of the pubs. The truth was, selling stories out by the wall was not a lucrative prospect, but he'd always liked the romance of being a Raconteur, even if the reality was decidedly less alluring.

However, the tokens might, potentially, represent a problem. If someone was willing to lay down four tokens, well, that kind of person was obviously very serious about their stories. The kind of serious that might also get seriously angry if they didn't feel they were getting what they traded for.

Still, with four tokens, he could rent a room for a few months, try to set himself up properly. Visions danced behind his eyes... A *real* dragon's den, with his name above the door...

The Raconteur reached a decision. He also reached out and grabbed the tokens. He half expected the customer to try to stop him, but he just sat there, watching him with those mournful, brown eyes.

The Raconteur set his features and adopted the soft, dreamy lilt of the professional storysell:

"Are you sitting comfortably? Then I'll begin. Once upon a time, there was a lowly cabbage fairy who dreamed of becoming a Fiction Management Executive—and not just any kind of Fiction Management Executive, a *godmother*. But all was not well for the cabbage fairy. The General Administration, kind and benevolent in all other things, did not accept fairies to train—"

"Excuse me, but I know all that," the customer interrupted gently. "Everyone knows how this city feels about fairies, and that despite that the General Administration accepted her into the Academy to train as an FME. Half the city was at the ceremony when the Head of the Plot Department thanked the cabbage fairy for her service."

The customer's tone of voice was friendly enough, but the meaning behind his words was clear: *Tell me something I don't know.*

"Oh. Er…"

"I'm in no hurry," the customer said, smiling. "Please, take your time."

The Raconteur found himself relaxing, his body choosing to let go of the tension he'd been holding without actually bothering to get his brain involved.

There was something about the customer's smile, something the Raconteur wasn't used to seeing in the faces of the inhabitants by the wall: friendliness.

"Well, I mean… there are a few stories going 'round, but they're nothing worth four tokens. They're rumours, really," he admitted. "Gossip." Later, when the customer was nothing more than a memory, he would wonder why he'd said such a thing.

"I tell you what," the customer said. "Why don't you let me be the judge of that?"

"Ahhh, well, yeah, alright. That sounds fair. I like to be fair, you know," he found himself adding.

"I don't doubt it." There was that smile again.

The Raconteur cleared his throat and began again.

"Once upon a time—"

"You really needn't worry about all that," the customer said. "Honestly. I'd much prefer to just hear the stories as they are."

"Oh—er. Right. Yes. Well, you're the boss. So... well, one thing they're saying is that she had help from someone in the GenAm."

"Do they know who?"

"I don't think so. But it seems a bit far-fetched, doesn't it? A fairy doing all that, finishing a Rags To Riches all on her own. Between you and me, it's caused quite a stir around these parts. Shaken things up, you know?"

"Assume I know nothing."

"Well, you know what fairies are like—"

"Ahhh?"

"Sorry, yes. So, the fairies are making a fuss. Agitating, you know—ahem, that is, they reckon if a cabbage fairy can do it, why not them, too? And, of course, this is making all the other tribes unhappy. No one likes it when the doormat gets tangled under your feet."

"Ha, yes. You have a way with words."

For a moment, professional pride overcame him. The Raconteur preened. "Thanks. I've always thought so. My mum wanted me to do something else, right? Something more stable, and there's this troll down our street who runs a stonemason's, offered me a job. But I said no, coz you gotta follow your dream, haven't you?"

"I couldn't agree more—I'm something of a follower myself. What else are they saying about the cabbage fairy?"

"Well... They say that the GenAm arrested her. There were brown suits outside her building for two days, apparently. Though I don't much hold with that. Whoever heard of the GenAm letting someone off? Plus, even if they had decided not to arrest her, they'd hardly let her join the Academy, would they? But either way, it's caused a lot of chatter out here."

"I can imagine. Is there anything else?"

"Not really."

The customer stood to leave.

"I tell you what, though," the Raconteur said, "She'll be better off at that Academy than round here. Trouble's brewing."

The customer paused. "But the Mirrors are working."

"Well, yes," the Raconteur conceded. "There's some as say we're gonna be entering a Golden Age. And they might be right, of course—the Teller, *whocaresaboutus,* knows what he's doing, don't get me wrong. But things are changing, and my guess is there's gonna be a lot of shifting around, a lot of seats being swapped."

"New masters, you mean?"

"I s'pose so," the Raconteur said. *Funny choice of words,* he thought. *But tokens talk, and four tokens can talk however weirdly they like.* "Still, not much we can do about it, is there? Them up top make the choices, and we have to live with them. S'way of the world, isn't it?"

"Yes," said the customer. "Yes, it is."

A new day grumbled into wakefulness. It was not the only thing in a bad mood.

"Oi! Not so fast!" Ivor shouted.

Bea stopped in her tracks, caught red-footed trying to race across the grotty reception of the block of flats where she lived.

"Where do you think you're running off to? Just you march yourself over here, Miss."

Bea glanced longingly at the exit. It wasn't often that one thought of Ænathlin fondly. As the last surviving city of the fae, Ænathlin had much in common with the sole toilet at a campsite—everyone used it, though none but the most masochistic of souls could be said to enjoy the experience.

But sometimes the only way to escape a bad situation is to face it head-on and try to stare it out or at least make it so embarrassed it leaves of its own accord.

Bea walked over to Ivor, who was hunched over the reception desk. Two large sacks were propped up against it, which she very deliberately did not acknowledge.

"Hello, Ivor," she said, her voice sugar sweet. "I'm so glad I caught you—I was worried I wouldn't get to see you before I left for the Academy."

She was gratified when the gnome's mouth twitched in a semi-smile at the outrageousness of her lie.

Technically Ivor was the building manager, though in all the time Bea had lived there she had never actually seen him anywhere else except swaddled up in his oversized woollen coat, sitting behind the reception desk playing solitary games to pass the time.

No, she corrected, *that isn't fair.*

Sometimes he sits in the back office, drinking.

Still, despite Ivor's lacklustre approach to his job, Bea liked him. After all, he had taken her in when no one else would: a cabbage fairy from the Sheltering Forest with nothing to her name except a dream of becoming a Fiction Management Executive, and a godmother at that, hadn't been a bet any of the other landlords had been willing to take. For whatever reason Ivor had, and Bea was grateful.

That didn't change the fact, however, that sometimes they did not see eye to eye.

Bea pulled herself up onto one of the stools that fringed the desk, turning slightly so she couldn't see the two sacks. Ivor had a deck of cards strewn out on the rough desktop. She smiled, recognising the deck. Idly she picked up one of the cards, turning it over.

"What're you playing?" she asked.

Ivor's bony hand snatched the card. "Never mind that, what'cha gonna do about all this? More of 'em arrived this morning."

Bea admitted defeat and finally looked at the sacks of letters. "I can't believe they're still arriving. You'd think no one had anything better to do," she said, trying and failing to defuse the situation.

Ivor snorted. "It's me that's got better things to do. S'not up to me to clean up after you."

"I thought collecting our post was one of your jobs?"

"Don't go getting smart with me, fairy. It don't suit you."

Bea grinned at him, stood up from her chair and walked over to the sacks, reaching her hand in to pull out a large package.

"I wouldn't open that one," Ivor said.

"Why not?"

It was Ivor's turn to smile. "It's squidgy."

The Academy

Bea dropped it. "You can't be...? That's disgusting." Now she thought about it, she could detect a certain 'midden-esque' smell in the air.

"Hah," the gnome laughed, showing off his brown and black teeth. "That's just the voice of the people, that is. Well, I say voice..."

Bea stepped away from the sack. "Mortal gods. This is ridiculous. You'd think I'd murdered a character, not completed a Plot."

Ivor rolled his eyes. "Come off it. Years you've been living here, banging on about how much everyone hates you fairies. You can't pretend you're surprised this is the reaction you're getting. You've broken in, ain't ya? No one likes a burglar."

"It's not my fault I'm a fairy," she muttered. Other things *were* her fault, she knew. But not that, at least.

"All I'm sayin' is, you wanted to get yourself noticed, and now you have. Take these letters. Some of 'em will be full of hugs and kisses, no doubt. Some of 'em ain't. That's what being noticed means. Take it from me, nothing ever ends, happily or otherwise."

Bea sighed. "You're right."

"Too right I'm right," Ivor agreed, looking smug. "You wanna play a game?" he added, changing topic with the speed of a weathercock in a hurricane.

"I can't right now," Bea said, feeling a pang of unexpected regret. "I'm on my way to see my friends."

Ivor shrugged. "Suit yourself. Don't forget to take that package with you—don't see why I should have to put up with the stink, thank you very much."

Bea managed a weak smile and grabbed the soft package between pinched fingers. Success definitely wasn't what she'd hoped it would be.

13

II

"Wasn't it *wonderful?*" Joan sighed, her eyes glazed.

Joan was a house fairy, small and slight boned, and a little beer went a long way. And she had consumed more than a little beer. As a result, she was now having trouble focusing.

Or rather, Joan was having trouble focusing her eyes; her conversation, on the other hand, had remained determinedly fixed on the Royal Wedding they had attended a few days ago, the grand finale to the Plot Bea had completed.

Melly, a red-haired elf, raised an eyebrow. "Wonderful. All that pomp and ceremony? Who wouldn't enjoy it?"

"Oh, shut up," Joan grinned. "I saw you having fun, you know. Bea saw you too, didn't you, Bea?"

Bea held her hands up, narrowly avoiding knocking over her glass of wine. This took a lot more skill than might initially be apparent. Their table, situated in a corner of the type of pub that would consider spit and sawdust to be showing off, looked like a battle was being fought between two opposing armies.

It was obvious already who the victors would be.

The empty glasses had taken control of the field, their troops amassing in greater numbers around the perimeter, while the full drinks were fighting a losing stand from the centre. With all the inevitability of war, it was clear they would soon be joining their fallen comrades, only to be replaced by younger troops.

"Don't get me involved," Bea said. "It's my last night before leaving for the Academy, I don't want to spend it sitting in judgment over whether Melly had fun or not." She took a sip of her drink. "Although you clearly did."

The elf glared at her, but Bea knew Melly well enough to know she was trying to mask a smile.

"I might have enjoyed it. In parts," Melly admitted.

"Esh'pesh'ly that part where you were dancing on the table," Joan said.

"I think everyone enjoyed *that* part," Bea added.

"Well," Melly said, "I wanted to blend in. It was a wedding."

Joan stifled a burp. "I know what we should talk about. S'more important than Melly dancin' on tables."

Melly feigned puzzlement. "What's more important than me dancing?"

"Bea," Joan said, waving her hand enthusiastically at Bea, "Is wearing a new dress. And, I reckon, because it's still in one piece, it's one she had made. I'm right, aren't I? Bea? Bea? Bea? Or should I say, Miss Godmother!"

Bea fiddled with the sleeves of her grey dress, silently cursing the fact that when you owned so little, everything new was noticeable.

"I thought I needed a change. A fresh start, a new me, that kind of thing. I was thinking I might even let the grey dye grow out of my hair—you know, get back to my roots. Ahaha. And there's this meet-and-greet thingy tomorrow morning before we leave for the Academy. I want to make a good impression. Make friends. Influence people." Bea coughed, aware she was babbling.

Melly stared at her. And then she shook her head, obviously deciding that now wasn't the right time to say what was on her mind. Instead, she reached into her sleeve and pulled out a slim onyx case. She opened it up and extracted a thin, black cigarette, which she lit and drew on deeply.

Bea felt the whole activity was done with very pointed and over-the-top exactitude, but she didn't say anything, either.

"It's amazing, really," Joan said, the beer apparently making her oblivious to the sudden atmosphere between Melly and Bea. Or possibly she was choosing to ignore it. Growing up in a large family, Joan was used to what she called 'friendly disagreements'. "You're goin' to the Academy! All your dreams comin' true—the firs' fairy ever accepted to train! I never thought I'd see the day when the GenAm recognoged, no, no, I mean, recognished a fairy."

"Yup, that's me," Bea said, pasting a smile onto her face. "Cabbage fairy made good. Well almost, anyway. I'm not actually a Fiction Management Executive yet. For some reason, I have to *finish* the training before I can call myself that."

15

Joan's eyes were beginning to cross. "You'll finish," she said, "And then you'll become the best godmother ever, and then, then, after that, you'll be a Plotter too, and then Narrator."

"Woah, woah," Bea laughed, aware Melly's eyes were still on her. "I just want to keep my head down and get through training. I'm not going to cause any trouble. Not like last time." She wondered if she'd said that for Melly's benefit or her own.

"No, no, no," Joan said, shaking her head vigorously. "That's not right at all. I know you'll do something amazing, Bea. You will. You're gonna fall in a mystery or, or, or solve a love. You're gonna do a'nother Rags To Riches or one of the Hero Quests. You're not gonna sit around like some sitting around fairy. You're stubborn. You're nosy. You're—"

And with that Joan's head hit the table, the beer suddenly getting the better of her.

Bea reached across to check on her friend. "It always surprises me how quickly she goes when she goes. There's never any warning."

Melly drained her glass of red. "I don't think she gets any warning either. Let's get her home. And then you and I need to have a talk."

III

"G'night," Bea said as she handed Joan over to one of her numerous sisters. She turned to Melly, who was waiting in the street.

"So then. Do you want to come back to mine?"

Melly nodded. "We can't talk out here."

They made their way towards Bea's. For several years the GenAm had maintained a strict curfew, monitoring the streets, pulling in troublemakers and rabble-rousers, and generally making sure everyone knew exactly where they stood, i.e., under the boot of the GenAm.

The system had been legitimised by the fact the Mirrors were breaking. But now they were up and running, the curfew had been relaxed. As a result, the streets were not only full but were full of fae who for once felt able to let their hair down and their spirits up. It was a miracle no one had died.

Yet.

As if to illustrate the point, Bea was forced to sidestep the slumped body of a dwarf who was hopefully only passed out. You could never tell in Ænathlin, and even by its own low standards, the city's outer ring was considered a slum. It was also where both Joan and Bea lived. Fairies never made it into the wealthier centre.

"So you leave tomorrow?" Melly asked.

Bea nodded.

"Do you know—" A small body slammed into Melly, interrupting her. "What—?"

Bea knelt down, bringing herself eye level with what turned out to be a young flower fairy. His pink and blue hair was falling across his face, black blood was running from a cut above his eye, and one of his wings had been torn, explaining why he had been running in the first place.

Bea was horrified. In general, she found flower fairies extremely annoying; because they were colourful and had wings, the humans tended to believe in them longer than they did house or garden fairies. As a result, flower fairies managed to eke out a little more respect from the rest of the fae tribes, a fact they lauded over the other two fairy clans.

But, as much as Bea might dislike them, that didn't mean she wanted to see a child in such a state.

"What happened to you?" she asked.

"Sod off," the fairy spat.

Just then, a group of young imps, adhenes and elves burst around the corner, some carrying clubs. If Bea had been on her own, she was certain they would have attacked both her and the little flower fairy. But she had Melly with her—and Melly was not just a fully-grown elf; she was also a fully trained witch.

Unsurprisingly, the gang skidded to a halt when they saw Melly, straight-backed and regal, dressed all in black, her cigarette burning red hot in sharp contrast to the very cold look on her face.

"What exactly is going on?" Melly demanded, stalking over to the group.

A few of the more sensible ones at the back turned and ran, but those at the front weren't so lucky. Bea watched as Melly began to have a very quiet, very serious word with them, noticing the way the smallest one's trousers darkened. She wondered what Melly was saying to elicit such a response and then decided she was probably better off not knowing.

"What about you?" she said, turning her attention to the flower fairy wriggling in her grip. "What happened?"

"None of your business."

"I just want to know you're alright."

The little fairy laughed. "Alright? After what that cabbage fairy did?"

"What do you mean?"

"I told you, sod off. You ain't a brown suit, lemme go."

"Why are you worried I'm a brown suit?"

The flower fairy glared at Bea. "It's all that cabbage fairy's fault. I ain't done nothing. But they all reckon us fairies are up to something. Think we're too big for our boots. I was just filching. No laws against filching, not small stuff anyway."

Technically, of course, this was a lie. The GenAm took theft of any kind very seriously. But Bea refrained from making this point. "So why were they chasing you?"

"Like I said, they reckon us fairies got grand ideas now. They reckon we're coming after them, looking for higher stakes. Now everyone hates us even more coz of some stupid cabbage fairy, showing off."

The flower fairy squinted at Bea, eyeing her messy bun, her soft, heavy figure and her height, which was about two heads taller than the average flower or house fairy. "Here, you're a cabbage fairy, ain't you?"

Bea opened her mouth to reply when Melly called out.

"Bea!"

She turned her attention away from the flower fairy to see what her friend wanted, and a second later was yowling in pain. The flower fairy ran off up the street, into the darkness.

"He bit me! The little—"

"You shouldn't have had your hand where he could," Melly said reasonably, coming back to join her. "You know what the kids are like round here. They might as well have been raised by orcs."

Bea rubbed her wrist, grateful the skin hadn't broken. "Yes, but still... What did that lot have to say for themselves?"

Melly dropped her cigarette, putting it out with the heel of her boot. "Not much."

"Melly, what did they say?"

"Nothing. Let's go."

Bea folded her arms. "I know it was because of me."

"Bea, kids fight, it's what they do."

"Melly."

"It was probably just a gang thing."

"A gang? There was only one of him. Anyway, flower fairies don't join gangs. They're too busy prancing around in the stems, looking pretty for the humans. Just tell me the truth."

"Mortal gods," Melly sighed. "Yes. It was because of you. Is that what you want to hear?"

"No. But I don't want you to try to hide it from me either."

Melly pursed her lips, but after a moment, she nodded. "I didn't think you knew."

"I've been getting post," Bea said as they resumed their journey back to her building.

"Post?"

Bea bit her fingernail, unsure how much she should say. But the truth was she wanted to tell someone—and, *strictly* speaking, this wasn't covered by the conditions of her promise to the GenAm to behave herself.

The fact that it was logic like this that had got her into so much trouble in the past didn't occur to her. Sometimes life has to hammer its lessons home.

"A lot of them are pretty strange," Bea said. "And by strange, I mean totally off-the-wall crazy."

Melly didn't respond.

"Half of them are barely written in sentences, and you don't want to know what they say about my mum. I haven't even seen my mum in years. But I suppose it's easy to be horrible when you're anonymous. They say I don't deserve to be at the Academy, that I'm going to weaken the Plots or make the Mirrors break again."

She waited for Melly to answer.

"I mean, what else do I have to do to show them that a fairy is just as good as any of the other tribes?" Bea continued when it became clear Melly was missing her cues. "My Plot is the whole reason the Mirrors are working again. Don't get me wrong, I know it isn't exactly as simple as that. You were there, you saw what happened at the Ball with the ogre and the witchlein attack. But that's even more reason to see it through, isn't it? Otherwise, what was it all for?"

Again, the elf failed to take her prompt.

"It's not all bad though," Bea said. "Some of the letters, not many, but some of them are from fae who are pleased I've been accepted. Fairies, mostly."

"I see," Melly said at last. "Like Joan."

Bea stopped in her tracks. "What?"

"You didn't notice it tonight?" Melly said, stopping too.

Bea shook her head.

"Oh? Really? Well. She's always been a little awe-struck by you, even before you were accepted into the Academy."

"That's not true," Bea said.

"Yes, it is. You know it is."

That was the trouble with elves—well, one of the troubles with elves, anyway. They were beautiful. It was one of the reasons they commanded such high status: the stories worked better when beauty was involved.

But even ignoring her perfect features and long, red hair, Melly had a way of carrying herself that seemed to demand your attention. It was probably the thin, antlered crown she wore, its base decorated with mother-of-pearl. Either way, Melly didn't exactly make it easy to ignore her.

Right now, Bea really wished that wasn't the case.

They arrived at Bea's miserable block of flats. Melly waited while Bea unlocked the front door, her nose wrinkling at a particularly organic smell coming from the open gutter that ran the length of the street. Bea led the witch quietly through the reception and up the narrow staircase to her floor.

"Bea, I didn't come here to talk about the fairies," Melly said once they were safely inside her flat. "What do you think is going to happen at the Academy?"

"Lessons? Tests? Friendships that will last a lifetime?"

Melly received this answer with exactly the amount of humour Bea had imagined she would.

"I'm serious, Bea. Why did you even accept the place?"

Bea chewed her fingernail. She wasn't surprised by the question. The trouble was, she still wasn't sure what answer she could give. "It's what I've always wanted," she settled on. "And you can't say I didn't work for it."

"Yes, I appreciate that. But surely the GenAm must know having a fairy train to be an FME would attract attention. I don't understand why they agreed to it—and to have made such a public spectacle of it, too. It goes against everything they've ever done."

"Maybe the GenAm just wanted to keep its promise to me," Bea said hopefully. "I kept my end of the bargain, after all."

"Did you?"

"What do you want me to say? That the whole thing was a disaster from beginning to end? That I should have listened to you? That I was stupid and selfish and as a result people got hurt?"

"None of that was your fault—"

"How can it not be my fault? It happened on my Plot. The Redaction Department sent an ogre and a load of witchlein to attack the Ball and people died—*you* nearly died. My hero was maimed and will never walk again."

"But you saved me, and you stopped the ogre. You can't punish yourself for what happened. You didn't know how it was going to end."

"No. But now I have to do something to make it right, and joining the Academy is my best option. Once I'm a godmother, I'll have some clout. I can make changes—official changes. I'll make sure no one gets hurt again, fae or human."

The two friends fell silent. Bea and Melly had never seen things the same way, not when it came to the GenAm, but both of them knew that hurting characters was wrong, even if they did reach the same conclusion via different routes.

Melly lit another cigarette, inhaled, coughed, and inhaled again.

"Bea, I'm not trying to say you'll be a bad godmother, or that what happened to those people was your fault. But you must see that everything about the Plot they gave you was rotten from the very beginning. Everything that could possibly have gone wrong with it did: you had an Anti-Narrativist genie trying to disrupt your Plot, a heroine who didn't want to marry the hero, and then the Redaction Department attacked your final act—in front of the characters."

"I know that, but—"

"*And* now the GenAm is acting like it was all part of their plan. And the thing is, I can't help worrying that it was. None of it makes sense. Why would they accept you into the Academy, after all that?"

Bea went back to chewing her nails. She could feel Melly watching her, the elf's anxiety as thick and pungent as the smoke from her cigarette. She'd hoped to avoid this conversation, a hope she now realised was naïve in the extreme.

For a moment, she considered lying, but she threw the idea away. Melly had been there, she knew what had happened. And with a stab of guilt, Bea realised she wanted to tell her, even if meant dragging Melly further into her mess.

"My Plotter, Mistasinon, knows I changed my Plot," Bea admitted. "He told me to join the Academy to prove my loyalty, to keep the Redaction Department from looking too closely at me."

Melly dropped her cigarette, horrified.

Changing the Plots wasn't simply a crime; it was an abuse of every single fae living in Ænathlin. The sanctity of the Plots ran deep, something the GenAm were at constant pains to maintain. Changing the Plots put the Mirrors at risk, and without the Mirrors, the city would starve... or, more likely, devour itself.

Of course, at the time Bea hadn't exactly meant to change her Plot... Well, she had, in a way... It was confusing. She'd known what she was doing was wrong, but she hadn't done it with the intention of harming anyone, nor of derailing her story. She'd wanted to make it *better*, and then she'd wanted to help her heroine out of the mess she'd got her into.

But the chances of her being able to convince the Redaction Department of that, should they ever find out, were somewhere around the same as her chances of replacing the Teller as the next Narrator of the city, whatever Joan might think.

"Mortal gods, Bea," Melly exclaimed, snatching the cigarette up before it burned the floor. "How did he find out?"

"He knew from the beginning I was making changes, but he didn't care. He just wanted the Plot finished."

Bea waited while Melly absorbed this new information.

"But he hasn't reported you?" the elf finally asked.

"No."

"Why not?"

Bea looked at the wall. "I don't know."

"You must have some idea. He's a suit—he works for them. He can hardly turn a blind eye when he finds out someone has committed a Redactionable offence. Hells, it's a Redactionable offence to hide a Redactionable offence. He couldn't possibly hope to get away with it if he were caught."

"I didn't ask him about that," Bea answered. It was true—when Mistasinon had offered her the deal to join the Academy or explain herself to the Redaction Department, she really hadn't bothered asking whether his own safety was in question.

23

"Bea, none of this makes any sense. None of it. And you're really going to join the Academy?"

"What else can I do? Even if I did want to back out, everyone knows now I've been accepted. I'm going, and that's an end to it."

Bea waited for the eruption, but it never came.

Melly took a long drag on her cigarette. The smoke curled and twisted in the air, drifting slowly up to the ceiling.

Eventually, she asked, "How's your leg?"

"It's alright," Bea replied after a pause. In one of those strange twists of communication, the silence between them was speaking volumes. "The scars ache when it's cold."

"Let me see."

Bea lifted her skirt, not entirely sure if the change in conversation meant she'd convinced her friend. She had the feeling that, rather than seeing her point, Melly had simply decided to put an end to the argument.

Melly stubbed out her cigarette and inspected Bea's right leg, which was covered in pink scars, two lines of little slashes about two centimetres long. They ran from her ankle to mid-way up her thigh in an alternating pattern, not unlike footprints. Which, in a way, they were.

"They've healed well," Melly said once she'd finished checking them over. "Luckily for you, witchlein have sharp scales and they're clean—you could have lost the leg if it had got infected. You'll always have the scars though."

Bea pulled her skirt down. "Thanks."

"You'd better be careful while you're at the Academy," Melly said. "You don't want anyone asking how you got them."

"Mortal gods... I hadn't thought of that. I can hardly say I was attacked by a horde of witchlein and an ogre, all sent by the Redaction Department to capture a genie... No one would believe me." Bea paused. "Or worse, they would," she said, trying to lighten the mood.

"Wear long dresses or trousers, you should be alright. And they'll fade eventually. Just keep out of trouble from now on."

Bea stuck her tongue out at Melly. "You don't need to sound like that's such an impossibility."

"You do remember that I've actually met you, don't you?" Melly said with a slight twitch to the corner of her mouth that could have been a smile. "Bea, I'm going to give you some advice. Experience tells me you won't listen, but I'm going to do it, anyway."

Bea couldn't help smiling. "Alright."

"Here it is: I'm older than you—"

"I know that."

"I'm older than you," Melly repeated, giving Bea a look. "I've had to learn a lot of things the hard way, and I'd prefer it if you didn't. Whatever it is that happened at the Ball, whatever it is that made the Redaction Department attack all those characters— sometimes you have to accept things you don't like for the greater good."

"People died. How can that ever be justified?"

"I don't mean it's just. But it may have been *necessary*."

"I don't believe that."

"But can't you try?" Melly asked Bea, a hint of desperation slipping into her voice.

Bea grasped Melly's hands, trying to make her understand. "Why should I? If I become a proper FME, I can do something about it. Not like last time—not changing the Plots or getting involved with genies or anything like that, I promise. But I really could help the fairies and the humans. And after everything that happened, I think I have a responsibility to at least try."

Melly squeezed Bea's hands. "I can see you've made up your mind," she said sadly.

In that moment, it seemed to Bea that the elf had known all along how their conversation was going to end, but she'd had to go through it, anyway.

"I'd better go," Melly said, getting to her feet. "You've got a big day tomorrow."

Bea walked her down the hallway to the grey mould manufactory that served as the floor's shared bathroom.

Melly stepped into the bathroom, facing the little mirror above the sink, her reflection hidden behind black spots on the glass. It didn't matter, Melly wasn't using the mirror to check her face. She ran her hand over the mirror's surface, causing the solid glass to ripple. A moment later, it went completely black, taking on the viscous texture that indicated it had connected to a Mirror and was now a portal to another place.

And sure enough, the image in the glass was no longer Melly's face but a landing decorated with pretty flowered wallpaper and a white staircase running down to a small hallway. There was an occasional table at the bottom of the stairs, with a china statue of a sleeping dog on it.

Melly had made the connection to the Mirror in her cottage, which was beyond the city wall, in the Sheltering Forest.

Bea had no idea how Melly had come to own a magic Mirror— the official line from the GenAm was that all the Mirrors were housed in the Grand Reflection Station or, since they had started to break, in the Index. There were rumours that the high-ups in the GenAm had their own Mirrors, but that had never been officially confirmed.

Melly hadn't offered an explanation for her Mirror and Bea, having her own secrets, had decided not to press the matter.

"I've got something for you," the elf said. She rummaged in her sleeve and pulled out a thin silver chain with a heavy, steel triangle hanging from it via a hole in the base so that the point hung downwards. "It's the point of the sword you used to kill the ogre. I asked Ana to have the blacksmith make it for you."

Her throat catching, Bea took the necklace. The sword tip was maybe two inches wide across the base, the two legs a little shorter, tapering to the point. The chain was new, the silver polished to a shine, but the sword tip itself was notched, its engraving all but worn away with use.

"I don't know what to say…"

Melly shook her head, all business. "Don't say anything. Just promise me you'll be careful. Sometimes the only way to win is to surrender."

She turned back to the mirror, and then she was gone. The glass slowly returned to normal, as if she'd never been there.

Bea closed the bathroom door and stood alone in the hallway, looking at the necklace laying across her palm.

"But nobody wins when you surrender," she whispered to herself.

IV

Many things in life turn.

A page of a book. A phrase. A blind eye. And, of course, people. And some, for reasons both complex and arbitrary, turn bad.

Julia looked up from her desk at the knocking at her door. She was annoyed at the interruption, even though she knew it would be something important. No one knocked on her door unless they absolutely had to.

"Come."

She closed the files she was working on with a quick movement of her pale green hand. Everything Julia did was precise, like a knife in the hands of a professional. And in truth, if you watched her long enough, you'd find yourself looking for the sharp edges.

But in the case of this visitor, Julia's natural proclivities were blunted, at least a little.

The goblin entered the room like a puppet on fraying strings, her large, saucer-shaped eyes—so good for seeing in the dark, but now eerily empty—blinking slowly in the glow from the oil lamps.

Not that she would complain. Julia wondered if she even knew her eyes were stinging her, or if that awareness had been taken away as well, along with the goblin's memories, her personality, her *her*.

Such is the nature of Redaction.

The GenAm didn't execute, not anymore. They Redacted, erasing everything that made a person a person. It was a much better system: kill a dissenting voice and all you'd have was a dead body. But Redaction served a double purpose, offering both a walking, talking reminder of what could happen to you if you answered back *and* providing free, loyal labour.

For most of the fae, the Redacted 'dead-heads' were unbearable, a reminder of the power the General Administration had over them. Julia, however, enjoyed seeing them out and about. They gave her an enormous sense of job satisfaction.

27

"my lady i have returned from the inspection" intoned the goblin in the flat, disjointed way the dead-heads spoke. Her eyes were beginning to weep in the light.

"It was a success?"

"west is pleased my lady but there are still some problems with the process"

Julia's mouth formed a thin line, though not, it must be said, one as thin as her patience. "In what way? She resolved the issues she had with the first ETP."

"yes my lady this is a new problem it does not last long enough but west believes she knows where the error is and has begun a trial using the new formula she will have the latest etp tested tomorrow so that she might see if this one fails"

"Very good. And West? Is she stable?"

"we have delivered some more medicine to her and she is grateful the troll barret looks after her he is concerned about the arrival of the recruits"

"Did he say this to you?"

"no my lady but you instructed me to watch him i saw that he checks the rooms and the locks and he orders the brown suits to be wary and then he checks again and orders again and this is behaviour that is born of anxiety"

"Yes. It is."

Julia stared at the goblin, watching with vague interest the way her round eyes were turning bloodshot. Anxiety was useful if it was channelled in the right way. Left undirected, it might lead to recklessness. But she'd chosen Barret, and she had no reason to doubt her choice.

It was, after all, hers.

"he would have me ask you a question"

"Speak."

"he asks my lady if the rumours are true about the cabbage fairy he feels this may cause difficulties if so"

Julia wondered how he'd heard about the fairy. One of the brown suits probably, bringing gossip with them from the city. She didn't like loose talk—or, more precisely, she didn't like loose talk when it was detrimental to her own efforts. Under her command, the

28

Redaction Department had done very well out of paying informers for information.

But she'd known there would be risks when she'd made her bargain with West. Risks, yes. But, potentially, rewards. The greatest reward any member of the fae could ever hope for. And, as the saying went, you can't change minds without cracking a few heads. Or something like that, anyway.

"You may tell him the rumours are true, but that he need not worry about Buttercup Snowblossom. She's an indulgence. A token of friendship." She smiled. "Give a dog a bone."

"i will deliver this reply"

"No, no." Julia sighed. That was the only problem with the Redacted. No sense of humour. "Tell Barret not to concern himself with the cabbage fairy. His task is to focus on helping West achieve success with the ETPs."

"yes my lady"

Julia waved the goblin away and returned to her work.

She had a city to save, after all.

F. D. Lee

V

Joan had a headache. Every time, *every bloody time*, she scolded herself while she waited in line. Bea was three times the size of Joan and could handle her drink much better than she could. And Melly was old and sensible enough to know when to stop. But it didn't seem to matter how much Joan told herself she wouldn't overindulge, she always seemed to.

No matter how good her intentions were at the beginning of the night, she somehow managed to convince herself to stay for one more, and then to have another to keep it company, and then a third because, for the fae, three was an important number. And then, somewhere around the fifth or sixth drink, the voice inside her head that suggested caution would end up curled in the metaphorical corner of her mind, blackout drunk, usually with Joan not too far behind it.

She knew she should pay more attention to her limits when it came to beer, but she had fun when she was out with Bea and Melly.

Melly might sometimes be too stern and serious, but underneath it, she was also kind and funny. And Bea was as bloody-minded as they came, but she would fight for her friends and knew the difference between right and wrong or, if came to it, easy and difficult. Plus, it was interesting listening to Bea talk about her Plot-watches and, Joan was happy to admit, a little bit thrilling to hear her so openly complain about the GenAm and the fairy-haters.

Joan had grown up in Ænathlin, and as a result, the general hatred of the fairies was so ingrained into the fabric of her life that most of the time it wasn't even worth paying attention to, like learning to live with a thorn stuck permanently in one's heel. Of course it was unpleasant, but concentrating on it made it worse, not better.

But Bea out and out refused to be included in the narrative that said fairies were useless, that fairies were responsible for the King and Queen, that the characters always stopped believing in fairies, that fairies did nothing to help the city or the Mirrors. And Joan, who had put aside her own dreams a long time before she met Bea, enjoyed listening to her talking about how she was going to become an FME and show them all what a fairy could do.

Joan smiled—a brave move considering the top of her head felt like it was being sawn off.

Bea had actually *done it*, as well. Not only had she been accepted into the Academy, but she was training to be a godmother. Godmothering was direct involvement with characters—it was real storytelling, working at the sharp end of the pencil. There was no way anyone could say fairies were useless, not if one of their tribe was a godmother.

The line moved forward, shaking Joan out of her thoughts.

She usually visited the Library of Faces once a week or so, and this morning had seemed as good a time as any; better, even, with a hangover.

The Library of Faces was cool and dark and had a working fountain in the centre of the main auditorium. Fresh, clean water was rare in Ænathlin, the Sheltering Forest taking up most of what remained underground, so the majority of the fae drank weak beer or boiled water. But it was traditional to wash the little tiles that represented your family members, and no one minded if, while you were doing your duty, you happened to steal a cup or two of freshwater for yourself.

Joan scuffed her heavy boots against the cobbles, trying to distract herself from her headache as she waited to get into the Library of Faces. If she'd known it was going to be so busy today, she wouldn't have come. She debated giving up and going home, but she was very nearly at the entrance. And anyway, she wanted to see her mum.

Once inside, Joan understood why it was so busy. Whole families of fae were visiting their dead, bringing with them gifts and offerings—no doubt partly out of guilt for not coming more regularly, and partly because the Mirrors were open again and trade from Thaiana was flowing.

She wandered, not needing to pay attention to her steps, through the auditorium with the huge fountain at its centre and carved friezes on the walls, taking the sixth memory lane from the entrance. Each section was divided by tribe and then again by clan, and finally by family. She passed by hundreds of little recesses carved into the stone walls like honeycomb until she reached the hole with the name 'ó Cuilinn' carved above it.

Joan reached in and gently removed the small, white tile that was all that remained of her mother.

The tile was carved from a piece of her bone. It had been taken before the body was burned, and carefully shaped and sanded down until it shone with a pearlescent beauty that enhanced, rather than mocked, its origins. Onto the tile had been carved a holly leaf, the symbol of Joan's clan, and Joan's mother's name, Margaret.

Joan slid down the wall, grateful for the cool stone against her skin, and started to tell her mum all about Bea and her Plot, and the Mirrors, and the resulting changes to the city.

❄

Bea looked surprised to find Joan waiting for her outside her apartment block, and said as much.

"Ah well, I thought it'd be nice for you to have someone to walk with," Joan said with a smile. She winced. "And, to be honest, I was hoping you might have some of that hangover plant…?"

Bea rummaged in her bag and pulled out some milk thistle. "Here you go."

"Thanks," Joan said, relieved.

They started to make their way through the narrow streets, keeping to the edges as much as possible to avoid the crowds. Neither felt in the mood to deal with a confrontation for banging into the wrong person.

They chatted about nothing, passing the street sellers and hawkers while the early morning shopkeepers removed their shutters. By the wall, glass was a luxury, and so most of the stores boarded up their fronts when closed and removed the boards during opening times.

A pixie was currently in the middle of opening his shop. Or rather, he should have been. Instead, he was huffing and puffing to

32

an increasingly large audience. The boards were resting against the shop wall, and one was attracting a lot of attention.

"What's going on?" Bea wondered aloud as they drew nearer.

"Probably he had his shop robbed," Joan suggested. Burglary and robbery weren't uncommon, especially near the wall. The GenAm took a hard line on such things, understandably given the erratic reliability of the Mirrors and the subsequent problems importing goods stolen from Thaiana. But as fearsome as the GenAm were, starvation has a way of changing the boundaries on what qualifies as a 'worthwhile risk'.

"C'mon," Bea said. "Let's see what's going on."

Joan hesitated. "I think we should probably keep moving." She wasn't by nature an anxious person, but she was more in tune with the rhythms of the city than Bea, who'd been born and raised in the Sheltering Forest. And right now, Joan was pretty certain she was hearing the beat of a death march.

"What? No," Bea said, stepping towards the crowd. "I want to see what's happening."

"I'm not sure—" Joan began, but she recognised the look on Bea's face. She took off her cape and shoved it into Bea's arms. "Alright, stay here. I'll go look."

Bea started to protest, but Joan was too quick. The little house fairy darted around the crowd and down a narrow alleyway between the buildings. A moment later, she appeared on the roof of the neighbouring building, moving quickly and quietly above the circle of fae standing outside the shop.

No one noticed her. Even with a hangover, Joan was an experienced tooth fairy, and she was good at her job. There had been times when she'd had to sneak into castles swarming with characters or into hovels with the child snuggled up in the same bed as their siblings or parents. There were even times when she had crept into prisons or slave pits. Climbing a wall and darting across the roof of one building, jumping the narrow gap and landing silently on the roof of the other was, frankly, easy.

Joan perched on the edge of the shop roof, expertly balanced, and listened. After a few minutes, she retreated from the eaves and retraced her journey across the roof, jumping to the other building and then nimbly down into the shadows of the alleyway. She reappeared and darted over to where Bea was standing.

"What's happening?" Bea asked.

"Let's move," Joan said, grabbing Bea's arm and dragging her away from the scene. When they were a few blocks away, Joan slowed down.

"What on Thaiana happened? What did you hear?" Bea asked.

"I don't know… it shouldn't have mattered… but the things they were saying…"

"Joan, you're scaring me."

Joan clapped her hands together, trying to organise her thoughts. "The shop was vandalised last night. Someone wrote something on the shutters."

"So? That kind of thing happens all time."

"Ah well, yes, that's true."

"But…?"

"I don't know… They were really upset. I mean, *really* upset. Someone had written 'F.U.' on the boards."

"F.U.? What does that mean?"

"I don't know. They were saying it's the fairies, and that something's going to have to be done about us."

"Listen, it'll blow over," Bea said. She sounded exactly like someone trying very hard not to sound like they were worried. "It's just because I've been accepted into the Academy."

"But that's not fair," Joan said. "You did an amazing thing. They shouldn't be so angry… it doesn't… it's just not *right*."

Bea offered her a smile. "Cheer up. A fairy *is* still going to the Academy. Things are changing. It just takes time, that's all."

"But how can you accept that?"

"Well… Because I think there's a lot happening at the moment. You know, the Mirrors and the Anties and so on. It's a lot of change. And I—" Bea stopped and then started again. "Look, you're right. I don't like it. I've never liked it. And once I've graduated, there might be something I can do about it. But right now I'm still just a fairy and so are you."

The pair walked on in silence through Ænathlin, lost in their own thoughts, dodging the general hubbub. Eventually, the streets began to widen as they reached the centre.

"It's so much nicer here," Joan said, taking in the ornate buildings, built before the Great Redaction.

The city centre was certainly different from the outer ring. It was almost hard to believe it was all still Ænathlin. The cobbled streets, though worn, were clean. The street lamps, though old and rusting, were beautifully rendered and always lit. The fae, though still subject to the Teller and the General Administration, though still in danger of Redaction, were confident and better fed.

The GenAm certainly seemed to favour the centre if the propaganda posters were anything to go by. Where Joan and Bea lived, the GenAm took a simple line, replicating the same few slogans over and over, bars to a cage so large it was impossible to see:

"The Teller Cares About You"

"Carelessness Creates Crossed Plots"

"Anti-Narrativists Operate In Thaiana"

"The Redaction Department: Protecting Your Safety"

But in the centre, the GenAm opted for a more nuanced approach. Here, the fae were allowed the luxury of pretending that everything was alright.

The GenAm posted artistic and subtle drawings, images made up of fine lines and intricate borders, showing stylised depictions of the Beast, three heads baying at the moon, snouts black with blood, or of Robin Goodfellow, leader of the Anti-Narrativists, burning Books, the flames beautifully rendered in simple print.

In the centre of the city, even the oppression was beautiful.

"I think because they don't know any better," Bea said. "Here, everything is Happy *Always* After."

"Happy Always After," Joan repeated. "Yes. That makes sense. For them, everything's always easy."

"Joan, please listen to me," Bea said, taking her by the shoulders. "The GenAm is dangerous. Don't get involved in any of this. The Teller Cares About Us."

"The Teller Cares About Us," Joan repeated, and then she smiled. "You sound like you think I'm about to join the Anties! Come on, you numpty. I'm just saying you're right. It *is* unfair. Now, off you go. I'm so proud of you, Bea. I know you're going to be fantastic at the Academy. Just keep being yourself, promise me?"

Bea looked away. "I'll do my best."

"Well, of course you will. That's my point," Joan replied.

They said their goodbyes and Joan watched as Bea walked across the main square, past the Redaction Block, and into the Plot Department.

VI

The two elves regarded the girl.

"Right then. We'd better get started," said one, a shade of reluctance in her voice.

"Marry, art thou afeared?" replied the other.

The first elf rolled her eyes. That was the problem with apprentices. They didn't know the ropes. She, on the other hand, was very familiar with ropes. And knives. And, on one memorable occasion, a wooden spoon. It didn't do to get stuck in a rut, after all.

"No, of course I'm not afraid," she said. "And do you have to speak like that?"

"It's traditional," grumbled the apprentice.

"It's bloody pretentious is what it is. You've read the instructions, have you?"

"Twice," said the apprentice, hooking his thumbs under the lapels of his filthy jacket. He'd obviously made it himself. No doubt he'd been trying for some kind of suit, but he lacked both the talent and the means to produce one. He'd cut his jacket from rough leather and animal fur, while his trousers—too tight to be practical, especially in their line of work—were already showing holes. But, and this was the important thing, he looked the part.

"What shall we do first?" he asked, toying with his knife, shifting it from hand to hand in graceful movements. It was an elf blade, made of silver and inlaid with a delicately engraved leaf pattern. Much like the rest of him, it harkened back to an older time. She supposed he would say 'a Golden Era'.

"We do it in the order we've been told to," she said. "Lesson number one: don't get creative. We do what we're paid to do, we keep it quiet, and we collect our payment."

"I suppose so," the apprentice replied sullenly.

Again, they regarded the girl. She was sitting quietly on a chair in the centre of the room, her thick, black hair framing her pretty face, smiling and occasionally humming snatches of a tune, half-familiar and half-unknown.

They hadn't tied her up. They hadn't needed to. She'd been happily compliant ever since the troll brought her to them.

"You'd think she'd say something," the master elf muttered.

"Characters are dumb, though, aren't they? Everyone knows that."

"Mmm. If you say so," the master elf said, her eyes still fixed on the girl.

The girl was unsettling. The snatches of song were bad enough, but there was something else... It took the elf a moment to realise what it was, and when she worked it out, it didn't make anything better.

Her smile. The girl's smile was absolutely genuine and yet completely devoid of any real understanding. It reached her hazel eyes and made them shine, all without seeming to engage her brain on the way.

The master elf stepped forward and clicked her slender fingers in front of the girl's face. The girl turned to the sound. Not deaf, then.

She'd worked in Thaiana a couple of times, when someone had been caught doing something that, while prohibited, wasn't the kind of thing anyone wanted to get the Redaction Department involved with.

The Teller banned the fae from any indulgences with the characters, but for some, the temptation was too strong. And so, when interested parties—usually parents from the wealthy trade families—found out what had been happening, they thought it prudent to call in her services to make the problem go away. It was risky, but ultimately better to have a character disappear than have their family name tarnished because of little Tabitha or Tarquin's Redaction.

It was a grim job, but someone had to do it, so why not her, the master elf told herself.

This is, of course, the perennial excuse for wicked acts. "It was going to happen anyway," or "If I don't do it, they will," or "Better them than me." No one ever sees themselves as the villain.

Besides, she was good at it. Elves were quick and nimble, and their tribal talent was the ability to heal. This was her major selling point—less mess meant fewer questions. But even allowing for her limited experience in Thaiana, she'd never met a character like this before. Not one who made it so easy. It was almost like the girl was giving them permission.

"What's first, then?" the master elf said.

The apprentice consulted the instruction sheet. "Eyes first," he said. "Traditional, ain't it? Eyes. It's like in the old stories. You know, before the Teller, *whocaresaboutus*, came along and took it all away."

"Less of that, thank you. We don't want the Beast paying us a visit."

"The Beast ain't gonna bother us. I heard it ain't been seen for months. Off chasing some super Anti or something." And then, remembering his image, he added, "I faith."

"Let's not push our luck."

They set to work. The girl didn't even try to stop them, though she did cry out in pain. Now that they'd finished, she was again just sitting there, the skin around her empty eye sockets creasing in a mockery of happiness.

The master elf wiped a cloth across her knife. "Pass me that list," she instructed.

She skimmed over the items requested. It was going to be a long day. The mortal gods alone knew why anyone would want to put someone though it all, even if that person were just a character. But that was the job: 'See how far you get before she complains or dies.'

She doubted they'd manage to get through the entire list before the girl's body gave out, even with healing. It wasn't that it was a long list, but it *was* very specific. Some of the things they'd been instructed to do were... well, they were like something out of a story.

No. It was very unlikely the girl would survive it all, but the master elf had a feeling that she wouldn't complain, not even once.

There was an unusual stinging in her chest, an echo of an emotion she thought she'd done away with years ago. She handed the list back to her apprentice. "Let's skip ahead to number four."

"Number four? Sew her mouth shut? But you said we had to do it all in order."

"I know what I said," the elf snapped. "I'm the master here, not you."

"Sister, tis nary a one—"

"And we'll have none of that nonsense, either. Go on, you can do it."

As the apprentice set to work with a needle and thread, the master elf looked again at the instructions they'd been given. If the girl did put up with all this, without even a word of complaint, perhaps the apprentice was right.

Perhaps the old ways were returning.

VII

Bea pulled at the strap of her oversized bag, trying to find a way to hold it comfortably. The sword point necklace was safely packed inside with her other treasures. She'd put it on when she'd dressed that morning in her new grey dress, but the feel of it against her skin had brought back unpleasant memories... her heart beating too fast in her chest; the slick, sticky sensation of walking on blood; the sound of hissing.

So she'd hidden it in her bag with the other items she couldn't bear to throw away, mementoes of things still too raw to touch without causing pain: old letters tied with a ribbon, a vial of perfume, a dried leaf... and now the sword point necklace.

Bea was standing in a large room in the Plot Department, trying very hard to ignore the unease she felt because of her conversation with Joan. To distract herself, she made a detailed surveillance of her surroundings.

At the top of the room was a raised stage, an empty chair set in the centre. Around her were about fifty other fae, all chatting in little groups. Bea got the impression they knew each other—either that, or everyone else was much better at starting conversations than she was. She saw a few faces she recognised from her inauguration the week before, but no one she knew well enough to say hello to.

She wasn't surprised to note that she was the only fairy in the room, but she hadn't expected to feel so out of place. The air buzzed with conversation while she stood inside a little bubble of discomfort.

She readjusted her bag again, and, for the sake of something to do, wandered away from the corner where she'd been standing. If she looked like she was moving around the room, perhaps no one would notice she didn't have anyone to talk to.

Rescue came in the form of a long table towards the left of the stage, groaning under the weight of food and drink. It seemed that the GenAm, like most of the city, was taking advantage of the recent surge in belief and the repaired Mirrors.

Supposing she had as much right as anyone, Bea took a plate and started to choose some food, grateful for both the distraction and the opportunity to look busy. She took her plate and her heavy bag back to the edge of the room, dropped her bag on the floor and sat on it. She ate quietly, watching the other recruits.

A ruddy-cheeked female dwarf, laughing loudly in the centre of a mixed group of fae, caught her attention. The dwarf had a halo of long, curly blonde hair which she wore in bunches tied with silver bands, and was dressed in a dark purple shirt over brown breeches, a wide belt around her sturdy waist. Even from this distance, Bea could tell the dwarf's clothes were well made, the material thick and expertly stitched.

Just then, the dwarf looked over to where Bea was sitting. She stared at Bea for just long enough to make her feel uncomfortable, and then turned back to her friends, laughing at something one of them said.

Bea swallowed her food, picked up her bag and moved as far away from the dwarf as the room would allow. Suddenly it seemed that a lot of the fae were looking at her, though more surreptitiously than the dwarf had done. Bea couldn't help thinking she should have worn a sign around her neck saying 'Yes, I'm A Fairy. Please Keep Your Gaping To A Minimum'.

Muttering swearwords, she found an empty spot towards the back and dropped her bag by her feet.

The room was filling up, which meant she stood out less and also that they would soon begin whatever it was the GenAm did when a new year's intake joined the Academy.

It occurred to Bea that perhaps she should have done more to find out exactly what happened when one started at the Academy. The trouble was that in order to find these things out, she should have had preparation meetings with her Plotter—who was still, technically, Mistasinon.

Absently, she lifted her hand to her mouth and bit her fingernail. She cried out in pain, drawing shocked looks from the nearest group of recruits. Bea looked down at her hand. Black blood was beading around what was left of her cuticle.

I'm not going to have any fingers left if I carry on like this, she scolded herself. And then she switched to another fingernail and started biting.

"I wondered if you'd have the nerve to show up."

Bea almost felt relieved. It was sort of nice to see a familiar face, even if it did belong to her sworn enemy, an imp called Carol. It was probably much the same feeling as someone who'd been sent to the gallows would have if they heard that the best executioner was on duty.

"Well met, Carol," she said.

"Cabbage mother," Carol replied.

Bea ignored the jibe, not about to give Carol the satisfaction of knowing the nickname bothered her. "Who'd have thought?" she said instead. "Here we are, two fae from the wall, both about to join the Academy."

Carol sniffed. "Well, you managed to worm your way in, certainly. You fairies really will do anything, won't you?"

"Oh? Really? You mean like actually working on a genuine Plot? Having direct involvement with the characters? Completing a Rags To Riches story that brings in so much belief the Mirrors start working again? That kind of 'anything'?"

Bea knew it was stupid to brag, but she couldn't help it, all her good intentions about behaving herself dissolving in the acid of her dislike. It was the first time she'd told the GenAm's official lie about her Plot and actually enjoyed it.

Carol's lip curled. "From what I've heard, you got a lot of help. A leg up, some might say. You honestly thought people wouldn't find out?"

Bea's bravado evaporated. "Find out what?" Miraculously her voice came out steady. "The GenAm saw my potential and offered me a Plot to run. I finished it. Now I'm here."

"'Potential'? Is that what they're calling it?" Carol's golden eyes were flecked with hatred. "Personally, I'm amazed you can show your face. You really are shameless, aren't you? I wonder if it's genetic. Oh look, here comes your Plotter. I expect you'll want to push your way to the front. It would hardly be the first time."

Bea looked up to see the Head of the Plot Department shuffling across the stage towards the chair. Walking behind her were a line of blue-suited Plotters, in the centre of which was Mistasinon. She felt the skin on her arms prickle and brought her hands up to rub away the goosebumps.

"The body doesn't lie," Carol said, catching the action.

"I have absolutely no idea what you're talking about," Bea hissed out of the corner of her mouth. "So why don't you—"

The end of her sentence was cut off by the sound of clapping. Bea dragged her attention back to the stage.

The Head Plotter took her seat, and a respectful silence fell over the room. The Head waved her hand dismissively at the assembly and sank back into her chair, already bored. She closed her eyes, and a moment later was asleep.

Then, horror of horrors, Mistasinon detached himself from the line of Plotters and took centre stage. Slender and tall, he was wearing a beautifully cut, three-piece blue suit over a pale amethyst shirt. His dark hair was slicked back, exposing his high forehead and thick eyebrows, his wide brown eyes blinking too quickly.

When Bea had first met him, she'd thought he looked kind. She'd liked his large, sad eyes and his smile that reminded her of summer rain. He'd struck her as being gentle and honest and, perhaps, as trapped by the expectations of others as she was.

She knew better than that now.

Mistasinon pulled a piece of paper from his jacket pocket and called out for silence.

Oh, mortal gods. He's going to give a speech.

"Hello, everyone," he began. "Welcome to the Academy." He glanced down at his notes and up again at the room. "Ahem. Yes. I'm speaking on behalf of the Head of the Plot Department who is, uh, not feeling very well."

The Head Plotter let rip a thunderous snore. The audience tittered.

Mistasinon brought his hand up and rubbed his neck. "Well, as I hope you all know, everyone at the General Administration is very proud to welcome you to the fold. So… Welcome!"

The crowded hall stared at him.

"Aha. Yes…. Um. I have it on good authority the Academy will be the best year of your life—that is, I don't mean the only year of your life... I mean, the best of many, many years. Um. Let me tell you a little about the Academy..."

As she watched him stumble through his speech, Bea realised again how unusual looking he was. Mistasinon was slender like an elf, but much taller. He must have been a little over six foot if she was any judge. Only trolls and ogres were taller, but they were also much bigger, so he definitely wasn't one of those tribes. Mistasinon's height and willowy frame made him look delicate somehow, like an animal bred to run or chase. But for all his apparent fragility, Bea had seen him attack a troll barehanded.

"...has a long tradition of nurturing the best and the brightest, and I'm certain you will be no exception. Indeed, I dare say you will all prove to be exceptional." Mistasinon looked up from his notes to offer the room one of his odd, sad little smiles and was rewarded with a few timid laughs.

Bea rolled her eyes and returned to her study of him.

It wasn't only his size and strength that were unusual. His skin was a warm brown, like someone who spent their time outside, in the sun. In fact, he was rather human-looking, now she thought about it. She wondered how she'd missed it before, but then she'd never really spent any proper time with the humans, before meeting him.

"...All of our Fiction Management Executives train at the Academy, from misks right up to godmothers and witches. The Academy will teach you everything you need to know about managing Plots and dealing with characters..."

All the fae had some kind of physical quality that marked them out as belonging to their tribe, whereas Mistasinon had none. Or, at least, none Bea recognised.

Elves had pointed ears. Goblins had large, saucer-shaped eyes. Flower fairies had wings. Garden fairies, like she was, had sturdy, plump bodies and green hair, hence the nickname 'cabbage fairies'. And the witchlein were covered in vicious, sharp scales that cut through your flesh—

Bea slammed the brakes on that thought before it had a chance to get started. Unfortunately, the psychological momentum caused by stopping one awful memory managed to propel her straight into another one.

She did know one thing about Mistasinon that might give her a clue to his tribe: he had a dapple of dark hair that ran across his chest and down his stomach, disappearing under the band of his trousers…

Bea felt her cheeks burn as she watched him on the stage while her mind conjured up the image of his half-naked body. Sometimes she hated her brain. But it *was* odd. For the fae, hair went on the head, or occasionally in the ears or nose, or on the knuckles. But that was it. Like so much else about him, the hair on Mistasinon's body just didn't make sense.

The truth was, he didn't really *fit* in either tribe, fae or human. He was too strong and fast to be a human, but he was also too hairy and too tall to be from the fae.

"…And so, you'll all be joining a long tradition. I'm sure you don't need me to remind you what an honour it is to be accepted into the Academy. And of course, the GenAm is lucky to have you."

Mistasinon looked straight at her.

And then he said, "All of you."

For a second Bea held his gaze.

The blush burning her cheeks reached critical heat levels. She dropped her eyes. When she glanced back, he was no longer looking at her.

Very deliberately, Bea turned her thoughts to Carol, whose scowling expression suggested she wasn't listening to Mistasinon's speech either.

She'd completely forgotten that Carol was also joining the Academy. What a *fun* surprise that was. But more importantly, what had Carol meant when she said she knew Bea had had help getting accepted?

It was probably nothing. Carol had always been Bea's loudest critic, and it was hardly a leap of the imagination to assume she would be unwilling to believe Bea had completed a Rags To Riches story.

The only problem was that Carol was right, wasn't she? Sort of, anyway.

"…The Academy was founded at the beginning of the Chapter in order to ensure that only the best fae, with the most detailed knowledge of the Plots, were entrusted with the task of running the stories and keeping the Mirrors working…"

Carol was probably just stirring things up like she always did. There was nothing to worry about—or, rather, there wasn't anything *new* to worry about. Bea smiled to herself. See? She was keeping positive.

"The Teller Cares About Us," chanted the room.

"—cares about us," Bea mumbled, hoping no one would notice she hadn't been paying attention.

Oh yes, she thought. *'The Teller Cares'*. Certainly, he'd brought order when there was chaos, but anything can be organised—just because you like to know where the knives and forks are doesn't mean you care about the cutlery drawer.

"Aren't you going to show your appreciation?" Carol said out of the corner of her mouth.

Bea started. The room was clapping, and Mistasinon was taking his place in the line of Plotters. The Head Plotter was still sleeping, despite the noise.

Bea offered up a half-hearted clap.

Carol's eyes narrowed. "You make me sick. Just keep out of my way when we get to the Academy. I don't want to get caught in your mess when the paper hits the shredders—which it will if there's any justice."

She was radiating anger. Bea stepped back.

"Just remember you're only a fairy. You might be trying to claw your way to the top of the pile, but you'll end up back in the Forest where you belong, left for the orcs and gnarls to feast on." Carol looked Bea up and down. "They'll get a good meal out of you."

"More than they'd get from you," Bea snapped back. But her heart wasn't it, and when Carol marched off, Bea didn't even bother making a rude gesture behind her back.

She started chewing her nails again, ignoring the taste of blood on her tongue.

Well, so much for keeping positive.

After Mistasinon's speech, the recruits wandered around, talking to each other or getting last-minute tips from their Plotters.

Bea sidled to the edge of the room, trying very hard to keep track of where Mistasinon was without actually looking at him, the effect of which made her eyes water and gave her a headache. The mortal gods were apparently on her side though, as Mistasinon had a quick conversation with some of the other blue-suited Plotters and then disappeared out a side door. He didn't even try to speak to Bea.

Which was good, of course. He was absolutely the last person she wanted to talk to.

Mind you, no one else seemed particularly keen to talk to her, either. She was having the same effect on the little groups of recruits as a potent but silent fart. It was almost funny. She'd drift, gaseous, up to a pocket of fae and watch as they noticed her. Their noses would wrinkle and, without doing anything so crass as mentioning the sudden intrusion, they would relocate their group about five feet away from her.

Bea decided it was like a game, as long as one redefined the term to mean an activity that was both infuriating and depressing. She was just wondering whether she had the monopoly on the idea when a voice cried out from behind her. From the volume of it, the speaker might as well have been at the other end of the room.

"What ho!"

Bea turned around to see the blonde dwarf who had been staring at her earlier.

"Hello," she said, smiling nervously.

"Hullo," the dwarf hallooed, her enthusiastic, booming voice marking her as coming from the wealthy inner circle. She stuck out her hand. "I did hope you'd come. We weren't sure if you wouldn't give it a miss."

Bea took the offered hand and nearly had her own pulled off when the dwarf shook it.

"A miss?" she asked, trying hard not to give in to the temptation to rub some life back into her fingers.

"Oh yes, darling. We took bets on it, aren't we wicked? I'm a magnum up on the deal, thanks to you. So, what do you think?

Isn't it just too dull for words? Hemmings is close to breaking point, all these people asking him about his troubles."

Bea tried to keep up. "Troubles?"

"*Ghastly* troubles. So, what did you think of your Plotter's speech?"

"I'm sorry? Why would I think anything about his speech?"

"Oh yes! Gosh! Silly me! Quite right, darling, it's so much better to be discreet, isn't it? What about the rest of it, then?"

Bea realised the dwarf assumed she knew what she was talking about; as if she was just coming back to the conversation after nipping to the toilet. But the dwarf was talking to her, which was more than anyone else was doing, and she certainly seemed friendly.

"You mean about all this?" Bea asked, gesturing around her. "It seems alright. Lots more fae than I expected."

"I should hope so," the dwarf laughed. "Considering how much our parents traded for us to be here, one'd hope we'd show up when the contract's to be signed. Oh! Aren't I wicked?"

She grinned at Bea.

"Now, let's get you caught up. That's Jones over there, his family owns the north-east markets, standing with Duskwood-Rumplestill—Tiff, to you and me—she was the one who jumped in the soup at Grainvale's bash. And there's Grimbo, who's Yonkie's cousin thrice removed, and Cheeser, who of course everyone knows. And that's Hemmings."

She pointed out an elf with dark shoulder-length hair, beautiful as the tribe always was, standing off to the edge of the group. He was dressed entirely in black: a long coat with a high neck above a frilled shirt with embroidered cuffs and a black waistcoat, thin-legged trousers and fancy shoes with metal buckles. He'd managed to get hold of a flower and was morosely plucking the petals from it.

"Hemmings is an elf?" Bea asked, incredulous. "An elf has troubles?"

"I should say so! There's simply no helping him. Still, he's my brother, and I am rather fond of him."

Bea looked at the elf and then back at the dwarf.

"Your brother? But—"

"Adopted, darling. We've had him since he was a baby. Papa found him at the Grand in the most dreadful circumstances."

Bea tried not to look too curious. "He was in danger?"

"Oh, no. In a handbag."

"A handbag?"

"A handbag, yes. A *frite-ful,* moth-eaten thing, only don't mention it to him or we'll never hear the end of it—he's terribly earnest. Oh, look! They're all looking at us! Go on, say hullo!"

Bea offered a little wave to the group, who smiled and waved back, all bar Hemmings. No doubt they'd heard every word the dwarf had said about them. Bea could feel herself blushing again.

"We're all dreadfully interested in you. Do you know there's never been a fairy train as an FME? They've never met a fairy before. Me neither, come to that. Oh, I'm quite certain we'll be the best of friends, Bea, aren't you?"

"You know my name?"

"Of course, darling. You've been the talk of all the parties this week. Buttercup Snowblossom—such an interesting name. Very 'ethnic'. Only why did you shorten it? Isn't it a terrible shame to give up your heritage?"

Bea opened her mouth to answer, but the dwarf cut her off.

"Oh well,"—she pronounced it '*h'oh whull*', changing the sound in the same way she pronounced frightful '*frite-ful*', making the first syllable somehow even more distinct. "I'd better head back to my chums, but I'll catch you outside. We'll be bunking together, isn't that well organised? We're going to be such great friends, I know it! My name's Dea'dora Kilumal Ogrechoker, by the way, but you can call me Chokey. Oh, and don't worry about all the rumours—gossip is what gossip does! Isn't this all wonderful fun?"

Half an hour later, Bea was standing outside the GenAm buildings with the rest of the new recruits, all of whom were chatting in happy groups. It seemed Bea was the only one who didn't already know somebody.

No, that's not true, she told herself. She knew Carol, who she'd spotted glaring at her from across the square. And it seemed she'd made a friend in the blonde dwarf Chokey, even if she wasn't entirely sure how it had happened.

Bea decided she would look for Chokey rather than standing around feeling sorry for herself. But instead, she spotted a group of elves, who were clearly drunk. Either that or she had been missing out on the wealth of humour a tompte trapped under a pint glass provided.

Bea squared her shoulders, ready to intervene when Chokey bounded up to her.

"Hullo, Buttercup! You don't mind, do you? Only I do think it a terrible shame not to use your real name." Somehow she'd managed to get hold of a bottle of wine. "Would you like some? Go on, might as well!"

"I just need to go over there and stop—"

"Nonsense! One of the brown suits will deal with the elves. Besides, that sort of thing builds character, don't you think? Here!"

Chokey shoved the bottle into Bea's hands.

"Bottoms up!" Chokey said encouragingly. "Oh look, see? Hemming's just spotted the elves. Poor dears. They'll wish it had been you that stopped them. He's *frite-fully* clever. Though sometimes I shouldn't wonder if that wasn't rather a handicap."

Bea watched as Hemmings went over to the drunken elves and started talking to them. She couldn't hear what he was saying, but whatever it was, it seemed to be having some effect—though not the one she'd expected.

The other elves stared at him, their perfect faces a picture of bemusement. Hemmings had his hand to his chest, his eyes closed as he spoke. Whatever he was saying was obviously very heartfelt. Then one of the other elves pushed him over.

They laughed and skipped away. Hemmings sat on the cobbles, a resigned look on his face. He reached over and lifted the jar, freeing the tompte.

Bea stepped forward, but Chokey rested her hand on her arm.

"Leave him, darling. He's perfectly alright."

"But—"

"Honestly. He'll enjoy it so much more later if he's left to suffer now."

Bea wasn't convinced, but she didn't know what to say. "Um. If you're sure…"

"Oh yes, quite sure! He is my brother, after all, I should know. He gets *frite-fully* upset by the other elves, poor dear. Finds them terribly low-minded. Go on, finish the bottle. It was only a couple of buttons, I'll get us another."

Chokey marched off, the silver bands in her hair catching the light.

Bea felt like she'd been caught in a whirlwind. She took a slug of wine to steady her nerves. The other recruits were looking at her, some wary, some with curiosity, most with ill-concealed disgust. Just then a red-headed brownie, her face covered in freckles, shot her a wide grin. Bea smiled back. The brownie ran off to her friend and whispered something in his ear. They both turned, looked at Bea, and started to giggle.

Bea took another gulp of wine.

"Alright, come on," shouted a brown-suited troll. "We're going through the Mirrors in groups of ten. You'll each be given a slip and—"

"Where are we going?" shouted a voice from the crowd. Bea realised it had been her. She felt herself begin to blush. Another dose of wine would help.

The troll turned to her. He had dark eyes that only got darker when he looked at her, reminding Bea of the public wells by the wall, dug deep into the earth in an attempt to find clean water. Nothing good ever came out of them, only brown liquid populated by thousand-legged insects dancing in crazed circles, trapped by the bucket. The water had to be boiled twice to drink, and even so it often made you sick.

Somehow, the troll's eyes contained the same poisonous potential.

"The fairy," he said, his mouth pinched with distaste. "The Academy is in the Fifth Kingdom."

"Voriias? But that doesn't make any sense," Bea said, the warmth of the wine insulating her from his chilly dislike. "The whole country's made of ice—there's no way to run Plots there.

Isn't the whole point of the Academy that we train to be FMEs? How can we practise Plots if we're in a place where none are run?"

The troll muttered something, and then said, "The Academy was officially relocated to Voriias about a year ago. That's all you need to know. You will go, you will study, and you," he said, glaring at Bea, "Will learn when to keep your fairy mouth shut."

Bea blushed furiously, her jaw tight with embarrassment and anger. Behind her, the drunken elves burst out laughing.

VIII

Bea stepped out of the mirror and into the Academy. Instantly she wrapped her arms around herself. It was freezing.

She walked forward, taking the steps from the platform gingerly. Strong wine and transworld travel did not mix. The fact that she knew why travelling by Mirror made one feel so sick didn't cheer her up.

The room was large, with GenAm banners inevitably hanging on the walls, slashes of red like open wounds against the dark wood panelling. Some of them she recognised from Ænathlin:

"The Teller Cares About You"

"Anti-Narrativists Operate In Thaiana"

"The Redaction Department: Protecting Your Safety"

And some she had never seen before:

"All Recruits Are Expected To Contribute"

"Do Not Trespass Beyond Your House"

Brushing her hair behind her ears, Bea diverted her gaze from the banners, already feeling quite miserable enough without deliberately adding to it.

The room really was… strange.

The walls were covered from floor to ceiling in dark wooden panels, varnished to a dull gleam. They looked handsome enough and must have cost whoever owned the building a fortune to install, but Bea couldn't bring herself to like them.

This much old wood shouldn't be kept together. Wood didn't really die, it just lost itself when it was taken away from its roots.

But it could still sense things, in a way, and to have so much of it made her feel uneasy.

You can take the fairy out of the garden, but you can't take the garden out of the fairy, Bea thought wryly as she continued looking around her.

There was furniture here and there, old, solid chairs with woven covers. In the centre of one wall was an ornate fireplace, but there were only a few logs burning forlornly in the hearth. There were no windows; oil lamps were set into the wood-panelled walls at regular intervals and burned on full. In between the oil lamps were mounted animal heads, staring down at the new recruits with glassy-eyed disinterest. The floor beneath Bea's feet was bare stone, and she could feel the chill of it through the thin soles of her boots. The scars on her leg began to pinch, making their own feelings about the cold known.

The room might have been handsome, but it lacked any sense of feeling, of warmth. There was nothing in it that spoke of a space for living—as if the person who had decorated it had spent too many nights with only their thoughts and bottle of laudanum for company. It was lonely and sombre and reminded Bea of the feeling she'd had the night she'd snuck out of her clan's camp to run away to Ænathlin.

She swallowed the bitter memory along with her disappointment. She'd always imagined that the Academy was some kind of fantastic place, filled with equal minded people, all eager to learn and improve themselves. She'd pictured bright, open, airy rooms filled with intelligent conversation.

Then she remembered what the troll with the dark eyes had said before, about the Academy only moving here a year ago. Perhaps it was just more of her bad luck. Perhaps all the previous recruits had studied in some beautiful castle in the warm climes of south-east Ehinenden.

She tutted, cross with herself. It didn't matter what the building was like. She was only going to be here a year, and besides, she *was here*. She was studying at the Academy. That was the thing to hold on to. Bea's spirits lifted. One year, and she'd be a godmother. She'd be in a position to make things right. What else mattered, compared to that?

There were a dozen or so brown suits from the Contents Department, checking through some paperwork, and a few of her soon-to-be classmates, all looking queasy. Someone was being noisily sick into a bucket. Obviously, the other recruits weren't used to the nausea that came with Mirror travel. Bea recognised the vomiter as the red-headed brownie who had laughed at her outside the Plot Department. She rummaged in her bag and pulled out some mint.

"Chew this, you'll feel better," she said, proffering the mint.

The brownie hesitated.

"Or keep being sick," Bea shrugged. "Your choice."

The brownie grabbed the mint and started chewing it. The sickened expression on her face eased. She gave Bea a weak smile and wandered off without thanking her. Bea recalled what Chokey had said about her mother trading for her place, and wondered if any of the other recruits had travelled by Mirror before.

Bea was well used to the sickly feeling that came with transworld travel, a result of her years spent Plot-watching, travelling between Thaiana and Ænathlin. She had always thought that everyone got into the Academy the same way: Plot-watching for an official FME, who would then recommend you for a place. Of course, none of the FMEs Bea had spent years Plot-watching for had recommended *her*, no matter how hard she'd worked—no one wanted to be responsible for allowing a fairy into the system, least of all a cabbage fairy.

Well, apart from Mistasinon…

Bea shook her head as if she might physically dislodge the thought of him from her mind. Anyway, the way into the Academy apparently had nothing to do with working hard. Apart from her and presumably Carol, no one else had worked to get their place here—not if the number of decidedly unwell recruits was any indication. Clearly, the surest way into the Academy was to have parents who could pay.

As if on cue, Chokey's booming trill echoed through the room.

"Buttercup! Over here!"

Bea spotted the dwarf, who was sitting on a bench with a glass of water in her hands. Putting down the glass, she marched over to Bea.

"Gosh, darling, I shouldn't fancy feeling like that again! Does it get any better? What an awfully dank place this is," she continued without waiting for a reply. "This really isn't what we were told to expect, I must say. Honestly, I'm tempted to tell Mama to write in and complain. I can't begin to understand why they haven't more wood on the fire, at the very least."

Chokey looked around the room for a brown suit, her eyes landing on a yellow-scaled witchlein, his tongue flicking in and out of his sharp-toothed mouth.

Bea's stomach lurched.

What was one of *them* doing here?

"I'll ask him," Chokey announced happily. "I say! Hullooo! Hullooo!"

"Chokey—You mustn't—" she stammered as Chokey started to make her way over to the witchlein.

"Whatever's the matter?"

Bea grabbed hold of Chokey's arm. "Please, don't—"

"Why ever not? Darling, you've gone very wild."

"He's a witchlein. They work for the Redaction Department."

Chokey gently removed Bea's hand from her arm. "Nonsense. He's in a brown suit, not a white one. I must say, I didn't expect tribalism from you. Come on, darling."

Chokey pulled Bea over to where the witchlein was standing.

"I say, you there, be a dear and bring us some more firewood, won't you?"

"There isssn't any wood," he hissed.

Bea shuddered. She couldn't help it.

"What'sss wrong with you?" the witchlein said, eyeing her.

"She's freezing," Chokey said pointedly. "Look at her, bunched up all tight, skin white as a sheet. The GenAm can't expect us to live in this *frite-ful* cold. Just pop outside and gather some wood for the fire, won't you?"

The witchlein turned his attention back to Chokey. "No one leavesss the Academy without permisssion from Headmistresss Wessst."

"I thought Radcliffe was the Headmistress?"

"She wasss. Now Wessst isss."

"Really darling, are you quite sure? I'm certain Mama spoke to Radcliffe when she was organising our place here."

The witchlein shrugged. "Wessst is Headmistresss now."

"Oh well, if you say so. Still, I'm sure that West won't want us all to freeze to death. Go and get us some wood, don't be a bore, darling."

"Look," he said, his tone of voice suggesting this wasn't the first time that morning he'd had this conversation. "I don't make the rulesss. No one getsss in or out without permisssion. Anyway, you try leaving—the ssstorm'll get you before you're off the groundsss."

"The storm?"

"You'll sssee sssoon enough."

Chokey shook her head. "You make it sound like we're prisoners! Surely that can't be right?"

"Whether it can or can't, it isss," he said, and walked away from them.

There was a roaring in Bea's ears. The scars on her leg stung, and the room began to spin. She swayed, her head light. She felt Chokey's hands on her forearms.

"Gosh! That wine *has* gone to your head, hasn't it? I suppose you're not used to it," Chokey said. "Still, I must say, I thought he was dreadfully rude. I can see now why you don't like them. Oh Buttercup, though! The expression on your face—you looked like you'd seen a ghost. Thank the mortal gods I was here to help you, that's all I can say. Aren't we already the best of friends?"

Bea opened her mouth to reply and threw up.

***

Thankfully, Chokey assumed Bea's sudden funny turn was a result of her journey via the Mirrors.

After the attack on the Ball at the end of Bea's Plot, she had hoped she would go the rest of her life without ever hearing that snake-like hiss again. Still, she at least had plenty of time to calm down as she stood in various lines to pick up her timetables and get her course books, Chokey prattling cheerfully away all the while.

They were herded from one identical, wood-panelled room to another, in what was supposed to be a tour. By the end of it, Bea was more thoroughly lost than if she'd been left to wander the halls alone. The Academy was a rabbit warren if rabbit warrens were filled with complaining students and bored-looking brown suits.

Eventually, they were all ushered into the assembly hall. Bea couldn't stop the gasp of amazement that escaped her.

The entire ceiling was made of glass, with thick black bars between the panes. The only vaguely normal thing about it were the red GenAm banners hanging from the bars, long tabards hanging still in the dead air. But, as strange as a glass ceiling was, the thing that caused her and the other recruits to crane their necks painfully upwards was the sky.

It was as grey as old, dead skin, swashes of black and blue marring it like bruises. The snow swirled through the air, vicious winds whipping it into giddy insensibility. The wind pummelled the glass, screaming in anguish as it tried to break into the room.

There were no Plots set in Voriias, the Fifth Kingdom of Thaiana. Now, looking at the storm raging above her head, Bea began to understand why.

Theoretically, the humans here could be included in one of the Plots, but the Teller's stories were about love and happy endings. And, while love was indeed universal, an hour or two trying to engineer a Happy Ever After while the wind cut through your clothes likes a psychotic tailor was enough to convince even the most egalitarian of FMEs that romance worked better in the warm.

The weather outside the Academy was like the end of the world and Bea, still staring straight up, said as much.

Chokey shivered. "Oh, what a horrible thought. I wish we'd found Hemmings. You don't think he's lost, do you?"

Privately, Bea thought it not at all impossible for someone to get lost in all the identical, seemingly endless corridors and rooms in the Academy. Aloud, she said, "He'll show up, don't worry. I don't think there's anywhere else for him to go."

Along the length of the vast hall were vertical rows of wooden tables lined with benches. The sole fireplace was away from the tables and was only burning a few logs, anyway. The cold was clearly going to be a firm friend during her stay at the Academy.

59

F. D. Lee

About forty brown suits of varying tribes marched in, taking up position around the room. Bea scanned them for the witchlein. His tribe were small in stature, and it took her a moment to find him among the brown suits, even with his yellow scales.

"Is everything alright, Buttercup? You're shaking. Is it this beastly cold?"

Bea nodded, her eyes fixed on the witchlein. He'd stopped on the opposite side of the room and was chatting to the brown suit standing next to him. He was too casual, too relaxed. Bea was certain something was up.

"Well, I can't say I'm at all surprised," Chokey continued, oblivious. "I should think they could do a little more to make us comfortable. I mean, I'm not trying to make a fuss, darling, but really—"

"TAKE YOUR SEATS!" bellowed the black-eyed troll from the meet-and-greet.

Five very busy minutes followed, in which everyone tried to find a seat with their friends, or near to the fire, or simply somewhere they would fit.

Chokey grabbed Bea by the arm, looking all the while for Hemmings, but the room was too busy. Eventually, they found some space at the end of one of the benches. When everyone was seated, ten fae in long black robes walked into the hall and stood in a line, just in front of the troll. Bea supposed they were the teachers at the Academy, a supposition that was confirmed when one of them, a woman, called out for silence.

Bea turned in her seat to get a better look at the speaker. She was tall and full-figured, with chestnut brown hair tied in a complicated braid around the nape of her neck. She was wearing a long black dress with a knotted cord under her breasts. The dress was made of heavy material and fell in interesting folds like the pleats in heavy curtains. Brown-eyed and honey-skinned, she reminded Bea for a moment of Mistasinon. Perhaps they were from the same tribe? There had to be more than one, after all; or else, where would little Mistasinons come from?

"Welcome to my house," she said with a tight smile. "I am West, Headmistress of the Academy."

60

She paused for a moment, tilting her head to the side like she was listening to music. Then, remembering herself, she gestured towards the black-robed figures. "These are your Masters. You will be divided into classes, and each Master will teach you for six months. At which point you will be tested, the results of which will determine your future employment within the GenAm.

"And now the rules. You are not permitted beyond your dormitories and classrooms, all of which are situated here, in the east wing. You are not permitted to travel outside the Academy unless accompanied, and then only by prior arrangement. You are not permitted outside your rooms after lights out. You are not permitted to engage in any kind of romantic fraternisation."

She glared at the room.

"You are here to learn about the Plots, to further the work of the Teller, *whocaresaboutus,* and the General Administration. You are here to learn how to cultivate belief, belief that can be used to sustain the Mirrors. This is your purpose. Nothing more, nothing less."

Bea and the other recruits prepared to offer somewhat chastened applause, but West held up her hand, halting them.

"I am given to understand that this year we have something of a prodigy in our midst. A garden fairy by the name of Buttercup Snowblossom."

Every pair of eyes in the room turned to Bea. She wondered if she could slide under the table. Why was she being singled out? She didn't want to be singled out.

"Ah. Mistress Snowblossom," West said, her gaze landing on the suddenly open space around Bea, as the other recruits shifted away from her. "Allow me to congratulate you on your success. I understand from my colleagues that your Plot has seen a surge in belief that has powered many Mirrors."

Bea's cheeks were burning. At least she was probably helping to warm up the room.

"And that," West announced, her deep voice dropping lower, "Is all I wish to hear on the matter. Here at the Academy you, all of you, are nothing more nor less than students. I expect you all to see yourselves as vases to be filled and to behave accordingly. That is, inanimately."

Bea didn't dare blink.

The other recruits began clapping. West took her seat.

Chokey leaned over and whispered, "Gosh! You are lucky— imagine all the Masters already knowing who you are."

Bea couldn't think of a single way to reply, so she just nodded and clapped her hands along with everyone else.

IX

Bea was sitting on her new bed in her new bedroom. Well, not exactly *her* new bedroom. Like Chokey had promised, she and Bea had been put together.

The room itself wasn't half bad. Unsurprisingly, three of the four wood-panelled walls were covered with GenAm posters, but there was also a window set in a stone frame, looking out onto... Well, onto the storm, really, but it was nice to have it, nevertheless. There were four beds, and next to each was a slim wardrobe and a writing desk. Most exciting, though, was the bathroom adjoining the bedroom.

Bea had never had a bathroom of her own. Growing up in a nomadic tribe in the Sheltering Forest hadn't exactly allowed for plumbing, and while living at Ivor's, she'd had to share the bathroom with the entire floor. Thus, she was quite excited to only have to contend with Chokey and two other roommates for the privilege of peeing in peace. Plus, she could get dressed in there, without anyone seeing her scars.

On the downside, she was now sharing a bedroom. Ever since Bea had returned from her now infamous Plot, she had been plagued by nightmares. She could only hope that if they continued, she wouldn't wake everyone else up with her screaming.

"...And then, of course, Edgar decided he was going steal her teeth, can you imagine!" Chokey continued, chatting away as she unpacked her trunk. She certainly had a lot of clothes and bottles of scent and lotion. She even had a mini-portrait of her family, an expensive item to own.

Bea went to pick it up. "Do you mind?"

"What? Oh no, darling, if you like."

She studied the image. Chokey was front and centre, grinning widely. Standing on either side of her were a male and female dwarf, both wearing the slightly constipated expression of parents trying to project an image of stern kindness for the painter to immortalise. There was a much younger dwarf sitting fat and happy at the front, who looked like the only thing she would project was mischief. Finally, standing at the back of the scene, dressed entirely in black and with his long, dark hair hanging over his face, loomed the adopted elf, Hemmings.

"...Well, I don't need to tell you how he reacted to that. Darling, it was priceless!" said Chokey.

"Mmm? Sorry?" Bea replied, returning the painting to Chokey's desk.

"Edgar, darling, and the teeth! It was positively hysterical!"

"Oh, yes," Bea replied dutifully.

She went back to her own bed and continued her unpacking. She uncovered the little bag that contained her sword point necklace, feeling the shape of it through the material. She ran the ball of her thumb along the edge, her mind hurtling back to the Ballroom and the sight of the ogre heaving its mountainous frame towards the prone figure of Melly, collapsed on the floor, Ana standing in front of her, a paper doll facing up to a rock.

Bea remembered picking up the sword, the sound of the witchlein's hiss filling her ears, the sick giddiness of fear and panic in her stomach blocking out the pain of the witchlein crawling up her leg... Trying to breathe as she took aim at the ogre, while somewhere in the back of her mind she knew she was going to watch her friend die...

"It was rather cruel, I suppose, but, really, I do think he brought it on himself, don't you? And these things will happen, won't they?"

Bea blinked. "I'm sorry?"

"I said I thought it was cruel of them to hide the teeth after Edgar had gone to so much trouble getting them, but that he brought it on himself."

"Oh yes," Bea said vaguely, stuffing the bag under her pillow. "You're quite right."

The thing was, Chokey asked a lot of questions, but she didn't seem to need an answer to them, just reassurance that someone was listening. And after the horror of the last twenty-four hours, Bea was finding the fact she didn't have to contribute extremely relaxing.

"It is a shame about the weather here, isn't it?" Chokey complained again. "I should have thought they'd send us somewhere more hospitable, really. It's not at all what I was expecting, especially when one considers they moved the Academy here. I shouldn't be surprised if it's some sort of ploy to keep us working."

"Mmm."

"In fact, the whole place seems terribly dull. Don't do this, don't do that. You do know, darling, don't you, that I'm relying on you to get me through? You simply must tell me all about your Plot. What are the characters like? Are they truly as stupid as everyone says they are?"

"Mmm—what? Oh no, not really," Bea said, catching up. "They're actually not very different from us."

"Goodness, aren't you odd? The same as us, indeed! But I suppose as long as they do what they're told it all works out in the end."

"Well, it's not as—"

"And what about your Plotter, darling?" Chokey continued cheerfully. "Such sad eyes! Rather reminds one of a stray, doesn't he? I dare say he's suffered terribly, wouldn't you? I'm not at all shocked you—"

Chokey's speech was interrupted by the loud creak of the bedroom door. Hemmings slunk into the room.

"Darling!" Chokey screamed at the top of her voice, jumping off her bed and enveloping him in a hug. "How marvellous! I've been looking for you all evening! Everything here is so poorly arranged, I thought maybe there'd been a mistake, and they'd put you somewhere else!"

"Every time you part from someone it is a rehearsal for their eventual death, and so should be seen as useful practice," Hemmings said, his voice heavy with the weight of the worlds. His eyes landed on Bea. "You've taken the bed under the window?"

"You can have it if you want," she said.

"Keep it. A bed won't make my life any better."

"I don't mind swapping."

"No, no. I shall persevere. I had hoped to use the view to inspire me, but I expect I'll find the deprivation equally illustrative."

65

F. D. Lee

"Er, alright," Bea said, looking at Chokey for reassurance.

"Don't mind him. He's just as odd as you are if you ask me!"

Hemmings shot his sister a pained look, tucking his long, black hair behind one pointed ear.

Bea held back a gasp.

Down one side of Hemmings' face was a network of tiny, faint crisscrossing scars. They weren't exactly disfiguring, but equally, they were hard to ignore. Bea wondered if they had anything to do with the unfortunate circumstances surrounding his abandonment as a baby. Elves were supposed to be perfectly beautiful; perhaps his birth parents hadn't wanted a son who was anything less.

"My wonderful brother is something of an artist, aren't you, darling?" Chokey said, beaming encouragingly at Hemmings.

"Really? Do you paint?" Bea said, forcing herself not to stare at his cheek.

"I suppose it might be called painting. I am a thoughtsmith. I invented the term myself."

He waited.

"Oh. Um. What's a thoughtsmith?" Bea dutifully asked.

"A thoughtsmith is someone who sees the world as it truly is and then transcribes that understanding into something comprehensible to the average mind. It's a thankless task. I shall no doubt die a pauper by the wall before my genius is ever recognised."

"I'm sure it won't come to that," Bea said, ignoring the bit about the wall.

"No, no. I doubt my intellect will ever see the light of day, and I will suffer terribly the indignities of unrecognised accomplishment. I may even pick up a disease."

"Oh no, I'm sure—" Bea began.

"It's better that way," Hemmings glared at her. "To live alone is the ultimate fate of all truly great thinkers."

"Oh, I do *hope* not," said Chokey, putting extra emphasis on the word 'hope'. She winked at Bea, a wide grin on her face.

"Hope should be a Redactionable offence," Hemmings announced, taking the bait. "What is hope but endless subjugation, the waiting for an outcome that will never be? Hope is, by its nature, the wish for something impossible. It is a lie. Don't you agree?"

66

Privately, Bea wasn't sure the elf didn't have a point. But 'Happy Ever After' was the order of the day, and she wasn't about to publicly go against that. At least, not until she knew she could get away with it.

"Well... I think the GenAm, you know, I think they'd probably prefer you stick to love stories," she said. "I mean, love is much easier for people to believe in, isn't it?"

Chokey giggled, putting her arm around her brother. "Oh, Hemmings, you're so easily wound up! Poor Buttercup—she probably thinks you're an informer trying to catch her out."

"An informer? Absolutely not," Hemming said, pulling himself up straight, his hand to his chest. "The GenAm restrict information—they very antithesis of thoughtsmithing. But I didn't mean to make you feel uncomfortable," he added to Bea. "I often make people uncomfortable, but I never mean to."

Embarrassed, Bea changed the subject. "Do you know who the other person sharing—I mean, bunking with us is?"

"No one, darling," Chokey replied happily. "It's just us three. I made sure Mama organised it that way. Of course, when I said I wanted you included, she was quite scandalised! She's a dreadful bore, isn't she, Hemmings?"

The elf shrugged. "She's frugal."

"I don't understand," Bea said.

"She likes to get the most out of everything," Hemmings clarified. "She's been dining out on adopting me my entire life. I dare say, once she's calmed down, she'll quite enjoy the fact she traded for your room."

"She traded for my room? I didn't know—Oh, mortal gods... How much?"

"How should I know?" Chokey said happily. "Don't worry darling, we can spare it. Besides, I so wanted to have you as our roommate."

"But—"

"There's no point being embarrassed," Hemmings interrupted. "Besides, would you rather be in the dorms?"

Bea shut up. She'd never been in a dorm before, but she had an imagination. She'd just have to find a way to pay them back.

How had she ended up in this mess? She was indebted to someone she barely knew and trapped in the middle of nowhere, surrounded by brown suits. And then, as it had done so many times before, the hissing of the witchlein filled her memory.

Her heart beat faster, pushing against her lungs. Bea inhaled and counted the breath out through her nose.

Hemmings and Chokey returned to talking at each other.

Bea went into the bathroom, closing the door behind her. She sat on the toilet and stared at the wall until Chokey called through the door to tell her it was time for lights out.

X

A world away from Bea, Mistasinon sat with his eyes closed, watching the colours dance on the skin of his eyelids, faintly aware of the ache across his shoulders. He couldn't decide if the pain was real or if he was imagining it.

He opened his eyes. A polished table ran down the centre of the room, twelve chairs neatly placed around it, five of them filled. He was at a meeting of the Lords and Ladies of the General Administration. Everyone who mattered, bar the Teller himself, was present, which meant that something was seriously wrong.

Sitting to Mistasinon's right was the Head of the Contents Department, a dwarf named Henry. He had a wide nose and small, suspicious eyes that darted from side to side like rats trapped in a barrel. His skin was flushed red, and he was currently shouting at the Head Indexer, who was sitting opposite him.

The Head Indexer was almost as grey as her suit. She was a brownie with yellow hair cut close to her head. Sitting on either side of her were the Chief Cataloguer and the Primary Binder, also dressed in grey suits. Unlike the other GenAm departments, the Index had three top roles, a reflection of the craft involved in organising, cataloguing and maintaining the Books—and, more recently, housing the broken Mirrors.

Finally, there was the imp Julia, Head of the Redaction Department, dressed in white, her blonde hair hanging straight around her pale green face. She was watching Henry shouting at the Head Indexer, her expression calm. Nothing ever seemed to agitate her, or at least that's what it seemed like to Mistasinon. He wondered if she knew how lucky she was, to be so unaffected.

He represented the Plotters. He'd been asked to attend the meeting in place of the Head of the Plot Department, who had claimed exhaustion after her efforts at the Academy meet-and-greet that morning. Or at least, that's what the message had said.

Judging by the way the meeting was going, it was dawning on him that his presence here was to account for what he'd done.

It was almost relaxing, in a way. The shouting, the anger, the fear... the threat of punishment. There's a comfort in the known, even if the thing you recognise isn't itself very nice. At least you know what to expect.

"Please," Mistasinon said, raising his hand for silence. "Arguing amongst yourselves isn't helping. Things took an unexpected turn, but we have to look forward now."

Henry turned his ire onto Mistasinon. "An unexpected turn? The whole thing was a bloody disaster! And don't think I've forgotten that it was your idea not to send the Beast after the genie. The last surviving genie, I need not add. That genie was our only chance to get the Mirrors working again. The Plots don't provide enough belief to power the Mirrors on their own, they haven't done for years."

Mistasinon shook his head. "My Lord, please. We've been able to manage the events at the Ball, and so far, the characters have accepted the Plot. The belief from that region is pouring in. The Mirrors are stable."

"They won't stay that way forever. We needed that genie," Henry countered, slamming his fist on the table. "But instead of having the Beast capture it and forcing it to do what we want— something which worked perfectly well with all the others—you decided you wanted to *talk* to it."

"Yes, but—" Mistasinon began.

"Where's the Beast? Has it been sent out now, at least? What's the bloody point of having it if we don't use it, that's what I'd like to know."

Mistasinon's hands balled into fists. He released them, flexing his fingers. "I'm certain that we can find another way, without the genie's wishes, to sustain the Mirrors. And even if we had managed to capture the genie and force him to wish the Mirrors back to full strength, it wouldn't have lasted forever. The magic would have killed him eventually, just as it did all the others. The truth is, sooner or later we'd be right where we are now."

"Except we'd have had time to work on a solution," Henry snapped. "Now we've got, what, four, maybe five weeks before the belief starts running out? The characters won't keep retelling the story, not anymore. Not now they've got all their little 'inventions' to keep them occupied."

"We can find another way to fix the Mirrors, we just need time and patience."

"Time and patience?" Henry repeated, incredulous. "Mortal gods! You haven't got a clue, have you? Bloody blue suits, you're all the same. You think you're so much better than us boys and girls in brown, just because you manage the stories. Well, sonny, while you've got your nose in a Book, we're on the actual streets, doing actual work. So let me tell you a little something about your precious 'time and patience'. Right now, the city's working. Goods are coming in, and everyone's happy. And that'll last just as long as the Mirrors do."

Henry spat on the floor. "There's your 'time and patience'. As soon as the Mirrors go down again, they'll be a riot—another rush on the Grand Reflection Station. But of course, you Plotters didn't deal with that, did you? No. It was us brown suits who dispersed the mob and picked up the bodies. Damn your time and patience. We need a solution now."

Mistasinon wiped his hand across his face, stalling for time. Henry was right. They did need a solution, and he didn't have one to offer. He'd wanted the genie because he'd thought there might be something in the lamp, something they could use to power the Mirrors without killing the genie himself. He'd also hoped to talk to him, to ask him questions about magic and how it worked.

But his plan had gone wrong, and now they had nothing.

Henry was glaring at him, waiting for a response he simply didn't have. Mistasinon took a deep breath. His chest and ribs felt like something was crushing them. Ignoring it, he prepared himself to admit his failure and accept the consequences.

He didn't manage a word.

Julia very gently rapped her knuckles on the table. Everyone turned to look at her. "My Lord Henry, you are quite right to be angry. All of you are. But it is not my Lord Plotter's fault that we lost the genie. It is mine."

Stunned silence.

Julia continued. "The plan to send in the cabbage fairy to gain the genie's trust and then to have him volunteer his lamp to us was, I admit, a bold one." She glanced around the room. "And yes, some here may believe my Lord Plotter's suggestion to try to reason with the genie rather than have the Beast capture it was foolish, or that his late arrival at the Ball forced my hand. But I am the one who vouched for him, and I am the one who lost confidence and sent in the ogre and the witchlein. It's my fault the genie escaped."

Mistasinon's mind raced ahead, trying to chart the suddenly foreign landscape of the conversation. What was she playing at? She could easily have left him to hang for what had happened. Why was she putting her neck in the noose?

"My Lord Henry," Julia said, turning her gaze on the dwarf, who paled. "I want to apologise to you on behalf of the Redaction Department—I want to apologise to all of you. But it's still our job to decide what the right course of action is, and we can't do that if we're at each other's throats. Isn't that right, my Lord Plotter?"

Mistasinon met her bright blue eyes, searching for some clue to what she was thinking. He might as well have been trying to out outstare the sun.

"Yes. We were… over-eager."

"Over-eager?" Henry repeated incredulously, his dislike of Mistasinon momentarily overcoming his fear of Julia. "It'll take a miracle to undo the damage he's done. Why is he even here? He's not a Head. He's—"

Julia held up her hand; Henry fell silent. "My Lord Plotter is here because I want him here. And the fae don't expect a miracle. They expect a plan, and they trust us to provide them with one."

It was impossible, Mistasinon realised. She'd thrown him completely, and now Henry and the Indexers were all looking at him, waiting to see how he would respond to such a public show of preference.

"Yes... Yes, exactly. Things have been difficult for a long time now… And while I thank my Lady Redactionist for her support, I acknowledge my plan was flawed. But so was the plan to capture the last genie and wish him to death. We need something sustainable."

A flash of something passed over Julia's face, so quickly he couldn't be certain what it was. If there hadn't been so many people in the room, so many emotions running high, he might have tried to find out, but as it was, he had no choice but to let it go.

"I agree," Julia said. "The truth is, we know next to nothing about how the Mirrors work, and thanks to our misguided attempt to reason with a genie, we lost our only possible chance of sustaining them. Or so it seems, at the moment."

She stopped, letting the sentence hang in the air like a fishhook.

"You have a plan?" Henry asked, taking the bait.

Julia looked down the table at Mistasinon.

"I would like to suggest that you, my Lord Plotter, investigate the Mirrors. We need to know how they work."

No one in the room, including Mistasinon, could hide their surprise. Henry, in particular, looked like his eyes were about to pop out of his head, giving his already somewhat bug-eyed expression an added urgency.

Mistasinon leaned forward, addressing Julia across the table. "My Lady Redactionist, I... I'm honoured, of course. But if I'm honest, this is unexpected."

"I have turned the page, my Lord, as all sensible people must. We need solutions, and I believe you are the best person to find them for us. Does anyone really disagree?"

Mistasinon was absolutely certain everyone disagreed, but no one seemed inclined to say so. Then, very slowly, the Primary Binder raised a trembling hand.

"Yes?" Mistasinon said gently.

"I was just wondering... Why isn't the Teller, *whocaresaboutus,* here? I mean... shouldn't he be telling us what to do?" He glanced nervously at Julia. "I don't mean my Lady Redactionist is wrong, I only... I just feel like the Teller, *whocaresaboutus,* should be here. That's all," he finished, his voice barely above a whisper.

"Simon, isn't it?" Mistasinon asked, smiling at the Primary Binder.

If the Heads of the GenAm hadn't known better, they might have said that Mistasinon had magic in his smile. When he smiled, it was like being welcomed home after a long day by an old friend.

He had a way about his smile that made you believe that he really meant it.

Which was, in fact, his secret.

He stood up and walked around the table to kneel next to Simon, fixing him with his large brown eyes.

"He's not here because he trusts us," he said, resting his hand gently on the boy's thigh. "He trusts us to find out how the Mirrors work and to fix them, permanently. And we can. I'm certain of it. The Teller Cares About Us."

For a painful moment no one answered, but then Simon nodded his head. "The Teller Cares About Us," he said.

"The Teller Cares About Us," the rest of the room repeated.

Mistasinon beamed. "Exactly. Because we're worth caring about."

The meeting broke up, and the suits went back to their Departments, tired and drained. Not for the first time since joining the Plot Department, Mistasinon wondered if he'd made a mistake. He drummed his fingers on the tabletop. He needed to concentrate on what had happened in the meeting, not spin around in circles.

He was finding it harder to keep his thoughts organised. The distraction of being around other people helped, but even the GenAm didn't hold meetings in the middle of the night.

Well, not often, anyway.

Or, he corrected, certainly not what could be called a traditional 'meeting'. The kinds of meetings the GenAm held in the middle of the night usually only had one person talking, for example. Although there would be a number of people listening. The Redaction Department, especially, was very keen on listening.

Something in the air caught his attention, momentarily settling him as Julia's familiar scent washed over his frazzled senses.

"Come in, Julia."

The door opened, and Julia re-entered the room.

"You haven't lost the knack, I see," she said. "Always sniffing things out."

Mistasinon stood and bowed. "My Lady," he replied noncommittally.

The Head Redactionist returned the bow and took her seat at the foot of the table. Although, Mistasinon thought, it could just as easily be the head. Everything was a matter of perspective, wasn't it?

"I was surprised you invited me to the meeting. And by your admission," he said, sitting.

"You thought you were going to be held to account?"

"Yes."

"Whatever for? You had a plan, which is more than any of the Heads have managed."

"A plan that didn't work."

Julia waved the statement away. "These things happen, my Lord. Especially when one is striving for change, for a better world."

He dropped his eyes. "You make it sound easy. People died."

"We both have blood on our hands, my Lord. There's no point wasting time lamenting it. And as you said, the belief is pouring in."

"Because I sanctioned a Plot in which people died," Mistasinon repeated.

Julia sighed. "You did that for that fairy of yours, and you got what you wanted, didn't you? Even if I were so inclined, I could hardly Redact her now, not after she was so publicly accepted. No, no, I'm not saying that I would," she added quickly, seeing the look that passed over his face. "I simply mean, why should you bother second-guessing yourself over it? And what harm has that Plot done, really? The Mirrors are working. Fear always creates belief, isn't that so?"

Distaste soured Mistasinon's expression. "We can't return to the old stories, to the blood and bone. They were cruel—the fae were cruel. They treated the characters like slaves."

"Hardly. Slaves would have done what we wanted them to."

"But all slaves rebel, sooner or later."

"And what would be your solution?"

"The other pathways—I know it's only a story, a legend, but if it's true, we could bypass the Mirrors completely. We wouldn't need—"

75

Julia shot him a look so old-fashioned it had come back into style again. "You're not a character. You shouldn't rely on stories. Belief is too easily manipulated."

"Then why do you continue to vouch for me, if you think I'm wrong?"

"My Lord, let me stop you. You think this is personal, and it isn't. When the Teller... what shall we say? Changed your role? You went to the Plotters even though we'd been colleagues for so long. But I understand why, and I forgive you for it. The truth is, I don't need your friendship, but I suspect you need mine. And I'm prepared to offer it to you because, despite our differences, I'm not your enemy. We're both working towards the same goal."

"We are?"

"We want what's best for the city. We want to avoid another civil war. Isn't that right?"

Mistasinon paused. "Yes. That's right."

"You're wary. I understand. All this must be very hard for you, considering." She fixed him with her cool blue stare. "How long has it been—a year? Tell me, do you miss him?"

A lump formed in his throat. Mistasinon swallowed. "Yes. But I understand the need for secrecy."

"You're loyal." Julia leaned forward, closing the gap between them. "He knew that, and so do I. That's why I want you to be the one to investigate the Mirrors. Will you do it?"

"Of course I will," Mistasinon said, trying to focus. The conversation had flowed too quickly, prying at cracks in the dam, threatening the release of painful memories. He felt like he was in danger of drowning. "But if I research the Mirrors and find nothing? What then?"

"I won't be able to save you a second time."

"I'll be Redacted, then."

"I'd prefer not. We need to show the other Heads your value, that's all."

"And what if I don't have any value anymore? You heard what Henry said."

The words were out of his mouth before he could stop them, spoken by another part of him, one he didn't know how to silence.

Julia tilted her head, her expression softening. A wave of humiliation washed over him as he realised he was grateful for her pity.

"You know more than anyone about the Mirrors," Julia said. "You were here when the GenAm was founded, and you've worked with all the Heads of the Departments, past and present. You've lived a long life. There's always value in knowledge if you know how to use it. But I've taken up too much of your time, my Lord. Remember, my door is always open if you need me."

With that, she bowed and left the meeting room.

Mistasinon sat, stood up, and sat down again. He placed his hands on the table, staring at his fingers. He needed to clip his nails. It was important to keep himself tidy, well-groomed. To look the part.

A muscle jumped in his jaw.

He pulled his hands back, no longer wanting to look at them.

Perhaps he was wrong about Julia.

Perhaps, if he had official access to the Mirrors, he could still discover something about where they came from, how they worked.

Perhaps he could still keep his promise.

He brought his hands to his neck, squeezing the long column of his throat. There were too many possibilities, too many choices, all pulling him in different directions. And then, with the inevitability of a misbalanced scale, a new thought rose up from the chaotic shadows of his mind.

Julia hadn't seemed interested in Bea.

It wasn't that guilt was a new feeling for him. He'd known the burning heat of shame in his stomach for as long as he could remember, but it was a fire that had been stoked by others. Now it was his own choices fuelling it.

He'd been terrified that Bea would take the fall for his mistakes. Even when he'd got her into the Academy, he hadn't been able to relax. He should never have told her the truth about the genics and the Mirrors. The knowledge put her in danger. More than that, it burdened her.

So why had he told her? What had he been thinking? He could have lied. He could have protected her—protected himself. But instead, he'd told her the truth.

Mortal gods... Did everyone feel like this, all the time? Or was it just him?

Just him...

What did that even mean? How could he even be sure which thoughts were his own... and now he had to make decisions and fix the things he'd broken. He had to balance it all with crooked scales, using measurements he didn't understand.

Mistasinon dropped his head into his hands, while behind his eyes, thoughts clamoured for his attention.

He wished someone would tell him what to do.

XI

The Academy served breakfast early, while most of the recruits were still half-asleep. Bea very quickly reached the conclusion this was probably to mask the dreadful quality of the food.

She tried to stir the grey porridge she'd been given, but gave up when her wrist started to hurt. They were back in the assembly hall, with its long wooden tables and GenAm banners hanging from the ceiling, the storm still raging above their heads, visible through the glass. The weather matched her mood, at least. Bea had managed to snatch a couple of hours of sleep the night before, her insomnia not helped by her very real fear she'd wake up Chokey or Hemmings if she had another nightmare.

"Hullo, Buttercup!" Chokey said, taking the seat next to Bea. Hemmings flopped down opposite. "You snuck out early—I had hoped we might get dressed together. I really wanted to have a go at your hair. It's so thick, it's no wonder you have such trouble keeping it tidy. Of course, there's nothing wrong with having messy hair, I suppose."

"I just wanted to get a good start on the day," Bea replied vaguely.

"I can't imagine why," Hemming said, inspecting his food. He took a mouthful, chewed, and then swallowed. "This is better than the muck our governess made for us," he explained, seeing the impressed look Bea was giving him.

"Seriously? I thought life was supposed to be better for you inner-circlers."

Hemmings' lip twitched.

"Gosh, Buttercup, why so glum?" Chokey said, missing the sarcasm. "I suppose it's because of the test?"

Bea's spoon froze, halfway to her mouth.

Once, she'd missed one of the steps on a staircase and tumbled, head over heels, down the flight of stairs. She still remembered the feeling when she'd realised that her entire equilibrium was balanced on a leg that had absolutely nothing to stand on and that it was too late to do anything about it.

How she felt now was exactly like that.

"Test?"

"The form test, darling."

"What's a form test?"

Chokey gave her a quizzical look. "It's the exam you take to decide which class you'll go in. If you do well, you'll be put in with the best Masters. They say if you're well placed, you're guaranteed to graduate a top tier FME."

Bea put her spoon down. "And what happens if, you know, someone were to fail?"

"Well, I expect it depends on how badly they failed. They could be expelled if they really ploughed it. Didn't you cover all this before you arrived?"

"Oh. Yes. I must have forgotten," Bea lied. She couldn't face trying to explain to Chokey that she didn't have the faintest idea what was happening. It was bound to all circle back to Mistasinon and the circumstances of her recommendation to the Academy.

"Well, nothing to worry about then. Oh look, there's Tiff! I must say hullo!"

Chokey bustled off to speak to her friend. Hemmings leaned forward and picked up Chokey's bowl, spooning the remains of her food into his own.

"I should eat up if I were you," he said. "It won't get any better if it's cold."

Bea nodded glumly and had another go at her breakfast.

How in the worlds was she going to pass a test she hadn't revised for? All her plans for getting through the Academy and graduating as a godmother, for working her way into the GenAm and then pulling the whole damn thing to pieces from the inside, were flittering away like birds at the beginning of winter.

"Besides, it's only a test," Hemming said from behind the curtain of his hair, his concentration fixed on his bowl. "What does it matter what kind of FME you are, as long as you're contributing? The trouble is, no one realises a leaf is a tree. Except me, of course."

Bea swallowed a mouthful of her breakfast. It took some effort.

"Pardon?"

"You think a leaf is an individual thing?" Hemmings asked, still not looking up. He ran his finger around the edge of his bowl, scraping up the bits of porridge stuck there.

Bea nodded. "Yes, of course. But you just said it was a tree."

"And so it is, really. A leaf comes from the bark, from the roots. Where were you born?"

"The Sheltering Forest," Bea answered, absently taking another spoonful of porridge.

Hemmings shook his head, finally looking at her, his eyes bright in his pale face. "No, no, no. You're from the Rhyme War, when so much of the Land was destroyed. You're from the bargain between Ænathlin and the Forest to protect each other. You're from, I don't know, the time your mother got lost when she was young and felt afraid, or when your great-grandfather decided he wanted to live in the north of the Forest and not the south. All those choices and feelings changed the world you grew up in and made you, you. You're from the garden fairies, and the court of the King and Queen, and the GenAm. You're a leaf, yes, but you're also the tree."

"And that's how you see yourself?" Bea asked, fascinated. "As a leaf stuck to a tree?"

"Of course."

"But then, how can you ever change anything? How can you make things better?"

"By thoughtsmithing and helping the tree to grow. Leaves capture the sun. I'm only a small leaf, though. You're a big leaf."

"What? No you're not—no I'm not."

"Really?" Hemmings nodded at one of the other long tables. "What about that imp, over there? She's been staring at you all through breakfast."

Bea looked over her shoulder, in the direction Hemmings had indicated. Two tables over, Carol was glaring at her. Bea waved. Carol frowned and turned her attention to her breakfast, which was congealing rapidly. Bea fancied she saw the imp's scowl deepen. Who'd have thought? The appalling standard of the food was a unifying force.

"Oh, her. She's always hated me, ever since we Plot-watched together," Bea said.

"Really? Mmm. One rather wonders how her branch is connected to yours."

"Alright, I see what you mean. We're all made up of our pasts, right? Our environment, the choices made by people who died before we were even born, and the things we did and didn't do. But we're still alive now, we still have a responsibility for how we behave. Carol's still a fairy-hater, for example. Just because almost everyone is, doesn't excuse her."

"No. But isn't that why we need to help the tree?"

"You make it sound like I should be friends with her," Bea said, incredulous.

"Perhaps. Enmity is often a very important ingredient in friendships," Hemmings mused. "A friend who holds us in absolute esteem probably doesn't know us very well. Or else they are a liar, and shouldn't be our friend anyway."

"Even if I wanted to make friends with her, which I don't, she wouldn't be friends with me," Bea said.

"If you say so."

"You disagree?"

"No one's ever taken such an interest in me, that's all. People don't like to be faced by their intellectual betters, I suppose. Are you going to finish that?"

Bea pushed her half-empty bowl across the table and watched as Hemmings dug in. She looked down at her hands. The skin around her fingernails was starting to fray, a result of her chewing them too much.

When Seven had crashed into her life, telling her things she didn't want to know, making her see the characters and the Plots for what they truly were, she'd done the unthinkable and changed them, despite the risk to herself.

Then Mistasinon had told her the real reason the Redactionists had attacked the Ball, killing and injuring all those people. The GenAm had murdered almost the entire genie tribe to keep the Mirrors working and the Plots churning, to maintain their power and control over everyone's lives.

But for better or worse, she knew the truth. So it didn't matter if she was a big leaf or a small one—hells, it was more likely she was a mushroom, growing in the muck at the bottom of the trunk. It was up to her to save the tree, because who else would?

And now it was all going to end, not with a bang, not even with a whimper, but with a failed test.

The room wasn't really small. It just seemed that way thanks to the rows of desks, all spaced out like little islands.

Bea checked the list hanging on the door and sat at the desk assigned to her. She'd never taken an exam before, but she recognised the atmosphere, which had a hard emphasis on the final syllable of the word.

The space was filled with the soft buzz of people trying very hard to be quiet, the scrape of wooden chair legs against the stone floor, and dozens of hearts beating too fast. Bea glanced around, noting the expressions on her fellow recruits' faces. Most were managing only to look like they wanted to be sick. Some, however, appeared to have given up on life altogether and were sitting, pale and sweaty, waiting for death to do the decent thing and claim them.

Bea waited while the rest of the recruits took their seats. Chokey and Hemmings were sitting near her, but annoyingly Carol's allotted desk was closer. The imp caught Bea's shoulder with her elbow as she walked past. On her other side, Bea recognised the red-haired brownie who she'd given the mint to the day before. None of the other recruits were familiar, though she saw Chokey waving surreptitiously at her friends.

A somehow more silent silence fell over the room, and Bea turned her head forward. West was standing at the top of the room, as stern and uncompromising as the night before, the large troll with the black eyes from the meet-and-greet next to her. He glared furiously at the room, his gaze remaining on Bea a beat longer than anyone else.

Mortal gods, he really does hate me, Bea realised. And then she reminded herself that most people hated fairies and tried to be comforted by the thought.

"The test will take three hours, and there will be no break," West announced.

A muted groan rose up from the rest of the recruits. Bea wasn't worried. She'd been through worse waits while Plot-watching and knew she could hold her concentration—and her bladder—for three hours. Besides, she hadn't revised. It was hardly going to be a challenging exam, considering she knew she was going to fail anyway.

"Before we begin, there are some questions," West said, looking over the recruits.

Bea's forehead creased. There was something wrong in what West had said, but she couldn't place what it was. Perhaps it was just the fact she'd asked for questions? No one ever took up the offer—it was a pointless formality and only made waiting even worse. So decided, Bea started lining her pencils up, so they lay neatly parallel to the edge of her desk.

"Is this test peer marked, or is it based on a scheme?" Carol said, her voice ringing out like a bell in the silence.

Bea's head snapped up. She couldn't believe it.

"You will be marked according to a scheme," West answered matter-of-factly. She seemed to be the only person in the room not in a state of shock.

"I've another question if you don't mind," Carol continued, her hand still raised.

"Yes, you do."

"When will we get the results?"

"Tomorrow evening," West replied. "Classes will begin the following day."

"And will we be given feedback?"

"I can give you all your feedback now," West said to the room. "You will pass, or you will fail. If you pass, you are merely good enough to begin the process of learning how to work for the GenAm. And if you fail, your feedback is that you are not good enough, and you will be sent home. Now, the papers will be handed out. Do not touch them until I give permission."

A group of brown suits picked up the papers and started handing them out. The witchlein was thankfully absent.

"You may begin," West announced. The room filled with the ominous creak of paper being handled and an air of terrified concentration.

Bea stared at her test. The irony was not lost on her that after everything she'd done—changing Plots, befriending genies, fighting ogres, nearly dying—it was a piece of paper that was going to see her fail. Sighing, she opened the booklet.

Her heart missed a beat.

She stared at the first page of the exam.

That couldn't be right…

Confused, she looked up at the other recruits. They were all hunched over their papers, getting on with their exams, which probably meant they had exams to be getting on with.

Bea looked back down at the near-blank sheet of paper in front of her. All that marked the page was one question. She flicked through the other pages, but all they said was 'please refer to question #1'.

Something was definitely amiss. The question in front of her had, could *only* have, one answer. In fact, the harder question was, who had written this test for her?

Because there was no doubt in her mind that the question in front of her was unique, and that she was the only recruit to be posed with it:

DO YOU BELIEVE THAT THE TELLER CARES ABOUT YOU?

Bea fiddled with her pencil and pondered stubbornly what to do. But she realised she had no options. Sure, she could write an essay on the various merits of the Teller and the GenAm; she could even risk being critical. But ultimately there was only one answer she could give.

She pressed her pencil to the page and wrote:

Yes.

XII

Outside the exam room, Bea grabbed Chokey.

"How did you do?"

"Gosh, darling, awfully, I'm sure. Can you believe they included that one about the five facial qualities of a hero? I know they come in different styles and so on, but they always look the same to me. I can't help it. Our governess used to jump out at me with flashcards, you know? '*Tall, dark and handsome*', '*blond-haired and blue-eyed*'. All it did was make me terrified of walking down the hallways. And Papa was never best pleased when the woodcutter's bills came through—she'd always have them printed in colour, just to add insult to injury. Oh look, there's Tiff. Let's ask her. Tiff! Tiff!"

A dark-haired imp with emerald skin and a wide smile wandered over to them.

"Well, that was a bloody shambles. I'd like to know who thought of question twelve," she said.

"Question twelve?" Bea asked weakly.

"The one about the eighteenth amendment to the sub-Plots. I mean, who cares? No one in their right mind would run more than one sub-Plot, anyway. The whole point is that the Teller, *whocaresaboutus,* made the stories simple."

"Gosh yes," said Chokey, nodding her head like it was on a counter-weight. "The characters couldn't keep up otherwise."

"Exactly. Stupid creatures."

"Although Buttercup's rather fond of them, aren't you, darling?"

Bea woke up from her thoughts about her test. "Yes, I am. They're nice if you get to know them."

Tiff and Chokey exchanged looks, and then Tiff burst out laughing.

"Well, you were right about her, Chokes. I can see why you wanted her all to yourself. You're both to come to my room tonight, d'you hear? I'm having a little get-together, while we still have the chance. Once classes start, this place is going to be a positive tomb."

"Wonderful!" Chokey exclaimed. "We'll see you there. Only, can Hemmings come too? I really do feel awful when he's left out. He is my brother, after all."

"Oh, if you insist," Tiff said. "My bloody cousin's coming, so I suppose he might as well, too. But I don't want any of his nonsense. He brings down the whole mood."

"I shall make him swear to it," Chokey said.

Tiff didn't look entirely convinced that this would be enough to contain Hemmings' enthusiasm for thoughtsmithing, but she smiled and said her goodbyes without mentioning it again.

"Well, that's a nice surprise, in any event," said Chokey. "Tiff always puts on the most amazing bashes. She's got her own room, too. Family's ever so wealthy, they've a series of dragon's dens, and they own part of the Grand Reflection Station. They're distantly related to Rumpelstiltskin, did you know? Of course, they were sensible enough to renounce the connection when the Teller, *whocaresaboutus*, came in. A party! I can't think of anything better!"

***

"I have news, my Lady," Barret said as he entered West's office, his dark eyes softening when they landed on her. "I think you'll be..." he stopped. 'Surprised' wasn't the right word, not exactly. "Interested," he settled on.

West looked up. "Oh?"

"The report has come back from the elves. The most recent iteration of the process was a success. The ETP didn't wake up, not once, and I set very rigorous conditions. I can assure you, the formula now works," he added proudly.

"Mmm. That's encouraging." West glanced over at the corner of the room where the original ETP was kept.

They couldn't keep it with the later versions. There was something about the original that set them off. Although that didn't exactly explain why West kept it in her office. Barret had offered to dispose of it, but West had declined. She seemed attached to it, for some reason.

"We run a story, next," West instructed. "A small one, but with some punch. That's how things get started. I'm so nearly where I'm meant to be, Barret—so nearly there. Your associates are up to the task?"

Barret wasn't sure if it was a question or not. West had a funny way with questions. She said the words in the right order, but the cadence of her voice didn't match them. Her questions had a habit of sounding like statements; as if she already knew the answer. It had taken him a good few months to get used to it. Still, this time she was looking at him expectantly.

"There are some issues," he admitted. "The new ones are still singing. The smiling's more of a problem, though—it's a little, ah, unnerving. But yes, we could run a pilot, now we know it works. I'll have one of the fresh ETPs delivered to the elves."

West cocked her head.

"She'll hear it again."

"My Lady?"

West's eyes were losing focus. When she spoke next, her voice sounded distant, like she was speaking from the bottom of a well.

"Singing, Barret, you were talking about the singing.... She'll hear the song again when the sky opens and the air tastes of saltwater."

Barret checked his pocket watch, the one he'd been given especially for this purpose. The hours twelve, four and eight had large red marks on the glass above them. But it was only six fifteen. He made a mental note to let the dead-head goblin know when she next came to the Academy.

"I'm here, my Lady," he said, taking a pair of heavy gloves out of his suit pocket and pulling them on. "Don't worry, I'm here."

"In the woods, in the woods," West said. "When he sees the girl. That's the moment it all splinters. Which one gets the body?"

"I don't know, my Lady," Barret said, humouring her.

Stepping around her, he pulled open the top drawer of her desk. He took out the bottle of medicine as carefully as he could, the heavy gloves making his actions clumsy. It was a bloody tricky

thing: wear the gloves and risk a spill, don't wear the gloves and...
well, Barret didn't like to think about that too much.

He gingerly placed the bottle next to her and, while not exactly
jumping, managed to distance himself from it almost immediately
he set it down.

West's eyes focused on the bottle. Inside it, a chalky, dirty white
substance glooped thickly against the glass. She looked up at
Barret. "You always know... how do you know...?"

"It's my job to know, my Lady," he said gently.

West grabbed Barret's thick arm, squeezing him. "Go left," West
said. "Left. Promise me."

"I promise."

"Do you believe me, Barret?"

"Of course, my Lady," he said diplomatically. "Now drink up,
and you'll feel more like yourself." Or less. He hadn't quite
worked it out.

Grasping the bottle, West brought it greedily to her lips. She
chugged the contents in a matter of seconds, so quickly Barret was
worried she might choke—the mortal gods knew what he would do
if she did. But this time, as with all the times before, she was safe.

She took a deep breath, regaining her composure. "Very good,
Barret. Thank you, as always. Now, I think we should try altering
the words we use when we're emptying them..."

Barret sat opposite West and started taking notes.

He'd long given up trying to understand how her mind worked.
He had been sent to aid West because of his size and his loyalty,
not because of his brains. He wasn't here to second-guess a genius,
nor was he here to question the plan. No matter what the GenAm
told everyone else, Barret knew the truth: the Mirrors were
breaking.

Here, with West, he had a chance to be part of the solution.
Barret allowed himself a small smile.

Whatever else was happening, it felt good to be important, to
matter.

XIII

Thaiana, the human world, was made up of five Kingdoms, each of which had their own version of hell, just as they had their own gods.

The Land of the Fae had nothing so spiritual, and so they had taken to stealing mythology from the characters. It made sense, in a twisted kind of way. The fae stole everything else from the characters, so why not their faiths too?

And so, like most narratives that are told, retold, and rarely thought about, the humans' religions seeped into fae society to the point where they weren't even noticed anymore. The 'mortal gods' were thanked when things went well and cursed when things went badly; the 'five hells' invoked in surprise or anger. And all without any of the fae ever wondering how strange it was that they relied so exclusively on the stories of a culture they despised.

Bea, however, was currently giving the five hells a great deal of thought.

She made a mental note that the next time she was working on a Plot, she would find the time to sit the heroine down and really try to get to the bottom of what the five hells actually were, and how one ended up there. She had a sinking feeling she might have stumbled into one accidentally.

Tiff's room was much bigger than the one Bea shared with Chokey and Hemmings, and it seemed that she had it all to herself. There was a large, wide bed in one corner and a number of sofas and chairs dotted around the floor, comfortably spaced thanks to the generous proportions of the room. There was a makeshift bar along one wall, its surface already sticky with spilt liquor and wines. Food had been provided, though not nearly in enough quantity to counter-balance the alcohol. Dotted around were bulb-shaped pipes with long arms coming off them, on which some of the guests were happily sucking. The faint smell, sweet and musky, of calaris root and fenlandriz filled the air.

The only things that seemed familiar were the GenAm banners hanging from the walls, dark red with black writing, reminding everyone that 'The Teller Cares About You'. But then Bea supposed even someone as important as Tiff couldn't escape the influence of the Teller completely.

She had been here an hour and had hated every minute of it.

It wasn't that she didn't like parties. She had no issue with people drinking or enjoying their free time. Mortal gods, she'd been drunk enough herself not to begrudge others the same enjoyment. But there was something wrong here, and she couldn't put her finger on what it was.

On the surface, it seemed like any other party. Everyone was laughing and chatting, little bubbles of conversation springing up as if from a blocked drain. And yet, she could see that no one was really listening to each other; their eyes were always darting around, looking for a better person to talk to or stand with. And when she did catch snippets of conversation, it struck her that it was always at someone else's expense.

There were moves being made, turns and counter turns, that reminded Bea of a game Ivor had taught her, the one with the figures that fought each other across a chequered board. It had looked easy when Ivor had invited her to play, but as he'd started explaining to her how each figure could or couldn't move, she'd realised it was in fact extremely complicated and required huge amounts of concentration.

The interactions between Tiff's guests were the same. Someone would say something to someone else that sounded innocent enough, even friendly, like, "Oh, darling, you decided to come! I'm so pleased." But then they'd add, "Aren't you brave! I truly admire your spirit, especially considering what happened at Jilly's". Bea would then watch the face of the other person go tight, and they'd soon make their excuses and move to another group. The ones left behind would laugh as if something very funny had just happened.

The whole thing smacked of bullying, but it wasn't the kind that Bea was used to. Whenever anyone had wanted to put her down, they'd just focused on her being a fairy, and a garden fairy to boot. So roundly disliked were the fairies, there was very little need to be subtle. Whereas the party guests seemed to take pleasure in masking their nastiness behind kind words.

Bea looked around for Chokey and Hemmings. They'd come in together, but she'd wanted to use the bathroom and when she'd returned, they'd both disappeared. After ten minutes of looking, she eventually heard Chokey's voice, not quite drowned out by the sounds of the party. She found the dwarf sat on the arm of a chair, chatting to a group of friends. Every now and again, Chokey would tear off a chunk of bread from a roll she had in her hand and lob it into the room. The dwarf looked unhappy, but when she spotted Bea, she grinned widely.

"Oh, isn't it too funny, Buttercup? I was trying to get Wilkie, but I kept missing, and now I think I'll just keep it up all night. No one's worked out it's me yet!"

Bea shrugged. "Seems like a waste of bread to me."

Chokey's friends roared with laughter. A male dwarf with a thick, red beard that clashed with his nose shoved a glass of wine into Bea's hands. "So, what's it like being a fairy then?"

"What's it like being a dwarf?"

"Bloody terrific," he guffawed, spilling his drink over Bea as he waved his hand around. "No one expects much from a dwarf! We get to work on most stories, and we didn't have any involvement with the King and Queen, so the Great Redaction didn't hurt us. Life's grand, ain't that right, Chokeroo?"

Chokey threw another lump of bread into the room, hitting a brownie on the ear. "Grand, darling, ever so. Oh, look! I think I've started a fight!"

Bea put her wine glass down, untouched. "Chokey, I think I'm going to head back to the room."

"What? Buttercup, don't be silly! It's only just getting started."

"I know, but I've got a headache," Bea said, pulling out the old lie. Classics are classics for a reason, after all.

"Hah," barked the red-bearded dwarf. "Probably spending too much time with Chokes. Never met anyone so bloody loud before, I'll bet? Oh, but we're all incredibly fond of her. Her and her ward. What a pair! One shouting and the other moping. Bloody hilarious!"

"Oh, Roo! You know Hemmings can't help it," Chokey admonished. She jumped off the chair and grabbed Bea by the arm, pulling her away from the group. "Come on, Buttercup, I want to show you off."

"I'm sorry," Bea said when they were out of earshot. "I didn't mean to give him a way to be mean to you."

Chokey turned to Bea, a brittle smile on her face. "Whatever do you mean? He was just teasing, darling. Builds character, a good bit of teasing. Oh, look! There's Hemmings. Hemmings! Hemmings!"

Hemmings, no doubt in an ill-thought-out bid to bring some enlightenment to his tribe, had entered into a conversation with a group of elves. They were now singing and dancing a merry-go-round around him, wrapping him up in ribbons every time the dance brought them in close. As a result, Hemmings, dressed entirely in black and with an equally dark expression on his pretty face, looked not unlike a maypole at a funeral.

"Oh dear, how *frite-fully* funny," Chokey wheezed. "He does invite this kind of thing, poor dear. Hold on, I'll go and rescue him."

Even Bea had to stop herself laughing. "No, wait—I've got an idea. Watch."

She marched up to the group of elves. "What ho and marry, gentle elves! You know, we fairies love this dance—it's all the rage by the wall!"

A look of horror rippled across the nearest elf's elegant features. "You know this dance?"

"I should say so! It's a classic!" Bea replied. "Will you do the bumps at the end? That's the best bit, isn't it?" She bowed and held her hand out. "Mind if I join in?"

The elf recoiled. "Marry, fairy, do not deign to touch me!"

"Oops, sorry," Bea said, trying not to grin. "But I can hardly dance with you without touching, can I?"

The elf looked like she was going to faint. "Brothers and sisters, I fancy I am tired of the dance. Let us find a new distraction."

"Oh, dear! Please do accept my warmest congratulations for your efforts—I hear you were simply splendid at the Trumpeting-

Beanfarts' hootenanny last month!" Bea shouted at the elves as they marched off.

She turned to Hemmings. "How about you, Mister Elf? Dance?"

Hemmings started disentangling himself from the ribbons. "I hate dancing. It is the mind that should be exercised, not the body. Still… Thank you," he said, offering her a grateful smile.

Bea couldn't help noticing the tiny scars on his face. When he smiled and the apples of his cheeks scrunched up, they were clearly visible, delicate cross-hatching of fine white lines.

Now she could see them properly, she noticed that his scars were thinner than the ones on her leg. It might be that time had softened them, but Bea suspected not. She wondered again what had happened to him. Chokey had said her father had found him at the Grand Reflection Station in bad circumstances… but then, she'd also said that those circumstances had been a rather unfashionable handbag.

Either way, Bea felt unable to ask Hemmings directly. Not only did she think it would be extremely rude, but she also had a sense that Hemmings knew very well that the scars showed when he smiled, which was why he did it so rarely. But he'd smiled at her, so she wasn't going to ruin it.

"Let's get Chokey and find a corner to sit in," Hemmings said, offering her his arm. "I think I've made my point well enough."

Bea took his arm. "Absolutely," she said.

❄

"I did rather hope that this might be a bit more interesting," Chokey said. "Since we're away from home. But it's all the same old round."

They were sat on the edge of Tiff's bath, hiding. So far they'd been lucky, and no one had needed the bathroom. The occasional rattling of the locked door was, no doubt, some lost soul looking for the exit and nothing to do with them.

Bea grinned. "You sound like Hemmings."

"I hardly think that's fair," Hemmings chided.

"Sorry."

"*I* always knew this party would be dreadful."

Bea ducked her head so that he wouldn't see her smiling. "You know, none of this is what I expected," she said when she'd regained her composure. "The Academy and everything, I mean."

"What did you expect?" Chokey asked.

"I don't know really," Bea said, nibbling what remained of her thumbnail. "I guess I didn't really think about the actual Academy at all. I wanted to be a godmother so badly it blinded me to a lot of things."

"Aren't you glad now you're here?"

"Oh… well… yes, of course I am."

Bea knew she didn't sound very convincing. She could taste the subtle tang of the lie on her tongue, and, had she been speaking to anyone else, she was certain they would have smelled it on her breath.

But Chokey was protected from all the nasty smells and tastes of the world. Bea didn't know how she managed it. Once, she might have thought it was Chokey's upbringing, but she was less convinced of that now. Hemmings came from the same home, but he couldn't be more different from his sister. Whatever it was that kept Chokey safe from the world hadn't been taught to the dark-haired elf.

But then, Bea thought, *brothers and sisters aren't always the same, are they?* After all, she'd run away while Mustard Seed, her brother, had chosen to stay in the Sheltering Forest with her mother and her clan. She'd told him there were opportunities in the city, that they could make something of their lives there, and that he was a fool to stay.

And now here she was, hiding in a toilet.

"That's good then!" Chokey replied happily, pulling Bea back from the chilly clutches of her memories.

Bea, Chokey and Hemmings exited the toilet to the great relief of the sizable queue waiting outside. Bea decided she wanted to leave, and, after a brief, albeit friendly, argument with Chokey, the dwarf agreed to let her go. Hemmings seemed torn, but in the end, he chose to stay with his sister.

Bea made her way through the roar of the party. Someone had produced a horn and was playing a jig. The lively tune jumped around the room, mixing with ease with all the different groups, pulling guests up to join it as it danced. Part of Bea longed to join in, but she didn't have the courage to dance alone.

She made her way towards the exit, her gaze fixed on the makeshift dance floor appearing in the middle of the room as pieces of Tiff's heavy furniture were dragged aside.

Which was how she banged into Carol.

For the briefest moment, before the imp's features settled into their familiar expression of disgust, Bea was almost certain Carol was looking wistfully at the dancers. But whatever she thought she saw vanished the second Carol realised who had bumped into her.

"Mortal gods, you clumsy ogre. What are you doing here, anyway?"

"I was invited, actually," Bea replied. She wanted to add that she'd seen an ogre and it had been anything but clumsy, but like everything else related to her Plot, she knew she couldn't.

"Invited?" Carol frowned. "Who invited you?"

Bea nodded at Tiff, who was being spun around in the centre of the dance. "She did."

"Tiffany…?"

"Yes, but I'm leaving now, anyway."

Carol's eyes narrowed. "So we're not good enough for you, is that it?"

Bea nearly staggered. "You *want* me to stay?"

"No."

"So why do you care if I leave?"

"I don't care what you do," Carol snapped. "The only thing you could possibly do to interest me would be to drop dead."

"Well, when I do, I'll be sure to come and haunt you." It wasn't the best retort ever, but Bea was proud of herself for keeping her cool.

"That doesn't surprise me. You're good at worming your way into places you're not wanted."

"I was invited," Bea repeated through clenched teeth.

Carol shrugged, apparently unaware of the supreme effort Bea was going to not to scream at her and make a scene. "Yes, well. I think we both know by now that being invited isn't the same as being wanted."

"Seriously, Carol—"

Bea had been about to swear at Carol, but something gave her pause. She looked the imp up and down. She was small and fine-boned, her long, blonde hair piled up on her head. She was wearing make-up and a pretty, pale pink dress. She looked like she'd made an effort.

And yet, like Bea, Carol had been standing alone, watching the dancers.

"Carol, are you—"

"Am I what?"

"Are you... I don't know... are you alright?"

Carol looked like she'd just had cold water unexpectedly dumped on her.

"Of course I'm 'alright'. I'm here with my peers. I've worked my *entire* life to be here—I *belong* here. The only thing that's ruining my evening is knowing that you're here. Mortal gods, it's like finding out the ugly sister's won the handsome prince, or the wicked old woman was right all along. It just shouldn't be. You're in the wrong story, cabbage mother—you're in my story. And just because no one else can see it yet doesn't mean you'll get away with it. Everyone here will see what you are, and you'll be written out soon enough."

XIV

Bea sat on her bed. She'd dug her bag of treasures out from under her pillow and lain them on the mattress.

The sword point necklace didn't glint or glitter. It was old steel, well-used. She picked it up, feeling the weight of it in her palm, remembering the moment she'd held the sword above her head, trying not to think about what would happen if she missed, trying not to notice the crumpled body of King John in a heap on the floor.

It had been heavier than the spears she'd used growing up, and the muscles in her arm had screamed at her while she tried to take aim.

She remembered she'd closed her eyes in the seconds between the sword leaving her hand and landing in the back of the ogre.

A tremor ran through her. Shaking it off, Bea packed up the necklace and her other private possessions and shoved them back under her pillow. She turned her attention to the window, deciding she ought to get some use out of the view, especially since she'd deprived Hemmings of it.

She ran her finger against the windowpane, watching as it cut a path through the condensation. The storm raged, flashes of white against black, a migraine made real. And then, suddenly, a flash of yellow.

"What…?"

Wiping the window, Bea pressed her face up to the glass.

In the distance lay what looked like a building against the dark mass of the forest, though the falling snow made it hard to be certain. Again there was a flash of yellow, a speck of light in the thick snowfall, emanating from the shadowy structure.

The bedroom door banged open, and Chokey bounded in, her cheeks flushed.

"Hemmings is just behind me—let's hide in the bathroom and jump out at him! Oh," she said, taking in the sight of Bea pressed up against the window. "Whatever are you doing?"

"Do you know if there are any other buildings here?" Bea asked, not moving.

"I should hardly think so. Quite frankly, I'm amazed anyone bothered with this one—it's hardly hospitable, is it?"

"I think I can see a light," Bea replied. She wiped the window again, trying to keep the glass clear. "Look, over there."

Chokey joined Bea on the bed.

"I can't see anything," she said.

"Look, just over there," Bea repeated.

"Where?"

"There. See?"

"I don't think this is funny, you know. You're just teasing me." Chokey grumbled. "Come on, he'll be here in a minute—it'll be such a hoot to scare him."

"There's definitely a light," Bea said, ignoring her. "It's hard to see because of the snow. Mortal gods, there could be anything going on out there, and no one would ever know."

"Well, even if there is another building, that doesn't mean anything," Chokey sighed, flopping down on her bed. "Big houses usually have outbuildings. Stables and woodsheds and so on. Besides, this is a school, not some kind of sinister haunted house with secret passageways and ominous goings-on."

Without thinking, Bea blurted out, "What about all the brown suits?"

"Whatever do you mean?"

Bea drummed her fingers on the windowsill, ignoring the dull pain from her bitten-down nails. Now she had to think of a way to explain what she'd meant without sounding like she was suspicious of the GenAm.

"Well... don't you think it would be better to have the brown suits policing Ænathlin, rather than here? That's where the Mirrors are."

"I expect they're here to stop Anties getting at us," Chokey said.

99

Now would be a really good time to let the conversation drop. Bea knew that. And yet she found herself saying, "Any Anti would freeze to death before they got close."

Bea gave herself a mental kick. Really, it was getting the point where if she kept opening her mouth without thinking she'd be invited to work in politics.

Chokey began untying her hair. "Not if they were a troll. They're built for the cold. Take that one that's always following West around. He's huge, I'm sure the weather wouldn't bother him. Not straight away, anyway."

"True," Bea conceded, "But we'd notice a troll sneaking up on us." She looked again at the landscape, obscured by the white haze of the snow. "Probably."

"An Anti could always come in via the Mirrors like we did."

Bea doubted it. The mirrors in the Academy, like all the mirrors in Thaiana, were normal glass. Thus, they could only be used to connect to one of the magic Mirrors in the Grand Reflection Station, where any fae passing through had to have their papers checked. So, in much the same way the Academy's mirrors were no escape, they weren't any kind of entry, either.

Anyway, why would the GenAm entrust the capturing of an Anti to a load of brown suits from the Contents Department when that was what the Beast was for?

The Beast's whole reason for being was to hunt down and capture Anties and then deliver them to the Redactionists. It was good at it. If it wasn't for the Beast, after all, the Teller never would have caught all those genies.

And then Bea remembered the witchlein.

They worked for the Redactionists, didn't they? Even if he was wearing a brown suit, that didn't mean anything. The Redaction Department were famous for using informers.

She realised she hadn't seen the witchlein since they'd arrived.

Somehow, that was worse. It was one thing to have a spider sitting in plain view in the corner of your room, but it was quite another to see the spider once and then never again.

Finally waking from its nap, Bea's good sense stepped in and advised her against saying any more on the subject. She pulled the curtains closed. "You're right. I must have imagined the light."

"I suppose it's not your fault, darling," Chokey said sympathetically. "Everyone knows fairies have a very over-active imagination. Aren't you lucky you're bunked up here with me to keep an eye on you?"

Just then, Hemmings stormed into the room, slamming the door behind him.

"Why did you run off like that," he snapped at Chokey. "I got cornered by that awful pixie girl, the one who always pretends she wants to talk about thoughtsmithing but then gets drunk and tries to kiss me."

Chokey burst out laughing. "Oh darling, it's your own fault for being so pretty and clever," she teased. "Who could resist you?"

"Beauty is an abstract concept, it's not my fault she finds me attractive. Anyway, you wouldn't say that if it was *you* she jumped on," Hemmings grumbled, quite rightly. "She says I'm 'intense'."

"Well, that's absolute nonsense, darling," Chokey grinned. "You've never been camping in your life."

Hemmings launched himself across the room, grabbed Chokey and demanded she apologise—which, between gulps of laughter, she steadfastly refused to do.

Bea watched them, wondering if she'd accidentally fallen through a Mirror. Chokey and Hemmings seemed to occupy another world, one of which she had no knowledge. A world in which things could be laughed off, where family arguments didn't end in running away.

And then she laughed and joined in as best she could, taking sides and teasing them both in equal measure. A while later, a brown suit knocked on the door, signalling lights out.

Bea lay in the darkness, the little leather bag causing a lump in her pillow which she couldn't be bothered to correct. Besides, if she was uncomfortable, she was less likely to fall asleep; less likely to wake Chokey and Hemmings if she had another nightmare.

She turned her mind to other things, such as why there were so many brown suits at the Academy, and why one of them was a witchlein. And what did the light she'd seen through the storm signify? Because it certainly meant something. If someone was

101

risking the cold to work away from the main building, what were they hiding?

In fact, very little at the Academy made any sense, now she had a moment to think about it. And, most alarming of all, who was altering tests to keep her here?

XV

"Welcome to Basic Plotting. My name is Master Dafi. Over the next six months, we will cover all the Plot structures, character profiles and common locations used by the GenAm."

Sat in the front row, Bea was trying to contain her nerves. She'd lined her pencils up neatly, opened her notebook to a fresh page, and written the date carefully in the top right corner. She was now resting her hands on her knees in an attempt to stop her legs fidgeting. Her hair was escaping its bun, but she didn't dare fix it less she drew attention to herself.

"The purpose of this module," Dafi continued, "Is to give you the foundational knowledge you will need if—and I say *if*—you are to become Fiction Management Executives. In six months, there will be a field test, after which you will be placed into classes for your specific roles. Do not think that because you passed the form test, you are on your way to becoming high tier FMEs like goal creators, facilitators or adversaries. You could just as easily be selected as mild perils or information givers."

The recruits exchanged nervous glances. No one wanted to be put in the morals stream, which was what Dafi was alluding to.

Morals were FMEs, at least technically. They tended to work on Young Belief and Tradition, and as such, the stories they ran were minor things with simplistic morals—hence their name. Morals' stories needed frequent repeating and, while very young characters provided a surge in belief, it didn't last long. As a result, morals were, despite their official status, in fact only one or two steps up from tooth fairies and Plot-watchers: odd-jobbers who did the dull work mainly because they were unqualified or unable to do anything else.

Perhaps that was why they had tampered with Bea's test—to make her a moral? It would make sense. She'd never have passed it otherwise, and now the GenAm could claim they'd given her the training, but she just hadn't been up to standard. No doubt they'd say it was because she was a fairy. It was unlikely anyone would argue the point.

Dafi fixed the room with a beady stare, his gaze lingering on Bea. "There are some of you who, quite frankly, I doubt will pass. In my day, the GenAm took recruitment seriously, but apparently, diversity is more important than ability. We shall see. Right then, I want you to break into small groups. You're going to tell stories about yourself. Each story will contain facts about your life, but one of these will be a lie. Your teammates must guess which is the lie."

Well, I'm off to a great start, Bea thought. It was painfully clear Dafi didn't want her in the class, and, judging from the sudden shifting of seats and averting of eyes from the other recruits, she wasn't the only one to have picked up on this.

She looked around her, at a loss. Who was she supposed to team up with? Chokey and Hemmings had been placed with different Masters, and the only other person she knew in Dafi's class was Carol, who so far had studiously ignored her. She was about to stand up and try to find a group to join when the freckled brownie with red hair came up to her desk, smiling nervously.

"Would you like to join us? You know, to thank you for the other day. The mint you gave me made me feel much better."

"Oh, um. Yes, please," Bea said gratefully, gathering up her pens and notebook.

The brownie led her over to her desk, where another brownie, a boy, had already pulled up his chair.

"Hi," Bea said.

"Hullo! You know, I never really believed they'd accepted a fairy until I saw you," grinned the boy. "I can't wait to tell my friends back home!"

"Oh. Um. Well, here I am," Bea said.

"We've heard *all* about you," added the girl. "Shall we do three facts?"

"Two facts, one lie," interrupted the boy.

"Yes, Harry, obviously," snapped the redhead, glaring at the interrupter before shooting Bea an apologetic look. "Well, my name's Aideen—"

"Truth!" Harry shouted gleefully.

Aideen spun on her chair. "*That* wasn't part of the game, Harry. I do apologise for him, Buttercup."

"That's alright," Bea said quickly. "And please, call me Bea."

"Oh, oh, oh, yes, of course. *Bea.* Gosh, this is fun! Well. Let's see. When I was younger, I got lost in the city, and Mama had to get ten brown suits out to find me. Ah, and then…. Oh, yes, we've got a well in our garden that can actually draw fresh water. And I've got a cousin who works in the Plot Department."

Bea waited for the other brownie, Harry, to guess. He fixed her with a wide grin, nodding encouragingly. Apparently, this was not going to be a team game.

"Erm," Bea said, "I think the one about having a working well is a lie?"

Harry burst out laughing.

"I guessed wrong?" Bea asked.

"No, no," Harry said. "You got it right!"

"No she didn't," Aideen snapped at him. She turned to Bea. "It *does* work."

"It doesn't," Harry said, wiping his eyes. "The water comes up all muddy."

"You're just jealous because you don't have a garden at all. The lie was that I got lost and Mama called out ten brown suits to find me."

"Ah, yes," Bea said. "I should have—"

"It was actually twenty."

"Oh. Right."

"But I can see why you guessed it was the well," Aideen said, her expression taking on the drippy look of the chronically sympathetic. "I expect you've never seen freshwater."

"What? Of course I have," Bea said. "I have been in Thaiana before, you know. There's plenty of clean water here."

If Aideen was chastised, her expression didn't show it. Bea was beginning to think none of these inner-circlers bothered with such inconvenient emotions as embarrassment. "Oh yes, I forgot you got here through your Plotter. How thrilling! I suppose you know Althaus?"

"Oh yes, absolutely," Bea lied. Apparently, the other thing about the inner-circlers was that they all assumed everyone knew everyone else. "Isn't she Tarquin's cousin, five times removed?"

Aideen frowned. "No, Tarquin's cousin fifth removed is Bunty. Althaus is—"

"Shall we carry on with the game?" Bea said desperately. "Why don't you go now, Harry?"

"Easy," Harry said. "There's a ghost in the Academy. Second, I've snuck into a dragon's den in the centre. Third, my family's been in the city since the 6th."

Bea felt relieved. At least this was an easy one. "The ghost is the lie."

Harry smiled beatifically. "Nope! That one's true."

"No it isn't," said Aideen.

"Yes it is, shut up—"

"Mortal gods, Harry, you're so embarrassing."

"And what do you know about it, Aideen?"

Aideen looked like she was about to turn Harry into a ghost. "Alright then, how do you know there's a ghost? You've seen it, have you?"

Harry gave Aideen a pitying look. "No, of course not. But I heard the brown suits talking about it when we were all signing in. They were saying they heard it the other night when they were patrolling. They said it screams."

"It was probably one of the elves. You know they like to play games," suggested Bea, trying to defuse the argument.

"I doubt it," Harry said. "The elves prefer their entertainment to be more... how shall I put it... immediate."

"How did the brown suits know it was a ghost?" Aideen asked.

Harry shrugged. "I've never seen an orc, but I think I'd recognise one if I did."

"Alright then, why would a ghost be here?"

"Why shouldn't a ghost be here? We're in Thaiana, aren't we? And this used to be a character's home, once. They're always dying."

"Really?" Bea asked, intrigued.

"Oh yes," Harry nodded wisely. "They only last about seventy years. Eighty, if you're lucky."

"I mean," Bea said, choosing her words with more care, "This place really belonged to a character, once upon a time?"

"Oh, right. So I heard. Anyway, I win the round. Now it's your turn, Bea."

"I haven't got anything to say," Bea said.

"Oh, come on!" said Harry.

"You must have something!" said Aideen.

"Of course you do!" said Harry.

"Play the game!" said Aideen.

"We want to know all about you!" said Harry.

"Oh, yes! Tell how you got that character to become Royal Adviser!" said Aideen.

"And how you managed the wedding!" said Harry.

"And tell us about your Plotter!" said Aideen.

Bea stared at them. It was like some kind of horrible relay race, in which her life was the baton.

Thankfully, Dafi saved her from having to answer their questions by signalling the end of the game. Bea started towards her desk, but Dafi shot her sour look.

"I think you'd be more comfortable at the back, don't you?" he said. "I'm sure you wouldn't want to feel you were getting in the way, isn't that right?"

Carol giggled.

Bea swallowed her immediate reply, not wanting to give Carol the satisfaction of knowing she was bothered. She couldn't help thinking that the whole 'game' had been set up just so Dafi could get her away from him without actually being so crass as telling her he didn't want her at the front. Choosing a desk at the back, she pulled out her notebook, held her pen to the page, and looked up expectantly at Dafi, a smile plastered to her face, masking her humiliation.

"Right class," Dafi said, taking a piece of chalk and writing on the blackboard. "Now that fun has been had and friendships forged, we'll get on with what we're actually here to do. We'll begin by memorising Plot 510b. In this one, a heroine is lucky enough to be a poor, downtrodden stepsister who is allowed to Fall In Love and live Happily Ever After. It begins when she meets a handsome hero in the forest..."

Bea slumped on her desk.

✳

At the end of their first fortnight, Dafi set a short test. He was a great believer in the effectiveness of tests, it transpired.

They were asked to prepare a presentation on a particular character type. Bea had been given the task of presenting on the secondary character, probably because Dafi couldn't think of a way to exclude her completely while still, technically, doing his job.

In the Teller's Plots, secondary characters were little more than an afterthought—most stories didn't even bother to include them. But Bea was determined to prove her merit, or at the very least get through the test without doing anything that would add to Dafi's growing dislike of her.

Bea, however, quickly realised she was at a massive disadvantage.

While she had spent her years in Ænathlin chasing Plot-watches, trying to catch the attention of some FME, the other recruits had been receiving an education; or, at least, they had been put in the way of a lot of facts and complicated words, which was apparently the same thing.

To her horror, Bea found that all the Plots, stories she thought she knew so well, were organised and categorised using an impossibly complex alphanumerical code, including thirty-one possible Plot stages and seven character archetypes, which all the other recruits had learnt prior to joining the Academy. When she asked Chokey about it, the dwarf explained that she and Hemmings had been taught for years by their governess to memorise the system.

Bea had two days to prepare for her presentation.

She spent all her free time in the Academy common room, a lifeless space given over to a few threadbare sofas and a small library of GenAm approved books, trying to embed lists of numbers and paragraphs of dry descriptions in her mind. Chokey and Hemmings helped as best they could, testing her long after lights out, but nothing seemed to stay in her head.

The problem was, the facts she had to memorise about the Plots and the characters were just that: facts. It was all decontextualised, devoid of any thought or opinion that might help her understand.

By the morning of her presentation, Bea was thoroughly depressed. It seemed to her that any FME who graduated from the Academy would have a very good idea of exactly what something was called without ever knowing what it really was.

Bea made her way to the front of the classroom. She'd done the best she could, and she already knew it wasn't going to be enough. Nevertheless, she'd filled her notebook with keywords and phrases, and practised in front of Chokey and Hemmings that morning. If she was going to fail, it wouldn't be in want of terminology, she'd decided.

"Ahem," Bea said, looking out at a sea of bored faces. Only Dafi, who was watching her closely, his pen poised above his correction sheet, and Carol, who was sitting in the front row glaring at her, seemed at all interested in her presentation.

"So... well, I think everyone's covered a lot of really, uh, interesting points about the hu—I mean, the characters. I've been asked to talk about the deuteragonist, that is, the secondary character."

At the back of the classroom, someone let rip a loud, fake snore. Bea carried on.

"The secondary character has one clear role: to help the hero. Accordingly, most deuteragonists are less intelligent than the hero, and they usually don't get to take part in the Happily Ever After. Um. Most Plots don't include a secondary character anymore, but 301 and 303 sometimes do."

Dafi grunted, clearly bored.

Bea glanced down at her notes. All the carefully written lines and columns seemed to dance across the page, blurring into each other.

Swallowing, she looked up and continued, "Typically, the secondary character would know the hero from childhood, and occasionally provide him with some kind of useful information, but more often than not, if we use them at all, their purpose is to allow the hero to do something extra, like rescue them. This maximises the retell potential of the Plot resulting from a more dynamic hero, which creates more belief. That's it."

Bea closed her notebook, relieved, and started back to her desk.

Carol put her hand up.

Bea froze.

"Yes?" Dafi sighed.

"She's barely said anything, and you're letting her finish?"

"Thank you, Carol," Dafi said. "But I really don't think there's very much more to say on the subject of deuteragonists. Of all the characters, they really are the most straightforward."

Bea made a noise that could only be interpreted as a snort. Dafi turned to look at her.

"You disagree?"

Apologise, Bea told herself. *Apologise, agree with him, and go back to your seat. It's not worth it. You can't change how any of them think. Go on. Say you're sorry for thinking that there might be more to people than labels and numbers.*

"Actually, yes. I do disagree," Bea heard herself say. She swore under her breath, but it was too late now.

She continued, "The only difference between a hero and a sidekick is that we focus on the hero—we let the hero be the hero because of the events we put him in. In fact, most of the time we make the sidekick look stupid because we engineer it that way. I understand why—to add more validity to the hero. But, really, there's no reason why a story can't have more than one protagonist. And also, even if there is a sidekick, why should their only purpose be to serve the hero?"

"For the Mirrors, of course," Dafi snapped. "For the belief. Simple is easier to understand and accept." He turned his attention to the whole classroom, spotting an opportunity to lecture. "The fairy's stupidity raises an important point. The trouble with the characters is that they may try to be individual, 'unique', if you will. Which, of course, is a tremendous problem if you encounter it. Who can tell me why?"

Again, Carol's hand shot up.

"If the characters are allowed to express individuality, they may not behave as they should within the Plot. They could, for example, refuse to participate, or demand a different ending. We need our main characters *and* our secondary characters to do exactly what we want them to do," Carol finished, shooting Bea a smug look.

"Yes, yes. I think we all know why it's a problem if the characters refuse the Plot," Dafi said, his manner indicating some annoyance that Carol had got the question right. "But can you tell us why it matters if they try to change their Happy Ending or their role?"

Carol hesitated. And then she said, "That problem is related to the retellers?"

Dafi nodded grudgingly. "Carry on."

"The retellers are the characters who hear about the Plot and spread it. They're our main source of belief, in real terms. And, for them, the Plot needs to be something they expect... It needs to be something easy that they don't question or think too much about. The best kind of stories for mass retelling are the ones that follow the strongest lines, like True Love or Rags To Riches. The ones that they want to believe anyway. The ones that don't challenge them."

"And so...?" Dafi prompted.

"And so if the characters try to change their role—for example, if the 'prize' decides she wants to be the 'hero'—then the story doesn't spread so quickly, because it isn't so easy to retell. Therefore, the best characters are the ones that do as they're told, as they're expected to do," Carol said.

"Exactly," Dafi said. "The beauty of the Teller's Plots is that they perpetrate the same narratives. Thus, for the retellers, they know exactly what they're going to get. And for us, this means that—if the Plot is done well, and followed to the letter—the story gets told again and again. The very best run Plots, in fact, are the ones the characters tell each other without even realising they're doing it, they are so conducive to their already held expectations and beliefs. This," he continued, turning his beady eyes back on Bea, "Is why the role of the deuteragonist is to service the hero. If he were to suddenly try to be his own 'person' within the Plot, it would require more effort from both the retellers and the listeners.

Belief would be risked. And the Plots and therefore the Mirrors would suffer. Simple is stronger."

"But in the long run, wouldn't we get more belief if we had stories for everyone?" Bea said. "Why do we—"

"Why do *you* keep asking questions? What do you think this is— some kind of debate? This is a school, and I am your Master. You will listen to what I have to say, and you will be grateful for the opportunity. Now get out—and rest assured I will be discussing your behaviour with West."

Bea pressed her lips together, her throat stinging as she tried to control herself. Grabbing her pencils and notebook, she stormed out of the class, slamming the door behind her.

Chokey and Hemmings were sympathetic when she told them what had happened, but at dinner that evening, she overheard Carol telling anyone who would listen about the stupidity of fairies and Bea in particular.

XVI

The door to West's office opened before Dafi had a chance to knock. The troll was there, of course, holding it open for him.

Dafi stuck his little nose in the air and marched past the troll, straight up to West's desk. He'd had enough, and he wasn't about to be intimated again. This time he would speak his mind, and he would be heard.

"Headmistress," he began, his litany of complaints well-rehearsed. "I'm afraid to say this situation cannot continue. It is untenable—untenable. I have kept my silence too long, and now I feel I am forced to speak out. Not only for myself, you understand, but for all the recruits of the Academy, past and present, who have struggled so tirelessly to—"

"You want to stop teaching the cabbage fairy," West said mildly. It wasn't a question.

Dafi wobbled for a moment. "Well, yes. As a matter of fact, I do." And then he rallied. "Never in all my years have I seen such a disgrace to these hallowed halls—"

"But the Academy only moved here this year," West interjected. "When I took over as Headmistress."

"Er... That is..." The conversation wasn't going the way Dafi had planned. Nonetheless, he decided to keep to his script. "It is up to me, as a long-serving and respected member of the faculty to see to it that this *farce* continues no longer. I have a—"

"A moral duty, yes, I understand," West finished for him.

"Er. Yes." Mortal gods, it was like she was reading his mind. "Exactly. For too long, the views of the silent majority have been ignored, but now it is up to me to stand and be counted. A fairy in the Academy! I never thought—"

"You'd live to see the day," West said. "Well, luckily for me, it appears you have. Dafi, do you know why I placed Buttercup Snowblossom in your class?"

"No, I—"

113

F. D. Lee

"It is because I was assured that you are the very best Master we have. The *very* best, they told me. When I was made aware of this burden we were expected to bear, I thought I would never be able to carry it. Oh, I said to myself, how can I ever hope to be the *first-ever Master of the Academy* to successfully take a fairy and turn her into a Fiction Management Executive? I was going to refuse her myself. And then, do you know what I thought?"

"Mmm? Pardon?" Dafi said, distracted by thoughts of unexpected fame.

"I thought to myself, as long as I have Dafi's support, I can do this. With, of course, full credit shared with my esteemed colleague. That is, with you."

"Ahem. Well, I suppose if anyone were able to form such a misshapen lump of clay into a thing of value—"

"Then that someone would be you. I couldn't agree more. Thank you, Dafi, for your continued support."

Barret led a somewhat confused Dafi out of the office.

"That won't work again," he warned.

West had stood up from her desk and was admiring one of her decorated vases. On it was a depiction of a woman, her dress torn, with her hands held up in entreaty to another woman. This second woman was sitting above her, holding a shield and a spear, seemingly unmoved by her pleas for rescue. Looming behind the supplicant woman was a naked man, grabbing her hair, pulling her towards him. Despite the woman's clear distress, the man in the image was showing every sign of enjoyment.

Barret hated the vase, but West always seemed drawn to it.

"It doesn't need to," West said. "He doesn't complain again."

Barret shook his head. "But why bother at all, my Lady? Fairies aren't good for anything, everyone knows that. None of the characters believe in them, not once they've grown up. And they're dumb. It's not like Dafi's classes are difficult, all she's got to do is repeat back what he tells her, and by all accounts, she can't even do that."

"I suspect she's not dumb, rather the opposite in fact," West replied, turning away from the vase. "No one listens to her, that's all. Still, if she is so publicly failing her classes, something must be done."

114

"What, my Lady?"

"I don't know yet," West said. "But I will."

XVII

Months passed, time piling up with the same dull monotony as the snow outside the Academy. Bea was almost halfway through her year, which meant she only had a few weeks to go until she could take the field test and, if the mortal gods were kind, leave Dafi's class behind.

The Master in question was currently wrapping up the morning's lesson with his usual damp-firework flair, and Bea was trying to balance the fact she knew she needed to memorise everything he was saying if she ever hoped to enter the high tier FME stream with the fact that she fundamentally disagreed with it all.

"And so, in conclusion, originally there were ninety-nine structural elements to the tales, features of which included many of the motifs latterly codified by the Teller, *whocaresaboutus*. However, it should be noted that features 316, 326, and, of course, 327b are among those that were retired by the Plot Department."

Bea stifled a yawn.

Once again, she'd been up late trying to revise. And, once again, to no avail, if today's lesson was anything to go by. Plus she still wasn't sleeping well, her dreams haunted by nightmares, and, beneath that, a drumbeat, a rhythm that seemed to rise up not from her memories, but from her bones.

She woke every morning covered in sweat, her heart racing, and lay staring at the ceiling, trying to forget the image of her friends' and family's bodies piled up in a heap, the black blood of Melly, Joan and her abandoned mother and brother mixing with King John, Sindy and Ana's red human blood. Sometimes the blood would rise up, and she'd drown; other times she'd run across the Ballroom, trying to reach them, only to find she couldn't move, her legs ripped into useless strands by the witchlein's claws, while the ogre smashed their bodies to a pulp.

She was yet to have a dream in which she saved them.

116

Still, Bea comforted herself that in terms of graduating from the Academy and becoming an FME, the nightmares were at least a fantastic motivational tool. The mortal gods knew she needed motivating.

She started packing away her pencils and notebook, only half listening as Dafi finished wrapping up his lecture when something he said caught her attention.

She raised her hand.

"Mortal gods—yes, Buttercup, what is it?"

"Did you just say class this afternoon is cancelled?" Bea asked, trying to keep the hope out of her voice. Judging by the look that swept over Dafi's face, she'd been unsuccessful.

"Yes, Buttercup, I did. And if you were capable of paying attention for more than two minutes at a time, you'd know that. You'll be spending the afternoon in private tuition with your mentor. I will see you all tomorrow."

The smile slid off Bea's face like grease on a hotplate. She had a dreadful feeling she knew where the conversation was heading, but she couldn't stop herself from following it.

"My mentor?"

"Yes, Buttercup. Your mentor. I assume you know the word?"

"I do, yes. But I don't know who my mentor is."

Dafi didn't bother to hide his annoyance. "Mortal gods. The person who recommended you, obviously. It's their fault you're here, after all—the least they can do is take some responsibility for your education."

"The person who recommended me?" Bea repeated, her voice sounding distant. For some reason, all she could currently hear was a high-pitched buzzing.

"For the love of—yes, that's what I literally just said. Must I spell everything out for you?"

Bea didn't reply. She was too busy trying not to vomit.

Mistasinon was coming to the Academy.

❄

"Did you know about this?" Bea asked Chokey and Hemmings over lunch.

"Well, of course," Chokey said, swallowing the limp, overcooked vegetables they'd been served that day. "It's only a formality, darling, to make sure we're on track for the field test. I suppose it's meant to give everyone in charge a chance to compare notes about our progress."

Bea's shoulders slumped.

Chokey and Hemmings exchanged a look.

"Oh dear," Chokey said. "I know you're not doing very well in your class, but honestly, they won't chuck you out yet."

Bea let her head bang against the table.

"'Yet', she says. Mortal gods..."

Chokey patted her on the head. "I didn't mean it like that, darling. Hemmings, I didn't mean it like that, did I?"

The elf looked panicked. He opened and closed his mouth, but for once was lost for words. Chokey shot him a murderous look and turned her attention back to the top of Bea's head.

"Aren't you pleased to be seeing your Plotter? I'm sure he'll be delighted to see you! I bet he won't notice how tired you look. And your hair is growing out so interestingly! You can really see the green now. Though you ought to fix your bun—it's always coming loose. You might as well wear it down and have done with it. Honestly, darling, it doesn't take any time at all to look nice," Chokey finished, indicating her own curly, blonde bunches, tied with silver bands.

Bea sighed, but she lifted up her head and managed a smile for Chokey and Hemmings.

She didn't want to see Mistasinon. The thought of spending a whole afternoon with him, shut away in some stuffy private room, made her feel decidedly unpleasant, like that feeling you get when you stand at the top of a high building and look down. But she could hardly explain that to them, could she?

All too quickly, their mealtime ended, and Bea shuffled out of the assembly hall with the other recruits. Carol shouldered into her as they funnelled out the door.

"I'm watching you, cabbage mother," she hissed. "Don't think you'll be able to get away with anything just because your pet Plotter's here."

"He's not my 'pet' anything," Bea snapped. "Believe me, I'd rather have a normal FME as my mentor."

"Easy to be humble when you've got a blue suit at your beck and call," Carol replied before flouncing away.

Each mentor had been assigned a room on the top three floors of the east wing in which to meet their recruits. Mistasinon's room was last on the list. Bea trudged up the stairs, the sea of other recruits thinning out the higher she got, until she was alone.

Initially, she felt relieved that no one would see her with him. She wasn't sure why, but the idea of others witnessing their meeting filled her with embarrassment. Probably because of what Carol had said—everyone must think she was a complete idiot, needing an actual Plotter to get her into the Academy. Yes, that explained why she kept hoping she might miss a step and fall and break her leg.

But as she climbed higher, her relief gave way to anxiety. What if Mistasinon now regretted telling her about the Mirrors and the genies, and had decided she was a threat? Wouldn't this be a perfect way to make her disappear? Maybe when she eventually found his room, it wouldn't be Mistasinon waiting for her.

Maybe it would be the Beast…

A butterfly flutter of fear trembled in her chest. She tried to bite her thumbnail, but there was so little left of it now it was impossible. She switched to one of her fingernails instead.

Eventually, she found herself on a landing in the attic of the east wing. She spotted a window to her right, letting in a beam of jaundiced sunlight. How high up was she? She went over and leaned on the stone sill, looking out. The snow was still falling thick and heavy, but the window was facing inwards, unlike the one in her room, and the high wall offered some protection from the storm.

The Academy lay below her, a sort of squared 'U' shape, with a garret on the opposite arm, suggesting that she was now standing in something similar. A dark shadow in the distance made Bea wonder if the layout was repeated on the further edge, where the storm blocked her view. West has said no one could leave the east wing, hadn't she? That implied that there was a central part to the Academy, and then another wing, hidden in the fog of snow.

119

Immediately below her was a thin ledge, barely a foot wide, and then a long stretch of nothingness, before the glass ceiling of the assembly room filled the bowl of the 'U'. The red GenAm banners were faintly visible despite the snow, hanging limply above the long tables where they ate their meals.

Not wanting to think about the GenAm at that particular moment, Bea turned her attention to the sky, if such a simple, friendly word could be used to describe it. It wasn't simply that the clouds were dark and heavy, though they were; it was the way they seemed to hang over the world, like a raised first moments before it slams into a face.

She pulled away from the window and looked around. On the opposite side of the hallway was another window. She went over and peered out of that one. The Academy was a sheer wall on this side, the dark brickwork fading away into nothingness. She was grateful the glass was there. There was no way anyone could survive a fall like that.

Lifting her gaze, she spotted the coach.

It was coursing over the ground at a good speed, given the thick snowfall and the strength of the wind. She squinted, trying to make out what breed of horse could negotiate such terrain. In fact, if she hadn't known better, she might have thought they were kelpi, the water horse tribe.

Perhaps they are kelpi, Bea mused. Kelpi wouldn't mind the snow… in fact, they might quite like it, as it would melt against their flanks, keeping them cool. And for all that the Academy was in Thaiana, it was still a fae building, so why not?

The keener question, Bea realised, was why there was a coach arriving at the Academy at all.

Along with the post, all their supplies were delivered via Mirror from Ænathlin, and surely the only reason to have the Academy in this gods' forsaken place was to keep outsiders, well, out?

Her gaze followed the coach as it rode past the building. Perhaps it didn't have anything to do with the Academy at all, and it was going to drive past them, into the woods. But then, just before it reached what looked to be the edge of the forest, it slowed down.

A light flashed on and off in the grey haze of the storm. Bea nearly hollered. There *was* a building out there—she'd been right all along!

The light flashed again, guiding the coach towards it. The coach disappeared, lost in the snow, and a moment later the light went out.

Bea turned from the window. Standing at the bottom of the stairs was the brown-suited witchlein, watching her.

"Aren't you sssuposssed to be at your mentor meeting?" he asked in his slithering voice.

"Yes," Bea croaked.

"Well, go on then. The attic room behind you."

Bea turned and ran. Her heart pounding, she pushed the door open without even thinking to knock, just wanting to put the solid wood between her and the yellow-scaled creature. She slammed it shut and stood for a moment with both hands pressed against the door as if she expected someone to try to break it down at any moment.

Time ticked by, and with it, Bea became increasingly aware that she'd just barged into her meeting with Mistasinon and was now standing, practically hugging the door.

She took a deep breath and turned around.

The room was a world away—hah, literally—from Mistasinon's office at the GenAm. His office in the Plot Department was little more than a cupboard, with barely enough room for him, let alone all the Books and files he kept there.

This room, however, was long and spacious, even allowing for the low walls and sloped ceiling caused by the pointed roof of the Academy. In fact, it was quite... what?

Cosy, her mind supplied.

There was a large, green sofa in the middle of the room, its seat and arms worn with age, and a very wide desk, with two chairs on one side and another on the side by the wall, presumably for Mistasinon. There were short bookshelves, half-filled, a small china sink set into a wooden housing, and a round window in the wall at the far end, its glass tinted green. There were no mirrors, and Bea assumed the green glass would make it difficult for anyone to use the window to spy through, via a Mirror.

There was also no Mistasinon.

Bea stood, dumb.

He hadn't come.

For some inexplicable reason, she felt a wave of anger wash over her, settling in her stomach like a flood.

He'd pushed her into taking the Plot, and then when Seven had shown up and she'd wanted to leave it, he'd talked her into staying. He'd lied to her from the beginning, playing her for a fool—though, if she was being fair, she could admit she hadn't made it particularly difficult.

But worst of all, he'd made her trust him. She'd thought he understood her somehow, that he knew what it was like to not belong anywhere. And now he couldn't even be bothered to show up for one measly afternoon and pretend to tutor her?

Bea screamed.

She screamed until her throat hurt, and then she crumpled onto the floor and cried. Ugly, fat tears rolled down her face, mixing with her snot and spit as she sobbed. It was not gentle, nor was it in any way attractive. But once she'd finished, she felt better.

Wiping her nose with her sleeve, she picked herself up from the floor and decided to have a look around. She rattled the drawers of his desk but found they were locked. She turned her attention to his bookshelves. There weren't many books, and Bea didn't really expect to find anything exciting in them.

Instead, what she found both confused and surprised her.

Originally they had clearly been regular books, cheaply printed and mass-produced by the Contents Department, like the kind that Dafi insisted they study. But in the margins of *these* books were hundreds of little notes, like the person who had been reading them had been trying to understand the whole of the GenAm and the Plots as quickly as possible.

The notes were written in what she presumed was Mistasinon's handwriting. It was elegant, with long lines and flourishes, but also neat and easy to read. The notes cross-referenced different pages in the book, and in others. But what was even more amazing was what they said. There were… Criticisms. Suggestions. Questions.

Bea skim read two of them in the space of an hour. And then she slowed down and started making notes in her notebook, so she had something she could take away.

By the time a brown suit knocked on the door to tell her to go to bed, she realised she was disappointed her 'tutorial' was finished. She even wondered if she might actually pass the Academy, now she had all this information to help her. Mistasinon must be feeling guilty for lying to her, and this was his way of making it up to her…

Well, if that was the case, it wasn't nearly enough. But she grudgingly conceded it was a good start.

All in all, things were looking up.

❆

The two men sat on the dry-stone wall, watching the sheep. It was still warm in the south of Ehinenden, and they were enjoying the lazy feel of the sun on their backs while the sheep were busy doing what sheep do: turning grass into wool, milk and, most efficiently, flatulence.

"Did you hear about that girl, up in Skraq?" said one, the piece of straw in his mouth shifting as he spoke.

"Hmn," replied the other.

"'parently, some bloke was away from home, lost, and he comes across this little old man, by the side of the road. Well, the bloke, he's tired, hungry, not thinking clearly, and he asks the old man if he has any food."

"Hmn."

"So's the old man says he's got food, water, gold, whatever, which the bloke can have—in exchange for the first thing he sees once he gets home. The bloke, he's all for it, int he? Reckons it'll be the dog, running out to greet him."

"Hmn?"

"Course, it's his girl what runs out, all happy to see her daddy. So the bloke thinks to himself, well, I can't let my girl go off with some old man what lives by the side of the road, tricking travellers and so on, so when the old guy turns up to collect, the bloke pretends it was the dog what he saw first."

"Hmn."

"Damn right. The old geezer int buying it. So to punish the bloke for lying, he says something like 'I'll take exactly the first thing you saw', which turns out t'be the girl's hands."

"Hmn?"

"Nah, I don't know how either, doesn't matter. So the old man, he produces this axe out of nowhere and chops of her hands, t'teach the dad a lesson. And the girl, she's so ashamed of her father for lying, she goes off with the old man anyway."

The other lifted his bushy eyebrows at this. "Hmn?"

"Nah, cause, y'see, turns out the old man were under a spell, and he was really a handsome prince. So the girl's alright in the end, int she?"

The two men fell silent.

The sheep continued to graze.

"S'good story I thought," said the first.

"Hmn."

"They stay in the head, don't they, the nasty ones? Used to get 'em like that when I were a kid, before everyone went soft. Course, you wouldn't get a local man behaving so stupid. But it int hard to believe of them lot up north."

"Hmn."

The sheep baa'd and frolicked, while the two men thought about the story.

XVIII

To the south of Voriias, where the Academy was situated, lay Ehinenden, the Third Kingdom of Thaiana. And within Ehinenden was Llanotterly, a small city-state nestled between the forest and the Shared Sea.

Llanotterly was facing bankruptcy, a situation not aided by the fact it was the location in which Bea's Plot had been set. The simple truth was that when a Kingdom holds a Ball in order to attract investors, it's not a good idea to then have an ogre attack, killing a number of guests and maiming the King. Nor was it particularly helpful to have your Royal Adviser kidnap one of your guests and disappear.

In the grand game of political chess, Llanotterly had achieved in one evening the diplomatic equivalent of throwing all the pieces on the floor and then setting fire to the board.

Melly opened her eyes, dropped her hands and stepped away from King John.

"How are you feeling, Your Majesty?"

John frowned. "Damned worried, and that's a fact. Just received word from the Six Points that the Roove-Starrens are backing out of their contract. Bloody bad sports, what? We've got half the army out looking for that blasted Countess Seven ran off with, what more can we do?"

"I meant, how does your back feel?" Melly clarified.

"What? Oh, I don't know. Annoying? Be pleased when they get that wheeled chair thingy working properly and I can move m'self around. Bloody thing tipped me over when I went round a corner." A smile twitched at his lips. "Actually, the whole thing was a bit of a hoot, but don't let on to Ana I said so. Never known anyone take everybody else's business so seriously."

Melly started to gather her things. "I've made you some more ointment, and I've left instructions with the maid to make sure you don't sit for hours in the same position."

"I'm quite capable of moving myself, Madam."

"Of course, Your Majesty," Melly said. "But being capable and actually doing it are different things. You'd sit reading all day if someone didn't remind you to move. You'll get sores. Again."

John rolled his eyes. "So, when's the next sesh?" he said, pointedly lifting himself further up the bed.

"To be honest, Sire, there isn't very much more I can do for you. Your bones are set as best they can be, and the muscle has healed well. Now it's more a question of you getting better at caring for yourself."

"Righto," John said. "Onwards and upwards."

Melly paused in her packing. She turned to him and laid a hand on his shoulder. "You're doing very well."

He smiled at her. "Can't keep a good dog down. I say, you couldn't pop in and see Ana on your way out?"

"Well, I should probably—"

"Won't take you a minute, there's a good gel," John said. "Spit spot and don't spare the horses and so on. She's in her office."

For a moment, Melly considered all the things she could do to him, starting with but not limited to giving him a hard slap. She swallowed her immediate reaction rather like one might swallow cod liver oil: ultimately it's good for you, but not very nice on the way down.

John was a King. And while Melly had spent enough time with him to know he was also a nice man, Kings were Kings first and foremost, and so were used to being obeyed. He wasn't really ordering her around. He was just, well, ordering her around. But there *was* a difference, and Melly knew enough to recognise it.

So she told John she would be happy to visit Ana and left him to his work. She made her way through the castle and arrived at Ana's office. She knocked, and a moment later, Ana pulled open the door, a pen held between her teeth.

"How's he doing?" Ana asked, removing the pen.

"He's well enough."

"And how well is well?" Ana mused, walking over to a side table where a decanter and a half dozen glasses sat. She waved the bottle at Melly, who inclined her head. Ana poured them both a drink.

"You're still worried about him?" Melly enquired, accepting the glass.

"I don't know," Ana said. She sounded angry, but Melly suspected she was trying to mask her worry. "He's chatty. He's involved in everything we're doing, including the smuggling. Especially the smuggling. The armoury is making him this chair with wheels on—though God knows, I wouldn't be surprised if it's that that finishes him off. He keeps making jokes about not having to ride horses and get saddle sores anymore. He says he's alright."

"You think he's lying?" Melly asked.

"I think he's trying too hard."

"Perhaps. Injuries like his are complicated. He's got to adjust to a new way of life, a new way of being him. Plus, he's King. He can hardly give in to despair or show weakness. Ruling isn't just about controlling the land or the people. You have to control yourself as well."

"It's bloody stupid. No one would judge him. I wouldn't judge him."

"Maybe he's coping better than you think he is?"

Ana pulled a face. "Do you do requests?"

"I'm a witch," Melly said, allowing herself a small smile. "I don't know much about Happy Endings."

"You weren't always a witch though," Ana replied. "You're as bad as he is. Always pretending. All these stupid games."

"Ruling isn't a game."

"No," Ana said. "Games are more fun."

"Is everything alright?"

Ana shook her head. "Not really."

"John mentioned the difficulties the Kingdom is facing, since the Ball."

"You'd think we were infected with the plague, the amount of nobles and investors keeping their distance from us. God damn Seven. If I ever get my hands on him, I swear... But anyway. I just wish I knew why he felt the need to kidnap that bloody Countess. Her husband is looking to make an alliance with Cerne Bralksteld against us. He's convinced we orchestrated the whole thing, despite what happened to John. Idiot."

"Is an alliance likely?"

"Hard to say. The Baron seems to have cut off communication with the rest of Ehinenden, which could be a good thing."

"Or?"

"Or it could mean something worse is coming." Ana pinched the bridge of her nose, looking for a moment terribly young. "Come with me, there's something I want to show you."

Melly hesitated. The GenAm had given her permission to be in Ehinenden to heal the King, but that was all. It was a concession to the fact that the ogre sent by the Redactionists had broken his spine.

Although it was probably more accurate to say it was a concession to the fact the King and Ana had both seen the ogre, and John's role within the characters' world was such that they couldn't afford to have him die as a result. Of course, once upon a time, things had been very different...

Ana, never one to beg, folded her arms and glared. "Five minutes. Besides, you'll want to see this."

Melly glanced over her shoulder, though she had no idea what she expected to see. The Beast, perhaps? But there was nothing.

She weighed up her options. Ana could hardly stop her from leaving, not really. Even if she called the guard, Melly was an elf first and a witch second. They wouldn't stand a chance of holding her, not unless they thought to bring iron with them, and Melly was certain they would not. It had been a long time since the characters had had to worry about the fair folk, and most had forgotten the old ways.

She *should* leave. It had taken her years to earn the disinterest of the General Administration, and now she was in danger of being back in their gaze. Not that she resented healing the King. Of course she didn't. If the GenAm asked for something, it was her duty to acquiesce. And now she'd done all she could, it was time to walk away.

But Melly was fond of Ana. The girl was sensible and stubborn. Fearless. *Mark you,* Melly thought, *I'm fond of Bea as well, and look where that's got me.*

Nevertheless, she reached a decision.

"What is it?"

"It's easier to show you," Ana replied, her tone grim. "Though God knows, I'd rather not see it again."

Melly followed Ana through the castle, passing all the weird and wonderful amendments John's forebears had made to the original stone structure. Llanotterly Castle was a building created by both competing egos and imaginations. Each successive ruler had been determined to make his or her mark on what had, at one time, been nothing more than a very practical, very study, stone keep.

Ana led her through the castle and into one of the many subterranean basements. They entered a bitterly cold room, in the corner of which was a dome, made out of stone. Melly might have asked what it was, and Ana might have replied that she'd brought the witch to one of the castle's ice houses, where they kept any perishable foodstuffs stored.

But what Melly wanted to know about was the dead body, lying mutilated on a cot in the middle of the room.

"Mortal gods," she breathed, stepping closer. "What happened to her?"

"I've got no idea," Ana replied darkly. "But I intend to find out. It looks like she's been tortured."

Melly could see that. Someone had taken the girl's eyes, sewn her mouth shut, and cut off her hands.

"Was there anything else done to her?" she asked. Something was stirring in the back of her mind, but she couldn't put her finger on it. Something she knew. Something she'd seen before. Something that made her stomach knot and her throat contract.

"You'd think they'd done enough, wouldn't you?" Ana said. "But no, you're right. There's more. They cut her open, filled her with rocks, and then stitched her up again."

"Who did this?"

"I don't know. She was left in the woods, just thrown away like a bag of rubbish. A huntsman found her and brought her to me. Frankly, if it hadn't been for the snow, I doubt there'd have been anything to find. I never thought I'd be grateful we didn't live further south. Sindy came to look at the body, and she reckons the girl's been dead a few months."

"Do you know who she is?"

129

"No. The huntsman assumed she was an escapee from the Baron, that's why he brought her to me. But I don't think she is."

Melly stepped closer to the body. She picked up the dead girl's arm and inspected the stump. The skin closed neatly over it.

"Why not?" she asked Ana.

"Because that's not how the Baron works. He kidnaps people as slaves. He wants them to work in his manufactories and, God forgive me, it's not exactly a sound investment to start mutilating your primary workforce, is it? And then I thought about you. Fairies and ogres and elves—and it occurred to me that maybe this is something you'd do."

A shiver of warning flickered through Melly. "We don't do stories like that. Not anymore."

"Really?" Ana said, the look on her face showing she didn't believe her. "So you're not branching out, then? Don't forget you and your friend Bea told me all about your little stories, and how you like to mess with our lives. How much did you get out of crippling John? I bet that story's been told a few times, right? And you can't pretend that any of this is normal. Look at her wounds. They're perfect, for want of a better word."

Frowning, Melly checked the stitching over the girl's mouth. Like her wrists, the skin was perfectly healed. The eye sockets, as well, were clean, with no damage to the surrounding skin. Next, Melly lifted the dead girl's dress and looked at her stomach. There was a long line running across her midriff, sewn up with black thread.

"That was Sindy," Ana said from behind her. "There wasn't a single scar on her when she came in."

Eyes pulled out. Hands and feet removed. Mouth sewn shut. Stomach filled with rocks.

Mortal gods. Ana was right.

Who *could* do this to someone, and heal them so well? Certainly not the characters. They had medicine, Melly knew, and they could perform amputations and other surgical procedures... but not so neatly. Not so cleanly.

Only the fae could do something like this, with such skill and such minimal damage. Only an elf. Melly paused. On the edge of her mind, an idea lurked. She slowed her thinking, trying not to scare it away.

Not one story, but many. All enacted on one character.

Like someone was practising...

Mortal gods.

"What are you thinking?" Ana said.

Melly shook her head. "We don't do things like this. Not anymore," she repeated.

"You don't sound very convinced. I want to know what's going on, Melly."

"It doesn't make sense to do this to a character. It's all about belief. When we did stories like this, the characters rebelled—they didn't want to be part of it."

"Since when did any of you care what we 'characters' wanted?"

"You're right," Melly said. "We didn't care. But *you* did. Too many villages lost babies, too many young girls went missing, too many musicians went mad. You started thinking and building, shutting us out. We... we couldn't keep up with you. We couldn't control you. You were full of ideas, and anger, and desperation to get away from us... To get away from the full moon and the long nights. That's why the Teller, *whocaresaboutus*, changed the Plots."

She didn't add what she was thinking, which was that killing the girl in such a brutal manner, if it had been done for a story, was pointless. Even if it worked, it would only work a few times before the characters refused to be part of the stories again.

Fear created belief, that was true—strong belief, as well. But love was safer.

Most characters wanted to be in a love story; only a very few refused, and when they did, the story was abandoned. That was the mistake Bea had made with her Plot: because she'd been desperate and thought she'd never be given another chance, she hadn't walked away.

Unlike me, Melly thought.

"So what do you think happened to her?" Ana asked, watching her intently.

A beat, and then Melly said, "I'm not sure."

Ana's lips pursed. "Why don't I believe you?"

"Look," Melly said, turning away from the body. "I'm not lying when I say I'm not sure. If this was done for a story, it's against all our laws. Only a mad person would risk it."

Or someone who knew they could get away with it...

Melly stepped on the thought before it had a chance to show in her expression.

"I'll see what I can find out," she said.

Ana added a heavy frown to her pursed lips, completing the 'something's-going-on-and-I-know-it' set of facial expressions. But for whatever reason, and to Melly's great relief, she simply said, "Make sure when you've got something to tell me, you do."

"I will, you have my word," Melly said.

She left the room as casually as she dared. If she could, she would have run.

XIX

Melly lit another cigarette, waving the smoke away from her eyes.

Her cottage was beginning to smell stale, no doubt because of the dozens of overflowing ashtrays and half-empty wine glasses. Walking over to the window, she twitched the curtain aside. There was no one there. The Sheltering Forest looked normal. But that didn't mean anything, did it? Looks could be deceiving.

Melly pulled the curtains closed and turned back to her living room. A hiss escaped one of the pipes that zigzagged across the walls of her cottage, and she nearly choked on her cigarette. She closed her eyes and took a deep breath. She needed to calm down.

She perched on the arm of her favourite chair, the one with the cushions she'd embroidered herself, and tried to think. She stared mindlessly at her china figurines, safely displayed on the shelves of her dresser, and smoked. Her hand was shaking so much the light of the cigarette moved like a firefly with an inner-ear infection.

On the floor next to the sofa, her wastepaper bin was overflowing with crumpled letters. Each one was addressed to Bea, and each one had been discarded. What could she possibly say? And how could she be certain that the letters wouldn't be intercepted by the Redaction Department?

Standing up, she left her living room and climbed the stairs to the first-floor landing, where her Mirror hung on the wall. It reflected her face, her countenance marred by dark shadows under her eyes.

Another pull on her cigarette as she took a moment to centre herself. Mirror travel worked best when you had a memory of the place you wanted to go. This was the reason the Teller set the Plots in such a limited amount of locations. Failing memory, a good description would work as long as it was clear enough to visualise where you wanted to be, and the Mirror was fully functional.

Melly had neither. She'd never studied at the Academy, and even if she had, she was unaware it had moved to Voriias.

But there was another way.

If you were old and strong, it was possible to create a connection based only on emotion. It was a dangerous, tricky thing to attempt. Get it wrong, and the best thing that would happen was it wouldn't work—the worst was that you might end up thinking you'd actually made the journey while spending the rest your life being fed soup through a straw in a room with soft walls.

She ran her hands over the glass, holding a picture of Bea in her mind, pouring her anxiety, her fear, and her love for her friend into the glass.

The edges of the Mirror turned black, slowly spreading over the glass like oil seeping into a lake. For a moment, the whole Mirror went dark, but then the connection failed, and the glass returned.

Frowning, Melly tried again.

The Mirror flickered, alternating between black and Melly's reflection. Clenching her jaw, Melly put all her energy into the connection. Beads of sweat formed on her forehead and ran into her eyes, making them sting.

The connection faltered, but for a second Melly saw a room with a woman dressed in black standing in the centre, a bottle at her mouth, guzzling a thick, dirty white liquid.

The image shuddered. The Mirror went black and then faded back into Melly's own reflection. Her face was shiny with sweat, a thin trail of black blood running from her nose. She wiped it away.

Perhaps if she'd been calmer, or if she'd eaten something in the last twenty-four hours, it might have worked. As it was, she realised she'd been lucky to get away from the experience with only a nosebleed and the glooping nausea that the Mirrors always induced.

Her hands shaking, Melly finished her cigarette. When the hissing in her ears had quietened, and she didn't feel like she was going to vomit or faint, she made her way back downstairs, to her sofa.

It was no good. She couldn't get hold of Bea, and she couldn't keep hiding. If what she thought was happening was true, she had to try to stop it. But how? She wasn't a fighter, not like Bea or Ana.

And the truth was, she was afraid.

"It's all falling apart," Melly whispered.

At the end of Bea's Plot, the Redaction Department had sent a small army into a room full of characters, all to catch an Anti-Narrativist. Admittedly, the Anti had been a genie, but still… That wasn't how things were done. The Teller and the GenAm maintained control, keeping the stories working and the belief coming in to power the Mirrors. That was why the King and Queen had been usurped, and everything sanitised.

She reached up and removed the delicate antlered crown she wore, turning it gently in her hands.

It was difficult, yes, living under such strict boundaries, having to give up your own dreams for the sake of the greater good. And of course some tribes had suffered as a result of the enforced simplicity of the Teller's Plots. The fairies, the mortal gods knew, had been punished for their loyalty to the King and Queen.

But *that* was the deal. Give up a little freedom for a lot of security.

And now someone was threatening that, and she, Melly, was the only who knew it was happening. And she didn't know what to do about it.

Grabbing her cigarette case and purse, Melly left her cottage and began the long walk to Ænathlin.

What she needed was a friend.

❄

"Aaaaaaah!" Melly screamed.

Then the perspectives clicked into place.

"Ahhh—ahoy there," she said, trying to cover her outburst. She coughed. "Hello, Domhnal. I was wondering if Joan was in?"

"Joany?" he said, a frown creasing his forehead. His new expression did nothing to ease Melly's shock upon his opening the door. She fixed her gaze on a point to the left of his face.

F. D. Lee

"I'm not sure—she went out a few hours ago. Hang on." Joan's father turned in the doorway and called up the stairs. "Anyone know where Joany's gone?"

There was a general hollering around the house as the question was relayed from room to room. Joan lived with her father and sisters in a tall, thin house that abutted the wall surrounding Ænathlin. Like many of the original houses by the wall, it was a hodgepodge of different elements, all stolen over the years from Thaiana. So it was that while Joan's front door was tall and painted bright red, there were also pillars holding up the lintel and a gargoyle set in the stone transom above the door.

It was not this, though, that had startled Melly.

"Give it a minute, one of them's bound to know," Domhnal said, once the shouts had died down. "Haven't seen you for a while, Mistress. How's you?"

"Fine, thank you."

"We were all very proud of that friend of yours, Bea. She's done us a good turn and no mistake."

"Oh?"

"Oh yes. Course, you don't live 'round here, do you, Mistress? 'Spect you've not heard."

Melly tried to concentrate on what Domhnal was saying, but it was difficult when she was also trying, at the same time, not look at him.

"Are you sure you're alright?" he asked. "You seem a little, what's the word, distracted."

"How are the girls?"

"Oh, good, good, thank you for asking."

Melly's eyes darted back to his face and away again. Reds, pinks and blues flashed across her vision.

"Keeping you busy?" she asked, her tone carefully neutral.

Domhnal hooked his thumbs into his pockets. "Well, you know what kids are like. Thank the mortal gods for Joany, that's what I say."

"Yes, she's a credit to you."

"She certainly is."

"Yes."

"Yup."

136

Melly bit her lip.

"I was just wondering… I didn't disturb you, did I?"

"No at all, Mistress. I was just taking a nap, as it happens."

"Oh."

"Why do you ask?"

"I think there's a little something on your… your…" For once lost for words, Melly gestured around her face.

Domhnal's hand shot up to his left cheek. "Here?" He began rubbing furiously at his face. "Did that get it?"

"Most of it," she said, covering her mouth with her hand.

Domhnal started rubbing furiously at his other cheek. Unfortunately, this did not make matters better.

Before rubbing frantically at his face, Domhnal had had fuchsia pink lips, bright red cheeks and blue shadow on his eyelids, like a clown. Now he still resembled a clown, only one who had fallen asleep without removing his make-up. If an impressionist painter had caught a glimpse of Domhnal's face, they would have retired their paintbrushes there and then, knowing that nothing they could create would match it.

Apparently, one of Joan's sisters had seen the opportunity for comedy presented in the form of her sleeping father and had grasped it with both hands. And a lipstick, blusher and mascara.

You had to admire her initiative. Which, it turned out, far outstripped her skill.

"Here," Melly said, trying not to laugh. She passed him her ebony cigarette case. "There's a mirror inside."

Domhnal took the case and popped it open. His eyes widened as he looked at his reflection.

"That little…!"

He handed Melly back her cigarette case and marched inside, yelling at the top of his voice. "Mags! Mags! I know it was you— come here this instant! That's the fourth time this week!"

Melly pocketed the case and turned to leave. There was a tug at her dress.

"Ello."

A little, curly-haired fairy stood in the doorway, her hands suspiciously clean when compared to the rest of her.

Melly made an educated guess. "Mags?"

"Yup," Mags grinned.

"You painted your father's face. That was very naughty," Melly said.

"Ah well… it was funny too," Mags replied, unchastised.

Melly's lips twitched. "Maybe. A little bit."

"More'n a little bit, I reckon. Joan's with her new friends, if you're looking for her."

"Her new friends?"

"Yeah," Mags said, twirling her hair in her fingers. "They hang out in the top room of The Quill And Ink, on Double Fortune Lane."

Melly knew the pub. "Thanks."

"No problem," Mags said.

A sudden burst of laughter erupted from inside the house. Melly guessed that Joan's other sisters had just laid eyes on their father. She reached into her purse and pulled out a small bag of salt.

"For your trouble," she said, handing the salt over to Mags. "Make sure you give some to your father—I think he's earned it, don't you?"

Mags grinned again, already imagining the make-up she could trade for with her share. She ran inside, shouting for her father.

Melly headed towards The Quill And Ink.

XX

"What you want with the fairies?" rumbled the troll behind the bar.

Melly leaned forward. "I want to speak to my friend."

"Elves and fairies ain't friends."

"I'll have a glass of red wine, then."

The troll grunted and poured her wine. She handed him a half piece of chalk and went to sit at a table near the front of the pub, where she could see the stairs leading to the top room.

An hour and another glass of wine later, she saw Joan come down the stairs.

She was with a group of about fifteen other fairies, all chatting to each other. The majority of them were house fairies, like Joan, though there were a few flower fairies and even a couple of garden fairies, a rare clan in Ænathlin. Melly decided to wait until Joan had finished speaking with her new friends before approaching her.

It was unusual to see so many fairies together. Not that there were any rules against it, but the fairies tended to keep their distance from each other. The hierarchy of oppression, so prevalent in the walled-in city, had been most internalised by those who suffered from it most severely.

The flower fairies, with their colourful hair and wings, loved by the characters far longer than either the house or the garden clans, looked down on their fellows. "Fairies we may be," they said, "But we're not *house* fairies, collecting teeth and tidying kitchens like slaves. Love us for what we're not if you cannot love us for what we are."

And the house fairies, unable to compete with the flower fairies' success, and not recognising that the game was rigged anyway, instead turned the ire down the chain, to the garden fairies. "Fairies we may be," they said, "But we're not *garden* fairies, living uncivilised lives in the forests, talking to plants, doing nothing for the characters. Love us for what we're not if you cannot love us for what we are."

Finally, there were the garden fairies, who were too big to be tooth fairies and too plain to excite the imaginations of the characters for very long. They could say nothing at all because they had no one else to look down on. And so they simply looked up and hated.

Melly had never really thought about it, but now she was watching Joan chatting earnestly with the other fairies, it occurred to her how unique her little friendship group was. An elf, a house fairy and a garden fairy. How had that happened?

Bea, of course.

Melly had met Bea on a Plot. She'd been the wicked witch and had gone through the usual show of being defeated by the hero. Bea had been Plot-watching. The story had ended, and both Melly and Bea should have returned to Ænathlin.

But instead, Bea had stolen a bottle of wine and taken herself off into a disused part of the gardens, where Melly had found her, drunk as anything. She'd demanded to know what Bea was doing, and had received in reply an angry invective about how unfair life was, and that Bea was going to show them all, whoever 'they' were, what a fairy could do if given the chance.

In defiance of all her carefully husbanded good sense, Melly hadn't walked away, nor had she reported her. There'd been something about Bea, her ferocious, misguided indignation perhaps, which had ignited something forgotten in the elf.

So Bea had snatched a further two bottles of wine, her plump figure and dyed grey hair making her similar enough to the characters not to draw attention, and she and Melly had drunk them together. By the time the sun rose, they were friends. After that, Bea had introduced her to Joan, and the rest was history.

"Hello, Melly! What are you doing here?"

Melly looked up from her wine and her thoughts. "Well met, Joan. I don't want to interrupt..?"

Joan pulled up a seat at Melly's table. "No, no, we've finished. I haven't seen you for ages—not since Bea's leaving party. I've joined this amazing group, Fairies United. We meet up once or twice a week."

Melly found herself smiling, despite her anxiety. "I was just thinking how nice it is to see so many fairies spending time together."

"Yes, it is nice. We've got a lot in common, actually. A lot *not* in common too, of course. There have been some spectacular rows. But I think we should have done it ages ago."

"So what's changed?"

"Bea, really. She's changed everything," Joan said, echoing Melly's own thoughts.

"Oh?"

"Yes. We're planning to write a letter to the GenAm—like Bea did—asking to be included in the Plots. I mean, I know there's Plot-watching, and the flower fairies get called in to help out with Young Belief And Tradition, but it's not the same. And we were thinking we might try to set up some job shares, so, you see, for example, I could invite some of the other tribes to come and do some tooth collecting with me. That way, they can see how hard we work. We think it's about time the GenAm and Ænathlin started recognising our talent. We provide a lot to the city, really. At least as much as everyone else does, anyway. So why not?"

Melly hesitated.

"You don't agree?" Joan asked.

"Is that a good idea—writing to the GenAm?"

"It didn't hurt Bea."

Melly looked past Joan at the remaining members of Fairies United. Most had already left the pub, but a couple were standing by the bar, deep in conversation. She leaned forward and lowered her voice.

"Joan, you know what happened to Bea because of that Plot. It's a miracle she wasn't Redacted."

"Ah, well, that's true. But that wasn't because she wrote letters, was it?" Joan answered, also lowering her voice. "That was because of the *you-know-what*, and the fact she changed her Plot. We obviously won't do any of that. But writing letters, standing up for ourselves, how is that a bad thing?"

"I don't think it's that simple."

"So you think we should just keep on being bullied by everyone?"

"No, of course not. I just think you need to be careful. The Mirrors—"

"The Mirrors are working, finally," Joan said, pulling back from Melly. "Bea's Plot helped them get started again. A Plot a fairy completed."

"Yes, I know that."

"Then why do you look so worried?"

Joan's tone was calm enough, but it was obvious from her expression she was annoyed. "You've always been sympathetic to our plight. Now we're trying to do something about it, and you're acting like we've just suggested going for tea with a gnarl."

Melly did the only thing she could think of. She pulled her cigarette case from her sleeve, extracted a slim black cigarette and lit up, taking her time over the endeavour. Joan waited.

"It's not that I don't support you," Melly said, once she'd finished coughing. "I just don't think you should be confronting the GenAm, at least not now."

"Why?"

Melly looked down at the tip of her cigarette, burning red. "Is there somewhere we can talk?"

Joan led Melly upstairs to the Fairies United meeting room. It was in the rafters of the pub, and Melly, who was much taller than a fairy, had to duck her head not to hit it against the beams. She glanced around. There were no mirrors, and the noise from the pub must muffle any conversation, no doubt why the fairies had chosen it. It was probably safe.

Melly told Joan about the dead girl.

"Tooth and nail, that's… it's horrific," Joan said, once she'd had a moment to gather her thoughts. The little house fairy had paled at Melly's description of the body and was now looking like she wanted to be sick. "Why would anyone do that?"

"That's the problem. It doesn't make sense." Melly glanced around her. She knew she was being paranoid, but she also knew how to survive in a city that used informers to find dissidents. "I think one of the fae did it. I think they were experimenting on her, putting her through multiple Plots at once. And…" Melly took a deep breath. "The things they did to her… they're from the stories. The old stories."

Joan fisted her hands in her hair. "That can't be right. The GenAm would never allow it. The Beast would be sent out."

"I know," Melly said.

"And anyway, the characters all refused those stories. It wouldn't work."

"I know."

"And why would anyone want to use one character for multiple stories, even without the… the… eyes and stuff? A heroine is hardly going to marry a hero, and then two minutes later begin another Plot. I know a lot of fae don't think much of the characters, but they must at least realise that a Happy Ending is an *ending*?"

"I know."

"None of it makes sense. And don't say 'I know'. I know you know," Joan snapped uncharacteristically. And then, more like herself, she said, "Sorry. It's just… this is awful."

"If I'm right, we should tell the Redaction Department." Melly said this in the kind of tone that indicated she had absolutely no intention of doing so.

"You don't trust them?"

"They sent an ogre into a room full of characters."

"But that was to catch an Anti. I mean, they should have sent the Beast in, of course, but it *is* their job. Are you worried they'll blame you for it? I'm sure they wouldn't… But then, you never know, do you, not with the white suits. I know! We could leave an anonymous note, just letting them know what you've found. That would work, wouldn't it?"

Melly ran her hands over her face like she was trying to rub dirt off her skin.

"I'm not worried about them blaming me. The GenAm knows I'm loyal."

"What is it, then? What's wrong?"

"When The Great Redaction happened, no one saw it coming. One moment the King and Queen were Narrating the Chapter and then the park was burning, and the Teller, *whocaresaboutus*, was in his tower as if he'd always been there. He took over in the space of a night." Melly snapped her fingers. "One night. We had no idea. We weren't prepared. He had all his Plots ready to go, and the Beast on his side. He must have been planning it for years."

Realisation dawned on the little fairy's face. "You think that someone's trying to change the Chapter?"

"Maybe. And we have no idea who's behind it—but if I'm right, whoever's doing it is connected. There's no way anyone could get away with mutilating a character, not unless they worked for the GenAm already. We can't go into the Redaction Department and announce something like this, not without knowing what's really happening."

"But still, that doesn't mean we shouldn't try. The old stories didn't work—trying to bring them back would be madness. We've only just got the Mirrors working properly. Why would anyone risk the characters refusing us again?"

"You're not listening," Melly said, trying to keep the frustration out of her voice. "If someone in the GenAm is vying to be the next Narrator—"

"All I'm saying is, we need to do something. If we can—"

"I was married," Melly said, silencing Joan. "Before the Great Redaction. My husband stood up to the Teller, *whocaresaboutus*. He spoke out. I saw the Beast take him away, and then I never saw him again. That's what happens when you stand up to someone whose power you don't understand. You lose."

Joan stood silent for a moment, lost. And then she said, "I'm sorry… I didn't know."

Melly was shivering. Joan unclasped her thick, woollen cape and handed it over to her. "I'd put it on you, but I can't reach," she said with a smile.

Melly laughed, a small thing that echoed with embarrassment and sadness. But she took the cape and wrapped it around her shoulders. On Joan, it reached nearly to the floor, but on Melly, it skirted her wrists.

"What happened to you?" Joan said. "I mean, after your husband…?"

"I became a witch. I started my new life, and after a while everything settled down. I suppose you think that sounds strange. But what else could I do? When the Teller's, *whocaresaboutus*, Plots started working, and the characters started believing in our stories again… Well, I accepted it. It all seemed worthwhile, in a way."

"Until the Mirrors started breaking again."

"Yes," Melly sighed. "Until the Mirrors started breaking again… And then the Redaction Department attacked the characters at Bea's Ball." Her voice hardened. "They shouldn't have done that. Even in the bad old days, we never did anything like that, not on that scale. But then they offered Bea a way out, and they asked me to help heal King John, and I thought… I thought perhaps that was it. An aberration, a one-off—a desperate act carried out because of the genie."

"But now there's the dead character."

"Yes. We can't return to the old stories. They weren't sustainable. We'll lose the characters. Even if we manage a few stories that way, they won't stand for it, not in the long run. I don't understand why anyone would even consider it."

Joan tugged at her hair, thinking. "Alright," she said. "So first of all, we need to try to find out who tortured and killed that girl, and what it is they think they're doing."

Melly wrapped the cape tighter around her shoulders. "Agreed. But how?"

"What we need is someone who knows the GenAm, and who can ask questions without raising any suspicion." Joan remembered a word from all her old detective books. "We need someone undercover."

"Who?"

It was at this moment that Joan had one of the worst ideas of her life.

"I've got a brilliant idea," she said, grinning.

XXI

W hat is belief but a very special kind of certainty?

There were things that simply *were*. If the sun rises, it also sets. If you drop a glass, it falls. If you heat water, it boils. Think what you want, it makes no difference to them.

But belief? You *had* to be certain, beyond doubt, beyond distraction, or else it wasn't belief. Without that conviction, all you had was an idea; a tendency, a mannerism, a habit. Your belief had to be as intrinsic as your beating heart. And, like your heart, belief worked best if it was shut away inside you, protected from harm, from interference, from the disease of doubt.

Protected from uncertainty.

Mistasinon had believed, once. And he'd been... not happy, not as such. Not even content, not if he really forced himself to think about it. But his belief had given him a certainty that he longed for, now it was absent.

He pinched the bridge of his nose, his eyes burning with tiredness. For all his obsessive dedication to the task, he still knew nothing about how the Mirrors worked; *why* they worked.

Magic gave them their power, but magic was deadly to the fae. Belief worked as a substitute, but it was unreliable. And there was no way the fae could live without the Mirrors. The Rhyme War had killed the Land, devastating it so that only the Sheltering Forest remained, protecting the city from the wastelands where the orcs and gnarls roamed.

That was why the Cerberus had been sent out to capture the genies. They could wish the Mirrors repaired. Yes, the wish magic killed them, eventually... but the argument had been that one life was worth many. And then one life had become two, two had become four, four eight... and now there was only one genie left, and he'd lost him.

Mistasinon shivered, though his office wasn't cold.

Kill the genies, borrow some time. Run the stories, borrow some time. But that was all it was—a loan. Eventually the Mirrors demanded more, a never-ending cycle of rising interest.

"And now we've got nothing to pay the ferryman with," Mistasinon said to himself.

Shaking his head, he stood up from his cluttered desk in his cramped office and went to stand in front of the Mirror, placed there by the Indexical Department for his investigations. He ran his fingertips over the surface. Wherever they touched, little inky bubbles instantly appeared.

He pulled his hand back. Then, slowly, he placed it on the cool glass, pressing his palm against the surface.

His stomach lurched as the connection was made. He had no idea what he would see. He never knew what the Mirrors would show him, not anymore. There were too many thoughts, too many memories fighting inside him, for him to use the Mirrors with any level of accuracy.

Under his hand, the Mirror went black instantly, clearing just as quickly. A grainy image appeared in the glass, flickering like a candle flame caught in the wind. A hillside, the green of the grass diluted by both the distance of the other world and the confusion inside him.

Mistasinon gripped the Mirror's frame, his knuckles white as he stared at the scene. It didn't matter that the connection wavered, black spots or flashes of his face occasionally obscuring it. He knew what he was looking at.

A gentle breeze buffeted the grass, and somewhere in the distance, he could hear seagulls calling out to each other. On top of the hill was a farmer's house, made of wood. The weather was so temperate there, it didn't need to be built with anything sturdier.

Mistasinon's throat caught.

With no cattle to tend it, the grass was overgrown. The farmer's house was rundown, the paint peeling. One of the windows was broken. It was obvious no one lived there anymore.

That was worse, somehow. It would be better if strangers had moved in, or even hero-worshippers—those bizarre fanatics who had followed him around on his labours, collecting up his old clothes or discarded belongings. Surely the house would have been a grand prize for one of them?

But instead it had been abandoned as if it meant nothing.

Wiping his eyes with the heels of his hands, he brushed aside the tears that were pooling at their corners.

The connection failed.

Mistasinon stared at his reflection. His eyes were bloodshot, silver trails of tears running from their edges down his cheeks, dripping off his clenched jaw.

A strange face. There were parts of it he recognised. The colour of his skin and hair reminded him of the men and women of his homeland, but the mouth was too narrow, the nose too short, the ears too low. Whose face was it, really?

Sometimes, in the middle of the night when he was alone with his thoughts, he wondered where his face had come from. Did he look like someone else, or was it completely new? He'd sat for hours once, trying to see his parents or his siblings in his features, but there was nothing of them.

His reflection brought its hand up to the base of its throat, massaging its neck.

My neck, he corrected. Yes. He could feel the skin and muscle under his hand. It was still so strange, even after all these months... no, a year now. A year without him... a year without himself...

Mistasinon yelped, pulling his hand away from his neck.

Blood.

To anyone else his blood might have been beautiful, a black liquid with red flecks, like the polished surface of a bloodstone—a rare mineral he remembered from his past. Foreign to his homeland, it had been imported at great expense and prized for its eerie beauty. He remembered seeing it on the necklaces of wealthy women as they passed him by and wondering what it would look like with the sunlight on it.

But the red and black plasma inside him wasn't beautiful, not to him. It was a confusion, a mess, a tangle of worlds neither of which he belonged to. It betrayed him.

Mistasinon rubbed his thumb and forefinger together until there was nothing more than a faint stain against his tanned skin. Tilting his head in the Mirror, he saw four raised lumps where he'd dug his nails into the flesh at the base of his neck.

He needed to get out of his office. He had to find people, noise, distraction. Pausing only to throw a blanket over the Mirror and to pick up his old leather satchel, he all but ran from his office.

Outside, the air was blissfully cool. The seasons didn't exactly change in the city, but the muggy heat of summer had long since given way to the sharp tang of winter. Slowing, he trotted down the steps from the GenAm, the large bronze doors shining like fire in the light of the setting sun. He lifted his face to the light, letting it warm his skin. He realised he'd spent too long with only himself for company.

Mistasinon took a deep sniff of the city air, wanting to centre himself and quiet his mind. He might not know who he was, but at least he always knew where he was.

But something was wrong...

Too late, the air was inside him...

Mistasinon staggered, clutching his head.

The smell was overwhelming. Oil, brick, cotton... anger, boredom, fear, hope... Sprays of blinding white, burning orange, vivid yellow, frozen blue... Flowers coming into instant bloom behind his eyes, infecting his senses with their stinging pollen, planting their seeds inside him. Crackling, electric roots of pain spread across the inside of his skull, coiling around his brain.

Someone was running, their skin tacky with sweat... A baker, mixing sawdust into the dough... Burning paper and tobacco plant... Lovers, salty sweat dampening their skin... Meat, roasting over a fire, the fat popping at it dripped onto the coals... A chamber pot emptied out a window, its contents hitting the cobbles...

And with that, the one that was Mistasinon lost its purchase. The colours swirled in a cyclone, spinning, bleeding, combining into a dark shadow.

From the shadow, the second one surfaced. *You're not in control, you're not doing it right, we don't know what we're doing... They'll be nothing left...*

It moved the eyes, shooting the body's gaze up to the Teller's tower, rising like a beacon above the city.

Find his voice, listen, listen... Be good... Do as you're told...

The third one stirred, snapping at the other two.

He did this to us. He said he loved you. Loved me. How can you be so weak? Little thing, looking for a lap, for a hand to lick...

It doesn't matter. We can't go there, the one that was probably Mistasinon stated, struggling to overpower the other two. *Not there. There's nothing there anymore.* He shifted the body's gaze, landing its sight on a window, high in the Redaction Department. *But maybe her? She knows about us. Me. Me. She knows... She'll tell me what to do...*

Like the fairy? the third one sneered. *But she hates us.*

We nearly killed her, I should never have allowed it.

I let me do it.

Isn't it always so? Disgusting monster, now worse than before. Deformed bea—

Something tugged at the body's elbow.

For once in unison, all three recoiled, bringing the arms across the narrow frame, trying to protect themselves.

"Hello! Are you alright? You look like you were going to faint."

For a moment, they held the body dumb, trying to comprehend the strange noises the little creature was making.

And then Mistasinon scrambled to the surface, pushing the other two back down into the shadows. He shifted his breathing, and the darkness went away, taking the smells of the city with it.

A blonde house fairy was standing in front of him, her eyes wide with concern. Next to her stood a striking, red-headed elf, smoking a black cigarette and glaring at him. There was something about her that disturbed him, but his thoughts were too fragmented to do more than vaguely register the feeling.

"No. I mean, yes. I'm fine, I mean," he said, glancing over his shoulder at Julia's window. "But I need to go. I have to go back. Back to work. Um. Sorry if I worried you. Enjoy the rest of your day."

The fairy tugged at her thick yellow hair. "Ah, well... You see, actually, we wanted to talk to you. I mean, you specifically."

"Me? But I don't know... Why? Have I done something?"

"Don't you remember us?"

A hundred possibilities suggested themselves, and then the correct memory flickered into life.

"Oh. Yes... I met you at Bea's inauguration. Your name's... Jane?"

"Joan. And this is our friend, Melly."

"Ah, yes. Now I remember you, too."

The elf gave him a sharp look. "We've never met."

"Oh. No. Well, I mean, you've never met me. I, uh, I saw you at the Ball. After the..." He faltered, not sure how much he should reveal. "You were unconscious," he settled on.

She stared at him. Mistasinon felt his hands twitch and forced himself to relax.

"That's not why we're here," she finally said.

The house fairy tugged again at his sleeve, glancing suspiciously around her. Then, in a very loud voice, she announced, "We would like to talk to you about the GenAm posters near the wall. They have been vandalised. It is a disgrace. The Teller Cares About Us."

"The Teller Cares About Us," repeated Melly and Mistasinon dutifully. He said, "That's probably something for the brown suits. If you go inside, they can give you a form to fill in."

"Ah, no," Joan said, again too loudly. "It is a very serious matter, and my friend and I are too community-minded to leave it to the brown suits."

A cold thought slid into his brain. Kneeling down so he was level with the fairy, Mistasinon said, "Is this about Bea—I mean, is everything alright?"

"We thought we should take you there, to show you the crime," Joan declared. Then, also lowering her voice, she added, "You really need to come with us. Please."

Mistasinon pulled himself to his feet. He looked again at the Redaction Department. And then he turned back to the fairy and the elf.

"You'd better lead the way."

XXII

The woman came home, setting down her bag in the hallway, removing her jacket and hat, taking off her shoes, and finally removing the clips that held her curly, black hair away from her face. It had been a long day, but a good one. She'd managed to solve the problem with the wheel at the mill and sold three of her clockwork door mechanisms.

She called her husband, who appeared out of the living room, their baby in his arms. The baby was put to bed, and she and her husband sat in the living room, snuggled on the sofa, watching the fire burn in the grate.

"Oh, you'll never guess what I heard today," she said.

"You know I hate guessing games," he replied mildly.

She smiled. "John was telling me this story about a girl, in one of those little villages they have down south."

"Let me guess—she gave birth to a three-headed cow?"

"What? No," she said, punching him playfully. "Listen, it's good. So there was a young girl whose father traded her for a bag of gold."

"I wonder how much gold we'd get for Sophie..."

"Not much, considering how sticky you let her get. Anyway, the point is, the father hadn't meant to trade his daughter. He met this little old man on the side of the road, and they struck a deal. The father thought he was trading for his dog, but it turns out it was his daughter. When the time comes for the trade, he can't part with her, so he tries to trick the old man. But the old man knows what he's doing, and he cuts off the girl's hands to punish the father for his deceit. The girl, horrified at her father's dishonesty, agrees to go with the old man because, even without her hands, she's beautiful and kind."

"Sounds like you," the husband replied.

"Stop interrupting. So the girl works for the old man, and she suffers. He works her so hard her hair goes grey and all that kind of thing. But in the end, the old man turns into a Prince! It turns out the elves had put a curse on him, one only the girl could break with her kindness. So he marries the girl, and they live happily ever after. Isn't that a good story?"

The man thought about it. "Yes, actually. It reminds me of the ones my gran used to tell me. Nasty, though. Losing her hands and all that."

"But that's what makes it good, isn't it?" the woman replied. "And it's only a story. Nothing like that would really happen— what kind of girl would go off with a stranger, especially after he cut her hands off? It's one of those allegory things, that's all."

The man dropped a kiss on his wife's head and wondered if his friend Nora had heard the story. He'd ask her tomorrow.

Joan waited while the Plotter took in the information about the dead girl.

They were taking a huge risk telling him, but he was the only person she could think of who might be able to find out what was going on. She was basing this on Bea's rather vague accounts of her meetings with him, and the fact that Joan was certain she'd detected some fondness for Bea on his behalf.

There were straw houses on the edges of cliffs in hurricane country that were less flimsy than this logic—something Melly had been keen to point out.

They'd taken him to Bea's bedsit. It was the only place she could think of that was private enough for a clandestine meeting with a GenAm official about a tortured character and a possible return to the old stories. Melly hadn't liked *that* suggestion either, but she'd not come up with any alternative locations.

The Plotter hadn't commented.

They'd had to strip him of his dark blue coat and waistcoat to get him past Ivor, and he was now pacing the room in a pale pink shirt, his sleeves rolled up his brown forearms.

"That doesn't make any sense," he finally said.

"That's what I thought when she told me," Joan replied, glancing at Melly, who was sitting on Bea's sofa, smoking. "So, do you think someone was trying out the old stories on her? What do you think we should do about it?"

Joan held her breath. If he was like any of the other suits—hells, anyone else in Ænathlin—he would report them now and let the white suits sort it out.

Time stood still, too nervous to move. The only sound was the crackle of Melly's cigarette as the paper burned.

Joan swallowed, her throat dry.

He'd been silent for a long time, just standing there, rubbing his neck.

She glanced over at Melly, who was sitting, her back stiff, watching the Plotter.

A cylinder of ash formed on the end of Melly's cigarette and fell to the floor.

And then the Plotter spoke:

"Honestly? You should report it to the Redactionists—it's their job to deal with Anties and... other things."

"I knew it," Melly snapped, glaring at Joan. "He just wants to get the white suits and the Beast involved." She stood up. "I told you this was a mistake. I'm leaving. I won't have anything to do with that three-headed monster."

The Plotter's face went blank. When he spoke next, there was an edge to his voice. "The Cerberus might be a monster, but he's served the city loyally. Besides, I said that was what you *should* do. I can see why you don't want to, given what you've said."

"That's why we came to you," Joan said, waving Melly back onto her seat. "We thought perhaps... We thought you could find out what's going on first, so we know what we're getting into." And then she played what she hoped was her winning card. "Bea said you were different from the usual suits."

Colour flooded the Plotter's face. He walked over to the window, so his back was to the room.

Joan caught Melly's eye and, grinning, mouthed the words '*I told you so*'.

The elf scowled and went back to her cigarette.

"So, will you help us?" Joan asked.

"I... Yes. I don't think I've got any choice, anyway," he added, still staring out the window. "It's my job."

Joan clapped her hands. "Excellent!"

Mistasinon gathered up his things and made for the door. His exit was impeded, however, by Melly, who ducked in front of him, blocking the doorway.

"I want your word you won't tell Bea about this," she said.

"Oh, Melly, I'm sure—" Joan began, but the elf cut her off.

"I'm serious. She won't leave things well alone. If she finds out, she'll find a way to feel responsible for it, especially given where the girl was found and by whom."

"Yes, of course," Mistasinon replied, something akin to relief darting across his features. "You have my word."

Melly stared at him, long enough for even Joan to feel uncomfortable. She couldn't imagine how it must be making the Plotter feel. Melly had a very good stare. She put a lot into it, the main ingredient right now being intimidation.

Still, having apparently satisfied herself that the Plotter was telling the truth, Melly stepped aside. "Thank you. For your help," she said grudgingly.

The Plotter looked like he wanted to say something more, but whatever it was it never made its way out of his mouth. He bowed to them both and let himself out of Bea's flat.

"See? That went well," Joan said.

"Shh," Melly hissed.

She went up to the door and pressed her ear to the thin wood. Joan waited. After a moment or two, her friend relaxed and stepped back.

"He didn't listen at the door," Melly conceded.

"I knew it was a good idea to ask him. All's well that ends well."

"I've heard that before. It's very rarely true." Melly looked back at the door. "Everything casts a shadow."

XXIII

It took Mistasinon a week to find the courage to leave the GenAm again.

When he did, it was with a cautiousness that bordered on paranoia. He sat for a long time at his desk, long legs crossed, hunched over his hands, filing his nails. Once he was satisfied they were short and neat, he dressed not in his blue suit, but instead in a pale woollen tunic and soft trousers. It felt strange not to be collared to his GenAm blues, but he didn't want to be noticed.

He went to the Mirror and, careful not to touch the glass, looked at his reflection. Of course, he was still conspicuous, his frame, his height, his warm brown skin… if it were summer, he might have been able to wrap a cloth around his head and shoulders, covering part of his face the way the characters did in the hot countries to keep cool. But in winter such a device would no doubt draw more attention, not less. In the end, he settled for ruffling his hair, so that it hung in curtains across his face.

For a moment he considered sending a runner to the Raconteur's, but quickly dismissed the idea, just as he'd done for the last seven days.

Next, he practised his breathing. Closing his eyes, he took a shallow breath in through his nose, visualising the air dropping quickly in his chest, skimming the surface of his lungs, and then he expelled it. Shallow breaths that rolled in and out of him, too gentle to overpower the fragile balance he sought to maintain over the other parts of himself.

He wondered for a moment if he was losing his mind, and then he laughed at his own ridiculousness. Losing his mind would, in the circumstances, be something of an advantage.

Returning to his desk, he grabbed his satchel and checked the contents. Satisfied that everything that should be in the bag was, he stood for a moment in his poky office, staring at the Mirror.

And then, pulling his shoulders back as if he were bracing against a heavy weight, he left the GenAm.

In the depths of the Indexical Department, hidden deep below ground, the broken Mirrors were kept.

Row upon row of Mirrors lined the vast space, a maze of fractured light and crazed reflections. The oldest Mirrors, the ones that had first shattered, were monstrous things, looming high above their descendants like the guilty memory of old traditions no longer observed.

They were relics now. Souvenirs from the time before the Rhyme War, when none of the fae had ever thought the Mirrors could break or that their Land would be ravaged, violated by greed and hubris, until all that remained was the walled city of Ænathlin, concealed within the remains of the Sheltering Forest, protected from the desert wasteland the Land had become.

Within the underground graveyard, it was possible to chart the slow demise of the fae in the diminishing magnificence of the Mirrors. Time was made physical as they shrank from the giant pathways of old to the most recent ones, only slightly taller than a troll, their glass cracked and their power lost.

With no genies left to wish them repaired, the broken Mirrors had been all but abandoned, their tomb visited only by a loyal few, whose sense of duty still outweighed their growing despair.

In the silence, a sound.

The creak of wood straining, and the soft chime of glass.

Mistasinon sat in the pub, ignoring the weak beer in front of him. He'd ordered it only because he knew it was what was expected of him, but he was too anxious to lift the glass to his lips. He was certain his hands would shake, spilling the warm, sticky liquid. So it sat forlornly while he concentrated on his breathing.

A shape caught his attention, and he watched the Raconteur make his way over to his table. He dipped into his satchel and pulled out the ration tokens.

"Well met," he said as the Raconteur took his seat. "I didn't expect it to take you so long to arrive. Business is going well?"

"That it is, that it is. With all thanks to you," the Raconteur added, smiling in what he probably thought was a winning manner.

"I'm pleased to hear it," Mistasinon said, meaning it. Trade was good for the city. He handed over the four tokens. The Raconteur looked at them and then back up at him.

"Is there a problem?" Mistasinon asked.

"Well, not a problem. Not as such. Only…"

"Yes?"

The Raconteur didn't need to hold his hand out. Everything else about him was doing it for him. "Well, what with me having a business to run now, people in my employ… I'm sure you understand. I even took on a couple of fairies the other day," the Raconteur said. "Can you believe it?"

"Why shouldn't I?"

"Werrrrll, no reason, no reason," the Raconteur said hastily, sensing he might have said the wrong thing. "I wanna set myself up as a serious concern, you know how it is. A while ago, no one would have come to a den that employed fairies. They wouldn't have trusted the stories to be any good—course, that's all fairy-hater nonsense, never bought into it myself. But business is business. Only since that group of theirs, Fairies United, got going, it's becoming a bit more acceptable to have them. Only out the back, naturally."

"Naturally?"

"Yeah, well, I can't have them mixing with the clientele. But still, everyone 'round here knows I've got them," he added, eyes darting to Mistasinon's satchel.

Subduing his frustration, Mistasinon pulled another ration token from his bag. The Raconteur grabbed it and squirrelled it away in what he now noticed was a new jacket.

"So, what can you tell me about the city?" Mistasinon said, adding with a note of sourness, "Other than the emancipation of the local fairies, I mean."

"Right, yeah. So the big news is the Mirrors, right? Ain't had any breaks for a few months now."

"So I gather. Any idea why that might be?"

"Course I do. That's what you pay me for, isn't it?" The Raconteur leaned forwards. "I heard from someone who works in the Contents Department that the Plotters have got something new going on, and that's why the Mirrors are working so well. They're keeping it hushed up at the moment, but my source reckons they've been trialling it for a few months now. She says it won't be long until they're ready to announce it."

"Does your source know what this new thing is?"

"Well, it'll be a Plot, won't it? That's what the Plot Department does. Perhaps the Teller, *whocaresaboutus*, has written a new one? Must be, right? It's not like anyone would be running an unsanctioned Plot, not unless they wanted to find out if the Beast really does have teeth stained black with blood."

"I'm not here to talk about the Cerberus. Tell me why you think the Teller, *whocaresaboutus,* has written a new Plot."

"Look around you," the Raconteur said. "Everyone's got more now. Trade's opened up, the restrictions on the Mirrors are relaxing. I heard the GenAm's even gonna let regular folks use the Mirrors soon, no papers required. It's a return to the good ol' days and no mistake. Stands to reason it's a new Plot."

"And does your source know when this new Plot is going to be announced?"

"If she does, she didn't tell me—which means that she doesn't know," the Raconteur amended. "You can rely on my information."

Mistasinon stood up, hooking his satchel over his shoulder, and shook the Raconteur's hand. "Thank you again for meeting me."

"No problem, no problem. I won't forget it was you who gave me my start. You're one of the good ones and no mistake."

Mistasinon smiled thinly. "I'm glad somebody thinks so."

After he left, the Raconteur ordered a pint of beer, killing some time before his next meeting. Business was going well and no mistake, but that didn't mean he could turn down trade. And, while it didn't do to speak ill of the GenAm, he wasn't about to go believing that the current boost in the Mirrors would last. No, better to hedge his bets.

Still, a little bit of extra courage before seeing his next client didn't go amiss.

He finished his beer and left the pub.

"Get out the bloody way!"

"Move it!"

"Watch where you're going!"

"You give that back, you little—!"

He ducked around and through the crowd, not even minding all the shouting and shoving. It did the heart good to see the streets so busy, even if meant you had to keep an eye on your belongings— this was still the outer ring, after all. If anyone tried to gentrify it out here, they'd soon find themselves tied up in an alleyway with a splitting headache and an empty space where their purse used to be. Or their kidneys.

Nevertheless, there was no denying it. Ænathlin had lost something in the last few months, and that something was its anxiety.

For almost as long as he could remember, the Mirrors had been breaking, and there had been shortages of food and goods. But now the Mirrors were—for the moment at least—working. And so the streets were full of fae, bustling in and out of stores, trading for things they wanted instead of things they needed.

He arrived at the designated building and pushed open the door. It was waiting for him, standing still in the middle of the room, that horrible, vacant look on its face. Mortal gods, they made his skin crawl.

"you have news for me" the dead-head goblin intoned, her saucer-shaped eyes blinking slowly.

"As a matter of fact, I do, yes, yes."

He took the payment from the dead-head, not bothering to try to haggle anything extra out of her. It wasn't just that there was no point trying to bargain with a dead-head, though there wasn't— they didn't have the imagination for it, not anymore. No, he didn't bother trying to haggle because he knew which Department the dead-head worked for, and no one needed that kind of trouble.

At least the meeting would be quick. The dead-head never asked for anything to be repeated. The Redacted had excellent memories on account of the fact they didn't use up any space in their heads on things like a personality.

The Raconteur began recounting his meeting with Mistasinon.

F. D. Lee

XXIV

Unaware that he was currently the focus of a story, Mistasinon walked through the city, his head ducked, concentrating on his breathing, holding his satchel close to his body. He bumped into a few people who swore at him and accused him of drunkenness, but no one stopped to confront him. Eventually, he found himself in the centre ring of the city, by the Grand Reflection Station.

He loitered for an hour or two, watching the crowds coming and going, all using the Mirrors. He thought about what the Raconteur had said and realised he had locked himself away in his office for too long, obsessing over the Mirrors.

So what are you going to do? he asked himself.

In the past, when he'd been called upon to find someone, it had been easy. The Mirrors were the only way from Ænathlin into Thaiana, and they gave off a strange, crackling scent, one that cloyed in his nostrils and churned in his stomach like a bad meal. He'd never thought about it before, but he supposed now it wasn't the Mirrors so much as the magic that they used.

The genies had smelled the same, which was how he'd found them. And, he was now certain, how he'd lost Seven, Bea's genie—he must have stopped using his magic, right until the moment he'd arrived in Llanotterly, and Mistasinon had hatched his plan to try bringing him in without violence.

He'd come to the Grand because he'd hoped he might be able to sniff something out, to find someone who stank of nerves and magic. But looking at the masses coming in and going out, it was clear he needed another plan. There was no way, not anymore, that he would be able to isolate one scent within so many…

But if not that, what else could he do?

His head lifted towards the Teller's spire, always visible in the overcrowded city thanks to its exceptional height.

For the second time in his life, he'd been cast out, abandoned by his master. And, while rationally he could understand that this time was different from the last, the pain of it felt exactly the same.

"Keep your promise," he muttered. "Do what you said you'd do. Be good."

Closing his eyes, Mistasinon counted to three, and then took a deep breath in through his nose, bracing himself for another onslaught.

Nothing.

Another deep breath.

Again, nothing.

He opened his eyes.

What was happening?

Confusion washed over him. He ran away from the Grand, towards the covered market. Coming upon a baker's, he charged into the shop, grabbed a loaf of bread and split it open, burying his face in its warm softness.

"Hey! Hey! What in the five hells do you think you're doing?"

Mistasinon ignored the voice, breathing in the scent of the bread.

"Excuse me," the baker snapped, "You can't just come barging in here, sticking your face in my bread—I've got orders, customers. This isn't the wall, you know."

She grabbed his arm—

—and landed on the floor on the opposite side of her shop.

Mistasinon dropped the bread, staring in horror.

"I'm sorry, I'm sorry, I'm sorry," he babbled, racing over to the baker, trying to help her to her feet.

"Get away from me!" she shouted.

The other customers, waking up from their shock, came to her rescue, encircling her, pushing him away.

"I didn't mean to—she startled me," he said, lifting his hands above his head.

"Startled you?" the baker repeated, climbing to her feet. "Who in the five hells do you think you are? I should call the brown suits on you, coming in here, stealing, causing fights."

"Nah, Cath, don't bother with the brown suits," said a dwarf, reaching behind the counter and producing a large bat. "I can deal with this."

F. D. Lee

The dwarf moved towards him, his face hard with intent.

Mistasinon held his satchel close, turning his body away from the advancing dwarf, guarding it.

A handful of the other customers joined the dwarf, flanking him.

Mistasinon's breath quickened.

And then the colours came.

Anger... Fear... Excitement... Red, white, yellow...

He couldn't breathe, he couldn't see... he was suffocating, drowning...

Something slammed into him, knocking him off balance...

A pink lightning bolt crackled across his senses... Satisfaction... A job well done... Another whack, this time to his ribs. Green explosions behind his eyes... Indignation... Coming here, thinking you own the place... Dirty yellow... No one understands what it's like to work so hard... Icy blue... Please stop, won't they stop... Magenta... I should get help...

Pushing its way to the surface, the third one snarled, the noise escaping from his throat, curling his lips and baring his teeth.

Mistasinon lost purchase, falling into the shadows...

...

...And then he was in the street.

His tunic was torn, his ribs aching, his left shoulder and hip bruised and tender.

Frantically, he reassured himself he still had his satchel and its contents. And then, ignoring the pain in his side, he ran back to the safety of the GenAm.

XXV

Bea looked up when she heard the shouting.

She was sitting by herself in the common room, trying to do her homework. She closed her book and retied her hair before following the sound of raised voices.

"Let him go!" shouted Aideen, the red-haired brownie from Bea's class. Harry, the other brownie, was being held down by two elves. But it was the third person who caught Bea's attention.

Carol was sitting cross-legged on the floor in front of Harry. She was leaning forward, her pale green hand grasping his chin as she spoke to him in a quiet voice. Aideen was off to the left, tugging at the arm of one of the elves holding Harry. But despite her desperate shouting, she wasn't really pulling very hard.

That was the thing about elves. They were beautiful, and they used their beauty against you. They made you feel weak and inconsequential, guilty for bespoiling them.

If you let them, that was.

Bea marched over to the scene.

"What in the five hells is going on?" she demanded.

Carol looked up. "Get lost, cabbage mother. This isn't your business."

"I'll be the judge of that," Bea said, grabbing one of the elves holding Harry and dragging him off. The elf screamed, unused to being fairy-handled.

"Oh for goodness' sake, grow up," Bea snapped.

The elf rubbed his arm and turned the full force of his beauty onto her. "Who do you think you are, touching me?"

"I think I'm the person stopping you bullying Harry," Bea replied, sticking her chin out. Elven glamour didn't have much effect on her—after all, she'd seen Melly dancing on tables and coughing up a lung after smoking her pungent cigarettes. It was hard to be frightened of a tribe en masse once you'd got to know one of them.

"I said get lost," Carol said, rising to her feet. "We weren't going to hurt him. We were instructing him."

Bea rolled her eyes. "Oh yes, that's exactly what it looked like."

"You don't know anything, cabbage mother. You don't belong here."

Scrambling to his feet, Harry said, "I was only talking to Aideen about the ghost, that's all. Then these three jumped on me."

"That's right," Aideen corroborated. "We were minding our own business. We weren't doing anything wrong."

Carol's eyes narrowed. "Liar."

Bea moved in front of Harry, so she was facing Carol. "Well, I know who I believe."

"Mortal gods. Fine. Since you've chosen to involve yourself in things that don't concern you, you might at least know the truth. These brownies were planning to sneak into the west wing."

"What do you care if they do?"

"Stupid fairy. We're not allowed out of this wing, are we? If they went off, they'd get us all into trouble—even you, although I know you think you're untouchable. We were simply explaining to them why they shouldn't."

"And this explanation took you and two elves, did it?"

Carol shrugged. "Whatever it takes. I'd have thought you'd understand that."

The two elves sniggered.

"What's so funny?" Bea said, turning on them.

"We all know how you got your place," replied the elf she'd dragged off Harry, his pretty nose curled.

"What's that supposed to mean? I got here the same way Carol did."

Suddenly, Bea's cheek exploded in pain.

"Don't you dare say I'm the same as you," Carol hissed, shaking some life back into her hand. She turned to the elves. "Come on. We'll find another way."

Swearing, Bea rubbed her face where Carol had slapped her. She turned back to the brownies. "Was what Carol said true? Were you planning to sneak out?"

"Well... Yes," Harry admitted. "But only to find out if there really is a ghost. I was the first person to learn about it, so it should be us who finds it. It's only fair, isn't it? We weren't trying to get everyone into trouble."

"Look," Bea said, hoping to sound friendly and not like she might also want to hold Harry down and knock some sense into him. "Firstly, there's no such thing as ghosts. And secondly, the GenAm doesn't take very kindly to rule-breakers. Famously so, in fact. Haven't you ever been to one of the public Redactions?"

"Oh, they wouldn't Redact *us*," Harry said.

Bea started to explain that people had been Redacted for less when she realised what Harry meant. He didn't mean they wouldn't Redact Aideen and him for breaking such a small rule. He meant they wouldn't Redact someone from the inner circle.

"I'm not sure you should rely on that," Bea said carefully. "They Redacted almost everyone during the Great Redaction, didn't they? Even the King and Queen."

"But they were the King and Queen of the fairies, and no one cares about fairies—"

Aideen kicked him.

"What?" Harry said, shocked. Aideen waggled her eyebrows at him, nodding her head towards Bea.

"Oh, right," he said. "Sorry."

Bea sighed. "Listen, you've got to look after yourself, and the best way to do that is to not get into trouble in the first place. Understand?"

"But you just rescued us," Aideen said.

"Yes, well, trouble's different for different people, I guess. Anyway—"

"What'sss going on here? I've just had two elvesss and an imp complaining about you three. They sssaid you're causssing fightsss."

Bea froze.

She knew what was behind her. No other fae had voices that slithered like that. But she couldn't stop herself. It was like when someone said something tasted bad and then handed it to you to try—you didn't want to, you knew what was going to happen, and yet somehow you always found yourself reaching out, mouth opening...

She turned.

F. D. Lee

The brown-suited witchlein was glaring up at them, his arms folded. Bea noticed that the yellow scales covering his body caused thousands of little bumps in the cheap material of his suit.

Her mouth went dry, probably because the rest of her body had broken into a cold sweat.

"We weren't starting fights," Aideen denied hotly. "They were bullying us. They attacked Harry."

"Isss that true?"

Harry stepped forward. "Absolutely. You know what elves are like."

The witchlein pursed his lips, thinking. After a moment, he nodded his head. "You're lucky it wasss me they complained too. Not everyone here isss asss understanding. Jussst keep out of trouble."

And then he smiled at them, his mouth full of razor-sharp teeth.

Bea staggered backwards.

"Isss your friend alright?"

"I don't know," Harry said. "Bea?"

Bea opened her mouth, but all that came out was a croak. She felt dizzy, as if the room were spinning around her. Her ears were burning, and yet the rest of her was ice cold.

The witchlein stepped forward, reaching out.

His scaled hand landed on her...

Bea flinched, her whole body spasming violently, trying to shake him off as if he were some grotesque creepy crawly.

The witchlein, so much smaller than Bea, went flying.

"What in the five hellsss did you do that for?" he said, picking himself up from the floor.

"I didn't mean to..." Bea said, shaking. "You came at me..."

"Gosh, I've never seen anyone fight a brown suit before," Aideen said, clearly rapt. "I thought fairies were supposed to be very docile."

"I... I..."

"Calm down, it'sss alright. You're Buttercup Sssnowblosssom, aren't you?"

"Yes. Buttercup. Buttercup Snowblossom. Um. Bea."

"Right, Bea, my name'sss Luca," the witchlein said. "I think I know what happened. I sssurprisssed you. You and your friendsss

168

have jussst had a run-in with sssome elvesss, tensssions were high, and you forgot yourssself. Isss that right?"

Bea didn't know what to say, so she just nodded.

"No harm done," Luca said. He looked down at his suit, which was ripped to shreds thanks to his yellow spikes, which had risen involuntarily. "No ssseriousss harm, anyway." The spikes on his body shivered and then settled back into neat scales. "I think you ssshould go to your roomsss, all three of you. Get an early night."

Bea watched him walk away. She rubbed the scars on her leg through her dress, remembering the scene at the Ballroom, the ogre smashing people out the way, while all around her tiny yellow witchlein, their scales raised, swarmed. Guests had tried to escape, only to be pulled to the ground by the tiny yellow monsters, while the huge room echoed with the witchleins' hissing.

Even after she killed the ogre, the witchlein didn't stop. Bruised and bloodied, her right leg freshly wounded, Bea had stood, facing an ever-tightening circle of them. The hissing in her ears, Melly unconscious behind her, and Ana, human and terrified, next to her, Bea had thought she was going to die.

The witchlein at the Academy, Luca, may not be wearing a white suit, but he was still a GenAm worker. Bea realised she was going to have to do something about him or risk the situation escalating beyond her control.

❄

"How did it happen?" the Chief Cataloguer asked, looking at the Mirror. Her reflection stared back at her, sharing her anxious expression.

"I don't know, my Lady. It was like this when I found it."

They stared at the Mirror. It was almost completely fixed, only a faint spider web of thin lines hinting at its previous state.

"No one's been down here?"

"There's no other signature in the book," the Indexer replied.

The Chief Cataloguer nodded her head. The Indexical Department took paperwork very seriously. If no one had signed in, then no one had been down here. Besides, why would anyone bother visiting the broken Mirrors, unless they had to?

The Mirror stood in front of them. It was one of the smaller ones—still much taller than the Chief Cataloguer, certainly, but small when compared to some of the really old ones.

And it had fixed itself.

"I'd better tell the other Heads," the Chief Cataloguer said. *Although*, she added to herself, *Julia probably knows already*.

Bea moved silently through the hallways of the Academy, listening carefully at corners and ducking into empty rooms when she heard footsteps. The other recruits should all be upstairs in the common room or else in their bedrooms. But then, she was where she shouldn't be, so there was no reason to assume that others weren't as well.

Thankfully, she reached the assembly hall without being discovered. Bea cracked the door open and slipped in, holding the heavy bottle tight, reassured by its weight.

Chokey had a small collection of drinks under her bed that she thought no one knew about. It hadn't been difficult for Bea to wait until her roommates were out to steal the largest bottle she could find.

The witchlein was walking along one of the tables, dragging a bag behind him, into which he was chucking the dirty cutlery from dinner. Bea swore under her breath. She hadn't planned on him having a bag of sharp implements, but then she supposed that the witchlein already had weapons built in, as it were.

Overhead, the storm continued to rage.

Luca turned and saw her.

"What are you doing here? You ssshould be up in the common room," he said, putting down the bag.

"I just—" Bea croaked. She coughed and started again. "I just wanted to speak to you. Um. If you've got time."

Luca's yellow eyes narrowed suspiciously. "You're not allowed down here on your own."

"This won't take long."

Bea wondered if he could hear the sound of her heart beating, or if the roar of the wind covered it. She held the bottle tightly, hidden behind her back. Mortal gods, she hoped he'd answer soon. Her palms were sweaty, she was certain she'd drop the bottle any moment now. If it smashed on the floor, not only would he know something was up, but, more crucially, she'd never get the chance to use it on him.

Luca's mouth thinned as he contemplated speaking to her. Still, to Bea's great relief, he obviously decided to give her the benefit of the doubt, and, leaving his bag of knives and forks behind him, he walked along the table towards her.

"Well… if it'sss quick," he said.

Bea managed not to shudder.

"Oh, it will be," she said, raising the bottle.

XXVI

The dark, wood-panelled corridors of the Academy wound, seemingly endlessly, throughout the old building. The Academy was a nightmare made solid, a twisting labyrinth that offered no way to predict where you were or what would happen to you.

Better to try to wake up. Better *never* to go to sleep. Better anything than to be caught in the nightmare's web; because perhaps, one day, you would never find your way back again.

And yet, somewhere deep within the tangle of rooms, there was laughter.

"You should've seen this dress," Bea said. "It was as wide as a bookcase, an' it was covered in these little pink butterflies that fluttered when I walked."

"It sssoundsss very traditional."

"That's what I said."

Bea leaned back against the wall and sighed happily.

She and Luca had finished the bottle of wine she'd brought as a peace offering-slash-apology, and Luca had stolen another from the kitchens. They were now sitting in the laundry room, getting thoroughly drunk.

"Thanks for speakin' to me," she said again. "I am sorry for how I reacted."

Luca shrugged. "People are alwaysss nervousss around usss. I'm usssed to it."

"Mortal gods, that makes me feel even worse."

"You're here now," he said, reaching into his pocket and pulling out some tobacco. He started rolling a cigarette. "Lotsss of people wouldn't have bothered."

Bea watched as his little hands moved quickly over the paper, creating a thin cylinder. That morning, the sight of his yellow-scaled fingers would have sent her into shock. Now she was just fascinated with how quickly he was able to create something from nothing. She was pleased she'd plucked up the courage to apologise to him.

"You're very quick," she said.

"Nimble fingersss. I used to cut my friendsss' hair when we were younger. I liked cutting hair." He gave Bea an appraising look, drawing thoughtfully on his roll-up. "I could cut yoursss if you like. If I put some layersss in, you could wear it down. It never ssstaysss in that bun you wear."

"That'd be nice." Bea reached for the bottle, missed, and tried again. "But maybe after less wine?"

Luca laughed, taking another drag.

"You know that stuff's addictive?"

"Really? I hadn't noticed. I sssupossse I wasss too busssy sssmokin' it. Hey, can I tell you a sssecret?"

"If you wan' to." Bea stifled a hiccup. "It can keep all mine company."

"I wasss very pleasssed when you got into the Academy."

Bea took another big gulp of wine and handed him the bottle. "You're the only one. How come?"

"Becaussse it'sss not jussst about fairiesss, isss it? Everyone getsss dumped on. I don't wanna work for the Contentsss Department, but the only other GenAm job they give to the witchlein isss with the Redactionisssstsss. It'sss already bad enough trying to get ssserved in a pub, without wearing white."

He burped. "Everyone hasss to be where they put usss. Fairiesss get it worssse, I know that, but it'sss not much better for usss witchlein, either."

"Huh. You know, I got all these letters before I came here. They were from fae who felt the same way. Well, some of them, anyway."

"Sssee? It'sss good you're here. Ssshowsss it can be done."

Bea squinted up at the lantern. She was mildly interested to note that where there had once been one light, there were now three.

A thought occurred to her.

"Did you change my test an' leave me those notes?"

Luca frowned. "What?"

"Nothing. Forget it. 'm drunk."

173

Luca laughed, and then a serious expression settled on his face "Isss it true what they sssay about you?"

Bea giggled. "Depends what they're saying, to be honest." She waved the bottle. "If it's the one about fairies all being shiftless drunks, that might have some truth in it."

"I mean about how you got your place here?"

"Oh. Right."

Through the fog of alcohol, a warning light blinked. Bea took another mouthful of wine, trying to organise her thoughts. This is one of the many neat tricks of drunkenness: reach a certain point, and your thinking is so muddled that the only reasonable solution is to drink more.

"It started out as a Happily Ever After story," Bea said. "But it changed while I was working on it. The humans didn't do what they were supposed t'do, and the girl, the heroine, didn't wanna marry the hero, you know? She didn't wanna be in a story, not my story, anyway. And then, then, there was this... this... this thing happened, an' this other girl, bossy girl but nice, you know? She became Adviser to the King. So by the end, it was a Rags To Riches. Everything worked out. Or so 'm told."

Luca seemed to be thinking about something. "Humansss? Y'mean the charactersss?"

"What? Oh, yes. The characters."

"Tha'sss a good story. Better'n the one I heard 'bout you."

Bea harrumphed. "Everyone's got something bad t'say about me. Not all of it's true... I don' have the time. Hey, have you ever been to Thaiana? I mean, properly. Not stuck here in the snow."

Luca nodded. "Once, yeah. I didn't like it."

"I've been loads of times. Plot-watchin'. Wait—you didn't like it? Why not?"

"I dunno. There were too many charactersss—humansss. They ssscare me. I kept thinking they were gonna ssstep on me."

Bea couldn't help it. She laughed. "'m sorry," she said when Luca thumped her on the arm. "It just seems strange for a witchlein t'be scared of something. Would it hurt you if one stepped on you?"

"Oh, yesss. We're not very thick ssskinned, dessspite the ssscalesss."

"Hah. You an' me both."

They sat for a while, both lost in their own thoughts. The only sound was the occasional glug of the wine bottle, getting steadily deeper as they emptied it.

"Can I ask you a question?" Bea said.

"Sssure."

"Is there somethin' goin' on here?"

Luca sat up and looked at her. "What makesss you asssk?"

"No reason. I just... I thought I saw a coach arriving, an' there's this light that goes off every few weeks. I've seen it, but no one else has."

"How do you know it'sss real if no one elssse hasss ssseen it?"

"'cause I've seen it. I know I have. An' half the recruits think the building's haunted. 's what the brownies were fightin' about with Carol an' the elves."

"Haunted? Like, by a ghossst?"

"Yeah. That's what they think."

Luca almost laughed, but then he saw the serious expression on Bea's face and changed his mind. "Y'know what it'sss like when people are cooped up for a long time. Everyone goesss a little mad."

"So there isn't anything... I don't know... clandestine happening?"

"I don't think ssso. I'm sssure they'd have told usss if there wasss."

Bea rather felt he'd missed the point, but she decided not to question him further. Either he knew nothing, or he was a much better liar when he was drunk than she was. A yawn escaped her.

"We should prob'ly go. Mortal gods, I'll get in so much trouble if I'm caught."

"I'll sssay you were helpin' me." Luca grinned, gesturing at the now empty bottle. "We were cleanin' out the old ssstores."

Bea burst out laughing. Well, that answered that question at least—Luca was clearly not an expert when it came to subterfuge.

They left the storeroom, trying to be stealthy but mostly falling about, laughing at each other. Still, they managed to make their way back to one of the corridors and Luca tottered off, waving goodbye.

175

Bea walked in the opposite direction. It occurred to her, as she cannoned off a corner, that she was probably quite a bit drunker than she realised. What would she do if one of the other brown suits found her? She giggled. Maybe they would expel her *and* Redact her. Take a belt and braces approach. The Teller Cares, after all.

At the thought of the Teller, Bea's mood lurched drunkenly from hysteria to depression. She flopped onto the floor, looking down at her grey skirt. The stitching was coming loose. She started to pick at it.

Perhaps it hadn't been such a good idea to try to find her way back to her room alone.

Pick pick pick.

Perhaps, in fact, a lot of her most recent ideas hadn't been that good.

Pick pick pick.

Perhaps she was going to fail everyone, all over again.

Pick pick pick.

Bea ripped a hole in her dress.

She swore.

It was time to get up and go back to her room. She stood up and toppled over, the alcohol spinning her around like a gyroscope.

Yup. Definitely drunk.

She half-shuffled, half-crawled to the edge of the floor, in order to use the wall to help her up. She pressed her bare hand against the wood, and—

Was thrown backwards, landing heavily.

Bea stared at the wall, cradling her hand against her breast. Now almost entirely sober, she pulled herself to her feet and walked back over to the wall. She stood for a moment in front of it, looking at it.

The wood had screamed at her.

Cautiously, Bea brought her hand up to the wall, letting it hover a few centimetres above its surface. Now she knew what she was listening for, she could sense it: a very slight prickle was coming off the wooden panels, not dissimilar to the feeling you get when you know someone is looking at you.

Bea looked up and down the hallway. It was empty, except for herself and the spectral sounds of the recruits, far away. She looked down at her hand, still hovering over the wood.

All the tribes had unique qualities that marked them out. Bea was a garden fairy, and the garden fairies' talent was that they could talk to plants.

She'd never seen much point in it if she were honest. A few times, it had come in handy—for example, when she'd needed to make a pumpkin grow to the size of a coach. But the fact of the matter was, there were a limited number of occasions in life when a giant squash was the answer to the question, 'what now?'.

It wasn't even like she could make friends with them. Plants weren't intelligent, at least, not in the way most people understood the term. They had a kind of basic need, a desire that pushed them to grow, to flower, to pollinate. In her more cynical moments, Bea thought a lot of her fellow fae weren't that much more advanced. But still, plants didn't think, not exactly. They felt.

And the wood that panelled the walls in the academy felt *afraid*. So afraid that it had sent a shock through her when she touched it.

It was unlikely that the wood had meant to talk to her. Whatever reasoning it might have once had, it had lost long ago, when it was severed from its roots. The wood-panelled walls weren't alive… but they also weren't dead, not completely. They could still feel. And Bea, thanks to her birth, was able to sense it.

Swallowing, she pressed her hand to the wood.

She was ready for it this time, and even so the force of the scream caused her to drop to her knees, her hand still against the wall. Steadying herself, Bea attempted to question the wood. She put all her uncertainty and concern into a ball of emotion and sent it travelling down her arm and out through the palm of her hand, into the wall.

What she got back was jumbled and incoherent. There was, above everything else, fear. It was cold and sharp, running over Bea's hand and up her arm to dance across her chest in a flurry of pinpricks, strangely reminiscent of the snowstorm raging outside the Academy. But beneath that were other feelings, less distinct but, if she concentrated, there.

Loneliness…

Confusion…

Anger…

Bea pulled her hand away. She looked around her at the walls of the Academy, each one covered in wood, surrounding her from all sides. Now she was paying attention, she could very faintly sense it, even without touching the walls.

The Academy was screaming.

XXVII

Someone was torturing her.

The fact that Bea knew her current misery was self-inflicted did nothing to ease her suffering. Her head pounding, wishing the Academy served something other than lukewarm porridge, she tried to organise her thoughts. She might as well have tried to herd cats.

Why were the walls screaming? What on Thaiana was happening here?

Because Bea was now certain that something was very amiss at the Academy. The problem was she had no idea what the problem actually *was*, just that she was certain there was one. Nor, come to that, did she have the slightest clue what to do about it.

Strange lights and phantom coach visits were suspicious, certainly, but they didn't actually *mean* anything. Her test had been altered, but she hadn't raised it at the time, and now she worried she'd missed her opportunity to do so without getting expelled. Ditto the books in the attic—if she mentioned them now, along with Mistasinon's absence from the tutorial, she was certain it would be twisted against her.

Added to all that was the fact that the screaming walls was a complete non-starter, at least in terms of asking anyone about them. None of the other fae could talk to plants, so there was only her word that it was even happening. Bea pessimistically, but very accurately, predicted the word of a cabbage fairy wouldn't carry much weight.

Thus it was occurring to her that, as certain as she was that something was wrong, absolutely no one would believe her if she told them. This was frustrating enough, but she was also not entirely convinced she *should* voice her concerns, even if she could find someone who would listen to her.

The most important thing was to become an FME. She would never be able to change anything if she remained just a fairy. All those dead genies, all those dead people… Poor King John, who'd never walk again… She'd never be able to do anything about it, not if she wasn't a godmother. It was the only way anyone would take her seriously.

But…

If something was going on, shouldn't she at least try to find out what it was? The GenAm was capable of anything. And, if she really was serious about making a difference, could she ignore something she was certain was wrong? She'd tried that before, and all that had happened was she'd caused even more pain. Hells, she'd got her hero paralysed.

But again, she'd also tried barging into situations she didn't fully understand before, and that had hardly worked out well, either.

It was, she was prepared to admit, a bit of a pickle.

"Hullo, Buttercup! Don't you look glum?" Chokey said, taking the seat next to her. Hemmings sat down opposite.

Bea ate some more of her porridge. "I didn't sleep very well."

It wasn't a lie. She actually *could* remember the last time she'd had a good night's sleep: It was the night before her Ball had been attacked by the Redaction Department.

"Are you worried about the field test in a fortnight?" Chokey asked, shovelling a spoonful of food into her mouth and pulling a face that said she instantly regretted it. "Honestly darling, nothing could be as bad as this food."

The field test. Now there was another problem.

They were almost halfway through the year, and the test would decide which classes they were streamed into for the final six months of training: godmother, witch, villain, peril, companion, information giver… moral. If Bea failed the test and was put in the moral stream, all her plans would be over before they began. No one took the morals seriously. Sure, she'd technically be a Fiction Management Executive, and she'd earn more tokens for her work, but to all intents and purposes, she might as well stay a Plot-watcher.

Hemmings scraped his spoon around his bowl with every sign of enjoyment—or at least, as close as he ever came to enjoyment. "Striving for anything is a great source of unhappiness."

"Oh, darling. You're not going to start on about trees again, are you? You know I adore your thoughtsmithing, but it's still dreadfully early," Chokey sighed. She sounded like someone who'd had this conversation before.

"Everyone here wants to become a suit," Hemmings continued, ignoring his sister. "Just to be able to say that they are suits. White, blue, grey, brown; what difference does it make? They're striving for something they've been told holds value. Horses, being whipped into a gallop by a driver they can't see."

"Lovely, darling," Chokey said, before quickly continuing. "Anyway, I'm certain none of us need to worry about the field test. My Master says as long as we've all learnt our classifications, it's easy enough to pass. Apparently, it's simply observing a few of the characters and making sure they behave themselves. Personally, I'm quite jealous of you, darling. I shouldn't think you've a thing to worry about."

"Why?"

"You've had some experience, haven't you? Both you and Althaus have been Plot-watching. I've never met a character before in my life."

"I suppose so, but—" Bea stopped. There was only one other person she knew of at the Academy who'd got their place by Plot-watching. "Althaus? You mean Carol?"

"Oh yes, darling. Do you know, when I first heard the rumour about her Plot-watching I couldn't believe it? But now I'm quite envious. Of course, Mama would never have allowed us to Plot-watch, even if I'd wanted to."

Bea gaped at Chokey. "You know Carol?"

"Didn't you know?" Dropping her voice to what she probably believed was a whisper, Chokey leaned forward. "The Althauses were once a very noble family—she's Tiff's cousin, isn't that just too strange for words? The Redaction was very hard on them, poor dears. Half the bloodline was dead-headed, and it's impossible really to maintain one's position after that, don't you think? What on Thaiana would anyone say to them over dinner? I must admit, I thought they'd gone into decline—so many of the old families simply refuse to participate at all, these days. They just sit in their townhouses and have the Raconteurs visit. But I suppose Althaus wanted a crack at the whip."

Bea whistled through her teeth. Well, she thought, that at least explains something about why Carol hates me.

Everyone blamed the fairies for the Redaction, even though it was the King and Queen who had given up their Chapter to the Teller. But they had followed the King and Queen, whom no one had seen since the Teller took control. The fairies, on the other hand, were everywhere. Blame is so much easier to dish out when there's someone there to take it.

"I never knew that," she said.

"I doubt it's something she advertises," Chokey replied.

"No. I suppose not," Bea said. But she couldn't help wondering if the walls weren't the only ones that were screaming, unheard, at the Academy.

West was drenched in sweat, her body shaking.

Barret pulled his hand back from her mouth. He looked down, suddenly realising he was holding the now empty vial of medicine in his bare hand. There'd been no time to put on his heavy gloves. He threw it away and gripped West's forearms, searching her face for some sign that she had returned to him.

"My Lady? Are you alright?"

West stared through him, focusing on something only she could see.

Barret resisted the urge to shake her, knowing his great strength could easily hurt her. This last turn had been worse than any he had seen thus far.

"My Lady? My Lady?"

West mumbled something unintelligible.

Stomach churning, his eyes darted around the room, looking for something to help her. But he only had the vials of medicine. If that didn't work, he had no idea what else to do. For all that West was a genius, she was also frail and delicate... She needed him to look after her. She relied on him. And he'd let her down.

Icy fear seeped into his blood.

What if she died?

West stirred.

"…Barret…"

"Yes, my Lady," Barret breathed, his heart beating madly. "I'm here. I'm with you."

Blinking, West groaned and tried to sit up.

"No, no, my Lady. Stay still," he implored her.

West smiled weakly. "I'll rest when I'm dead." She wiped her hands over her face and grimaced. "Pass me a towel, please."

Barret was reluctant to leave her, even for a second, but he did as she asked. West wiped the sweat off her face and neck, and then cleaned her hands. By the time she'd finished, she'd regained her composure, as if by cleaning her body she'd also cleaned her mind.

"I know what we do next, Barret. I want you to let the ETP out."

Barret frowned, confused. "Which one? Why?"

"If I told you, you wouldn't believe me," West said, a hint of something in her voice that made him think she wasn't simply trying to avoid his question. She sounded, if anything, disappointed. "And you know which one. *The* ETP."

All thoughts about West's condition vanished from Barret's mind. "You can't mean…?"

"Yes. The first one. The feisty one."

"But my Lady, it's broken—"

West met his eyes.

"Exactly."

183

XXVIII

Hidden behind the storm, the moon sat in a black sky, lonely in her singularity, surrounded by stars that could never understand her.

Far below, Bea lay in bed, listening for the soft sound of Chokey and Hemmings' snores. When she was certain they were asleep, she swung her legs out of bed and tiptoed across the room. She reached the door and carefully pulled it open, hoping to avoid the creak of the old hinges.

It was not the first time that evening that she would turn out to be unlucky.

The door groaned, complaining about having to work in the middle of the night. Bea held her breath, waiting for either Chokey or Hemmings to wake up and demand to know what she was doing out of bed.

But nothing happened, and she stepped out into the hallway. The cold hit her like a punch to the stomach.

Stupid, stupid, stupid, she scolded herself. She knew how cold the Academy was, and she'd come out in just her nightdress. She thought about going back to her room to get her cape but decided against it. Chokey and Hemmings had slept through one cacophonous creak, but she doubted she'd get away with it again.

So decided, she crept down the hallway on light feet, darting in and out of shadows and around corners whenever she heard the footsteps of a brown suit on patrol.

There is a certain type of person who would be surprised by how good Bea was at being stealthy, given her size. This was the same kind of person who'd be shocked to discover how fast a hippopotamus could lunge out of the water and bite their leg off. Or, at least, *would* be surprised, once they'd stopped screaming.

Bea was on her way to Mistasinon's attic office.

Not because she was looking for some kind of explanation for all the strange things happening at the Academy—of course not. That was the kind of behaviour that got one into trouble, and she definitely wasn't going to do that. Not again. No, she just wanted to revise for the field test, and Mistasinon's books were better than the ones in the common room.

Bea had done quite a good job of convincing herself all this was true. It's amazing what rationale the mind can produce when it really wants to.

Arms wrapped around her against the cold, she found her way to the assembly hall and paused. All the hallways looked the same. But the attic was up, wasn't it? That shouldn't be too difficult to find.

She wandered around the Academy until she found a staircase which led her to another floor and another maze of corridors. Choosing one at random, Bea followed it until she came to another flight of stairs, which she ascended. If she had it right, the assembly hall should stay to her right. Unless it was now on her left...

Mortal gods, where was she?

Luckily, the air was already so cold that when Bea's torrent of swear words turned it blue, it wasn't all that noticeable.

It occurred to her that this might, perhaps, not be one of her best ideas. She was almost impressed. The ranking for 'Bea's Worst Idea Ever' was quite a competitive field.

Wandering down yet more corridors, she eventually found another staircase. She followed it up as high as it went. Which, it turned out, was nowhere. There was an attic room, certainly, but it wasn't Mistasinon's.

She was in the wrong part of the building.

Like the landing outside Mistasinon's attic, here there were two windows. In an attempt to get her bearings, she went up to the one facing inwards, towards the Academy.

Bea cursed, looking through the window.

As best she could judge, she was in the west wing—exactly where she was forbidden to be.

Of course I am, she thought dismally. *Where else would I have ended up?*

She made as good a study of the view as she was able, given the driving snow and the way it distorted everything. Supposing she'd been wandering the corridors for about an hour, if she could get her bearings and find her way back to the east wing, she might still have time to find Mistasinon's office before anyone found out she'd left her room.

So resolved, Bea made her way back down the stairwell, trying to plot her course against the image of the Academy she had in her mind. She walked along the winding corridors, descending any staircase she found. Every now and again she would try a door handle, just in case it opened onto a room she recognised. Most were locked, but occasionally one would open. Every room she looked into was dusty and smelled of disuse.

So why keep us out of the west wing, she wondered. *There's clearly nothing here.*

Finally reaching the ground floor, she found one room that looked like it might have been recently used. It was still covered in dust and cobwebs, but there were some signs of life, absent in the other rooms, that implied that not too long ago it had had a purpose.

It was much larger than most of the rooms she'd seen in the Academy, aside from the assembly hall. This one didn't have a glass ceiling, but it did have tall shelves, now empty, running up the high walls.

Library, Bea's mind supplied.

Well, that made sense. The Academy was a huge, old building, and usually such property was owned by the wealthy, for whom a library was a sign of status. But where had all the books gone? She went up and inspected one of the shelves. It was covered in dust. She looked down at the flagstones, which were comparably clean.

Bea chewed her lip.

Now was the time to turn around. Forget about finding Mistasinon's attic. She was lost. She was somewhere she shouldn't be. There were mysterious lights and screaming walls, and what did she think she could do about it, anyway? Hadn't she learned her lesson about rushing into things, about acting on impulse instead of thinking things through?

She stepped further into the library.

In one corner was what looked like a storeroom, a heavy padlock on the door. Next to the door was a chalkboard sign. She went over to have a look.

The writing was faded, but she could still make it out:

Empty Protagonists, mk 5.
1/70th mes mxd x2, dbl boiled, 8 stns.
Sng/Sml = Stble.

Bea traced her finger over the letters. What in the five hells did any of that mean? Most of it was gobbledegook, but she could at least recognise the first line, even if it didn't make sense.

Empty Protagonists? She'd never heard of any such thing. Surely if Dafi had mentioned something like that, she would have paid attention? Besides, what good was an empty character?

The whole point was that the protagonist *did* something: Fell In Love, went from Rags To Riches, lived Happily Ever After. A hero or heroine did something that inspired others to retell the story. How could an empty thing ever do something? Who would want to listen to a story with a protagonist like that? How could that inspire belief?

There were too many questions and not enough answers.

She was just trying to work out what to do next when something caught her eye. A flash of light, like a reflection. She walked over to where she'd seen it, and, sure enough, wedged under the bottom of one the bookshelves was a glass vial. At the bottom of the vial was a white residue, caught somewhere in the drying-out process between liquid and solid. She picked it up and went to pull out the cork.

She hesitated.

While the fae were stronger than humans, they weren't immortal. Iron, for example, was poisonous, and Bea knew that it could be melted down. Could it be bottled?

She stared at the vial. Whatever was in it didn't look like iron. But there were a lot of strange things going on, and Bea was cynical enough to recognise the possibility that as bad as things currently seemed, they could always get worse. Better to be safe than sorry.

It never occurred to her that the safest thing would be to leave the vial well alone.

Putting the bottle carefully down, Bea ripped a length off the bottom of her nightdress. She wrapped it around her hand, wincing at the added exposure to the cold on her calves, especially against the tight skin around the scars on her right leg. Very slowly, every muscle in her arms singing, she eased the cork out of the vial.

She brought her nose to an inch above the neck of the container and sniffed.

Puzzled, she sniffed again.

Mineral water. She looked again at the white sludge. Chalk water, perhaps?

But why would anyone keep a sealed bottle of chalk water in an empty library? Perhaps if someone liked to sit and read after a big meal, they might suffer indigestion… Shrugging, Bea put the cork back in the vial and placed it on the shelf.

It was past time to leave. She'd snuck out of her room looking for answers. Instead, she now had even more questions. She exited the abandoned library, closing the door quietly behind her, and turned back the way she thought she had come.

It was then that Bea saw the ghost.

XXIX

The ghost was a blonde female, wearing a long white dress covered in stains and ragged at the hem. She was wandering down the hallway in a dazed fashion that suggested she wasn't aware of her surroundings.

Bea's mouth dried up, and for a moment she wasn't sure she could remember how to move. Part of her brain screamed at her to turn and run away—sneaking around the Academy was one, admittedly terrible, thing; but dealing with spirits from another plane of existence was beyond her, even she could admit that.

Frozen, Bea watched as the ghost drifted, disorientated, further down the long hallway. She'd never believed in ghosts. People died, and that was it—they were gone. Lost forever.

And yet here she was, standing at one end of a corridor with a ghost at the other. She was so far out of her depth, she might as well have been in the middle of an ocean. The ghost hadn't seen her… She should stick to her original plan, get back to her room and then think about what to do next.

The ghost thumped into a wall. Despite her alarm, Bea found herself frowning. While she was happy to admit that she was no expert on the paranormal, she was pretty certain ghosts shouldn't behave like flies trapped against windows.

If this was a ghost, then it couldn't hurt her, could it?

And if it wasn't a ghost, then it was very clearly someone who needed her help.

Bea whispered a very rude word, already regretting what she was about to do.

"Hello," she called out, her voice hollow as it bounced against the walls. "Are you alright?"

The ghost stilled.

Now that she had the creature's attention, Bea realised she had no idea what to do.

"Um," Bea said. "My name's Bea. Perhaps I can help?"

The ghost stood motionless, its back to Bea.

She realised something more than vague conversation fillers might be needed.

"I'm not going to hurt you. I'm a recruit here. I'm training to be a Fiction Management Executive." Then, because sometimes you just can't help yourself, she added, "A godmother, in fact."

The ghost turned around.

Bea's hand shot to her mouth.

The ghost's hair hung in long, lank tresses, framing her haunted expression. She was desperately thin, her eyes bloodshot, her cheeks hollow. Her mouth was hanging open, a trail of saliva running down her chin. Her hands twitched at the ends of her arms, jerky spasms that seemed unconscious.

The things that most alarmed Bea, however, were the dark red patches on the ghost's tattered white dress. Ruddy stains above her knees, at her elbows and along her arms, and smeared across her stomach.

Red blood.

"Mortal gods," Bea whispered. "You're human?"

The ghost started toward her.

Her breath coming in short gasps, Bea watched in mounting horror as the ghost lifted its arms, its fingers twisting into claws, its body twitching like a marionette under the control of a hiccupping puppeteer.

The ghost released a long, ragged sound, low and guttural:

"Gooooooooooooooooodmoooooooooooootttttthhhhhhhhhhhhuuu uuuuuurrrrrrrrrrrrrrrrrrrrrr."

Bea turned and ran.

Lungs burning, she hurtled back down the corridor, crashing into the far wall as she took the corner, running too fast to control her trajectory. She was momentarily overwhelmed by the screaming of the Academy, while behind her, the dreadful moan of the ghost echoed down the hallways as it pursued her.

"Gooooooooooooooooodmoooooooooooootttttthhhhhhhhhhhhuuu uuuuuurrrrrrrrrrrrrrrrrrrrrr."

Her mind a riot, Bea ran, no idea where she was going. Moonlight fell in bars across the floor, flashes of black and white as she sped past the windows of the Academy. The wind howled, the snow pummelling the glass.

"Goooooooooooooooodmooooooooooooottttttthhhhhhhhhhhhhuuu uuuuuuurrrrrrrrrrrrrrrrrrrr."

Bea was good on her feet. Usually. But now she was panicking, her heart beating a baião in her chest, her mind a thousand miles away from her feet, her thoughts scattered.

She took a corner too quickly and, some instinctual sense of self-preservation twisting her body so she wouldn't land against the wooden walls again, she ended up slipping on the smooth stone floors, landing heavily.

Gasping for breath, Bea twisted, scrambling to see behind her.

There was nothing there.

Getting to her feet, Bea pulled air into her exhausted lungs. A sudden pain stabbed her side—a stitch. She pressed her hand against her waist and strained her ears, listening for the wailing cries of the ghost.

Silence.

She'd lost it.

Still gasping for breath, Bea looked around her. She was standing at the top of a long corridor. Somewhere behind her was the ghost. In front of her, the new corridor stretched out, one side of it full-length windows, looking out onto the furiously swirling storm, the other a solid, wood-panelled wall. The only doorway the corridor offered was a double door set in the glass, leading out into the storm. At the end was another turning, presumably—hopefully—leading back to the east wing, and safety.

Gripping her waist, Bea started to inch down the corridor, trying to be as quiet as possible. Shying away from the wooden walls, turning her head behind her every few steps to check the ghost wasn't following, with nail-biting slowness she crept the length of the hallway.

Her heart started to slow its rhythm. Her breathing evened out. She was about halfway down the corridor now, nearing the double doors leading into the storm, stealing ever closer to the east wing.

And then she heard it:

"Goooooooooooooooodmooooooooooooottttttthhhhhhhhhhhhhuuu uuuuuuurrrrrrrrrrrrrrrrrrrr."

191

F. D. Lee

Bea spun around. The ghost was behind her, at the mouth of the corridor, its clawed hands reaching out, its empty face staring, mouth open, the ragged cry falling from its lips. The red bloodstains marring the ghost's white dress were clearly visible in the silvery moonlight.

The ghost shambled towards her.

Bea turned, ready to run—

At the eastern end of the corridor stood another figure, a huge dark shape, half-hidden in shadow.

Behind her, the ghost howled:

"Gooooooooooooooooodmoooooooooooooottttthhhhhhhhhhhhhhuuu uuuuuuurrrrrrrrrrrrrrrrrrr."

Bea was trapped in the middle of the corridor.

She did the only thing she could think of and pushed open the glass doors, incoherent babble tumbling unnoticed from her mouth.

The wind caught the door and ripped it from Bea's hand. Oblivious to this warning, she went through, into the blizzard.

The cold hit her, knocking the air from her lungs. Before she could get her bearings, the wind slammed into her, sending her flying head over heels. Bea landed in the snow, hitting it hard. As she stumbled to her feet, the wind took her again, tumbling her like she was nothing more than a balled-up piece of paper.

Teeth chattering, Bea lifted her head, trying to see through the haze of white that whirled around her.

The world had shrunk to the radius of a foot. Looking down, the snow stinging her eyes, Bea realised she couldn't see her hands, though she could still feel the biting cold of the snow against her palms.

If she had been a human, she would probably already be dead. As a fairy, she would last another five, maybe six minutes.

…whatdoIdowhatdoIdowhatdoIdo…

"Help me!" she screamed.

Her words were whipped away by the storm, stolen, unheard.

No one was going to rescue her.

Pulling herself onto her hands and knees, Bea steadied herself on her elbows, keeping as low to the ground as she could, denying the wind the chance to send her flying again. She squinted against the snow, trying to see.

Where was the Academy? Where had she come from?

Her hands and forearms were agony, the cold cutting against her exposed skin. Her nightdress was getting heavier, the weight of the snow sinking into the thin material.

Bea realised she may have been overly generous in her calculations of how long she could survive out here.

And then, somewhere in the distance, she saw a light.

It was small, a little yellow beacon, barely visible in the storm.

Legs stinging as the cold sank into her muscle, Bea started crawling towards the light. The wind battered her, tangling her long grey-green hair, scratching her skin. Tears fell from her eyes, turning to ice before they were halfway down her cheeks. Her teeth chattered uncontrollably, while her fingers were turning as white as the snow, her body pulling her blood into her centre, trying to keep her alive.

Head lowered, glancing up only to check the light was still there, Bea pushed on.

Slowly, painfully, she drew closer to the light. Her legs were heavy, stiff and frozen. Her hands and feet were numb, dead lumps of flesh, removed from her body.

Mortal gods, she was tired. She felt fuzzy, disembodied, her mind freewheeling like the snow in the wind.

Her wrist twisted, sending her sliding face first into the snow. She tried to right herself, but her arms were numb, her legs a dull throb of pain.

Heavy… Tired… Cold…

The pain drifted away, floating around her like an aura, removed but still, in a distant way, attached.

Through the fog of sleep, she realised she had fallen with her bum in the air, like a duck diving below the surface of the water. When spring came, if it ever did, they would find her like that. A frozen statue of a fairy-duck, trying to dive for pieces of bread.

Hemmings would be so jealous.

Bea smiled, too numb now to tell if the muscles in her face had moved.

Never mind.

This wasn't happening to Bea. Bea was asleep. Bea was dead. Dead again? Ahhhh, but then Dafi said she had to be told everything twice.

The snow fell on her frozen body, burying her.

Everything went black.

XXX

"How can I help you, my Lord?" Julia asked, bowing.

Returning the welcome, Mistasinon stepped into her office. Like most of the rooms in the GenAm, it was compact and decorated in a dreary style, despite her rank. She had a large window behind her desk and a heavy cabinet along the left-hand wall, which she kept locked. She also, unsurprisingly, had a Mirror, its surface covered by a heavy white cloth.

"May I?" he said, gesturing towards the empty seat in front of her desk.

"Of course."

"I wanted your advice, my Lady. If you don't mind?"

"About your incident in the baker's? They reported it, you know. It's not a problem," Julia said, offering him a friendly smile. "Things like that are easily dealt with. Mortal gods, I wish everything were so simple, truth be told. A few words in the right ear, a handful of tokens... All gone."

He should have expected this. Of course she'd know what had happened. And besides, wasn't her knowledge of him part of the reason he'd come here? With a flash of mortification, he knew it was true.

"I can control it," he said, not sure who he was trying to convince. "If I'm careful."

A flicker of something passed across her face, not quite compassion, but not revulsion either. "Hard though, to limit what you are. Is it really worth it, I wonder?"

"What I am?"

"Well, yes. Do you think you're something new, just because your appearance has changed? A blue suit doesn't cover *that* much, my Lord."

"No... No, I suppose not."

Julia sighed and leaned back in her chair. "I've never been one for introspection. I find it wastes time. Wailing at the moon, 'Who am I?', 'Why am I here?'... Mortal gods... 'Why do bad things happen to good people?'. It's boring and worse than that, it's selfish. I'm speaking to you as an equal, I hope you realise? Not as one might talk to a slave."

"Yes. Thank you."

Julia settled back in her chair. "You're very impressive, my Lord. I do wish you'd see it for yourself. You don't know your own strength, but I do."

Mistasinon shifted in his seat. "My body's getting weaker," he confessed. "I'm not as fast as I was. Not as strong."

"There are different kinds of strength, my Lord. And you broke that dwarf's arm when you fought your way out. Hardly the actions of a weak little pup. Oh, come now, don't look so alarmed. He's received the best healing, and no one knows it was you. Haven't I protected you all this time? Kept you out of the way, safe from prying eyes? And yet you still don't believe me when I say I have your best interests at heart."

Mistasinon felt sick. He had no idea he'd hurt anyone... but then, could he honestly say he was surprised? She was right. The blue suit didn't cover what he really was.

"Our situation reminds me of an illegal story I heard once," Julia continued, "About a woman who had the gift of prophecy. She could see the future, always with complete accuracy, but no one believed her. She had to watch her family murdered, and her city fall to war, knowing all the while that if only someone had listened to her, it could have all been avoided. Or so the story went."

All other thoughts evaporated from Mistasinon's mind, exorcised by the words falling from Julia's lips. His breath caught in his throat while a sudden pain across his shoulders pulled at him. Mistasinon grappled with himself, resisting the urge to breathe deeply, to rub his neck... all the little ticks he'd developed to help keep himself in his body, and which no longer seemed to be enough.

"How did... who told you that?"

Julia waved her hand dismissively. "I hear all kinds of things, my Lord. Does it matter? I only mention it because it seems apt. You don't believe me when I say I want to help you. You ran off to the

Plot Department at the first opportunity, despite all our years together. I wonder, do you mean to hurt my feelings?"

Mistasinon shook his head, pushing down his confusion. "No, no. I'm grateful for all your help."

"That means a lot. Remember, if you're lonely, you can talk to me. So then, if not to discuss your recent upset, why are you here?"

"Oh… Yes. I wanted to talk about the Mirrors. I think there's something wrong."

"Wrong? My Lord, are you sure? They've been working perfectly for months."

"I mean, it's why they're working. It doesn't make sense. They were breaking almost continuously, but now we've gone months without any new breakages. Doesn't that strike you as odd?"

"Why should it?" she asked. "We're running Plots, and then there are all the other little things we do to gather belief—the tooth fairies and so on. You should be relieved, my Lord. Apparently, we didn't need the genie, after all."

"I suppose so. I just… I wondered if you knew of anything unusual happening? Something new?"

"New? Goodness, no. The problem is the same as it ever was: the characters stopped believing, stopped taking part," Julia replied. "You're the one who's been studying the Mirrors. What else could it possibly be?"

"I don't know," Mistasinon sighed. She was right, wasn't she? He should know what the answer was… And he'd failed. Lost once again. Swallowing the mouldy taste that filled his mouth, he continued. "But… I heard a rumour that the Plot Department is experimenting with new stories."

"Shouldn't you be asking the Head of the Plot Department then, my Lord? Or does she still not trust you—after the incident with the cabbage fairy, I mean."

"No… I mean, yes, you're right—she doesn't know what to do with me. But I didn't ask her because—"

"Because she doesn't care what day it is, let alone what's happening in her own Department?"

"Yes."

Julia smiled. "You were right to come to me, and not just because of Deborah's disinterest in her own Department. The other Heads are wrong not to trust you. You have value."

He felt his cheeks colour at the swell of pleasure Julia's approval gave him. Her kindness was a buoy in the choppy waters of his confusion, something he could tether himself to if he'd let himself.

"Thank you. But there must be a reason the Mirrors are still working?"

"I'm afraid I don't know how to answer your question," Julia said. "Perhaps if you could tell me something more. What do you think is happening? What have you heard?"

Mistasinon opened his mouth to reply when there was a knock at the door.

"What?" Julia shouted. Then, in a more measured tone, "Come."

The door creaked open. A brown suit cautiously entered the room, the expression on his face indicating he'd rather be anywhere than where he currently was.

"Uh. Excuse me, my Lady."

"What is it?"

"Er," he looked at Mistasinon. "I was told you had a Plotter here... Um... Miztas... Meesta... Er...." His voice died away.

Mistasinon took pity on him. "That's me. How can I help?"

"Uh. There's been an accident, sir. You're needed."

"Isn't that something the brown suits deal with?" Julia asked.

"Er... I was told to come and find him, my Lady. Wherever he was. Er. It's something to do with the Academy."

Mistasinon paled. "The Academy?"

"Yes, sir. There's been an accident. The recruit you recommended—"

He was on his feet before the brown suit finished speaking, the chair clattering to the ground behind him.

"Take me," he instructed.

The brown suit glanced at Julia. She nodded her head, and both he and Mistasinon left her office.

Julia drummed her fingers on her desk while behind her eyes, her brain whirled.

It had often struck her as strange how limited other people were, spending all their time and energy worrying about petty things, refusing to see the bigger picture. And if something went wrong, how quickly they went to pieces. No one had any resilience. If they would only think things through clearly and logically, the city wouldn't be in its current mess.

She really didn't understand how their minds worked.

But she was learning. Always learning.

In the characters' world, the philosophy of elementis was gaining in popularity, much to the detriment of the Plots. Men and women from the First and Third Kingdoms spent happy days digging up bones, examining the earth and the stars, imagining impossible numbers. And some of these explorations into the sweaty jungles of knowledge involved the dissection of various small and harmless animals. Always, of course, on the understanding that such behaviour was a necessary evil.

Julia, however, would have happily taken a scalpel to a mouse just to hear the squeak.

So what did she know?

Mistasinon was vulnerable, guilty, and frightened of himself. That was good. Fear was always a fine quality, in other people. She knew how to use fear. Julia had a plan for Mistasinon, but she'd prefer it if he came to her of his own accord.

Before he changed, Mistasinon had been loyal to a fault. Following orders, getting things done, never answering back. Mortal gods, he'd been better than the dead-heads. And so, for the last year she'd been working on him, re-enforcing his training, making sure his new-found sense of self didn't ruin what he truly was. A treat, then the stick, and then another treat. It was almost too easy. He was half mad now, frantic for a strong hand and a guiding voice, and she was ready to provide both.

But still… Mistasinon was going to the Academy, and there was no way she could reasonably stop him. Perhaps it had been a mistake not to Redact the cabbage fairy? No, it would have turned him against her. By keeping the fairy around, she'd won his trust. Nevertheless, she shouldn't underestimate him, or the apparent sway the fairy had over him.

It appeared there was a contender for the role of his new master.

Julia laced her fingers together. Mistakes happen when people don't think. When they let their emotions get in the way of the facts. Happily, she herself didn't suffer from that particular affliction. She'd put work into Mistasinon, but that didn't mean she'd won him. She'd better make sure she had all her pieces in place.

She stood and picked up the chair Mistasinon had knocked over, carefully setting it in front of her desk. Then she walked to her office door, opened it, and called for her dead-head.

The goblin arrived.

"my lady"

"I want to know what happens at the Academy. Don't go yourself, I don't want Barret knowing I'm interested. Use a Mirror, speak to one of our informers there. I want to know how Mistasinon behaves around his cabbage fairy, what he does with her. No interference, just observation."

She paused, thinking through all the possibilities. The fairy could still prove useful, or she might have exhausted her purpose. Too early to tell. More immediately, Mistasinon was interested in the Mirrors, and that meant her work was getting noticed. Others would follow.

"And bring me anything that ties us to West. I suspect things at the Academy are coming to their end. If so, I want to make sure we're distanced."

"yes my lady"

"Oh, and do we still have eyes on those two elves? The ones Barret employed?"

"yes my lady"

"Good. They're Anti-Narrativists, make sure they're Redacted in the morning. Have it done publicly. You may leave."

The goblin closed the door softly behind her.

Julia walked over to the large cupboard in the corner of her office and, lifting a key from a chain around her neck, unlocked it. In front of her were rows of small glass bottles, each one filled with a dirty white liquid.

She smiled to herself, grateful that the city had someone like her looking after it.

XXXI

Someone was holding Bea's hand, a warm, gentle touch, skin against her skin, stroking her thumb, brushing against her knuckles.

She'd been dreaming. There had been music, a heavy drumbeat that pulsed through her, louder than any sound she'd ever heard. She could remember following the sound of the drums, searching for something... A tree.

She'd found a tree with nine branches, and at the end of each branch was a sphere, suspended in the air, one glowing red, another yellow, another blue... And right at the top, a black sphere with lightning crackling across its surface. She had stood at the bottom of the tree and looked up, the drumbeat growing louder and louder, filling her until she had...

Woken up, and felt someone holding her hand.

Bea groaned.

The touch left her hand.

"...are you there? Can you hear me? Bea? Bea? Wake up, Bea, it's time to wake up, Bea."

"Dun wan'ta."

Someone laughed. "Bloody minded as ever. Can you open your eyes?"

Bea supposed that she could, though she didn't see why she had to. It was so nice where she was. Warm and hazy, with nothing to worry about.

"Wossinit f'me if I do?"

Another trill of laughter. "How about a cup of sweet tea?"

"Wine. I was drinking wine with Luca."

"I don't think wine is a good idea."

Bea smiled lazily. "Spoilsport."

"Can you open your eyes?" the voice asked again. "The healer wants to check them."

Healer? Why did she need a healer? She was feeling brilliant, all warm and drowsy and comfortable.

Bea opened her eyes reluctantly, blinking against the fuzzy world of real life. Shapes and colours merged, perspectives clicked into place, and she saw Mistasinon gazing down at her, his thick eyebrows knotted in a frown.

"Hello, Mr Plotter," Bea said, her tongue heavy in her mouth. She smiled at him, reaching up to touch his face. "You do look odd, do you know that?" She giggled. "You've got hair on you, all over your chest. I *saw* it. You're all wrong. All wrong."

Mistasinon smiled. "Yes. Yes, I know. How are you?"

"Sleepy."

"How else do you feel?"

"Dunno. Hot."

The frown returned to his face, and he pulled away, disappearing from view. A muttered conversation, hushed tones, worried. She couldn't make it out, but it seemed silly to be worried. Everything was lovely and warm. Nice to be warm. She'd been cold for so long. So cold her bones hurt. Snow. She'd been in the snow, hadn't she?

A moment later, a tompte buzzed in front of her. She pressed her little hand against Bea's skin and darted in front of her eyes. Bea felt the tompte's touch against her eyelids, pushing them open, inspecting her pupils. And then she pinched Bea's cheeks until she opened her mouth, and popped a pill in.

"Swallow."

Bea couldn't think of any reason not to, so she did as she was told.

The tompte flew off, her tiny wings humming. Bea turned her head and saw her buzzing in front of Mistasinon's face, talking in whispers to him. Mistasinon stood with his arms folded, his long body rigid as he listened. He whispered something back to the tompte, who shrugged. Mistasinon looked over at Bea, saw her watching him, and quickly looked back at the tompte. The conversation between them continued for a few more hushed turns, and then the tompte flitted away.

Mistasinon came back to Bea, taking a seat next to her. She wondered vaguely where she was, but then the thought drifted back into the clouds. She was aware, in a dreamy sort of way, that she wasn't thinking clearly, but she didn't mind. It was nice, not to think.

"She says you're still ill," Mistasinon said. "I don't really understand it. You got too cold, and now you're too hot."

"Too this, too that. Buttercup Snowblossom. I remember. I got lost in the snow."

"Yes, you did."

In the fuzzy cotton wool of her mind, something scratched. White snow. Red blood. White snow, red blood. Whitesnow, redblood. Whitesnowredblood... Mortal gods, the girl. The human girl. The ghost.

Frantically, Bea reached out for Mistasinon, grabbing his hand, holding it tight.

"You found me? Did you see it?"

"I didn't find you," he said, shaking his head. "It was one of the brown suits, a troll. You were lucky. If you hadn't been seen.... Mortal gods, Bea, what were you doing?"

"It was the ghost, the ghost chased me. It wanted a godmother."

"Bea, you're not making any sense."

What did he mean, she wasn't making sense? What was there to misunderstand? It was perfectly simple. Bea dropped his hand, rubbed her eyes, trying to untangle the wooliness in her head.

"The ghost, but it isn't a ghost. It's a person... She's hurt. She's hurt, don't you understand? I have to help her... I have to save them..."

"Save who?"

"The girl, aren't you listening? They've done something to her. She wasn't right. I have to help her. Stop it, stop it all."

She could hear her voice, the frantic, near hysterical edge to it, but it sounded very far away. Everything was moving too slowly. Like she was submerged in the sloppy porridge the Academy served for breakfast.

"What was... what was in the medicine?" she asked, trying to make sense of the sluggish rhythm of the world. "Are you Redacting me?"

"No, of course not. It's to make you sleep, that's all. You need to rest."

"It's… I can't…" A memory fluttered for a moment across the surface of her mind. "Empty. Empty protagonists."

"I don't understand, I'm sorry."

A wave of tiredness hit her. Her head dropped, bounced back up. Blinking, she tried to remember what she'd been saying. Something was wrong…

Mistasinon was here. Why was he here?

"Have I failed? Are you sending me back?"

"No, you had an accident."

"Did I? Ah. I died, I remember now. And you told me I've got… got what it takes. You took me out f'dinner. D'you remember?"

"Yes, of course."

"You've got no friends."

"I… no. Not anymore."

"I was your friend. But you… You lied to me."

"…yes."

"Yes," Bea repeated. "I liked you."

"Really?"

"I had a dream… abou' a tree…"

A pause, and then Mistasinon said, "You need to sleep."

"…t'sleep. Did you save me?"

"No. It was a troll, remember? I didn't save you."

"Yes, you did… From the witchlein. They hurt my leg. The King… Mortal gods… All the blood…"

"Shhh. Go to sleep."

"I don' like sleepin'… The dreams… the drums…"

"You're safe. Nothing's going to happen."

"There was red blood, ev'rywhere…"

"Everything's alright now. Shhh."

"Shhh," Bea whispered. "Shhhh. I saw it. I saw the girl. I haf'ta help—"

And then she fell asleep, the medicine the tompte had given her finally taking full effect.

Mistasinon sat for a moment, replaying Bea's jumbled words, trying to make sense of them. But however he rearranged them, he couldn't get a clear idea of what she meant. Of course, she was sick. People said strange things when they were sick, didn't they?

He should probably go. He'd made sure she was alright, that was enough. He should keep trying to find out about the Mirrors, and the dead character. He had to speak to Julia again. He had to keep his promise.

But somehow he found himself settling back in his chair, stretching his long legs out in front of him.

After a while, he fell asleep too.

Barret knocked on West's door, as gently as his large hands would allow him.

"My Lady?" he asked when there was no reply.

He put his hand on the doorknob and felt it turn. Briefly, he wondered what he should do. He knew it wasn't right to enter a superior's office without permission... but he also knew what West was like, especially if she was having one of her funny turns.

He pushed the door open.

The office was empty.

He closed the door and made his way to West's *other* office. The one where she did her real work.

Mortal gods damn that fairy—who in the five hells did she think she was, anyway? Bringing that blue suit here, disrupting West's work, getting in the way of everything they were trying to achieve.

As Barret walked, he imagined all the things he'd like to do that bloody fairy, if he were allowed to. He knew the route off by heart, so he had plenty of time to really *stretch* his imagination.

He reached the west wing, entered the correct room and pressed the valve that opened the door. He wiped a cobweb from his face as he made his way along the tunnel to West's workshop. Bloody spiders. He'd have to come down here with the feather duster again.

That was another thing, wasn't it? Not only had the GenAm stuck them with some mentally deficient fairy, but they'd also forced them to work alongside all the recruits and Masters, pushing West out of her own home.

Oh sure, he knew the rationale: less conspicuous, attached to but still far away from the GenAm; autonomy, far removed from the

F. D. Lee

shallow, self-serving bureaucracy of the four Departments. Plus, crucially, ready participants to test the ETPs on.

Eventually, Barret appeared out the other end of the tunnel. He walked through the holding room, ignoring the ETPs and their strange snatches of song, and into the laboratory. On the floor was a trapdoor, its ring made of iron. For West, the iron wasn't a problem, but Barret didn't fancy getting a burn. He put his thick gloves on, pulled the trap door open, and descended the stairs into the basement, where West had set up her workshop.

She was sitting at her desk, staring at the wall, sipping from a bottle of her medicine.

"My Lady?"

"Ah, Barret. I was just thinking about you."

"My Lady—"

"You will go left, won't you?"

Barret's great forehead creased, and then remembered. "Yes, of course. I promise."

West's mouth twisted into what might, in dull light, have been mistaken for a smile. "You'll forgive me if I don't put much faith in that. Anyway, what can I do for you?"

"Nothing, my Lady. I just wanted to check on you."

"Kind of you. How is our patient?"

Barret squashed the ire that rose in him, though he couldn't stop the way his dark eyes narrowed. "She's recovering, my Lady."

"And the Plotter who came to attend to her? He remains?"

"Yes."

"Good. Good." West grinned. "Finally, everything is happening as I want it to. He's here, Barret! He's here!"

A sharp taste in his mouth, like metal. Barret swallowed. "And our work, my Lady?"

West looked up at him, momentarily confused. "Our work? Oh, the ETPs. Yes, yes, they're ready. Why? Is it time?"

"That's for you to decide, my Lady. The Redactionist gave you full jurisdiction."

"She's a clever one, Barret. Maps it out in her head, all the possible routes—and then she sends others walking. Clever, clever, clever. Of course, that didn't stop her ignoring me when I warned her, but never mind. This is what happens next. Send some of the

206

more recent ETPs out. The recruits use them for their field test. Thank the Gods you reminded me, Barret. Imagine, having done so much to get this far, and then to miss a step. What would I do without you?"

"I'm happy to help you. I'll always be happy to help you," Barret replied. He could hear the sincerity in his voice, and he hoped that she would notice it too. He wanted nothing more than to make West happy.

"I know I can be difficult sometimes," West said. "Hard to follow. I appreciate you, Barret. We're not just colleagues, are we? We're friends."

"Friends?" Barret repeated. He swallowed. "Yes. Yes, friends."

"I know you think I jeopardised our work here, releasing the original ETP, causing that girl, the fairy, to hurt herself." West reached forward and grasped him, holding onto him as if she were dying and he was life itself. "But everything is happening as it does. And now he's here. All I have to do is make him see, make him ready. He's going to rescue me, Barret, I... I'm certain he will. Isn't that wonderful?"

Her hands were warm, the heat from her skin reaching through the thin material of his brown suit. It almost matched the burning fire inside him.

She might not see it, not yet, but it was him, Barret, who was her rock, her island in a stormy sea, her refuge against a cruel world that could never understand her. If West needed rescuing, he would be the one to do it. Him, and no one else.

"I know you don't understand," West continued in her deep, husky voice. "But if you believe nothing else, please believe me when I say that I know what I'm doing. Besides, there's nothing you can say that will change what's going to happen."

West sighed, a sadness in her eyes that made Barret's heart hurt.

"That's a lesson I've learned the hard way," she said.

XXXII

Bea was pretty sure a rat had died in her head. There was no way normal biology could account for the way she currently felt.

Groaning, she sat up.

Now… this was odd.

She wasn't in her room. She was lying on a sofa, submerged under a blanket. She looked to her immediate right. An armchair sat as close as possible to her makeshift bed, a quilt piled up on it.

Bea rubbed her temples. Adding to the giddy sickness she already felt, vague memories spun behind her eyes. They were not particularly comfortable or welcome. She sat up slowly and looked around. She was in Mistasinon's attic. The desk was messy with folders, books and half-finished meals. A blue coat was hanging over the back of one of the chairs flanking it.

Uh-oh.

The door opened, and Mistasinon walked in, a book under his arm, his brown satchel hanging from his shoulder. He was wearing a pale yellow shirt, the sleeves rolled up to his elbows, a dark blue waistcoat and matching trousers. All were creased, and it occurred to Bea, seeing him so dishevelled, how neat and tidy he usually kept himself. She also noticed he looked thin, the fitted waistcoat accentuating his narrow torso. His brown eyes were anxious, his warm skin chilled by the oppressive cold of the Academy.

"You're awake," he said, breaking the silence.

"I am, yes. Sitting up, too. I mean, if we're playing 'I spy'."

A smile twitched at his lips. "How are you feeling?"

"Rotten. What happened? Why are you here?"

Mistasinon paused for a moment, a myriad of expressions darting across his face, each quickly extinguished by the next. He walked over to one of the chairs by his desk, turned it around to face Bea, took his satchel off, placed the book on his desk and, finally, sat down.

"You were very unwell," he said. "You've been in and out of consciousness for about a week. What do you remember?"

Bea stared at him. "A week?"

He nodded. "A troll found you outside, in the storm. He brought you in, and they contacted me—as your mentor. You didn't have any family entered on your forms. You didn't actually have any forms at all," he added, a shade reproachfully. "I filled them in for you. I put your friends, the elf and the house fairy, down as family members. You can change it if you want."

"Oh. Thank you. I guess. A week?"

"Seven days," he confirmed.

"And you've been here the entire time?"

"It's fine. I had work to do. The Mirrors."

Bea looked away. "Any luck deciding who's next on the GenAm's 'Mirror-fixing' hit list?"

"Not yet, no." He rubbed his neck. "That was a joke."

"I don't find murder very funny."

"No. Sorry."

Bea supposed he'd at least stopped trying to explain away what had happened to the genies. Her head was pounding. She reached up and rubbed her temples.

Mistasinon grabbed his bag and rummaged around in it. "I've got something here if it hurts."

"I'll be alright."

He put his satchel down and began fiddling with the buckle, his slender fingers working the clasp, his eyes fixed on the task. Bea watched the muscles in his forearm move, the tension between them made manifest in the rigidity of his body as he distracted himself with his bag.

"I should get back to class," Bea said.

Mistasinon looked up, his large brown eyes searching her face as if he were trying to find the words he was looking for, hidden in her expression. When he answered her, he sounded wary.

"That might be a problem. You were caught outside your room in the middle of the night. Not only that, but in an area of the house you had no right being anywhere near. The woman in charge, West, isn't very tolerant of rule-breakers, from what I can gather."

Bea shook her head. There was something very wrong here, and she needed to find out what it was. "I can't be expelled. I have to become a godmother."

Mistasinon didn't reply.

"Right then," Bea said. Kicking off the heavy blankets, she tried to stand up. It was a short-lived and highly unsuccessful endeavour. Her head spun, and she wobbled.

Mistasinon jumped up from his chair and moved across the room, managing to catch her before she fell over.

Time stretched, seconds strained far beyond their tolerance, while Bea and Mistasinon stood, their bodies brushing, his hands on her arms, hers on his, both caught by surprise. Neither spoke, each unsure what to make of what was happening.

And then Mistasinon shifted his stance, separating them. He helped her onto the sofa and stepped back, rubbing his neck anxiously.

"You're fast. That must be a useful one to have. Mine's not much help most of the time," Bea said in what she knew was a weak attempt to brush over whatever it was that had just happened. She pulled her blanket up to her shoulders.

Mistasinon looked confused. "I'm sorry?"

"Speed. Your tribal talents—speed and strength, right?"

"Oh."

"Mind you, you were slower just now. I nearly fell. It's probably the cold, though," Bea rattled on, wishing desperately she'd never started. Mortal gods, she'd take being in Dafi's class to being here, now, with Mistasinon. Hells, she'd even give the 'ghost' another go. "It gets into your bones, doesn't it? The cold. Everyone here's always complaining about it."

Turning away, Mistasinon walked over to the sink in the corner of the room and poured himself a glass of water. "Do you want one? The water's fresh. There's a butt on the roof."

Bea rather suspected there was a 'but' in the room as well, floating unspoken between them.

"Yes, please," she said.

He poured a glass for her and walked back to the sofa. He hesitated. And then he put the glass on the floor, where she could easily reach it. Bea picked it up and took a sip. The water was cold and clean and tasted amazing. She downed the whole thing.

"Could I have another?"

"Of course." He refreshed her glass, again putting it on the floor.

Bea sipped it this time, not so much because she didn't want to guzzle it, but because she couldn't bear the awkward way he kept not giving it to her.

"So," she said, moving back onto what she thought was safer ground, "How do I make sure I can keep my place here?"

"Is that really a good idea?" he replied, his forehead knitted in a frown.

"What? Yes, of course it is. I have to become a godmother. It's the only way I'll ever be able to change anything."

"You want to change the GenAm?"

"Somebody should."

Once again, he fell silent.

"So?" Bea prompted. "There must be something I can do."

"Pardon? Oh, sorry. Um. Well, I suppose we'll have to talk to West, see if we can convince her to let you stay."

"We?"

Mistasinon nodded. "I owe you, I think. I haven't been a very good mentor, I mean."

Bea was about to say something, though she had no idea what it would be, when he spoke again.

"Bea, you, ah, you mentioned something before… About a ghost, do you remember? I've been asking around. A lot of the recruits here seem to think there's a ghost. They say they hear things at night."

"The other recruits have never even been out of Ænathlin before. They don't know anything about anything."

Mistasinon moved, sitting on the chair next to her, pulling it up close. "No, but you do," he said, his hand squeezing the arm of the sofa, fingers brushing against the blanket that covered her. "You're not caught up in it all the way everyone else is. You think about things. You see what's really there—that's why I chose you to get the genie."

His words hit her like a hundredweight. And something inside her, something she didn't even realise she'd spent months trying to keep intact, shattered into a thousand pieces.

"Bullshit! Bullshit, horseshit, dog shit! All the shitty shit shit!" Bea shouted, pulling back from him. "You must think I'm so bloody stupid."

"No, of course I don't—"

"I trusted you, and people got hurt—why would I make that mistake again? You think that I'd *help* you? That you can turn up here and play doctor and suddenly everything will be forgiven? What in the five hells is wrong with you?"

"Nothing's wrong with me," he replied, drawing away, his back rigid. "I'm loyal. The Teller Cares About Us."

"Cares about us? Mortal gods... Is that what you really think? The Teller *controls* us, he doesn't care about anything, except maybe himself."

"And you're so different?" Mistasinon retorted, on his feet suddenly, grabbing his bag and jacket. "Everyone thinks about themselves, everyone. At least the Teller tried, *tries*, to make it better. You just want to prove a point—to show everyone how brilliant you are. I don't know why I thought you were any different."

"Excuse me? And where in the five hells are you going?" Bea demanded as he made his way to the door.

"Does it matter?" he answered, his arms wrapped tightly around his satchel. "You obviously don't want me here."

"I never asked you to come, did I? In fact, I never asked you to drag me into any of this!"

"Ah, yes, right. I see. It's all my fault, is it? My fault that you changed your Plots and that you ran around after that genie? That you did everything you could to sabotage the story I gave you? And I suppose it was me who wrote all those letters to the GenAm, begging for a place at the Academy?"

Bea gripped her blanket, scrunching it up in her fists, deforming it. "No. You're just the one who works for a mass murderer."

For a long moment, they stared at each other. And then Bea threw herself down on the sofa, pulling the blanket over her head.

The sound of the door slamming reverberated around the attic.

She lay in the darkness, the blanket pressing against her face, the wool scratching her skin; revenge, perhaps, for her cruel treatment of it moments before.

But everything she'd said was true, wasn't it? She was right to be angry with him. *Yes,* she told herself. *Push it away, move on. Leave it behind, let it go. It's only—*

The door banged open.

Bea scrambled out from under the covers.

"Why do you hate me and not the genie?" Mistasinon demanded from the doorway.

"What makes you think I don't hate Seven?"

"So you don't deny hating me?"

"Which question do you want me to answer? Are we playing the game of threes?"

He paused and then shook his head. Closing the door behind him, he stepped into the room, pulled up one of the chairs in front of the desk and sat down.

"No. I don't like those games, I never have. I just want to know what makes me bad. I have to know. Why is he the hero and I'm the villain?"

"It's not about heroes and villains, don't you understand that? Heroes are just the ones who win, that's all. It's about right and wrong. The GenAm, who you work for, is evil, and you've *known* all along what it's capable of. You went along with it."

"But what the GenAm did… it was for the city. It was to keep the Mirrors working and everyone safe."

"And that justifies it?" Bea asked. "A whole tribe, murdered? And what about the rest? The Beast and the Redaction Department, ready to punish anyone who doesn't agree? And the stories—they control everything. No one can think straight anymore. I mean, listen to you. Heroes? Seriously?"

"But I never wanted to hurt the genie," Mistasinon insisted, his hands on his neck. "I wanted to talk to him, to ask him to help us. I thought his lamp might be the key."

"And what if Seven had gone with you, but he couldn't help with the Mirrors, he didn't know anything more than you do about how they work—what would you have done then? Would you have let him go?"

A flash of anger shot across Mistasinon's face and then it was gone, replaced with something much worse: acceptance.

He shook his head, no.

"That's what I thought," Bea said, all her anger exhausted. Instead, for some reason, she only felt incredibly sad.

Mistasinon mumbled something.

"Pardon?" Bea said.

"I said, I don't understand," he repeated. "I... it's confusing. Everything pulling in different directions. It's not supposed to be so difficult, surely? Heroes do the right thing, and it's the right thing because they do it. We've always tried to do the right thing, and we're the monster..."

Bea stilled, watching him.

Somehow, he'd managed to curl his long body up without actually moving. He just seemed... smaller. Like he was trying to take up as little room as possible without doing anything as crass as drawing attention to himself.

"Look, Seven's not a hero," she finally said. "He ran away. He left me and everyone else to die. If I ever do see him again, I promise you I'll have something to say about that. But you're right. I don't hate him. He saw things differently, and he forced me to look at things differently, too. To be honest, I don't think he meant to, but by the end, we understood each other. He believed in me. That I could see what was wrong, too."

"I believed in you," Mistasinon said, meeting her eyes.

"You believed I'd do what you wanted me to do. That's not the same thing."

He dropped his gaze. "No. I suppose it isn't."

"But... I lied to you, as well," Bea found herself saying. "I didn't tell you about Seven when I first met him. I didn't tell you even though I knew you could get into trouble. I thought I could fix it all on my own. So I lied to you. And perhaps if I'd been more honest at the beginning, I could have stopped all those people getting hurt."

She ran her hands through her hair, closing her eyes. Colours danced across her eyelids, making her feel dizzy. She opened her eyes, blinking away the wooziness.

"You want me to tell you what I think makes a hero or a villain?" she continued. "The truth is, I don't know. You lied to me. You manipulated me. And the GenAm murdered all those genies—that will never be right. But you also said you didn't want to do that. And I suppose if you had, you wouldn't have got me involved in the first place, even if the way you did was utterly deceitful. You obviously haven't told anyone how I really feel about the GenAm, or I wouldn't be here, now. And you told me the truth, in the end. I'm grateful for that."

She paused. Then added, "But I'm not giving you any points for getting me into the Academy. I don't think I'm cut out for rote learning."

"Ah. No. I can see you'd have trouble being told what to think," he said, a smile lifting the corners of his mouth.

It was one of his rainy-day, melancholy smiles, the kind that made Bea feel the same way she had when she'd realised she could think about her abandoned family and her missing father without needing to cry.

She couldn't help thinking how much easier it would be if she just *knew* what she was supposed to do, to think. She supposed there had to be people out there who were never bothered by second thoughts, who never worried if they were doing the right thing, or how other people felt, or what might happen next. People who never wondered what it was that made them, them; who always knew they were right.

Lucky bastards.

"So what you're saying is that we're both liars?" Mistasinon asked. "That nothing makes any sense at all?"

"Seems so. Or at least, you have to try to make sense of it for yourself, I suppose."

Mistasinon leaned back in his chair, a thoughtful expression on his face. He didn't speak for a long time, and when he did, he changed the subject.

"There's someone who wants to see you if you feel well enough? A dwarf called, um, Dea'dora Kilumal Ogrechoker."

"Oh, that's Chokey," Bea said. "Yes, I'd like to see her."

F. D. Lee

"That's a relief. She's been quite insistent, I mean. She kept on mentioning her mother and what would happen to me if I tried to keep her away."

"Mortal gods, you don't want to pick that fight, believe me. Tell me, how does Chokey compare to the FMEs at the GenAm?"

He smiled nervously and then, when he saw Bea was grinning, he laughed. "I'm absolutely certain she'll fit in perfectly, once she graduates."

"You must be delighted to know the Academy is maintaining a high quality of alumni?"

"Absolutely. It's a great comfort to me. I've always admired the GenAm's ability to employ such, uh, affirmative people."

"Self-assured."

"Exactly. Firm of belief and steady of hand."

"'Bloody awful', I think you once called them?"

"Ah, yes. And I stand by it."

They grinned at each other.

And for just a moment they were friends again, or almost-friends—or whatever it was they'd been before she'd found out he'd been lying to her, and then before he'd finally told her the truth about the Mirrors and the genies and the GenAm.

And then the moment passed.

"Well then," Mistasinon said. "I'll just go and get her."

As the door closed behind him, Bea wondered if he'd felt it too. She thought about what he'd said to her about hating him. She was angry with him, with good cause, and she still wasn't sure if she trusted him, but was he right to say she hated him?

She was saved from having to answer her own question by Chokey bursting through the door, a bottle of wine in her hand and a thick ream of paper under her arm. Hemmings shuffled in behind her.

"Darling!" Chokey boomed, dumping the pile of paper on the floor and plonking herself on the sofa, next to Bea. "You look positively ghastly! Mortal gods, I don't know why they stuck you all the way up here in the attic like some mad old relative everyone would rather forget exists. What would have happened if there'd been a fire, that's what I'd like to know! Anyway, darling, it's been positively dire this past week, without you."

Bea wiggled, making room for her. Hemmings was instructed to bring two more glasses over and then took the armchair next to them. Chokey poured the wine.

"I'm not sure I should be drinking," Bea said, but her heart wasn't in it.

"Nonsense. If the storm didn't kill you, this won't," Chokey said cheerfully, pouring out three large measures. "Now then, how are you feeling? Did you know we all thought you were going to die? It was terribly exciting."

Bea sipped her wine, trying not to smile. "It takes more than a bit of snow to kill me off."

"Quite right! So, do you want to hear the gossip? They had us all locked in our rooms for two days—can you imagine? Thank the mortal gods we've got our own room, that's all I can say about that. And Althaus has been rubbishing you terribly. But Hemmings put her right, didn't you, darling?" she added, turning to her brother.

Hemmings tucked his dark hair behind his ear. "She said you did it deliberately, to get out of doing the field test. I explained to her that every person confines their perception to their own limits of understanding. I don't think she took it on board, though," he added sadly. "She just said she'd limit my perception if I kept on at her."

"Anyway," Chokey continued, "She soon shut up once we got out there. I don't know why, I'd have thought she'd have been pleased it was so easy, the characters were very well behaved, but she seemed awfully put out by it all."

Bea's heart sank. "You've done the field test?"

Chokey and Hemmings looked at each other. "Three days ago, I'm afraid," Chokey said. "Hemmings has already been placed to train as a villain because of his scars. They haven't told me yet what I shall be. But, darling, we simply won't have you being sent down, will we, Hemmings? I'm sure neither of us could imagine not having our little cabbage fairy around, isn't that right?"

"There must be something you can do?" Hemmings asked.

Bea shook her head. "Mistasinon might be able to stop me being expelled, but there's no way I can graduate as a godmother if I haven't passed the field test. They'll put me in the moral stream."

Chokey sloshed another measure of wine into Bea's already very full glass. "I've brought you all the homework from Dafi's class, so you can catch up on everything you've missed."

But even Chokey could tell this wasn't what Bea wanted to hear.

XXXIII

The day of Bea's meeting with West arrived.

She had woken up in her own bed, back in her room with Hemmings and Chokey. Mistasinon had returned to Ænathlin, but he'd promised her he'd come back and, against her better judgement, she believed him.

Hemmings and Chokey had left earlier for classes. Bea was still excluded, supposedly because of her health. Whether that would still be true by the end of the day remained to be seen.

She got washed, taking as long as possible in the bath, enjoying the feeling of the warm water and the luxury of privacy. When she was dry and dressed, she got on with packing her clothes and other belongings. If she were expelled, she didn't want to have to waste time packing. She wanted to be able to leave there and then.

Running away again, she mused to herself.

Once she'd finished, she rummaged under her pillow, looking for her little bag of treasures. Carefully, she laid her possessions out on the bed. There was an old letter, folded over many times, its paper yellowing and edges worn; a small vial of perfume, some seeds, and finally the sword point necklace Melly had given her. She opened the bottle of perfume and inhaled the scent. The smell brought back memories of her mother, and a time when she'd been happy.

Shaking herself out of the sudden funk she'd indulged in, she started putting everything back in the little leather bag, ready to go into her large bag. And then, for some reason, she undid the whole thing and took out the necklace. It lay across her palm, heavy and cool.

Did I really kill an ogre with this? It seemed too small, insignificant, to ever do anything so impossible.

She ran the tip of her finger across the point. It was blunt, of course. Melly wouldn't have given her something that she could accidentally hurt herself with. But still… It was a solid piece of metal, with a pointed end. With enough force, it could probably still do some damage.

She glanced up at the wooden walls and thought about the bloodied girl she'd found, wandering the halls. The 'ghost'. And then, telling herself she was being ridiculous and paranoid, Bea put the necklace on.

She spent the rest of the morning sitting in her room, looking out of her window at the snow. There was no sign of the light.

A knock at the door brought her back from her thoughts. Mistasinon stood in the hallway, his dark brown hair brushed back from his narrow face. There were dark shadows under his eyes, and beneath his tanned skin, he had a greenish tinge. It had only been a week since she'd last seen him, and yet he looked like he'd aged a dozen years.

"Are you alright?" Bea asked. "You look… tired," she finished lamely, not feeling it was appropriate to say what she really thought, which was that he looked like death warmed up.

He seemed surprised by the question. "Oh. Yes. I mean, no. I'm fine, I mean. I've just been busy. Shall we go?"

"Yes. Right. Lead on."

Bea turned to take one last look at her room and then followed Mistasinon into the hallway.

"Sssurprisse!" Luca hissed, grinning through his sharp teeth.

"Luca!" Bea cried. She sat on the stone floor, but even so, they weren't face to face. The witchlein really were tiny. "What are you doing here?"

"Sssomeone hasss to take you to Wessst, ssso I volunteered."

"Insisted, from what I heard," Mistasinon corrected, a smile playing at his lips.

The witchlein blushed, his yellow scales turning deep orange. It was one of the most amazing things Bea had ever seen.

"Thank you," she said, hugging him. "It means the worlds to me, truly."

Luca led Bea and Mistasinon through the corridors of the east wing of the Academy, chatting away to Bea about nothing. All too soon, they arrived outside West's office. There were two seats against the wall, which Luca ushered them into.

"I can't ssstay," he said apologetically. "I wasss lucky to be allowed off to essscort you."

"I understand," Bea said.

"Good luck," Luca said, glancing over his shoulder at her as he walked away.

"He seems nice," Mistasinon said, once they were alone.

"He is."

They sat in silence.

"Are you feeling better?"

"Yes, much."

The silence lengthened.

"I've been reading about your progress," he said. "To prepare for the meeting."

"Oh?"

"You seem to have had quite an impact on one of the Masters here. Dafi?"

"Aha. Yes. I'm not his favourite pupil."

"I would like to have seen your presentation on the secondary characters. His report said that you stood up in front of the class and argued that everyone should get to be the protagonist in their own story?"

"That I did," Bea smiled. "I got sent to my room for two days for that one."

The silence returned, stretching over them and down the length of the hallway.

"Bea?"

"Yes?"

"About the other day—"

"Darling!"

They both jumped as Chokey bounded down the hallway and skidded to a stop in front of them.

Bea stood up and hugged her. Over the top of her head, she saw Hemmings standing shyly a few feet away. Bea opened her arms and, after a second's thought, the elf bundled into the hug as well.

"We simply couldn't let you go into this ghastly meeting without coming to wish you luck."

Bea disentangled herself. "I'm sure it'll be fine," she said. *They all think I'm going to be expelled.*

Chokey turned to Mistasinon. "You will look after her, won't you? I should hate to have Mama write to your superior," she warned, giving him a serious look.

"I think I'd hate that too," he replied, nodding his head solemnly.

Chokey cocked her head, frowning. And then she burst out laughing. "I rather like him, darling," she said to Bea. "And he's quite handsome, isn't he? Even with those eyebrows. You know, a lot of my friends don't really support intertribalism, but, honestly, I do wonder sometimes if they haven't rather overblown the whole thing, don't you agree?" she finished, turning back to Mistasinon.

"I... er..." Mistasinon floundered.

"This is Chokey's brother, Hemmings," Bea said, shooting the dwarf a murderous look, which she completely ignored.

Mistasinon held his hand out.

Hemmings stared at it.

Mistasinon put his hand down.

"Hemmings is a thoughtsmith," Bea said before Chokey got it into her head to add anything else to the conversation. "That means he does a lot of thinking for other people."

"Oh? I've met a few people who could do with a bit of help when it comes to thinking," Mistasinon said to Hemmings. "Myself included."

Hemmings' eyes widened. "Really?"

"Yes, absolutely."

"When you have time, I'd be very happy to read to you from my journal. It's rare I meet someone who is prepared to admit their shortcomings."

"I'd be very happy to hear what you have to say."

"Gosh, aren't you brave?" Chokey said. "No one's ever *volunteered* to listen to Hemmings' stuff before."

"Really? Well, a person who writes for fools is guaranteed a large audience," Mistasinon said, "So I suppose the opposite must also be true."

Hemmings looked like he was going to cry. "Oh, yes, yes, I've often thought the same thing. Perhaps when you've finished helping Buttercup—"

The door to West's office opened, silencing him.

"West is ready for you now," Barret said.

Chokey enveloped Bea in another hug. "Good luck, darling. We'll be in the common room when all this nonsense is finished with," she added pointedly, looking at Mistasinon.

Bea and Mistasinon followed Barret into West's office.

It wasn't what she'd expected, although she would have been hard pushed to say exactly how she'd imagined West's office would look.

Like all the other rooms in the Academy, it had a stone floor and wood-panelled walls, from which Bea very carefully kept her distance. West's office was somewhere in the middle of the east wing, and so didn't have any windows. As a result, oil lamps burned on full in the walls, casting a warm, yellow haze over everything. There was a long mirror in the corner behind West's desk, its surface covered with a sheet. Along the left- and right-hand walls were freestanding bookcases, but there were no books on the shelves.

There was, however, a lot of pottery. Vases, jugs and urns, glazed black, orange and pale beige, were displayed on the shelves, each decorated with different scenes. Some showed humans fighting each other, while in others they were eating and drinking, surrounded by odd creatures Bea had never seen before. They looked like they were half-animal and half-human: they had goat or horse legs, with male and female human torsos and heads. The mortal gods knew what kind of fae they were supposed to be.

One of the vases showed a horse with wings sprouting out of its back. Bea wondered if it was some ancient clan related to the kelpi. Kelpi needed water to keep them cool, but maybe flying through the air would have the same effect? She wished she could look at it properly, but this wasn't the time for art appreciation.

West was sitting behind her desk, watching them with interest. She was wearing her dark hair down with a thick braid across the top of her head, and her usual black dress with the cord knotted under her breasts, looping around her midriff. Her honey skin glowed in the lamp light, and her dark eyes glittered with something that, had Bea not thought it was ridiculous, she would have said was excitement.

"Please, sit," West instructed, her voice as deep and heavy as the snow outside.

The troll took up position behind West. Bea wasn't sure why, but she got the impression he had chosen to stand there not to watch them, but so that he could be near West. It was something in the way he carried himself.

West turned her attention to Mistasinon. A triumphant expression ghosted over her face when she looked at him. Bea found herself frowning, and then wondered why. She looked away, only to see the troll glaring at Mistasinon like he was something he'd stepped in.

She became aware suddenly that there were a lot of currents in the room. Had Mistasinon picked up on them? Her eyes darted to her left, to where he was sitting. He was breathing strangely, quick and shallow—what in the five hells did that mean?

It occurred to her that maybe putting her future in his hands hadn't been the best idea, after all. But it was too late now.

"Now then," West began, talking directly to Mistasinon. "I understand you wish your recruit to keep her place?"

"That's what she wants," Mistasinon replied. "She went through a lot to get here, and I see from her records she passed the placement exam—"

"But it is her actions since then that are under examination now," West cut across him. "We've had numerous complaints from her Master." She held her hand out, and Barret produced a pile of papers. "All of these are negative reports regarding her behaviour in lessons. It says here... ah yes... 'Refuses to participate in lessons', 'participates too much in lessons', 'could try harder', 'tries too hard'. What do you make of that?"

"Honestly, it sounds to me like her Master is the one who needs to be reviewed," Mistasinon said mildly. "He seems somewhat confused."

Bea could have kissed him. She folded her hands in her lap and concentrated on her knuckles.

"You may have a point," West conceded. "But that doesn't account for the fact she was out of her room in the middle of the night, in an area of the Academy expressly forbidden."

"Youthful high spirits."

"Perhaps, but hardly the behaviour we wish to encourage. The Teller, *whocaresaboutus*, and, indeed, The General

224

Administration, for whom we work, take a very dim view of renegade behaviour. I am not inclined to be the first Headmistress to allow such a recruit to graduate."

Mistasinon crossed his legs, leaned forward on his elbows, and offered West one of his special little smiles. And... yes... West's cheeks flushed ever so faintly, her eyes widening. Bea was certain she wouldn't have noticed it if she hadn't been paying attention. She shifted her gaze and noted that the troll had also spotted West's reaction to Mistasinon.

"I sympathise," Mistasinon said, apparently the only one in the room oblivious to the effect he was having on West. "But I can assure you, Buttercup has learned her lesson. And she's already paid a high price for her actions."

"Another problem. Due to her illness, she's missed two weeks of classes."

"She can catch up. And she was Plot-watching for years before being accepted. That must count for something?"

West handed Dafi's reports back to Barret. "She missed the field test."

"Couldn't she retake it?"

"Let me be plain. All the recruits have taken the test, and so they know what it involved. What would stop her from asking one of her friends what happened? She could find out what the Plots were or the type of characters." West paused. "Although this may not be such a problem. I could, perhaps, source a new Plot for her to be tested with."

For the first time since the meeting began, West turned her attention to Bea. "However, none of the Masters will take you. Dafi may well be 'confused', but he is also very vocal, and after your adventures, you are seen as something of a liability."

Bea swallowed. "I have managed a Plot before," she said.

"So I understand. But I also understand that things did not go smoothly."

Bea stole a glance at Mistasinon. She was not reassured to see he looked as horrified at this statement as she was.

"Um... Yes. There were some problems," Bea said, trying to find a foothold in the conversation. She felt like a mountaineer who'd just realised she'd run out of crampons with half an alp to go before reaching the summit. "But I *did* finish it. And surely that's something that the GenAm needs as well? FMEs who can think on their feet, deal with unexpected complications, and still get the Plot finished?"

"But you had help, did you not? From this person sitting next to you?"

"Excuse me, but I think your information—" Mistasinon began.

West held her hand up. "You misunderstand me," she said to him. "I am suggesting that you help her again."

Mistasinon opened his mouth and then closed it. His thick eyebrows pulled together. "I'm afraid I don't follow you."

"I am willing to allow *you* to supervise her field test."

Bea wanted to jump up and dance around the room. She wasn't going to be expelled! She could run off a quick Plot-watch, which Mistasinon would sign off, and then she'd be back in classes, ready to find out why in the five hells there was a bloodied human woman wandering around the Academy, and she could still become a godmother. Finally, things were going her way!

It suddenly occurred to her that Mistasinon hadn't said anything.

"Mistasinon?"

He shifted in his seat. "I'm not sure that's such a good idea," he said.

"Why not?"

"I... I'm very busy at the moment," he said weakly, rubbing his neck. "I hadn't thought this would... That I would need to..."

"If I may intervene," West said. "This is the only offer I am prepared to make. Either you supervise her field test, or she leaves the Academy today."

XXXIV

"What do you mean, you're very busy at the moment?" Bea demanded.

West had allowed them a moment in the hallway outside her office to discuss her proposal.

"What do you want me to say? I don't think this is a good idea."

"Why not?"

Mistasinon closed his eyes. He seemed to be having trouble breathing again. His hands pumped like he was trying to keep them warm. Bea felt a pang of sympathy.

"Are you alright? It's quite oppressive here if you're not used to it."

His eyes snapped open. "I'm fine."

"Then please... listen to me. I have to be here." Bea picked up his hands, holding them still. "I have to pass this course and become a godmother, otherwise what was it all for?"

Scowling, he pulled his hands away.

"Has something happened?" she asked, searching his face for some clue to his sudden change of heart. "You said you'd help me. I thought we'd reached..." The sentence died on her tongue. What? What did she think they'd reached?

"I've had time to think, that's all," he said. "Besides, I need to be in the GenAm, not running around Thaiana."

"It won't take long, you just need to sign the form. You said you'd help me keep my place, I don't understand what's happened. If someone's said something to you, something to frighten you, you can tell me. You know I understand what the GenAm is capable of."

"Just stop it, Bea," Mistasinon snapped, shoving his hands in his pockets. "Why do you keep thinking I can help you? You say the GenAm is this evil institution, and yet you seem quite happy to make use of it when it suits you, and you don't have any problem coming to me when things aren't going your way. I *work* for them,

Bea. The GenAm took me in and looked after me, and you tell me you want to change it and expect me to help you. Have you even thought about that?"

Bea stared at him while around her, the world fell away. And yet somehow she was still standing.

"I was wrong. It's my mistake, I see that now," he said, a hint of remorse in his voice. "I think we should stop whatever this is. It's not real. You should go back to Plot-watching, and I'll go back to... to where I came from."

"You can go to one of the five hells, for all I care. But you said you'd help me," Bea answered, relieved to hear her voice come out steady. "All you have to do is take me on a Plot-watch. That's it. And then you can go back to your life, and I'll go back to mine. The end."

She folded her arms, stuck her chin out, and waited for him to reply.

On the other side of the doorway, Barret was having his own problems.

"Why are you encouraging this?" he said, trying to keep a lid on his anger. "Just get rid of her. Look at all the trouble she's caused. We've just completed the first-ever fully successful run with the ETPs, none of the recruits noticed anything was unusual. The test Plot the elves ran is working. We're nearly there." Then, playing what he thought was his trump card, Barret added, "And the Head Redactionist will want a status update soon. What will I tell her?"

"Whatever you think is best. The ETPs work. She's got what she wants. Now it's my turn."

"We still haven't located the missing ETP," Barret said, changing tack. "All the recruits think the place is haunted—that's that bloody fairy's fault too. What if they start poking around? Get rid of her and that Plotter, then all the rumours will die, and we can go back to our work."

"Barret, this is what happens," West said. "It's what *has* to happen. I've waited so long... I've worked so hard. Please. Please believe me."

"Waited for what? For him?" Barret cried, emotion overtaking him. "My Lady, what you're doing is bigger than anyone else. He doesn't understand, he'd never understand. You must have heard the rumours, he's only here because he and that cabbage fairy are—"

Before he could finish, the door opened, and the Plotter and the fairy re-entered the room.

"How long will this field test take?" Mistasinon asked.

West folded her hands in front of her. "A day. Two, at the most."

Barret held his breath. He realised he was hoping the Plotter was going to refuse.

"I'll do it. But after this, I think Bea, Buttercup, should have another mentor assigned to her. I trust that won't affect her progress?"

West smiled. "Of course not—once you've accompanied her on the field test, and reported back to me, personally, on her progress. You leave this evening. I have the details sent to you."

The Plotter looked momentarily confused, not used to West's strange turns of speech. What was that if not more evidence that the only one who would ever really understand her was Barret?

More so than ever before, he knew it was up to him to protect her, to keep her safe from herself. He couldn't understand what it was about the blue suit that had cast its spell over West, or why she had it in her head that he was going to rescue her. Rescue her from what? From her genius? Her future?

It didn't make sense. *He shouldn't even be at the Academy.* It was that stupid cabbage fairy's fault. He was an intruder, stealing West away from her work. Away from him.

Barret's dark eyes narrowed as he watched the Plotter and the fairy leave.

XXXV

Bea went to see Luca to tell him she wasn't being expelled, and then to the common room. She found Hemmings lounging along one of the tatty sofas, staring into space. Chokey was sitting on the arm, plaiting and unplaiting her hair.

"Guess what?" Bea grinned. "I'm taking the field test!"

Chokey dropped her braid. "Darling! Oh, well done! Everyone was saying that it was probably for the best, that you didn't really belong here anyway, but we just knew you'd find a way to stay on."

"We've been waiting here all afternoon," Hemmings said, adding, "I haven't been able to write a line, not even a poem."

"I'm sorry you were worried," Bea said, offering Hemmings an apologetic smile.

"Never mind that! This is simply too perfect!" Chokey said, stamping her feet in excitement. Hemmings pulled his legs away before she trampled them.

"You'll sail through the field test, I'm quite sure. Honestly, if anything it's rather dull. Really, I don't understand why you think there's so much to these characters. They weren't in the slightest bit entertaining, and there was barely anything for us to do. It was just a lot of young girls, sopping about, doing just as we told them to. One girl didn't even bother asking who she was off to marry, can you imagine?"

Bea frowned. Of course, there were humans who were happy to be in the Plots; she'd watched enough stories to know that. But there was something in the way Chokey described them that sent a shiver through her, and she couldn't quite work out what it was.

"Hemmings, were your hu—sorry, characters the same?"

"I'm afraid so. And I had quite a good Plot to watch, compared to some of the others. She had to sit up in this tower so her hero could rescue her. I was rather looking forward to explaining to her why it was such a good opportunity to do some proper reflection, but she just went up there, no questions asked."

Bea started chewing her nails.

"Oh, don't do that, darling. They've only just started growing back."

"What?"

"Your nails, Buttercup," Chokey clarified.

Bea pulled her hand away from her mouth. "Sorry. Um. Anyway, I'd better get going. I don't want to keep Mistasinon waiting."

"I shouldn't worry about him, darling, he's hardly likely to leave without you," Chokey called after her as she walked away.

Bea was prepared to admit she'd only ever met two characters properly, but she'd observed loads of them, doing Plot-watches. And, while they all had taken the news that they were going to be in a Plot differently, she'd never heard of one not asking a single question. Usually, they wanted to know if the hero was rich and handsome, at the very least.

Her thoughts returned to the 'ghost'. She had the sense that the woman wandering the Academy fitted in, but she had no idea how. And then she remembered the mysterious empty protagonists...

Was there some connection?

Of course there bloody well is, Bea thought. It was just too much of a coincidence, and, as she knew all too well, coincidences never happened by chance. There was always someone behind the scenes, manipulating events.

And then there was the question of Mistasinon. What did she know about him, really? She'd based her opinion of him on her instinct that he was a good person, that he understood, like she did, that there was something fundamentally wrong with controlling people, keeping them locked in place like the spiky-toothed wheels the humans used in their steam-powered machines.

But like he'd said himself, he was a suit.

He worked for the GenAm. She'd assumed he'd fallen into it somehow, the way most people did. It wasn't like there was an abundance of career choices in Ænathlin, and the GenAm was by far the safest way to earn a living, as long as you didn't mind conforming to their notion of what you should be. The Teller had kept things static for hundreds of years, and while that was clearly wrong, it did mean that the GenAm provided job security. Was it really that surprising to discover he was loyal?

You don't really believe that, though, do you?

Despite what he'd said, she was certain there was something else going on. Just a few days ago, when they'd been alone in the attic, he'd wanted to know more about what was happening. She supposed she could be imagining things, changing the world to make it fit her point of view... A poor little fairy who no one takes seriously, who ran away from her family when she couldn't cope with the disappearance of her father, who thinks she's cleverer than anyone else, despite the fact that everything she does usually makes things worse. Who doesn't know when to shut up, when to give up.

But on the other hand... She *knew* what the GenAm did was wrong. They'd murdered the genies, and they didn't care about the characters or even the fae, not really. They kept everyone locked up in their own heads with stories and threats of Redaction, with every day being exactly the same as the last, with no hope of anything ever changing.

Bea sighed. *Pick, pick, pick... Always picking things apart, that's your problem. Or you actually are just an idiot,* she added to herself. *Can't rule that out. You certainly seem to have a knack for making things difficult for yourself.*

"Psst, cabbage mother."

Bea looked up. Carol was standing in the doorway of one of the classrooms, beckoning her.

"Carol, I really don't have time for this."

"Yes, you do. Trust me."

For a moment, Bea wondered who she distrusted most: Carol or herself. But there was something in her tone of voice that made her pause.

"What is it?" she asked, wary.

Carol waved her over again. "Will you stop standing around like a lump and come here," she hissed.

Bea contemplated walking away. She really did. For about two seconds. Sighing theatrically, she walked over to the imp, who pulled her into the empty classroom and shut the door behind them.

"Well?"

"Are you going on the field test or not?"

"Really? Is that what this is about? Yes, I'm going on the field test. And yes, I dare say it is because I got here unfairly, and everything is unfair, and you're the best, and I'm the worst. Is that it?"

Carol shot her a venomous look. "Mortal gods, stop whining. So you *are* taking the test?"

"What of it?"

"Do you know which heroine you've been given?"

Bea frowned. "No. They gave the details straight to my mentor. He's supervising me."

"That figures," Carol muttered. "You have to go and see my heroine," she added.

"Excuse me, you want *me* to check up on *your* heroine? No way. Do your own work."

Carol looked like she was about to slap her. "Look. There's something wrong with the characters. None of these idiots here noticed it because they've never stepped outside of their own stupid circles. But you'll see it," she finished grudgingly.

Bea started to frame a snappy riposte and then reconsidered. Somewhere, buried behind her venomous tone and spiteful expression, Carol had just paid her a compliment. Well, sort of, anyway. At least, as close to one as Bea could probably hope to receive from the imp.

Ghosts, empty protagonists, Plotters who were confusing the plot, characters behaving out of character—and now mild recognition from Carol. Bea couldn't help wondering if she'd somehow fallen through a Mirror and ended in a bizarre, backwards world.

"Alright, give me the details. But I want you to tell me something in return," Bea said. "What's your problem with me? I always thought it was because I was a fairy. I mean, I heard about your family… about losing your position. But I think it's more than that. Almost everyone hates fairies, but with you, it feels personal. So what is it?"

"There's too many of you fairies. You don't do anything to help the Plots. It's your fault the Great Redaction happened, you and your King and Queen."

"Yes, fine," Bea said. She was actually disappointed. For some reason, she'd hoped Carol might have a better reason for—

"But I hate you more, now, because you cheated your way here."

Oh.

"Oh," Bea said.

"Everyone knows about it. You and your Plotter, carrying on together. It's disgusting."

"Listen, my Plot was—wait, what?" Bea said, coming to an abrupt stop, her brain catching up with her ears.

Her and Mistasinon?

Carrying on together?

"You want to know what really makes me hate you?" Carol continued, speaking clearly and slowly so that Bea wouldn't miss a word:

"It's not intertribalism if that's what you're thinking. I couldn't care less if someone wants to degrade themselves by sleeping with a fairy. It's the fact that you used your relationship with him to get your place here. You're worse than all of them. The Harkers and the Ogrechokers and the rest haven't got a clue what any of this really means. They bought their way in, and they'll buy their way out. But you know how hard I worked to get here, going on all those Plot-watches, sitting for hours watching some ridiculous girl wait for her hero to turn up and Make All Her Dreams Come True. It's worse than cheating. It's *insulting*. Just make sure you check on my heroine," Carol finished, before marching out of the classroom and slamming the door behind her.

Bea didn't try to follow her to set the record straight. Even if she could have told Carol the truth about how she got her place at the Academy, she wouldn't have been able to. Right now, her brain had completely shut down.

Everyone thought she and Mistasinon were…? That they'd…?

And then, as if stepping on a snake in long grass, she felt the stinging bite of understanding:

That was why he hadn't come to their tutorial, leaving those notes in his place. That was why he didn't want to go away with her. Why he thought she should go back to Plot-watching, with all the other fairies.

Mortal gods, she really was stupid.

All this time she'd thought it was because he felt guilty about lying to her, or even, since his outburst, because he genuinely didn't see anything wrong with the GenAm. Hells, both of those things could still be true; but she knew, with sudden clarity, that they weren't the main reasons for his determined absence.

He was embarrassed.

Embarrassed to be associated with a fairy.

Well, screw him—apparently, everyone thought she was anyway, ha bloody ha. If her time in Ænathlin had taught her anything, it was that it didn't matter what anyone thought about her, including him. She wasn't about to let a nasty rumour about her stop her doing what needed to be done.

She was going to find out what in the five hells was going on, just as soon as she'd got this bloody field test out of the way.

Barret thought he knew all about anger—anyone who had to fill out endless AN72 forms in triplicate, working for years under Osgood, Administrator Level 5, Sub-Section 7 Head, learnt how to manage their frustrations.

This was something new.

He stared at the wall in his room, trying to rein in his fury and resentment. He wouldn't be any good to West if he couldn't control himself. She needed him to be in control. She needed him to look after her. That was his job. Not managing all the other brown suits. Not even reporting back to the Head Redactionist about the ETPs.

West was his duty.

She was amazing. He'd never met anyone like her, never even imagined there could be anyone like her. The things she'd achieved, and he'd been there, standing next to her, helping to make it possible.

She said she wanted him to believe her, but he was doing one better than that: he believed *in* her. He could see what she needed because he knew her better than she knew herself.

It wasn't West's fault, that much was certain. She was a character. They were easily confused at the best of times, and

West's remarkable genius left her even more vulnerable. They were fragile, everyone knew that. That was why he'd been appointed to her, trusted to take care of her.

Yes. He was responsible for her. It was up to him to save her from herself.

The Plotter was dangerous. He was distracting her. Barret had seen the way she looked at him, heard her talk about him. What tribe was he? He didn't look like any tribe Barret recognised, but perhaps he had a bit of elf in him... Yes, he was slender like them... And the elves used their beauty to bewitch the characters. The Plotter wasn't beautiful; he was too scrawny and weak. But it was the only explanation that made sense.

Nevertheless, somewhere hidden away from the raging beast that was prowling through him, Barret was aware that he couldn't do anything to the Plotter. Sure, he could physically overpower him, the skinny little sap looked like he'd fall over in a strong breeze... But if anyone found out, it would be Barret on the Redaction block. He was a brown suit, while the Plotter was, naturally, a blue suit. More important.

More important—Mortal gods, it made him sick. Who could possibly be more important than him? He was the one making sure West could flourish, that her genius could work unimpeded so that she, he, *they,* could save the Mirrors.

It was always the same story, wasn't it? All the effluent, pouring from above onto the innocent below.

There had to be something he could do. Something to make the world right again.

It had all begun with that jumped-up, fat, *disgusting* cabbage fairy. That made it even worse. He knew the rumours about how she got her place here. How else would one of them make it to the Academy? She didn't deserve to be here, but as long as she was, her Plotter would keep sniffing around her, wouldn't he? Like a dog chasing a bitch in heat. It was revolting.

Yes. The fairy. If it wasn't for her, West would never have laid eyes on the Plotter. It would still be just him and her, working together in their secret little world, relying on each other for everything. Without the fairy, there'd be no reason for the Plotter to come back again.

And then West could get back to her work, back to him. She wouldn't think about the Plotter again, Barret knew it, and if she did, it would only be to marvel at how she'd almost lost everything over someone so insignificant.

He couldn't allow anything, or anyone, to get in their way.

It was his responsibility to rescue her.

XXXVI

Bea stepped through the Mirror and into the Grand Reflection Station in Ænathlin. She stood dumbstruck, awed by the scene in front of her.

The Grand was... organised.

If she hadn't seen it with her own eyes, she would never have believed it. To her left and right were rows of Mirrors, all functioning. Orderly lines queued up in the avenue in front of her, brown suits ushering them to whichever Mirror was free.

This was not the Grand she knew and hated.

Six months ago, when Bea had last used the Mirrors, the only reason she hadn't been able to describe the Grand as a riot was because riots usually didn't require you to have your papers stamped before you got to join in.

Suddenly, Mistasinon appeared behind her, having come through the Mirror. He only just managed to stop himself toppling off the small platform by grabbing hold of her.

"Mortal gods, sorry," he apologised. "I should have given you more time."

"Calm down," Bea said, ignoring the burning heat of mortification on her cheeks. "Or are you worried everyone's looking at us?"

"What? No. Why would...?" His eyes widened, horrified. And then he nearly fell off the platform anyway, practically jumping away from her. By unspoken agreement, they both very carefully descended the platform, self-consciously keeping a respectable distance from each other.

"It's so calm," Bea said, stating the obvious for want of anything else to say.

"Yes." Mistasinon paused. "There's been a lot of changes since you've been gone, actually."

"That sounds ominous."

"I can show you if you'd like?"

Bea eyed him cautiously. "I thought you wanted to get this over with?"

"Ah. Yes, of course," he said, rubbing his neck. He shot her a half-smile. "But we're here now, and it won't take a minute."

Telling herself she was a prize fool, Bea nevertheless allowed him to lead her through the Grand towards the exit, Mistasinon's blue suit making sure they didn't have to go through the Contents Department's checkpoints.

At least some things are still the same, she mused.

When she stepped through the arches of the Grand onto the streets of Ænathlin, she felt grateful she hadn't voiced her thoughts. She was still feeling queasy from travelling through the Mirror, and she would have had to eat her words.

Fae teemed around her, all going about their business in the happy, determined way of people with something to do and the means to make it happen. The city was like a colony of ants on stimulants.

"Welcome home," Mistasinon said.

"Are you sure we're in the right place?" Bea asked, unable to keep the disbelief out of her voice.

"Trust me, it's Ænathlin. This is just what the city is like when the Mirrors are working. I suppose you've never seen it like this?"

"No. When I came here, most of the Mirrors were broken or breaking. It was still busy, but..." Bea trailed off, lost for words.

She couldn't deny it was good to see the city so invigorated. The trouble was, she also knew what everyone else around her, with the exception of Mistasinon, didn't: that without the magical subsidy of the genies' wishes, eventually the Mirrors would break again.

Stepping backwards to get a better view, Bea crashed into a flower fairy who'd been standing, unnoticed, behind her.

"Sorry! Sorry!" she apologised frantically, helping the flower fairy to her feet.

"It's fine," the flower fairy replied, brushing herself down. She had yellow and red hair and orange and bronze wings. She also had a large badge pinned to her dress, emblazoned with the letters 'F.U.'

"Oh! You're a fairy too? Would you like to come to our meeting tonight?"

"Er. I can't tonight," Bea said. "Sorry."

"No problem. We have meetings every week." The flower fairy shoved a small, cheaply printed sheet of paper into her hands. "Here, have an informative pamphlet. Fairies United Cannot Be Divided!"

"Er... really?" Bea said.

"Absolutely! We're looking for people to doorstep, and you could also join the march outside the GenAm, and then there are the coffee mornings—"

"I'm sorry," Bea said, backing away. "I don't really have the time."

The flower fairy gave her a disappointed look. "You're just like my uncle Tom," she said sadly. She darted away to bestow her pamphlets on more deserving people.

"What was that all about?" Bea asked Mistasinon as they headed back inside.

"I should read the pamphlet if I were you," he said.

Bea flattened out the crumpled piece of paper, skimming it. Then she read it again, slowly. And then she read it once more, closer still.

"Fairies United is a group of fairies' rights activists?"

"They like to call themselves fairyists. But yes, you've got the gist. I thought you'd be pleased?" he said as he guided them through the checkpoints.

Bea wasn't sure how she felt. "How did it happen? Hasn't anyone tried to stop them? Isn't it dangerous?"

He offered her a smile. "You started it, or at least, when the Head Plotter thanked you so publicly, it started. Though I suspect it's been coming for a while. And yes, lots of fae are trying to stop them, but there are some who are trying to help, as well. Sometimes the right thing to do is dangerous."

Bea looked down at the pamphlet again.

"Your friend Joan's involved with them," Mistasinon continued, as they lined up for the next free Mirror to take them back to Thaiana and the location of Bea's field test.

"Joan? How do you know that?"

"Oh, you know," he said. "Word gets around."

"But if it's dangerous, she shouldn't be doing it."

Mistasinon stopped, ignoring the complaints from the fae lining up behind them. "Tell me, do you think your friends were worried about you when you were doing your Plot?"

He didn't actually say, '*When you were running around with a genie, changing your Plot and basically inviting the Redaction Department to send the Beast out for you,*' but Bea got the point.

"I suppose so."

"And did that stop you?"

"No."

"Well then. Everyone has to be the protagonist in their own story, isn't that right?"

"S'pose so," Bea mumbled, annoyed to be so easily caught out.

Mistasinon, perhaps out of kindness, left it at that. They started moving again, to the satisfaction of the queue.

They finally reached a free Mirror. Mistasinon stepped onto the small platform in front of it, while Bea waited for him to make the connection. One minute ticked by, and then another. He just stood in front of the glass, rubbing his neck.

"Don't you know where we're going?" she asked.

"Yes, I'm just... trying to concentrate."

"Oh. Right."

"I don't want to connect to the wrong place," he clarified, staring intently at the Mirror.

Bea was about to say it would hardly matter as they could just start again. But then she wondered if he'd think she was trying to prolong their time together and kept quiet.

Yet still he stood there, glaring at the Mirror like it had insulted him.

"Do you want me to read the description?"

"It's fine," Mistasinon said. He rubbed his hand across his mouth and nose, and then pressed both hands against the Mirror, pulling them away almost immediately they touched the glass.

It shouldn't have been long enough to make a connection, but Bea watched, incredulous, as inky little spots appeared on the surface and then bubbled away, quick as water on hot metal. An image of a small village appeared in the Mirror.

Mistasinon exhaled, and Bea realised he'd been holding his breath. She didn't understand why he'd been so nervous about

F. D. Lee

making a mistake with the connection. If anything, she was extremely impressed. She'd never seen anyone connect a Mirror that quickly—it had barely had time to go dark before he'd found the place they were looking for.

Before she could say anything, Mistasinon disappeared through the Mirror. She counted a minute under her breath, took one last look around the Grand, and then followed him through.

It was time to find out what was going on with the characters.

XXXVII

"It's spring," Bea said. "I didn't realise."

They were standing on the edge of a forest in Sausendorf, in the south-east of Ehinenden.

"Yes. But then, the winter never really hits this far south," Mistasinon replied. "And you've been at the Academy for six months."

Bea lifted her arms, raising her face to the sky. The sun felt wonderful against her skin, its gentle warmth sinking into her, calming and comforting.

There were faint smells she'd forgotten she knew: the leaves turning to mulch under the dark cover of the trees, the sap and the bark, sweet and slightly smoky, a heady scent charged with the promise of growth and life. And, of course, yes, the rustle of the forest, the leaves whispering in the breeze, birds chirruping to each other, the soft ground beneath her boots...

"You like being in the outdoors?" Mistasinon asked. "Does it remind you of home?"

Bea's eyes snapped open. He was watching her, tanned cheeks flushed, lips slightly parted. She coughed, dropping her arms.

"No," she said. "I left the forest behind. So, what are we supposed to do?"

A frown fluttered across his high forehead. He pulled the Book out of his satchel and flipped the pages.

"Your heroine's due for a Sacrifice/Reward. From what I can see here, the FME in charge has already got the thing started. All you have to do to is give the heroine her call to action, and then tomorrow I'll check she's properly on the Plot. If she is, you've passed. It's actually quite straightforward, considering it's supposed to be such an important test."

"At least it won't take long then. Who's the FME running it?"

Mistasinon turned to another section of the Book. "She's a mild peril. A troll called Alice. Do you know her?"

F. D. Lee

"Vaguely. I've watched a few of her Plots before. She seemed alright."

Bea looked down at the heroine's house. The girl was isolated—but then, they often were, weren't they?

Belief was a resource that required careful husbandry: the idea of Happy Every Afters and trolls and witches and elves was a fun one, but only when it was also a *distant* one. It had to start with "My sister's cousin's brother lives over in Skraq, and did you hear…" or "A few years ago there was this girl, and according to my grandad…", and then the best ones, like the Teller's, became "Once upon a time…"

If the Plot Department ran stories too close to each other or too frequently, then people would start paying attention, and that was when things went wrong for the fae. One reaction would be the iron again, the fires, the hunts. That was bad, true enough, but the other was worse: the humans could start thinking.

They turned their belief into curiosity, into questions, inventions, ideas. And when the time came for the fae to run a Plot, the hero or heroine would tilt their head, and say, "But why should I? Go and find someone else, I'm actually quite busy at the moment, working on this theory I've got about imaginary numbers. Besides, aren't fairies and so on just for children?"

They started to shine a light into the dark places, not in the world, but in their minds. And the kind of belief the Mirrors needed withered and died in the light.

Mistasinon closed the Book with a snap, making Bea jump.

"What is it?"

"I think there's been a mistake," he said, trying to open his satchel while also holding the Book away from her. "We should go back."

Without thinking, Bea sprang forward to grab the Book.

A confused two minutes followed, in which Mistasinon, taken off guard, tried to keep the Book above Bea's head, while at the same time not lose his balance. Bea took advantage of his discombobulation to twist around him and, half jumping and half climbing up him, she managed to snatch the Book from his grasp.

244

Panting, she flicked through the pages, her eyes dancing across the words until they landed on something that made her stop. She looked up at him.

"This can't be right?"

"It's a mistake," Mistasinon said, brushing his hair out of his eyes. "It must be. The Plot Department hasn't issued stories like this for hundreds of years—they're too risky. Hells, they were risky back then, and it was a lot easier then than it is now."

Bea read the page again. "She'll refuse. It's pointless. Is this deliberate? Are they trying to get rid of me? There's no way I can pass with a Plot like this."

Mistasinon looked at the heroine's cottage, nestled snug in the clearing below them. "Look, I know I said some... things... before, and I regret the way they came out, but—"

"But nothing," Bea said, her grip tightening on the Book. "If you don't want me to go down there, you'll have to stop me. I'm not giving up without a fight."

As the words left her mouth, it dawned on her that he probably could, too. He was strong; she'd seen him fight a troll barehanded and come out the victor. He could easily just pick her up and deposit her back in Ænathlin. But she'd said it now, and she wasn't going to back down.

The wind rustled the leaves in the trees. Birds chirruped. Mistasinon stood in an agony of indecision. Bea held her ground.

"Fine," he said. "Let's go."

The heroine, Dionne, sat on her bed, smiling happily as Bea told her about the Plot and what was expected of her.

"that sounds fine," she said when Bea had finished.

Bea glanced over at Mistasinon, who was standing in the corner of the room, watching them intently. She turned her attention back to the girl.

Two facts were immediately obvious. The first was that no one was trying to sabotage her field test. The girl had agreed to it all, without a moment's hesitation. The second was that there was something very wrong with that fact.

Bea thought about what she *shouldn't* do. She shouldn't try to talk the heroine out of it. She definitely shouldn't try to talk the heroine out of it while in front of an official General Administration Plotter, in the middle of her official General Administration field test. Such behaviour was exactly the sort of thing that not only ensured a fail but also guaranteed a visit from the Beast in the middle of the night, a short trip to the Redactionists, and then… nothing.

She looked down at the Book, resting on her lap. And then she looked up at the girl, her smile plastered on her dark face.

Bea muttered a swear word. Of course she was going to do it, wasn't she? She'd just have to hope Mistasinon wouldn't want the added hassle of failing her—or worse, reporting her—and would just pass her and walk away.

"Are you quite sure you understand?" she said to the girl. "You're agreeing to seven years of servitude, to having your mouth sewn shut… it's a bit—" *insane, barbaric, stupid* "—extreme, don't you think?"

"that sounds fine," Dionne said again, still smiling.

Bea felt her patience flicker, like a candle on the last of its wax.

"How about… how about instead of sewing your lips shut and basically selling yourself into slavery, you go and work for the troll for a set number of hours every day, but promise not to speak unless spoken to?"

Bea wasn't entirely happy with this suggestion either, but it had to be better than what the Plot demanded.

Dionne's smile faltered. "but that isn't what i am supposed to do."

Bea opened her mouth to speak and then caught sight of Mistasinon. He was standing by the window, gingerly sniffing the curtains. What on Thaiana did he think he was doing? But then, if he was busy being strange, that meant he wasn't paying attention to her.

"it is a noble sacrifice to save my brothers," Dionne said, rallying. Her smiled returned full strength.

"Well, yes, of course," Bea said, focusing her attention back on the girl. "But I don't think that means indenturing yourself for seven years to a troll—not to mention disfiguring yourself so that you can't answer back. And besides, didn't at least *one* of your brothers think to himself 'oh look, all my other brothers have gone to kill this big bad troll and have been trapped in stone'?"

"Turned into swans," corrected Mistasinon, making Bea jump.

He'd moved away from the curtains and was now poking around Dionne's make-up stand. He picked up a small, almost empty bottle of dirty white liquid, holding it up to the light. And then, apparently committed to acting extremely strangely, he sniffed it.

"No, no, trolls can't transfigure—" Bea stopped herself. There was no point arguing with him over the intricacies of tribal talents. Back to the girl and her eerie smile. "What I mean is, why didn't any of your brothers consider trying something that didn't involve running directly at the troll, waving their swords around?"

"it's my job to save them. i would like to do it."

Bea stared at Dionne, struggling to find a way to make her see sense—one that didn't involve picking her up and carrying her away. But it wasn't up to her, was it? Not in the end. She couldn't force the heroine *not* to be in the story. She felt something on her shoulder. It was Mistasinon's hand.

"You're not going to change her mind."

"This isn't right," Bea said. "You can't think this is right?"

Dionne's head moved as they spoke, following the flow of their conversation. *Like she's waiting for one of us to speak next*, Bea realised.

Waiting, listening… not thinking.

"Come on," Mistasinon said gently. "We should go."

"I… yes. Alright. Good luck, Dionne."

The girl didn't reply. She just sat on her bed, smiling happily.

⁂

Yawning, Luca tried to concentrate on his patrol, his feet heavy as he trudged along the corridor. It was dark in the Academy. It was always dark, a result of the wooden walls and the storm.

Things had not been going well for the brown suits, recently. A lot of them were blaming it on Bea, which made him feel bad. What made him feel worse was that he wasn't sure if they didn't

F. D. Lee

have a point. Ever since she'd had her accident, they'd been made to work longer hours, patrolling further around the Academy.

It was a bit strange, really. After Bea's accident, West had cancelled all the classes and Barret had gone off for two days, taking patrol while the rest of the brown suits wandered around the east wing, making sure the recruits stayed put. And then Barret had returned, had a long meeting with West, and the next day classes had resumed.

Barret was in a bad mood, too. Usually, the troll was alright to work for. He was strict, certainly, and he got really angry if they interrupted his work with West but other than that he made sure they got their ration tokens on time and gave them all decent shifts with good breaks.

Or, at least, he'd used to. For the last two weeks, everyone had been on doubles.

Luca switched his lamp from one hand to the other. He'd been told to patrol the west wing, which struck him as pointless since no one was allowed there, and anyway, West kept most of the rooms locked up. He'd found a few that were open, but after a quick inspection, they revealed themselves to be devoid of life.

Luca ruffled his scales, trying to keep warm.

He'd been on shift for hours, serving meals, tidying away, keeping a general eye on the recruits in the common room; but he was nearly finished now. Two or three more corridors and he'd be finished.

He arrived at the corridor joining the two sides of the Academy, its glass wall looking out onto the gardens.

Luca lifted his lamp, the scales on his neck tickling as the cold breeze snuck in through the cracks in the window frames and brushed against him. He fiddled with the lamp's blinkers and twiddled the regulator, trying to adjust the intensity of the light. Out of curiosity, he walked over to the windows and held his lamp up to the glass. Snowflakes danced in the beam of light, bright white against the blackness beyond.

Emptiness there, nothing more.

Luca sighed at his own silliness and turned away from the window.

248

Resuming his patrol of the west wing, he turned his back on the glass-lined corridor. It was very quiet. Even the storm outside was reduced to a faint wailing. Luca lifted his lamp a little higher, causing his shadow to bleed into the darkness behind him.

He walked on. The lamplight streaming over the hallways caused strange shadows. Luca shivered and then felt stupid. He was a witchlein, one of the most feared tribes of the fae. He shouldn't be letting a few shadows spook him. Still, he found himself fiddling again with the regulator and the shutters on his lamp, trying to further widen the flow of light.

And then he heard a strange sound as if someone were rapping their knuckles, *tap tap tap*, upon the wall.

"Hello?" His voice came out in a dry whisper. He swallowed and tried again. "Hello? Isss anyone there?"

He held his breath.

Nothing.

Luca breathed out.

It must have been his imagination, only this and—

Tap tap tap.

The scales on Luca's arms fluttered involuntarily. He let out a hiss. Lifting up his lamp, he peered down the corridor, at a line of closed doors. Each one was set back slightly in the thick wall, the cobwebs of long-starved spiders hanging in the corners of the frames.

Tap tap tap.

Luca glanced over his shoulder. He could go back the way he'd come... Find his way back to the east wing. No one would know he hadn't finished his patrol, he was sure.

But then, what kind of guard would he be? And what was he frightened of, anyway? He shook his head, amused suddenly at his childishness. What did he think he was going to find? The Beast, lurking behind some old forgotten door?

It was the weather getting to him, that was all.

Tap tap tap.

Luca adjusted his grip on the handle of the oil lamp and followed the sound of the tapping until he came to a door no different from any of the others, with the exception that it had fewer cobwebs.

Perhaps if Luca had been concentrating less on the tapping and more on his surroundings, he might have wondered about that.

Tap tap tap.

He reached out and tested the handle. To his surprise, it turned easily. He pushed it open and found himself in a windowless room, completely empty. He shook himself. It had been his imagination that had set his heart beating, tricking him into hearing the repeated sound—there was no one here.

He was just about to leave when there came again the strange tap, tap, tapping as if someone were rapping against the wooden wall.

Turning his attention to the wall, he fiddled again with the regulator on his oil lamp, opening up the valve, increasing the brightness as much as it would go. He set it on the ground, facing the wall, and walked up to it.

Tap tap tap.

"H-hello?"

Tap tap tap.

And again:

Tap tap tap.

And again:

Tap tap tap.

Forcing his resolve, he reached his hand to the wall and brushed his fingers against the wood, the sharp scales that overhung his fingertips leaving fine scratches on its surface.

The tapping stopped.

How was it possible...?

Pressing his palm, devoid of scales, against the wood, he half expected the tapping to resume. When it didn't, he ran his hand over the wall, feeling the smooth, varnished surface against his skin.

Dust danced in the light from the oil lamp.

Luca's hand moved across the wall.

Click.

He jumped back as the wall started to tremble, his yellow scales glinting in the bright light of the lamp.

With the sound of groaning metal, the section of the wall that had been beneath his hand shuddered and began to move, pulling back and grinding to the side, revealing a hidden corridor.

The tapping stopped, the silence once again unbroken.

All was stillness.

Luca stepped towards the portal, the darkness of the hidden corridor heavy as a black hole, pulling him forwards. He'd take a quick look and then go back and tell Barret what he'd found. It really was very dark. Even the light from his lamp wasn't picking up much—

Something white flashed in the darkness.

The spikes involuntarily rose on Luca's body, their razor-sharp edges ripping the thin material of his suit.

Like a body floating up from the depths of the ocean, the whiteness came forwards, revealing itself...

It might once have been a woman—what it was now Luca had no idea. Dressed in white, the creature blinked wide, dead eyes, its face framed by matted, tangled hair. Its hands and feet were stained red.

It rapped its knuckles against the jamb.

For a moment, the apparition seemed puzzled. And then it stepped through the hidden doorway and into the chamber, opened up its mouth, lips white and cracked, and screamed.

Luca stumbled backwards, losing his balance. He fell, his spiky body smashing into the lamp, breaking the glass.

Around him the fire rose, catching on his cheap suit, embers flying about him as he flailed, only to land, dying, upon the floor.

The last thing he saw, as the flames and oil engulfed him, was the contorted, vacant face of the dead-eyed creature that had been rapping on the other side of the wall, trapped within the hidden corridor.

XXXVIII

Mistasinon placed Bea's pint of beer on the table.

"Thanks," she said, taking a large mouthful of the cool beverage. They'd travelled to a nearby village, and Mistasinon had rented them each a room for the night, paying for it with silver coins produced from his satchel. Bea had considered objecting on principle, but after the events of that afternoon, the idea of sleeping on the forest floor did not appeal. She wanted to sleep in a bed, and she wanted a very hot bath. Every time she thought about Dionne, she felt dirty.

He took a seat on the bench next to her.

"That was... awful," Bea said, staring at the top of her drink, watching as the bubbles dispersed the white foam.

"Yes," he said.

"I don't understand why she agreed to it. Surely anyone in their right mind would have refused?"

"Yes."

"Why is the Academy even running a story like that? I mean, I know this is just a test, but it's also still a Plot. Surely the Teller wouldn't allow it?"

"I don't know."

"In the past, weren't more of the stories like that? Blood and bone stuff?" Bea continued, too busy trying to understand what she had just seen to notice the shadow that had fallen over Mistasinon's face. "It can't be that the Plot Department is going back to the old ways? That doesn't make sense. Wasn't that why the Mirrors began to break in the first place?"

"Yes."

An uncomfortable silence squeezed itself into the space between them. Bea desperately wanted to ask him if he thought Dionne had anything to do with the so-called empty protagonists; there was something about the way the girl had sat there, smiling at them while they told her what was going to happen to her, that made Bea certain there was a connection.

But she had to remind herself that Mistasinon wasn't her ally. For all his politeness, kindness even, since their argument outside West's office, it didn't change what he'd said, nor the fact that he wanted to disassociate himself from her. And, while he hadn't mentioned her attempt to talk the girl out of the Plot, he'd still heard it. He might fail her on that alone, or worse, report her. He was a suit, he'd said it himself. No, Mistasinon was not her confidante, no matter how much she wanted to unburden herself.

See? She was learning when to keep her mouth shut. Melly would be so impressed.

Bea took another gulp of her beer.

What did an 'empty protagonist' mean, anyway? Dionne had spoken, listened, and decided to be in the story. And yet, Bea couldn't confidently say that she thought Dionne had been behaving normally. The woman in the Academy, the so-called ghost, had seemed to want something, even if that something had been to chase Bea through the corridors and out into the snow. Dionne hadn't seemed to want anything at all, except to be told what to do.

The thought occurred to Bea that if there was a ghost, it certainly wasn't in the Academy.

Next to her, Mistasinon dipped one of his long fingers into his pint of beer, and then tentatively licked it.

"Everything alright?" Bea asked, ashamed of herself for being grateful for the distraction.

"Mmm? Oh, I don't often drink."

"Oh? No drinks with the other blue suits after a long day?"

He took a sip of his pint. "I don't really get on with the other suits. Or they don't get on with me, maybe."

"Oh. Well, what about before you became a Plotter?"

"I wasn't given alcohol then," he said vaguely.

Bea sensed there was a lot more to that statement. She was just trying to decide whether she had the energy to pry when the door to the inn burst open dramatically.

A young man stood in the open doorway, hands on hips, chest puffed out and head held high. He was very handsome, tall and broad-shouldered, with dark eyes and hair. He was also dressed in an extraordinarily fancy get-up. He had a long red cape, one shoulder left rakishly uncovered, green velvet breeches, a white shirt with a blue sash across his chest, knee-high boots, a thick sword belt around his waist, and a wide-brimmed hat with a purple plume. Bea thought he looked like a rooster who had taken psychedelic drugs and then been given access to the fancy-dress box.

"What a cock," she muttered.

"I say," announced the young man to the room, "I'm looking for the castle, but I seem to have become lost."

Bea noticed the locals exchange glances. An old woman, sitting at the table next to theirs, sniggered.

Mistasinon leaned over to her and whispered, his breath warm on her neck, "I think you'll enjoy this."

"What's happening?" she whispered back.

"Just watch."

A smile darted across the barman's face, his teeth flashing white against his black skin. He grabbed a dirty tea towel and started cleaning out one of the empty pint glasses that had been left on the bar, although what he in fact managed to do was smear the old suds around the inside of the glass. Bea looked down at her own beer. Her glass was spotlessly clean.

"Ooo arrr?" said the barman.

One of the patrons started to laugh and turned it into a cough.

"Yes, my good man," the fancy gentleman said, walking over to the bar. "You'll be pleased to know I'm here to kill the fearsome troll who resides there."

"Are ye now?" the barman replied. "Ye durnt wan' t'be abroad thiz night, sayz aye."

Bea shot Mistasinon a confused look. "Why is he talking like that?" she whispered. "He didn't talk like that when we took our rooms."

Grinning, he put his finger to his lips. "Shh. You'll see."

"Oh, there's no need to worry about me," the fancy man said. "I've my faithful steed outside, and of course Silver Wind won't let me down." He patted the sword at his waist. Both it and the belt it was carried in looked suspiciously new.

"Ye arrn't frrom rownd these parrtz, arrrre ye, lad?" the barman asked, spitting in the empty pint glass.

Bea was certain his 'r's were getting longer.

"Indeed, I am not," replied the fancy man, appraising the bar with genteel disdain. "I have travelled many leagues in order to save you all from the troll."

Behind him, Bea noticed one of the regulars silently take down the dartboard and replace it with a ram's skull.

"Ye nay wan' tae go there," piped up the old woman at the table next to Bea and Mistasinon. "Tis doom frae all who do. Dooooom! Dooooooom!"

"Worry not, old crone, I know what I am about," the fancy man said. Though it did appear to Bea that his confidence wobbled a bit when he saw the newly installed wall decoration.

"Ye be an adventurrrrrra, lad?" said the barman.

"What?" asked the fancy man, watching with ill-concealed horror as the barman used the cloth to wipe his spit around the pint glass.

"An adventurrrrra, are ye?"

"Oh, yes. I am here to make my fortune and win fair maid." He looked around the bar proudly, trying again for awed reverence. The couple sitting in the window started making odd gestures at him, waving their hands in bizarre and complicated patterns that were either very mystical or very rude.

"I say, are they feeling quite well?" he asked the barman.

"Darn't mind them, lad, they jurst be warrrnting tae orrrfferrr ye some pr'tection from the evils."

"Oh. Well. Very good. Now, about that castle?"

"Ye everrrr faced a trrrrrrol, my lad?" the barman asked.

"I've heard all the stories," he replied, pulling himself up to his full height. "And my father paid for my fencing lessons."

"Good Lord," muttered a woman across the room, only to be quickly shushed by her friends.

"Ye ma'be wantin' to forrrrrrgo ye hunt, lad, for tiz a terro'bul fate that awaits ye. Ye'd be welcome at yon harth, if'n ye chooziz."

"Certainly not. Now, are you going to tell me the way to the castle or not?" the fancy man snapped at the barman. He could tell things weren't going the way they should, but he didn't quite know why. Everything seemed right—the local inn, the stalwart barkeep, the rude mechanicals. But somehow, now he was actually here, he had the distinct sensation he wasn't the one in control. It was not a feeling he was used to.

"I'll take ye, Sirrah," piped up a young boy. "Cor blimey." The barman shot him a look. "I mean, oooo arrrrrr."

The boy held his hand out.

The fancy man looked down at it.

The whole bar held its breath.

Bea sat forward on the edge of her seat.

"Very well," said the fancy man. He dropped two silver pieces in the boy's outstretched hand. The boy led him out of the bar, turning round to drop a quick bow to the room.

Once the door had shut behind them, the whole bar burst into laughter.

"Drinks on the house," shouted the barman. "*One*, mind you. I won't have a repeat of 'Wolf Hunter Thursday'."

Everyone cheered and barrelled up to the bar for their drinks.

Bea was laughing so hard she was crying. "But what'll happen to him?" she said, wiping her eyes.

"I dare say the boy will lead him around the woods and then drop him off at a local hostel. That'll be another couple of silvers in the local economy."

"So you've seen this happen before?"

Mistasinon sipped his beer. "A few times. I'm pleased you got to see it. I thought it might cheer you up a bit. You know, considering…"

The spectre of Dionne hovered behind their eyes, smiling her horrible, empty smile.

Bea downed the last of her beer. "Do you want another? It's free, apparently."

Mistasinon considered his half-empty glass.

He reached a conclusion.

"Alright. Just one, though."

"Am I alive?" Mistasinon asked, blinking owlishly at the empty glasses in front of him.

"What?"

"Oh. Nothing."

Bea laughed. "You're drunk."

"Am I?"

"Well… how do you feel?"

Mistasinon thought for a moment. "Sad? I think. One of me is sad, but I don't know if that's the right one. I never know which one."

"Er… alright," Bea said. She spun around on the bench, sitting cross-legged so she could face him. "That didn't really make sense, so I think that confirms it. You're drunk—but worse, you're getting existential."

He shifted in his seat, rearranging his long legs, his knees brushing against hers. "Is that serious?"

"It can be. But I know a cure."

"Really?"

"We need to play a game. It's the only way out when the beer gets you all maudlin. Let's play 'guess my age'. Loser drinks."

"Alright. How do you play?"

"I try to guess your age. If I'm right, I win."

"You'll never get it," he warned her, reaching for his drink.

"Aha. A challenge."

He bowed his head. "Go on then."

Bea pursed her lips and looked him over. "Well. Let's see. I reckon you're older than me."

"Why do you think that?"

"Just some of the things you say. I think you're… mmm... two hundred?"

He laughed. "Noooooo."

"Three hundred? No? Older?"

He shook his head.

"You can't be younger," Bea said, incredulous.

"I have been in this body for about a year," he announced happily, taking another mouthful of beer. "So I win?"

"What? No. You're obviously too drunk to understand the rules."
She made a face at him. "Either that or you think I was born
yesterday."

"I know when you were born," he said, waving his finger under
her nose. "I've read your file, remember. You're older'n me.
C'mon. I won. Drink."

Bea rolled her eyes but took a long sip of her beer.

"You should drink two," Mistasinon said, grinning. "Because,
you see, I got your age and you didn't get mine."

"What? No! That's a fix!"

She'd meant it as a joke, but Mistasinon's face fell.

"You don't like playing with me?"

His hair had come loose, and he'd spilt beer down his shirt. His
tawny skin was flushed, and he was staring at her earnestly, his
wide, brown eyes slightly crossed.

Bea shifted a little away, aware suddenly that she was in real
danger from him.

"You're the one who didn't want to be here, not me," she said.

"I didn't mean it like that. I was, I was, I was trying to keep you
away. Safe. I'm a monster. You know it. You said I was the most
pitiless and evil creature ever writ. I remember."

"What are you talking about? I never said that."

"You did. You... I remember." Suddenly he had her hands,
holding them so tightly it hurt. "Everyone knows it, Bea. Everyone
knows. I'm sorry, I'm sorry. I should never have helped you. I
should never have met you."

Bea shook him off. "Go to bed. You're drunk."

Mistasinon opened his mouth and then closed it. He fumbled for
his satchel and tried to stand up. He fell back down on the bench,
landing with a thump.

"Fantastic," Bea muttered. She finished her beer and clambered
to her feet, holding her hand out for him to take. "Come on. I'll
take you to your room."

Mistasinon allowed her to help him up. He leaned on her
shoulders, and she put her arm around his waist. They stumbled,
Bea also not entirely sober. She had no idea how she managed to
get them both up the stairs and to their rooms. The thing about a
drunk Mistasinon, she realised, was that he was all legs.

"Here you are," she said.

"Bea?"

"Yes?"

"Do you ever think you'd like to stop being you?"

"Sometimes. Everybody does."

"Do they?"

"Uh-huh."

Mistasinon gave the idea some consideration. "And, when you're thinking, how do you know who it is thinking for you?"

"Er... I don't know. I suppose it's always me, isn't it?"

"Is it? I'm never sure. Sometimes I think I know, and then sometimes I don't. Maybe I'm all of me, squashed together in my head. Or there's shadow mes inside me, but I don't know if they're *me* me or one of the other mes. I haven't been me for very long, so maybe I'm not me. Maybe I'm a shadow me. Or a shadow of my shadow."

"Well, you're apparently very young," Bea said brightly, trying to lighten the mood so that he would go to bed. There was something about the way he was looking at her that disturbed her in a manner wholly different from the upset she'd felt over Dionne.

But Mistasinon was caught in full flow now, the alcohol loosening his tongue.

"Sometimes the other mes are so loud, and I get lost, and then I come back, but is it me who's come back? I mean, what do I mean?... I mean, where did *I* go when I went?"

"You're here with me."

"No, no, no. That's not... I think I'm disappearing."

Bea stared at him in bewilderment. And then she reached out and squeezed his arm. "Well, I don't know about all that, but you're an interesting drunk." A pause, and then she added, "I've had a nice evening with you, whoever you are."

"Really?"

"Really."

He smiled at her. "Thanks."

"Now go to bed. And drink some water."

Mistasinon went into his room. Bea stood for a moment in the hallway, the memory of his arm under her hand tickling her palm, trying to work out what had just happened. And then she gave up.

259

She would have a long bath, and a—well, a terrible night's sleep, but never mind that.

And tomorrow she would go and see Carol's heroine.

⁂

Bea found the girl's cottage in a secluded part of the forest, exactly where Carol's instructions said she would be.

According to Carol's Plot, the heroine was a Princess, kidnapped by a jealous old crone—an FME, a witch usually, with a fake hump and some make-up—until one day a Prince would find and marry her. It was a simple story, especially for a test. No wonder Chokey had been so annoyed with Carol for complaining about it.

The girl was in the garden, sweeping the paving stones, humming snatches of a tune Bea was certain she'd heard somewhere before. It all seemed quite idyllic, really. Which was why it took Bea a moment to realise what was wrong, and then when she did, she couldn't believe she'd missed it.

Long Plots like this took years to set up. The girl had to be taken when she was very young, in order to properly raise her as a peasant, believing the crone to be her mother. She would then work hard all her life, cleaning and making house, so that when the Prince found her, no one would be in any doubt that she deserved to suddenly find herself responsible for a whole Kingdom's wellbeing. Apparently, it was supposed to be a Happy Ending.

But this Plot had been set up for the test, and the girl in the garden had to be at least eighteen years old.

Bea walked over to her. "Hello," she said once she was in earshot.

The girl looked up, offering her a happy smile.

"hello."

"I think I'm lost. Have you lived here long? Could you tell me the way back to the town?"

"hello," the girl said again. The smile hadn't shifted. Surely she should at least have frowned? Or looked concerned? Or cross, even, at the interruption of her chores by a stranger?

"Um. Is your mother here?"

"my mother lives far away."

Mortal gods, that smile was getting on Bea's nerves.

"You live here alone?"

"a blonde lady with green skin brought me here and told me to wait for the Prince."

Right.

"And none of that struck you as a little… odd?" Bea asked.

The girl smiled at her in answer. She hadn't even stopped sweeping.

"Is anyone here with you?"

Smile, sweep, smile, sweep.

"someday my Prince will come."

Trying not to shudder, Bea left the girl, turning her attention to the cottage. The girl ignored her.

Inside there was… nothing. A mattress on the floor, a few days' worth of food in the kitchen and, Bea was relieved to see, some toilet paper, towels and soap in the bathroom.

And that was it. This wasn't a home, it was a holding cell.

Bea didn't bother saying goodbye to the girl when she left. There didn't seem to be much point.

By the time she got back to the inn, it was late afternoon. She looked around the bar, but there was no sign of Mistasinon. Going upstairs, she knocked on his bedroom door. There was no answer.

She returned to the bar.

"Excuse me, do you know where—"

"He's gone, love," said the barman, not without sympathy.

"How do you know—"

"Tall, skinny fella with the eyebrows? He left this for you and went."

The barman handed Bea a folder.

"Oh. Right. Thanks."

Bea opened the folder. It was her report. Mistasinon had passed her, though she wasn't wholly surprised by that.

What did surprise her was Mistasinon's spidery handwriting, his name scrawled along the bottom.

It was nothing like the notes in the books in his attic room, nothing at all. Which meant someone else had left her those books, someone who knew she needed help. Someone who had access to the Academy, and who wanted her there.

But who? And why? For all and everything, she'd been certain that the only authority who wanted Bea at the Academy was Mistasinon, even if she'd also been certain his motivations stemmed from guilt.

The Academy…

Bea said a word that caused the barman to raise his eyebrows. Mistasinon had left her. West had specifically said that he had to hand her report in, directly to her. And now he wasn't here.

Had he forgotten that part of the deal? Bea supposed it could be true. He must have woken up with a raging hangover, after all.

And yet, as she stood in the taproom, staring at the table they'd shared the night before, she couldn't help wondering if he'd run away from her.

XXXIX

Bea caught herself biting her nails and retied her hair to give her hands something to do. She was in the Plot Department of the General Administration, supposedly in a waiting room. She felt like she was visiting the place where beige came to die.

Everything around her was a muted shade of brown, from the carpet beneath her feet to the paper on the walls. She couldn't even say that it was horrendous. It wasn't inspiring enough for such a big, emotive word.

There were three rows of chairs, six chairs in a row, all thinly upholstered and uncomfortable. For some reason, the person who had designed the seats had decided to put the backrest at just the right height to dig into one's shoulder blades while also, and this was quite a trick, providing absolutely no support at all. It meant she either had to sit forwards on her elbows, or lean back and risk spinal realignment.

Around her, other fae wriggled and fidgeted, also apparently trying to locate the exact position that wouldn't cause them permanent injury.

This was ridiculous. She'd been waiting two hours trying to get in to see Mistasinon, to remind him that he had to return to the Academy with her. But apart from being given a ticket with a depressingly high number on it, nothing had happened. West was expecting her back that evening, with her completed field test and, crucially, Mistasinon along with it.

Perhaps this was a sign. Perhaps, like Mistasinon, she should run away. She'd done it before, hadn't she? When the spectre of her father sitting in his empty space by the fire had simply become too much, and no one would listen to her... not even her brother, who'd always understood her so well, right up the moment when he hadn't.

She looked down at the report, resting in her lap.

She'd come to Ænathlin to prove that a fairy could be something here, to show her brother that he was wrong, and then to rescue him and her mother and her clan from the dangers of life in the Forest. She hadn't come to get involved in conspiracies and GenAm sanctioned murders, nor to find herself mixed up with a strange Plotter with sad eyes.

The trouble with you, she told herself, *is that you never know when to stop pushing, to stop asking questions, to stop assuming everything is wrong.*

The fact that most of the time something *was* wrong wasn't much comfort. She wondered if anyone else ever had the kinds of problems she had, or if it was something about her, specifically. She had a gloomy suspicion it was the latter.

Shaking her head, Bea tucked her report in her bag. Years ago she'd run away, and all that had happened was that she'd taken herself with her. Perhaps she'd be expelled, perhaps she could talk her way out of it—she'd passed the test, after all. There were questions that needed answers, and she clearly wasn't going to find them here. So, she had to go back to the Academy, didn't she?

She was making her way out of the Plot Department when she saw someone she recognised.

"Excuse me! Wait!" she called out, running down the hallway. "You're... um... yes! Godwyve. I remember you—you introduced me to Mistasinon. Could you help me?"

The imp turned, blinking mechanically at her. His face hung slack, his eyes glassy.

"he has not been in the department for almost three weeks if you would like me to i can take a message would you like me to take a message"

Bea stared at the Redacted imp.

He was empty. A shell. A dead thing that was, inexplicably, horrifyingly, still walking and talking.

"what would you like me to do i am happy to help" Godwyve intoned.

Bea continued to stare. Behind her eyes, a mental avalanche had begun. It was moving slowly, but it was gathering speed. And, she knew, soon it would bury her.

"Would you do anything if I asked you to?"

"what would you like me to do"

Bea had to know. She had to know if she was right.

"Pinch yourself."

He did so. There was no question in his expression, no resistance. He just did as she told him to.

"Um. Good. Now… Um. Poke yourself in the eye."

Godwyve raised his finger and brought it sharply towards his eye. Bea was only just able to stop him in time.

"Sorry," she said. She knew it was pointless to apologise, but it made her feel better. "I changed my mind. Um. You'd better get back to work."

She watched the imp walk away from her. He didn't look back, didn't say goodbye. He just returned to whatever it was he'd been doing before she'd called out to him.

Bea ran all the way through the Plot Department, out through the high, bronze doors and past the Redaction Block in the square. She only stopped running when she was in very real danger of collapsing.

She knew what was wrong with Dionne and with Carol's character.

***

Joan settled back against the thick cushions and sighed.

"It's nice not to be working. But I'll have to pick up a new tooth quota tomorrow," she said.

"Joany, you work too hard. I have always said it is so," Delphine replied in her affected Marlaisian accent, shimmying up the bed as she spoke, her brown hair cloudy around her heart-shaped face.

"Ah, well. I don't mind. Anyway, you work harder than I do. I still can't believe how well you're doing. I'm very proud of you."

Delphine shrugged, an action at which she was singularly adept. She had a way about her that managed to convey absolute disinterest and, at the same time, total focus. Joan had never been sure if it was a gift of her tribe or a talent unique to Delphine herself. She was an adhene, a tribe famed for their ability to seduce the unwary. She was also a Raconteur and proprietor of The Golden Claw, one of the most successful dragon's dens in the city.

"Is this so? Let me tell you a story, Joany. Free of charge, of course." Delphine rolled over on the bed, so she could look up at Joan. "Once upon a time, there was an 'orrible, cruel little fairy who stole the heart of another."

"Oh, really?" Joan said, a wry smile on her face.

"Do not interrupt a story, Joany. It's bad luck. An 'orrible, cruel little fairy who stole the heart of another. This fairy took the heart and kept it in a black box. She never took the heart out of the box, not even once. You might wonder why she bothered taking it all, but fairies are very fickle creatures, and their behaviour rarely makes sense."

"Hey!"

Delphine smiled. "I am just the Raconteur, my dear. I do not write the stories. And so, the heart remained locked in a box, and the poor, dear, innocent adhene, from whom the heart had been stolen, was forced to live a half-life. Without her heart, all she could do was work. Luckily, she was also very clever, and so she worked hard and built for herself a wonderful castle."

Joan looked around Delphine's room. It was very well appointed. They were lying on a large bed under a silk canopy, and the floor was littered with expensive, brownie-made clothes. She knew that the other rooms in The Golden Claw were equally plush, though perhaps tidier.

Delphine caught her looking. "Is it not a castle?"

"It's a castle."

"So I may continue? The adhene was very happy in her castle, and she learned to live without her heart. Until one day, the 'orrible fairy returned! Can you imagine such a thing? The 'orrible fairy, we shall call her Jane, returned because she needed the help of the adhene—"

"Doris," Joan said, grinning.

Pulling a face, Delphine continued. "Very well. The adhene, *Doris*, who, despite missing her heart, was still good and kind, gave Jane this help, and Jane disappeared again. Just as you please. And Doris went back to her castle, unknowing if she would ever get her heart back. The end."

"That's not a very Happy Ending. I thought all the love stories had Happy Endings. And anyway, I'm pretty sure that Jane returned a week later, and thanked Doris very thoroughly for all her help."

Delphine twisted one of her curls around her finger, smiling. "So, what do you think the moral is?"

"That adhenes like to exaggerate?"

"It is that anyone can feel inferior, Joany. Even me. Especially when one is missing their heart."

"Ah so?" Joan said, wiggling closer to Delphine. "Well, as luck would have it, I happen to have enough heart for two."

"So perhaps the story is not yet finished, after all?"

Joan put her hands on Delphine's face and kissed her. "Perhaps not."

A knock at the door interrupted Joan's plans.

"*Merde*," Delphine said. She threw a slipper at the door. "Go away—I'm entertaining."

"It's not for you, Mistress. She says she's here to talk to the fairy," came a voice through the door.

Joan jumped off the bed and started grabbing her clothes. "It's probably about last night's meeting," she mumbled as she pulled her shirt over her head. "I'll just be a few minutes."

Waving Joan away, Delphine curled up under the covers. Joan looked at the shape of her for a moment and then went to find out what she was needed for.

Bea was standing in the hallway.

"Sorry, I didn't mean to disturb you, but I can't stay long and I really need help, and your dad said you'd be here, and—"

"Woah, it's alright," Joan said, holding her hands up to stem the flow of Bea's babble. "Follow me. Room four isn't being used at the moment. Delphine's having it redecorated," she added proudly, unable to resist the subtle boast.

"I can't believe you're here," she said, once they were safely inside and the door closed behind them. "I'm sorry I haven't written to you for a while, there's been so much going on. Oh, Bea, it's amazing! People are finally beginning to take us seriously— fairies I mean. It's been hard work, and we've had some trouble. Michael was taken in by the brown suits the other day for causing a disturbance, and all he was doing was handing out pamphlets. Sure, he was doing it inside the Contents Department, but still.

Anyway, we've decided we'll start going door to door, just around the wall to begin with, but maybe, once we've got more support, we can start focusing on the middle and inner circles. Goodness, Bea what is it? You look—"

Bea grabbed her in a tight hug, cutting her off.

"What's all this?" Joan asked, her voice muffled.

"Nothing," Bea replied from above her head. There was a tremor in her voice that made Joan think she might be crying. "I've missed you so much, that's all. It's just hit me."

Joan put her arms around Bea, or as far they would reach, and hugged her back.

They stood there for a while, breathing together.

And then Bea let her go, and Joan took a step back. She waited while Bea wiped her eyes.

"Oh, Joan... I'm sorry. You must think I only come to see you when I'm in a mess."

Joan rolled her eyes. "Course I don't. What's wrong? Is it to do with your Plotter and the dead character?"

Bea stared at her.

"Oh..." Joan said, the look of confusion on Bea's face indicating that she may have just put her foot in it.

"Joan, what do you mean, Mistasinon and the dead character?"

"Well, I'm sorry—he did promise Melly he wouldn't get you involved, but to be honest I didn't really believe him, and, well, you know..." Joan let her sentence drift off.

The two fairies stared at each other.

"I think you'd better tell me what happened," Bea said. "Because if I'm right, things might be even worse than I thought."

XL

Mistasinon pushed the door closed and leaned against it, staring at the circular room. He knew this room better than any other in the whole of the GenAm.

He shouldn't be up here. It was dangerous, and he couldn't honestly say he'd been careful enough to make sure no one had seen him. Julia had spies everywhere. Even if she didn't know he'd come up here, she'd certainly know by now that he was back in Ænathlin.

But where else could he go? This had been his home, once.

He walked over to the Teller's desk. His belongings were still laid out the way he'd liked it, neat and orderly, the edges of the folders aligned perfectly with the edges of the tabletop.

"You were always so in control," Mistasinon said, his voice echoing in the emptiness. "You always knew what was best for everyone."

Reaching out, he brushed his fingertips over the leather surface of the desk. He brought them to his nose and sniffed. The Teller's smell had faded into nothing, lost to time and the stronger scents of leather and wood varnish.

His throat stung. Massaging his neck, he stepped away from the desk and walked over to the Teller's Mirrors, lined up neatly against the wall. He remembered the Teller used to spend hours in front of them, in the early years. He'd watch his Plots being run, carefully noting down any potential changes that might improve the story.

Mistasinon looked at his reflection. He didn't recognise himself outside any more than he did inside.

"How do they manage it?" he asked his reflection.

They don't, they're lonely...

They're free...

No pack. No family. How is that freedom?

"They're used to it."

We're not. We're not like them.
If we die, maybe we can find our way back.
He wouldn't want us. He threw me away.
Only the Teller loved us.
We aren't good enough.
"But who's good and who's bad?"
That's not our decision. You wait to be told.
No, never again. Bite them, kill them, tear them to pieces.
Let me out. You're not one, we're one.
You don't know what you're doing.
Horror when you touched her in the Grand.
She knows what we are.
You revealed us.
Disgusting.
Weak.
Pet.

Mistasinon threw back his head and howled, no longer caring if anyone heard him. He reached for the Mirror, grabbing the frame, wanting, *needing*, to smash his reflection into a thousand pieces.

But when he tried, he couldn't move it.

Several frantic minutes passed, filled with the sound of his efforts to pick up the Mirror until he gave up, exhausted and defeated. Sweat dripping down his face, he crumpled to the floor. And then he spotted it.

The tower didn't have corners, but behind the Teller's desk, shoved up close to the wall, was a large cushion. Mistasinon crawled over to it. When he landed on it, a cloud of dust flew up into the air and floated gently down, landing unnoticed on him.

He lay on his old bed, his chest heaving as he tried to catch his breath.

Dirty, nasty thing, you couldn't even get us home.
Couldn't even do that right.
No wonder he didn't want us.
Monster, beast, and evermore shall be so.
We are what we are. We belong together. Back to the Shadow Land. Back where it makes sense.

He ran his hands over his face. But it wasn't his face, was it? It was a person's face, created for him, woven out of thin air and pasted onto him. It wasn't his face he saw in his reflection. He wasn't anything.

We have to keep our promise.

The Teller Cares About Us.

When Mistasinon had been the Cerberus and the Teller his master, everything had made sense. He'd had the Teller's voice, guiding him. And he'd had his heads, his other *hims*, to shoulder the burden of thought. He'd been a part of something, a family of sorts. A pack.

And then…

The Teller had wished him different. And then the Teller had died, leaving him trapped in this new body with its strange new way of seeing the world, and with no one to make sense of it all for him, no one to tell him what to do.

Mistasinon rolled onto his side, pulling his legs up to his chest and wrapping his arms around his knees.

She said the GenAm's evil. You know it's evil. We've seen evil all our life, we can smell it.

Don't be so weak. Swapping one master for another. Pathetic. The Teller knew what we are, that's why he changed us.

No, the Teller loved us. He loved us. He loved us.

The Teller threw us away, just like the Shadow Master did.

No, the Teller Cares About Us.

Do you really believe that? The Teller did this to us.

Shuddering, Mistasinon tightened his grip on his knees, pulling himself in as small as he could.

The Teller had shown the Cerberus kindness, but he'd also taught him to fear the kindness being taken away. The Teller had taught him a whole new kind of fear, without ever raising his hand to him.

Mistasinon pressed his face into the darkness between his arms and his legs, a desperate, guttural sound filling the silence of the tower. He had no idea it was coming from him.

There was no one telling him what to do, and he didn't know who he was. When he'd lost his other heads… what had been left behind? Which one was he? How did he know if what he was thinking was *his*? Where did he end and they begin?

There was a rock inside him, pulling him downwards, into the shadows. It exhausted him, fighting against the weight of it.

And the thing that hurt him most was how familiar the feeling was.

XLI

" . . . And then I realised what it was that Dionne and the other girl had in common. The GenAm is Redacting the humans, making them into perfect 'characters'."

Joan shook her head, unable to believe it.

"It's the only thing that makes sense," Bea said. "They must have been testing it on the dead girl Melly saw. Seeing how far they could go."

"But why would they do it?"

Bea paused. A hundred thoughts were running through her mind, and she was struggling to keep up with them. She began pacing the room, walking in ever-quickening lines as she caught up with herself.

"Because blood works, if you can get away with it. Blood is *easy*. Everyone believes in blood. Hells, we'd never have changed the stories if we hadn't had to, would we? Now we've found a way to get away with it. I mean, it's genius, really, isn't it?" she added sourly. "Simple is strong. Hah! Damn right it is."

"Bea, slow down. You're not making sense."

She pinched the bridge of her nose. "Sorry… It's all falling into place, but my mouth is moving slower than my thoughts. Alright, so imagine if we could stop the characters from ever going off-Plot. Imagine if we had a way to make sure that the heroine was always quiet and good and waited for her prince to come. Imagine what we could do if there was a way to make the characters submit to us, utterly."

Joan paled. "But that… that's awful… Everyone should have the chance to… I don't know… resist. Of course, the Teller's, *whocaresaboutus*, Plots are the best we've ever had, and I don't want the Mirrors to break," she added quickly, her fear of the GenAm and its informers bred into her. "But still… the characters should at least have the chance to say no if they really don't want to take part."

"But it's us against them, isn't it?" Bea replied. "It's a war, in a way. A war fought in the mind. Ha. A war fought with thoughts. And with Redacted protagonists, we have the ultimate weapon. They don't complain. They don't ask questions. They just follow the Plot. The GenAm could probably even *reuse* them. Marry one hero and then on to the next, no waiting! The Redacted characters wouldn't know any different, I'll bet. They're empty—empty protagonists, just moving through the story."

"I can't believe the GenAm would do such a thing." Joan tugged at her hair. She thought for a moment and then admitted, in a lower voice, "Ah well, maybe I can. But how can Redaction work on the characters? The dead-heads can barely think—if you don't tell them what to do, they just stand around, waiting. A character needs to be able to participate in some way."

"It can't work the same with them as it does with us, that's the only solution. When I was talking to Dionne, she wasn't like the dead-heads here. I mean, there was clearly something wrong with her... But it wasn't as obvious. Dionne was still human enough to seem human. Especially for most of the recruits, who've never even met one before. If I hadn't bumped into Godwyve so soon after seeing her, even I might not have realised what was wrong."

"That sort of makes sense," Joan replied. "After all, they're not the same tribe as us, are they? I mean, I know we're all different tribes, but we're all one tribe as well, really. We all come from here, from the Land. But the characters are from Thaiana. Perhaps Redaction works differently, depending on which world you're from?"

"Exactly. I bet even experienced FMEs wouldn't notice either, not really. They don't think of the humans as anything more than playing pieces."

"You're right," Joan sighed. "I hate to say it, but sometimes I only really think about them as a quota. But wouldn't their family or friends notice there's something wrong with them?"

Bea shook her head. "Think about it. Whoever meets our characters? Half the time they're orphans or step-children, or far away from home with no one who cares about them. We choose them with that in mind, because people like to hear stories about the meek winning out in the end, and because it's easier for us to manage the Plot when no one's really paying attention to the main character—"

"So there're no witnesses," Joan finished for her.

"And it's not like the Redacted humans are ever going to complain or tell anyone what's happened to them. I expect the GenAm started with the heroines because they're the simplest anyway. All they have to do is look pretty and get some hero to rescue them."

Joan looked like she was going to be sick. "But I still can't see how they think they'll get away with it. Even if the characters don't revolt, we will. Redacting characters is dangerous, and it's dark. The things Melly said they did to that dead girl... That's not from the Teller's Plots. That's the kind of stories we used before the Great Redaction. No one here would stand for it, not if they knew."

"Wouldn't they?" Bea asked, adding a generous portion of bitterness to her anger. "Look at Ænathlin. The Mirrors are working, everyone's happy, trade's moving. I dare say, if it was presented in the right way, if the GenAm explained it *just so*, no one here would make a fuss."

"Tooth and nail—wait! Bea, where are you going?"

Bea stood in the doorway, caught in the space between here and there, before and after.

"I'm going to stop it," she said.

***

West closed her eyes, concentrating on the images flickering in her mind. So far, everything had followed her predictions perfectly, but now it was... confused.

She could see the fairy, marching towards the line of Mirrors in their strange, distant city. At the same time, she could see her standing in a clearing, a branch of wood in her hands, ready to attack a bear. And she saw her, younger now, trying to understand where her father had gone and why he wasn't coming back. She saw the fairy and a blue-skinned man, walking through the sand.

She saw Julia, standing in front of the crowds, a large scroll in her hands. The crowd cheering, the scaffold looming ominously behind her. She saw her sitting quietly, pulling the wings off a tompte, while the other children played without her. She saw her carefully disposing of any evidence of their connection to each other, all except the jars of dirty white liquid. And she saw Julia standing in the middle of hundreds of Julias, an army of Julias, stretching to infinity.

She saw Barret, screaming with uncorked rage. She saw him in his youth, sitting on his grandmother's knee as she told him how special he was. She saw him working in the Contents Department, his frustration and resentment growing hard in his belly, a canker poisoning him. She saw who he could have been, and although she knew he wouldn't listen to her, it hurt. It always hurt.

She could see all of them. All the crucial moments, the choices that created their futures, that made them, them.

But she couldn't see *him*.

The Cerberus' future was a thousand scenes, all of them in disarray, like a jigsaw puzzle thrown to the floor. In one, he went to the imp and asked her to be his new master, to tell him what to do. In another, he returned to the Academy, and they met in the basement. In a third, he never got up again.

West opened her eyes and reached for her medicine. As she sipped the dirty white liquid, the images faded, leaving behind only the memory of what she had seen.

Was it the medicine that made it so difficult to see what the Cerberus would do? It allowed her to turn the visions off when she no longer wanted the burden, silencing that part of her mind that had been so cruelly altered. But no, she didn't think it was the medicine. When it wore off, everything came flooding back.

No... It was the Cerberus itself causing the problem.

She knew what had happened to it, of course. That they'd changed it. But it was still the Cerberus, even in its new body.

Three heads, three minds, three futures...

For the first time in years, West didn't know what was going to happen.

It was wonderful.

XLII

Bea returned to the Academy, back to the room where she'd first arrived all those months ago. This time, however, she wasn't nervous or frightened or guilty.

She was angry.

It was late, and most of the other recruits would either be in their rooms or in the common room. That was good. But that also meant that the brown suits would be patrolling, which was less helpful. Bea had an idea about what she was going to do, but she knew that being waylaid by some Content, even Luca, was not part of the plan.

She poked her head outside the door. The corridor was empty. Stepping back, she closed the door and took a deep breath. At least if she was thrown across the room again, there was no one around to hear her.

Pausing to retie her hair, she set her report down on the flagstones and cautiously approached the wooden walls.

She had to get to Mistasinon's attic. She needed to know more about Redaction and what she was getting involved in. No one really understood the process, the GenAm kept the secret under lock and key. Like most of the fae, she'd witnessed the public Redactions in the square outside the GenAm buildings, but she didn't actually *know* anything. The GenAm didn't approve of an informed citizenry.

When someone was Redacted, an Eraser, a small white stone, was placed on their forehead, the words were spoken by the Redactionist, and that was it. Where a moment ago there had been a thinking person, all that was left was an empty shell.

That wasn't enough to go on. Was it the words or the stone that emptied a person? A combination of both? The Redactionists always wore white gloves when carrying out the sentence... Did that mean that if someone simply touched an Eraser, they'd be dead-headed?

F. D. Lee

Bea wasn't going to make the mistake of barging into a situation without any idea what was happening, why or how. Not again.

Her plan was simple. She'd find her way back to Mistasinon's attic and the books there, and see if there was anything in the notes that might help her. Whoever had left them for her clearly wanted her to know more about the GenAm than was allowed in the regulation books and histories, and it might just be the same person who had gone to so much trouble with her tests.

In fact, someone had gone to a lot of effort to keep her at the Academy. Altering her placement test, allowing her to retake her field test, providing her with all those notebooks. Someone wanted her here, and there had to be a reason for it—and the more Bea thought about the 'ghost' and the Redacted women, the more convinced she was they were connected.

Coincidences never happen, not in real life.

The right person doesn't just turn up at exactly the right time. The villain never simply happens to mention how they intend to wipe out the entire village, oh, and incidentally, that big button over there will stop it all from happening, and there's a nice big countdown clock so you know just how much time you have left.

Real life doesn't work like that. In real life, people get hurt. In real life, bad things happen to good people. And in real life, if someone provides you with a score of oh-so-handy notes, detailing subjects and ideas that one wasn't even supposed to think let alone write down, there had to be a reason. And Bea was certain the reason was to help her stop what was happening.

The hitch was, she needed to get to Mistasinon's attic without getting lost on the way, and the only way she could think of doing that was by asking the walls. The walls which, last time she'd touched them, had thrown her through the air with the violence of their screaming.

Her hand fluttered to her sword point necklace. She fingered the point, trying to believe that she'd been brave when she'd thrown the sword at the ogre, and not terrified and hurt and full to the eye-teeth with panic.

That she'd saved some people, even if she'd let others get hurt.

The necklace was cool, highlighting the sweaty clamminess her hands. Try as she might, it didn't make her feel like a hero. If

278

anything, it made her even more acutely aware of the fact she was just a garden fairy from the Sheltering Forest, lost and out of her depth...

And yet, here she was, and she had to do something.

Rolling up the sleeves of her grey dress, Bea walked up to the wooden panels, took a deep breath, and pressed her hands to the wood.

Somewhere dark, with weeds growing through the stone...

Fear and anger and the realisation that she would never be found, that she would never see her husband, her child, her friends, her parents, ever again...

Bargaining, but the creature didn't listen...

Praying, but God didn't hear...

Walking down long corridors, yellow scaled hands pushing open a door...

Standing on the landing, looking out of the window...

Crying in the night...

So far from home...

Bea bit her lip so hard it hurt and pushed past the frantic, disjointed emotions the wall was giving her.

Up the stairs...

So alone...

Left, and then right...

Tears...

Left...

Cut away...

Chopped down...

Right...

Up...

Death, but not dead...

Up...

Please...

Left...

Empty...

The attic.

Bea pulled her hands away from the wall and stood, chest heaving. Absently, she wiped her hand across her mouth, and then wiped her black blood on her dress. She picked up her report and turned to face the wall again.

"I'm sorry," she whispered.

And then she left the mirror room and made her way to Mistasinon's attic.

West opened the door to Barret's room.

He looked up at her, startled. She'd never been to his room before—he hadn't even realised she knew where it was.

"My Lady?"

"She's here," West said. "The fairy has returned."

Barret looked at West, so small, so delicate. How could this be happening? With the return of the fairy and her blue-suited freak, he knew that everything would change. West would leave him. She'd cast him aside. All because some stupid fairy didn't know how to sit in a classroom and follow the rules.

He knew what they wanted to do: they were trying to take West away from him, to send him back to the Contents Department. Perhaps they'd found out about the ETPs? They wanted the glory for themselves; no doubt they'd devised the whole plan from their bed, after who knows what filthy activities.

He should have left the fairy to die—he would have done if he'd known what would happen. He'd only saved her so that West would avoid any unwanted attention from the GenAm.

If it were just the fairy, maybe he could have done something. Stopped her taking West away from him. But he couldn't do anything about a Plotter. Plotters were high ranking workers in the GenAm, and he was, technically at least, only a brown suit. He'd never get away with it.

"Would you like me to bring her to you?" Barret asked sullenly.

"You go to her," West replied. "I know you go, so go. She's in the same attic room."

And then, so quietly Barret wasn't even sure he'd heard it, she added, "Left, Barret. Like you promised."

XLIII

Bea arrived in the attic. Putting down her report, she went over to the bookshelves and grabbed a handful of books.

She took them over to the desk and settled down to read. Neat, elegant writing filled the margins, written with long lines and flourishes. Page after page, she skimmed through the notes, looking for anything that might give her some clue about the empty protagonists, or how Redaction worked.

Nothing. She grabbed another book, leaning over it, her eyes darting across the page.

Behind her, the door opened, but she didn't hear it.

Licking her finger, she turned the page and read on. There was so much information, but, maddeningly, also so little. Scores of notes detailed the GenAm, how things fitted together, comments on the official Plots—how to run them, what could be changed, potential outcomes if such and such were amended—but nothing useful on Redaction.

Closing that book, she grabbed another from the pile, missing the faint rustle of papers behind her, from the other end of the room.

She skimmed through another two books, checking the contents pages, scanning the margins, searching for anything that might be worth a closer look. She was conscious of the time. West would be waiting for Mistasinon to hand in her report. Would she be sent home if he didn't? Could she risk it? But how much longer could she spend here in the attic, either way?

Again, the current book provided nothing. It was as if whoever had written these notes had studied every aspect of the GenAm except Redaction. It was just so bloody *typical*, wasn't it? Pages and pages of notes on heroes, heroines and story points, on the advantages and disadvantages of different plots, on the GenAm and how the four Departments worked, but nothing on what Bea actually needed to know.

Frustrated, she ran her hands through her hair, tugging it free from its bun. Swearing, she leaned down to pick up her hair tie.

A shadow fell across her.

She looked up.

Looming above her was the troll who guarded West, a strange expression on his face.

"Oh. Um. Hi," she said, swallowing. "I was just... um..." What in the five hells could she say she was doing? "I was doing some extra work. Um. Because I missed so many classes. I've been ill."

The troll's dark eyes narrowed.

"Was it you who rescued me?" she continued. "I meant to say thank you, but I haven't had a chance. Um. Thank you. You saved my life."

This didn't have the effect on the troll she'd hoped it would. If anything, it seemed to annoy him.

"I should have said it before, but West and Mistasinon were there, and it didn't seem like a good moment," Bea babbled on, lamely. Something wasn't right, but she couldn't put her finger on it. Sure, she was out of her room and that was bad, but the troll looked like he was holding onto his temper by the tips of his fingers.

She stood up, hairband forgotten. "Um. Well. I guess I'd better be getting back to my room."

Barret pulled her report out of his jacket and flipped it open, his eyes never leaving her face. He must have picked it up from the bookshelf where she'd left it.

"Says here you've 'worked exceptionally hard'", he said. "That you've 'more than proven your capacity to be a Fiction Management Executive'. That the GenAm would be 'lucky to have you'."

"Er... yes. I've read it. Oh. Are you here to collect it? I know West wanted to see Mistasinon again, but—"

The troll slammed the report onto the desk, crumpling it under his enormous hand as if he wanted to smear it into the wood. What was going on? Sure, she knew he didn't like her. There were hundreds, thousands, of fairy-haters in Ænathlin, but this was different. There was something *hungry* in the blackness of his eyes.

"You don't know anything about what West wants," Barret growled.

Bea slid around the chair, so it was standing between them. Her heart was beating like an overwound clock, racing through the seconds.

"But she said that Mistasinon had to bring the report back to her personally," she said, "And I know he's not here. I don't know why he isn't here, but, I mean, the report's signed, so I don't think it should matter if he's not."

"Your Plotter isn't here?"

"Er. No. But I am, and my report—"

Barret released a great, guttural roar, his dark eyes gleaming, and lunged at her.

Bea jumped backwards, his fists barely missing her, and collided into the wall, banging her head and shoulders on the low eaves.

The chair that moments ago she'd been sitting on lay in pieces on the floor.

"What in the five hells!" Bea yelled, clinging to the wall. "Have you lost your mind?"

"I know what you're trying to do," Barret said, picking up a piece of the broken chair, testing its weight. "You're trying to steal it from me. West and the ETPs. All our work."

"I have no idea what you're talking about. You've made a mistake."

Barret snorted. He dropped the piece of chair he was holding and reached for a leg, which was much heavier and more solid.

"Listen, I'm sure we can work this out, whatever it is," Bea said as she sidled along the wall, trying to put the desk between herself and Barret. "I'm not trying to steal anything. I don't even know what an ETP is.... *Oh.*"

Suddenly, the penny dropped. And with it, Bea realised she was in very real danger. "ETP... Emp-Tee Protagonist. It's you. You and West. You're Redacting the women."

Barret gave the chair leg an experimental swing.

"We're saving the city. We're heroes," he said, apparently satisfied with his new toy. "I know your type. You pretend you're helpless and pathetic, but you're not. You worm your way in, under the covers, and cast your spell. But you can't fool me.

F. D. Lee

Entitled little cabbage fairy, expecting everything to be handed to you. I won't let you ruin West's work—*our* work. We were fine until you came here, dragging your weird-faced Plotter behind you. Now she's confused, and it's your fault."

While he spoke, Bea had managed to get behind the desk. Barret stood on the opposite side, hefting the chair leg.

"You think you're special, don't you?" he asked. If it wasn't for the murderous gleam in his black eyes, he would have almost seemed calm—serene.

"No, no. Honestly. Nothing special about me," Bea replied, frantically trying to work out how to escape.

"Damn right."

He swung the chair leg at her, putting all his trollish strength into it.

Bea ducked, feeling the *whoosh* as it passed just inches above her head.

"You can't murder me!"

Barret grinned. "You know what? I think I can."

Horrified, she realised he was right. And she knew from the way he smiled at her that he'd seen it in her expression.

"Fine, but you're not allowed to!" she snapped, her mind, riddled with panic, only throwing up semantics. "Someone will find out!"

"You really think so? Your Plotter isn't here. All I need to do is dump your body in the woods. It'd be easy: 'Stupid fairy, did it before, wouldn't listen, such a tragedy'. Blah, blah, blah."

And, still grinning, he swung the chair leg again.

Bea threw herself forwards, sliding under the chair leg and across the table, landing badly on the other side. She scrambled to her feet and ran for the door, heart racing.

She made it into the hallway before she felt his hands on her hair, tugging her backwards.

"What lovely long hair you have," Barret crowed from behind her. "All the better to catch you with."

Flashing white spots filled Bea's vision, pain tearing through her synapses, leaving stinging electric shocks behind it. The back of her head was beyond agony, entering some new and uncharted land where pain was heavy and hard and sizzling, and still the troll pulled at her, dragging her to him by her grey-green hair.

284

"Tell me, does your Plotter like your hair long? Is it part of his fetish?" Barret hissed in her ear, her hair bundled tight in his fist. "Did you set him up to seduce West, or was it his idea? You're disgusting, both of you. West would never see it, but I do. I see what you're trying to do."

Sickness filled Bea's stomach, roiling nausea and pin-sharp pain defining her. Barret's breath was hot and sour, the hate inside him congealing on his tongue. Reaching up behind her head, she tried to pry his hands from her hair.

But it was no use. He was too strong.

"You'll never get West," Barret whispered. "You'll never have her. She's mine."

Something cold brushed against Bea's wrist. For a moment she didn't register it, didn't understand what it was. And then it clicked.

Frantically she fumbled at the base of her neck. Barret's large, calloused hands landed on her shoulders, a creature from her nightmares. He spun her around, pulling his fist back to deliver the killing blow—

Bea sprang at him, the point of her necklace held tightly between her fore- and middle fingers, her thumb braced against the flat base.

She aimed for the most obvious part of him, a dark target near the centre of his face.

There was a moment of resistance, and then a soft acquiescence.

Barret screamed, shoving Bea away from him. The sword point necklace exited his eye with a sickening 'pop' and went flying into the shadows.

Bea tumbled and staggered, crashing into the wall.

Barret stood in front of her, his hand over his eye, a thick, clear liquid oozing between his fingers, down his face.

Neither moved, both of them trying to catch their breath, trying to rise above the wailing agony the other had inflicted.

And then Barret sidled, cautiously, around her. Bea mirrored him, trying to keep him in front of her.

It was only once they came to a stop that she realised what had happened. Barret was now blocking the staircase down from the attic.

How could she be so stupid? Even half blind and in obvious pain, Barret was a better, nastier fighter than she was.

Bea backed up, her mind awash with renewed panic. She felt something hard in the small of her back. The window. She was standing in front of the window that looked down onto the assembly hall. She glanced at the staircase, but knew the minute she made a move towards it, Barret would have her again.

So, the question was: guaranteed death here or probable death out there…?

"Why are you doing this?" Bea panted, trying to concentrate on her plan and not the searing agony at the back of her skull. She didn't expect an answer, but she needed to say something to distract him. "It seems like a lot of hard work, that's all I'm saying."

Reaching behind her, she fiddled with the window latch. The pain in her head was easing from a burning white fury to a wave of molten red anger.

"I'm sure West wouldn't like it," she continued, praying to the mortal gods she didn't believe in that she could keep him still and talking long enough.

Barret grunted, his hand still covering his ruined eye. "You don't know what West wants. You don't know anything. Fairy brains are smaller than normal brains."

"Oh, right. Yes, silly me," Bea replied. "I knew that one, too. Didn't even need to revise it. We learn it when we're young."

Her hands were shaking, and the window latch was old and sticky. She couldn't do it. She couldn't get it open. She was going to die, he was going kill her—and then the latch gave way, and the window shifted slightly as the pressure was lifted from it.

Pressing her hand against the glass, she pushed as hard as she could, working it like a loose tooth.

"You know, there's nothing going on between me and Mistasinon," she continued, desperately trying to keep him focused on her words, not on what she was doing. The tension in the window eased, a tiny change in the world that was, at the moment, as significant as the birth of a star.

"Liar. How else would one of you have made it into the Academy?"

"Hah. Yes, right. Well, I'm sorry to shatter your world view, but I haven't slept with him. And even if I had, it wouldn't make any difference. You'd still be just another fairy hater. An idiotic, closed-minded, old fairy hater—and I bet West knows it too."

Behind her, the window flung open.

Bea spat at Barret's feet. "I bet that's why she'd rather work with Mistasinon than with you."

Screaming, he launched himself at her.

Lifting herself up, Bea scrambled through the window, onto the ledge.

The cold hit her, but the wind did not. This side of the building was partially sheltered from the storm by the other wings. Not that it meant she wouldn't freeze to death, of course. She skirted along the ledge, away from the open window.

Barret's head and shoulders appeared through the window, his left eye screwed shut, a crusty shell already forming in his eyelashes, glueing it closed. He struggled and then screamed in rage. He disappeared back into the Academy.

He was too big! He couldn't fit through! She was safe! All she needed to do was continue edging her way along the ledge, find another way into the Academy, and once she was inside, she could find Luca or Chokey or Hemmings or *someone* and—

The window smashed into a thousand shards of glass.

Barret's bloodied fist pulled back inside.

Bea didn't waste time swearing. Head ducked, she kept moving down the ledge.

Behind her, the wall shuddered as Barret flung himself against it. The stone, old and unmaintained, started to crumble, dust and debris disappearing into the snow. Another almighty thump and the stone began to shift around the broken window frame. Another, and the brickwork began to fall away.

A distant crash, somewhere far below, marked the moment the old stone window frame fell through the glass ceiling of the assembly hall.

Barret pulled himself through the broken window, testing his weight on the ledge.

All in all, Bea's plan, flawed as it had been, was now completely useless. Clearly, Barret's determination to murder her was greater than whatever pain he felt from his eye or even from smashing a window out of its frame. But then, trolls were strong, weren't they? And their tribal talent was working stone…

Now he was on the ledge as well. How long did she have? He was hesitant, the ledge narrow and the stone crumbling under his immense size. But he was making his way towards her.

I'm going to die, I'm going to die, I'm going to die….

Ignoring the terrifying sight of the troll moving towards her, Bea reached another window. Hands shaking with cold and fear, she fumbled with the glass, trying to find a way to get it open. It was useless—the window was locked from the inside.

Stupid, stupid, stupid.

Barret shouted something, which the storm mercifully whipped away.

Bea looked down, but all she could see was the glass ceiling of the assembly room, too far below to risk jumping.

Her heart was beating in her throat, her fingers already turning white as the cold seeped in.

She couldn't go back, and she couldn't go down.

Up then.

Maybe… maybe… she could get in through the other window, on the opposite side. Maybe it wouldn't be locked… Maybe the mortal gods would finally do something to help her…

Of course, that meant climbing over the pointed roof, right into the storm.

Bea squinted up. The clouds above the Academy were black, bulbous cysts, infecting the sky, spewing snow. She started climbing up the roof, while behind her she heard what had to be the sound of Barret, following her up the shingles. Terror racked her, stabbing like needles.

Exhausted, she reached the arched roof. No longer protected by the walls of the Academy, the wind caught her, easily shifting her weight. She tumbled, skidding and bouncing across the tiles, the hard edge of the ridge pummelling her ribs and arms as she sought for purchase. Frantically she flailed, trying to find something to hold on to, something that might stop her being blown away.

A chimney saved her, though not gently. She slammed into it, knocking the breath from her lungs.

Against the black and purple sky, the snow spiralling around her, stinging her eyes and burning her skin, she saw Barret crest the top of the roof.

He was huge, a dark shadow of lumbering intent. The cold had no effect on him, only the force of the wind pounding his mountainous frame, caused him to slow down, hunkering as low as his bulk allowed him.

Bea pressed her back into the chimney. There was nowhere she could go. She inched up onto her feet, using the bricks to help her keep her balance.

She was too exposed, the cold reaching under her dress, pressing against her skin in unwanted and unwelcome ways. Her right leg, covered in scars, began to seize.

Barret drew closer, the wind harassing him as surely as it had Bea, his long brown coat streaming, his expression malformed, his remaining eye shining with hate.

Bea glanced to her right. The Academy was down there. And to her left, then, the woods. Could she do anything? Could she get back down to the open window? Could she—

Hunched over, struggling against the force of the storm, Barret charged at her.

Bea was leaning on her left leg, her wounded right leg protesting too much to take her full weight.

But to Barret, it seemed like she was preparing to jump right, towards the woods. He adjusted accordingly, shifting his trajectory to the right as he lunged at her.

Bea did the only thing she could think of. She dived left, towards the Academy, sliding and slipping down the roof, grasping for purchase, pressing her body against the icy tiles, scraping her hands on the rough shingle as she tried to slow her fall.

She landed against the gutter on her heels, sending shocks of pain up her legs.

For a moment, she was still.

And then her scarred leg gave out, and she tumbled over the edge off the roof, falling, falling, falling.

She hit the glass ceiling, smashing it as she crashed through.

Barret struggled to halt his charge, pulling himself up short to avoid slamming into the chimney breast. The wind seized its opportunity gleefully, grabbing him and hurling him from the roof.

Whether it was his size that stopped him finding purchase, or if it was the strength of the wind that dragged him from the roof, he would never know.

He tumbled and bounced; the storm batting him to and fro like a rag doll. For one brief moment, he was in the air, stretching out his fingers to grasp the shallow guttering of the Academy, floating in dead space, in dead time, in dead hope.

And then the world righted itself, and he fell, disappearing into the darkness.

XLIV

West sat, drinking her medicine, waiting.

In the room above her, the ETPs rustled around in their cell, occasionally singing snatches of song. It was quite pleasant, in a way.

She still hadn't worked out how to stop them singing, but now she thought she might leave the feature in. She'd managed to reduce it so that the ETPs weren't singing constantly. It shouldn't get in the way of the Plots that were so important to all these Gods and monsters.

No, let them have their snatches of song. It kept them calm, and it didn't hurt anyone.

Besides, West knew the song they were trying to find, the rhythm they could no longer hear, though they'd never known, when they were full, that it had been there.

She knew all about the rhythm, the beat, the song that joined all things together.

She took another sip of the chalky, dirty white liquid. She had no idea what the time was. She was just drinking it now, finishing one bottle and starting on another, a constant chain of self-medication.

Everything was laid out. She'd even cleaned the chair.

If he came to her, she'd be ready.

The GenAm banners saved Bea.

The wind, for once allowed access into the building via the hole caused by the falling masonry, was rushing around the assembly room, overexcited by its newfound freedom. It blew the banners across the open space, and Bea, her brain working on some ancient survival skill, reached out for one as she fell.

Her weight pulled it down, but it broke the momentum of her fall.

291

She lay on one of the dining tables, her chest heaving, her body bruised, bleeding and aching, swathed in the red GenAm banner.

But she was alive.

Pulling herself up on unsteady legs, Bea half walked, half hobbled, out of the assembly room. She was dazed and dumb, her mind empty. Whether by unconscious design or luck, she found a bathroom, and, stumbling into the nearest stall, was thoroughly sick.

Once she'd finished vomiting, she sat for a moment, her head resting against the cubicle wall. Her whole body hurt, but not nearly so much as her soul.

For a moment, she considered not getting up again. She could sit, hidden in the toilet stall, and perhaps no one would ever find her. Was Barret right—would nobody miss her if she just disappeared?

She had no idea whether the troll was still looking for her. She didn't even really understand why he'd attacked her in the first place. But he had... and he'd also unwittingly told her who was behind the empty protagonists.

West.

And she was the only one who knew, wasn't she?

Sighing, Bea pulled herself to her feet, left the stall and went over to the nearest sink, washing off the blood and grime from the roof. The hot water against her hands and face revived her somewhat, though not as much as a glass of wine and two weeks sleeping in a comfortable bed would have done.

She stared at her reflection. Amazingly, her face had escaped the attack with only a tiny graze across her cheek. Her hands and legs weren't so lucky, having taken the brunt of her fall, and the back of her head felt like it was being used as a drum by a particularly enthusiastic octopus. Nevertheless, she basically looked exactly the same as she had half an hour ago.

It struck her as intolerably unfair, considering. If she was going to be attacked on a rooftop during a storm by a gods damn troll and then nearly fall to her death through a glass ceiling, she rather thought she ought to at least have something to show for it. She'd even lost her necklace.

You've got to confront West, she told herself.

Yes, she replied, *but first I want some painkillers.*

She had some birch leaf and devil's claw in her bag—one of them would work, and if not, she'd take both. So decided, she left the bathroom and snuck back to her room. When she got back, she found Hemmings sitting on her bed, staring out of the window.

"The light's back," he said.

Bea frowned, muddled. "What light?"

"The one you said to Chokey you saw. Come, look."

Hemmings patted Bea's mattress, inviting her onto her own bed.

Bea stood for a moment in the doorway, too exhausted to move. And then she joined him at the window. The view was murky, the snowfall making it hard to see anything beyond the dark haze of the woods in the distance.

"Look, there," Hemmings said, pressing his fingers to the glass.

Sure enough, dancing in and out of existence between the snow flurry, was the light. For reasons Bea couldn't explain, she was certain it had been turned on for her so that she could find it. Perhaps Barret had damaged her head more seriously than she thought.

"When Chokey told me about it," Hemmings said, "I have to say, I did wonder. I've been watching for it. The last few weeks, since you had your accident, it's been there almost constantly. I don't think anyone else has seen it. They don't think to look," he added primly.

"What do you think it is?" he asked.

She said, "There's something in the woodshed."

Hemmings peered out, through the snow, at the flickering light.

"What an eerie feeling."

"Darlings!"

They both jumped.

Chokey stood in the doorway, a bag in her hand. She bounded over to them and landed heavily on the bed. "What's going on?"

"Buttercup's light's back," Hemmings informed her. "Look."

Bea busied herself making a herbal infusion with her painkilling plants while Chokey cosied up next to Hemmings at the window. She was just sipping her drink when the dwarf squealed with shock, having obviously caught sight of the light.

"Gosh! I must say, I thought it was just your imagination, Buttercup," she announced, turning away from the window, the mysterious light apparently not holding her interest as much as it did Bea or Hemmings.

"You won't believe what happened while you were on your test—how did that go, darling?—anyway, while you were away, I heard the most amazing thing from Harker. That witchlein brown suit, the one you dislike so terribly, you remember? Well, apparently, there was an accident last night, and he died. Can you imagine?"

There was a crash.

Bea looked down and realised she'd dropped her cup, the dregs of her drink spreading out across the flagstones, seeping into the cracks.

"What? Luca? What do you mean, he died?"

"Goodness, Buttercup, what has got into you? I thought you hated the witchlein?" Chokey said, bending down to pick up the pieces of Bea's shattered cup. "I don't really know what happened. He was wandering around the wings, you know, doing whatever it is the brown suits do, and he had an accident with his lamp."

Bea's arms dropped to her sides, lifeless. She stared at Chokey, not seeing her, her eyes stinging.

She hadn't known him well, but she'd liked Luca. He'd been kind and friendly. She rubbed her right leg, fancying she could feel the scars through the material of her dress.

The tears came. She didn't try to stop them.

"Oh," Chokey said, watching Bea's expression melted. "I'm sorry, Buttercup. I thought you didn't like him."

Hemmings put his arm around her, squeezing her tight. "You know, I've always thought that, after one dies they become what they were before they were born."

"Thanks," Bea sniffed.

Chokey carefully deposited the pieces of Bea's cup in the rubbish bin and grabbed her bag. "Come on, Hemmings. Let's go and... um... Give Buttercup some time alone."

Giving Bea one final squeeze, he and Chokey went into the bathroom, closing the door behind them. A moment later there was the click of the lock.

Wiping her eyes, Bea collapsed onto her bed, looking out the window. The light flickered on and off at irregular intervals, but for once, she wasn't paying it any attention.

Out there somewhere, beyond the snow, was the whole of Thaiana. It felt to her as if the human world was a dream, and all that truly existed was the dark, wooden walls and cold stone floors of the Academy, and the snow, and the wind.

Sindy, her first-ever heroine, was out there somewhere. No doubt she was working hard for someone else's betterment. Bea imagined her sitting with Will, her husband, laughing and joking about something that had happened that day. Or perhaps she was in the town square, working with the people of Llanotterly to help the refugees. Sindy was good at medicine, so good she'd even saved Bea's life once. Bea hoped that wherever she was, whatever she was doing, she was happy.

She also thought about Ana, Sindy's sister, who was working for the King now. She couldn't suppress a smile, in spite of her sadness. She had never in her life met anyone as self-righteous, heavy-handed and ultimately good as Ana. Even if she was a massive pain in the arse.

Pressing her face up against the cold glass, her thoughts stumbled from Ana to King John. He had suffered so much as a result of her Plot, his spine broken by the ogre the GenAm had sent, and he hadn't even made it into the final version, as far as she knew. The story had erased him, as the snow outside blanked out the world.

No matter that John had been brave, or that he'd been trying to do his best for his people. He hadn't fallen in love with the girl, hadn't done what he was supposed to do. Instead, he'd worked tirelessly and without thanks or appreciation to try to solve the problems of his Kingdom. But an unmarried, disabled King wasn't a 'happy ending', not according to the GenAm.

Luca's dead.

She hadn't known him well… but she'd known him well enough to care that he was gone. He probably had family and friends… People who, like her, would feel his absence in their lives, only more keenly, more sharply. A black hole had opened in their world, sucking up a possible future, leaving nothing behind but memories.

She knew what that felt like, and she wouldn't wish it on anybody.

Bea pulled her forehead away from the window. The snow hit the glass, melting as it landed, leaving behind trails of soft tears, falling in disjointed patterns, bleeding into each other in unpredictable ways.

Next came thoughts of her family, far away on another world, lost to another time. Her mother and her brother, presumably still wandering the Sheltering Forest with the clan. Time ran not so differently in Thaiana as in the Land, and as night was falling here, Bea knew it would be falling there.

When she was a child, before her father had vanished and she'd felt what it was to lose someone and know she would never, ever get them back, they had often sat together around a campfire, her brother on her father's knee, and her with her head resting on her mother's lap. The clan had told stories.

Not Plots, the cheap tales created to harvest easy belief from the humans. They'd told their own stories, the fairy stories. Stories about their clan and their history. Stories about running from orc and gnarl attacks. Stories about how people met and how people left. Stories about births and deaths.

Stories about stories about stories. All falling, individual snowflakes building up, amassing into a great storm in Bea's heart.

She knew that she couldn't have done anything. She couldn't have stopped John from losing the use of his legs. She couldn't have stopped Luca burning to death. She couldn't have prevented her father going out that day.

Her heart hardened.

But she could stop what was happening now.

It was time to let old ghosts go and live in the present.

Gathering up her cloak, Bea went to the door. She would have to ask the wood again to tell her where to go, not an experience she really wanted given the dull throb that still echoed at the back of her head, but needs must. For a moment she considered leaving a note for Chokey and Hemmings. But no, they were better off out of it, doing whatever the hells it was they were doing in the bathroom.

Bea pulled the door open.

Mistasinon stared at her, his hand raised, about to knock.

The ghost wandered through the hidden passageways of the Academy.

Whatever Isabella had been before that first, failed Redaction, she wasn't anymore. She was half-formed; alive, technically, but empty. Awake but dreaming. There, but not.

Now she was the original ETP; a ghost made of flesh and bone, a shadow of what she had once been.

And so the ghost of Isabella wandered the secret corridors, scattered thoughts spiralling through her fractured mind. Things were missing that should be there… Things were there that should be missing…

She had a vague memory of a man, warm hands on her hips, and of someone laughing.

There was a hole inside her mind where her heartbeat was supposed to be. No. That wasn't right. No, no, no, something else. Something else.

She was alive…

A shop, opening day, and everyone was clapping. She was wearing her golden dress, and he was so proud of her.

It hurt like a rotten tooth, the decay burying its way into her, sharp trails of white pain burning in its wake.

She was alive…

Where were the drums? Where had the music gone? It was so silent. How had she never noticed the music before, how had she never noticed it playing in her mind, playing in her soul? The drums, the rhythm, gone.

She was alive…

Pain, God, so much pain, but then a cry, the same cry that had been heard after the pain since the dawn of time, and then so, so much love.

Tears fell from the ghost of Isabella's eyes. They went unnoticed, unwiped.

Red blood ran in thick red streams from the cuts on her knees and hands. It went unnoticed, unwiped.

She was alive…

The voice, deep and husky, the voice that told her it would all go away, that told her someday her Prince would come, that told her she was happy.

A face, exhausted, shiny with sweat and tears, holding up her baby, showing her what they had created.

She was alive…

The voice again, telling her to leave, to find her godmother, to find her happy ever after. The dark-haired woman, with the dark eyes and the dark soul. The one who had done this to her, who had stolen her from herself.

She was alive…

And the ghost of Isabella was going to find her, and she was going to kill her.

XLV

Mistasinon didn't fall. He crumpled.

Bea found herself with him in her arms. She had no idea what had happened, why he'd disappeared or reappeared. She didn't ask. She just put her arms around him, stroking his back while he shivered, his chin resting on the top of her head.

After a few moments, she led him over to her bed. She sat and he lay next to her, curled up small, his arms around his knees, his body shaking. Not sure what else to do, she ran her hand up and down his side.

Time drifted over them.

The shivering stopped. Mistasinon pulled himself up, wiping his hands over his face.

"Hi," he said. He didn't merely look sheepish; a whole flock had taken up residence in his expression.

"Hi," she replied.

"Sorry."

"That's alright. It's been one of those kinds of days, apparently."

Mistasinon looked around him as if he hadn't realised where he was. He stood up and rubbed his neck. A thought seemed to occur to him.

"Did you get your report? You passed."

Bea laughed. It wasn't funny, not really, but she couldn't have stopped the laughter even if she'd wanted to. "Yes," she said, "I did. I don't think I'll be staying on, though."

"Ah?"

"No. I'm not sure being a godmother is right for me, after all."

"Ah. Well, no. Maybe not." He cleared his throat and glanced at the door, his hands drumming against his legs. "Well... I have something I need to do. Um. So... Yes. Well, goodbye, Bea."

"Why did you run away from the inn?"

Mistasinon looked at her, his face a mask of panic.

"I'm not angry," Bea said. "Well, no, I am. But there are other things I'm angrier about. I'd just rather know. Is it because of the rumours?"

"What rumours?"

"About us. Our relationship."

He seemed confused for a moment, and then the penny dropped. He blushed crimson but shook his head. "No, no. That's not why I left. I had to... I had to think, that's all."

"About the dead girl Melly told you about?"

She almost felt sorry for him. The conversation clearly wasn't going his way, judging from his floundering.

"I don't know what you mean," he tried.

Bea crossed her arms. "Yes you do. And you're here now because the GenAm is Redacting humans."

"What?"

"The humans—the characters. They're being Redacted, that's what's wrong with them. Don't tell me you don't know."

Mistasinon flopped down on Chokey's bed. "I... no. I didn't know. Honestly—I swear I didn't know. I knew something was wrong, but... How did you find out?"

Bea scrutinised him. If he was lying, it was an expert performance. She supposed she ought to assume he was lying, all things considered. But when she examined herself, she realised she didn't.

So she explained to him what had happened after he'd left her in the village inn, only omitting her conversation with Joan, not wanting to risk her friend's safety along with her own.

"...But why are you here, then?" she finished. "Not to hand in my report, like you promised," she couldn't help adding sourly. Perhaps things weren't quite as resolved between them as she was trying to pretend they were.

"Oh. No. Sorry," he answered, at least having the decency to look guilty. "There was a bottle in Dionne's room. It smelled—I mean, you know, it seemed strange. I realised I'd, um, I'd seen it before. On West. That is, *in* West's office. So I came here. I didn't mean to get you involved," he added quickly.

"It's fine," Bea sighed. "I got myself involved—despite popular opinion, I don't need your help. At least, not when it comes to getting myself into the middle of GenAm messes. Mind you, if I find out you've been lying to me about *anything*, I won't be held responsible for what happens to you."

There was a flicker of something in his eyes, but he nodded his head. "Understood."

"Right. Good. West has been Redacting humans, and I intended to stop her. So, are you going to help me?"

Mistasinon rubbed his neck.

Bea waited.

And then he said, "I don't know."

She opened her mouth to reply when the door to the bathroom burst open, and Chokey and Hemmings came crashing into the room. It was the kind of entrance that suggested they'd been pressed up against it, listening in. And sure enough, when Bea looked, she saw that the cheap lock was hanging, broken, from the door.

She'd completely forgotten they were in there.

Hemmings helped his sister to her feet.

Bea wondered what on Thaiana she was going to say to them, or what they were going to say to her, when something caught her eye.

"Hemmings, what is that in your hair?"

The elf turned his head left and right, shyly. He had two bright red streaks in his hair, hanging around his face. "Chokey dyed it for me."

"Doesn't he look gorgeous?" Chokey said, grinning with pride. "He was so taken with yours, Buttercup, the green roots and the grey ends I mean, not the mess. He just wouldn't stop going on about it, so I had Mama send us some red."

Hemmings shot his sister a death stare.

"Are they really Redacting the characters?" Chokey continued, ignoring her brother's embarrassment. "Honestly, we were riveted. I can't believe they'd do something like that—how gruesome. So what's the plan?"

Bea looked at Mistasinon.

He shook his head. "I'm sorry... but you can't, none of you... It's dangerous."

"It's dangerous to go alone," Hemmings said.

"Quite right," Chokey agreed. "Besides, we're hardly going to sit here doing our homework while you two bundle off, saving people. That's not what friends do, is it?"

"Well," said Bea, also turning on Mistasinon, "I'm certainly not staying put."

Mistasinon frowned, his jaw tight.

"I mean it," Bea said. "It's not up to you, anyway. What are you going to do, chain us up and keep us here?"

For one horrible moment, he seemed to consider it.

"No," he finally said. "But we need a plan. I don't want any of you getting hurt. If they're Redacting the characters, they could just as easily Redact you."

"Us, darling," Chokey corrected.

"Yes, that's what I meant." He turned to Bea. "Do you know where it's happening?"

"I think so," she said. "There's a woodshed. But it's outside. I don't know how we'd get there—wait. Chokey, where did you say Luca died?"

"Oh, well, somewhere in the west wing. Why?"

Bea pursed her lips. "That's where I was when I saw the ghost—the Redacted human."

"And that's where West's troll found you," Mistasinon said. "After you ran into the snow."

They looked at each other.

"There must be a way to the woodshed from there," Bea said.

"Gosh, isn't this thrilling!" Chokey exclaimed. "But, darling, how will we ever get there? The brown suits are patrolling all the time, and, besides, you know what this place is like. We'd just as likely get lost and never be found again."

"I'm a Plotter. If we run into any brown suits, I can tell them I'm supposed to be here, or there, or whatever. They won't argue with the blue suit," Mistasinon said.

Chokey grinned at him. "Aren't you wonderful? I should like to have my very own Plotter," she added, winking at Bea. "Handsome and useful!"

Bea didn't dare look at Mistasinon.

"But we still need to find our way there," Hemmings said.

"Hold on," Bea said. She went up to the wall and placed her hands against it.

The next moment she was on the other side of the room, sprawled on the floor. Hemmings jumped forward to help her, but Mistasinon was closer. He pulled her to her feet.

"What happened?" he asked, his eyes darting over her face, pausing at the scrape on her cheek.

Bea rubbed her head, swearing vigorously. "I tried to ask the wood, but I, um, had a fall earlier and hurt my head."

"What? Are you alright?"

"I can't make sense of what it's saying," Bea continued, ignoring him. "It's angry and confused enough, even when I can think straight. Basically, I can't find out where we need to go."

Gloom descended. The four fell silent.

"Luca… the brown suit witchlein?" Mistasinon asked. "The one who met you here and took us to see West?"

Bea nodded.

Mistasinon turned to Chokey. "And you think he, uh, passed away near where we need to be?"

"It certainly seems that way, darling."

Mistasinon strode out of the bedroom.

Chokey and Hemmings looked at Bea questioningly.

"Don't ask me," Bea said. "Seriously," she added as she saw Chokey open her mouth to say something.

They followed Mistasinon out into the hallway. They found him on his hands and knees, his face pressed up against the cold flagstones.

"What is he doing?" Chokey asked.

"He's smelling the floor," Hemmings said.

"I can see that, darling," Chokey said, pinching him. "But *what* is he doing?"

Hemmings rubbed his arm sulkily. "He's smelling the floor," he repeated.

Mistasinon crawled around, sniffing.

"I think I've got it. Come on." He got to his feet and marched off down the corridor.

Chokey, Hemmings and Bea looked at each other. And then, by mutual consent, they followed him.

"What now?" Chokey asked.

They were standing in an empty room. That was it. A dead end.

Mistasinon pinched the bridge of his nose. "He definitely came in here."

"Are you absolutely certain, darling? Only, I know they say one should follow one's nose, but—"

"He was here," Mistasinon affirmed. He was breathing strangely, heavy and hard like he'd just run a marathon. "I can still smell the lamp oil. Can't you?"

The other three dutifully sniffed the air.

"Yes…" Bea said. "Faintly."

"How terrible," Chokey said in a fascinated tone. "Just imagine burning to death."

Bea thought about telling her off but realised there wasn't much point. Chokey didn't mean to be cruel. She *wasn't* cruel. She was just thoughtless, sometimes.

"We could try one of the other rooms," Bea suggested.

Hemmings tucked his new red streaks behind his ears. He walked over to the wall and started running his hands over it.

"What are you doing?" Bea asked. She was beginning to think that both men were losing their minds. One sniffing everything, and now the other rubbing everything.

"Isn't it obvious?" Hemmings said over his shoulder. "There must be a secret passage somewhere."

"Oh, I doubt it," Chokey said. "I'm sure Collins or Stoker or James or Shelley would have mentioned a secret passage."

Hemmings turned around. "Only the unintelligent fail to see the mystery in the world." He went back to feeling the walls.

"Alright, alright," Chokey grumbled. "There's no need to be rude." She went up to another wall and started feeling for a catch.

Mistasinon looked at Bea, arching one of his thick eyebrows.

Bea shrugged. "I'm not touching them. You go ahead."

She watched, bemused, as the other three went about feeling the walls. She was just about to call a stop to the whole thing when, underneath Hemmings' hand, there was a click.

A section of the wood panelling groaned and then pulled aside, revealing a dark corridor carved out of stone.

"Yes! I knew it!" Hemmings shouted joyously, pumping his fist. "In your face!"

They stared at him.

He coughed. "That is, when one chooses to shake off the veil of—"

Chokey gave him a hug. "Well done, darling. That was very clever."

Hemmings blushed. It clashed with his red streaks, but no one mentioned it.

"Right," Bea said. "What now?"

"We go in," Chokey said.

They eyed the dank, dark corridor.

No one moved.

"Mortal gods," Bea said, exasperated. "Alright. Mistasinon, would you stick your head down there and tell us what you can see—I mean, smell?"

He hesitated and then did as she asked. "It's definitely the right way. Um. Bea…"

"Yes?"

"You said you saw a ghost? I mean, one ghost. I mean, *one* Redacted character."

"Yes, why?" Something in his expression was making her nervous.

"I can smell more than one person down there. Quite a few more than one, in fact."

Bea swore. Chokey looked shocked. She ignored it. "I suppose we shouldn't be surprised. They must have loads of them."

"What are we going to do with them all?" Mistasinon asked. He was leaning against the wall, a muscle jumping in his cheek, his jaw tight. He looked as bad as she felt.

"We can't leave them there," Hemmings replied. "It's the responsibility of all thinking people to show compassion."

"We could take them to the mirror room?" Chokey suggested.

"And then where?" Mistasinon snapped at the dwarf, both hands on his neck. "We can't bring a load of Redacted characters into Ænathlin. It'll cause a riot."

"And they'll die if we take them out into the storm," Hemmings answered, a steely edge in his voice Bea had never heard before. "They're only characters—Buttercup nearly died, and she's one of the fae."

"There must be something we can do," Chokey said.

Bea let them go round in circles. She was thinking.

Hemmings was right: there was no way a human could survive in the snow. And Mistasinon was right, as well: they couldn't take them through to the Mirrors in the Grand.

But Bea knew about another Mirror.

A secret Mirror.

Melly's Mirror.

"I think I have an idea," she said.

❄

"Will she take them?" Mistasinon asked once she'd explained.

"I don't know, but it's the only thing I can think of."

"It's very risky. It's still in the Land."

"Yes," Bea said, "But it's not in Ænathlin. Melly's cottage is in the Sheltering Forest. And she doesn't have to keep them. She can use her Mirror to take them somewhere else. Ehinenden maybe. Ana helps lost people, she might take them."

Mistasinon didn't look convinced.

"Does anyone else have a better idea?"

And that was it. Nobody did.

"Right then," Bea said. "Chokey, Hemmings, you stay here and keep watch. If any brown suits come, close the door and... think of a reason why you're here."

"Will do," Chokey said.

Bea rolled up her sleeves.

"Let's go be heroes."

❄

Far away from the Academy, the story of the handless girl was spreading slowly across Ehinenden.

But it was limited. It was only one story, and as strong as the blood and the bone were, eventually even the old tales ran out of imaginations to infect, just as the new ones did. Belief needed believers and believers needed constant tending.

In a small town in the province of Cierremont sat three men in the corner of the local inn, wallowing in gloomy self-pity.

"The new play isn't working," said one. "It's too complicated."

"It's the audience. Damn yokels, they wouldn't know great art from a turnip shaped like a di—"

"Oi, watch it," said the third, a stout man with a white beard carefully oiled into a point. His name was Christopher. He lowered his voice. "They might not know their art, but they know how to jam a pitchfork up our arses for offending them."

"I don't want to go back to the farm," lamented the first, who went by the name Alfonso. He was a delicate young man, short with narrow shoulders, the remains of the evening's greasepaint still smeared around his ears and along his hairline. "It's beneath me."

"This play is beneath anyone," grumbled Peter, the second. "We should be doing something new. We should be making plays about how life *really* is. Shake up the established order. We should do the one I wrote about the slaves in Cerne Bralksteld."

"Oh, yeah, that's genius," replied Christopher. "I'm sure the Baron would be absolutely delighted with that. I bet he'd give us a medal, with a play like that. I bet we wouldn't get thrown in the manufactories at all."

Alfonso stared miserably at his pint. He had the air of someone who'd heard this tune before and was bored of the dance. And then an idea struck him.

"How about something old?" he said. "I heard this story in the pub the other night about a girl who had her hands cut off..."

XLVI

Bea stumbled over a loose rock.

"Are you alright?" Mistasinon asked, in front of her. He was, as Chokey would say, following his nose.

"Yes. It's dark, that's all."

"Here." Mistasinon reached behind him and took Bea's hand.

They walked on in silence.

"Mistasinon?"

"Yes?"

"What's wrong? I mean, I know I don't know you very well… But it's obvious there's something wrong."

The darkness closed in, no doubt as anxious as Bea to hear what his reply was going to be.

"I'm not feeling myself lately, that's all," he said.

He couldn't have made it any more obvious he didn't want to continue the conversation without actually saying as much. They walked on for about twenty feet or so. The corridor was long and the ground underneath them uneven, slowing their pace to a crawl.

"You're not as strong as you used to be, are you? Or as fast?" Bea said, doggedly. She knew she should take the hint and let it drop, but her desire for the truth was stronger than her etiquette. Besides, there was something about walking through the blackness that made it easier to ask.

The only sound was the gentle whisper of their breath and the occasional rattle of loose stones beneath their feet. And then he answered.

"No, I'm not."

"Are you sick? Only I've never heard of someone losing their talent before. Having a talent is part of being in a tribe, isn't it?"

His flinched. Without thinking, she held his hand tighter, brushing her thumb against his.

"I don't think those were my talents," he admitted softly. "I think they were… left over. From my last job."

"Ah. I see," Bea said, though frankly, she didn't see at all. "So if there are guards or something like that...?"

"I don't know what help I'll be. I might be able to smell them before they get to us."

"Well, that's good," Bea said with overenthusiastic jollity. "Forewarned is forearmed."

"My sense of smell isn't as good as it used to be either. Since you're asking."

"Oh."

"It's harder to distinguish between smells," he continued. "Sometimes I can't see them at all, and then other times I get... overwhelmed."

"Overwhelmed?"

"There are too many colours, you know?"

"Not really," Bea admitted. "Smells just... smell."

"Ah. Yes. Of course."

"Maybe it will settle down," Bea suggested.

"Maybe."

They followed the corridor as it twisted and turned. They didn't speak again until, suddenly, Mistasinon pulled up. He let go of Bea's hand.

"We're here," he said.

Bea heard a click. Light spilt into the corridor. She covered her eyes, and then slowly took her hand down. Mistasinon stepped out of the corridor and into the room beyond. Once her eyes had adjusted, she followed him.

They entered a plainly decorated room. There was a door on the other wall, straw scattered on the floor, a well-stocked freestanding larder, and lamps burning in the walls.

There was also a cell containing ten Redacted women.

"Mortal gods," Bea whispered.

She walked over to the women. They didn't pay her much attention. They were milling around, vacant-eyed with vacant smiles plastered on their faces, humming snatches of a tune that was strangely familiar.

"Um. Hello," Bea said.

The women turned and looked at her.

"hello."

"hello."

"hello."

"hello."

"hello."

"hello."

"hello."

"hello."

"hello."

"hello."

Bea shuddered. "They're so——"

"Creepy?"

"Horrible, I was going to say. Do you think… is there a way to change them back?"

Mistasinon reached out, perhaps to put his arm around her. But he seemed to change his mind, and instead patted her tentatively on the shoulder.

"I don't think so," he said. "I think once you've been Redacted… I think that's it. But I could be wrong," he added helplessly.

"Well, they look clean and well-fed, at least," Bea said, sidestepping her horror by focusing on practicalities. "Let's see if we can find a key. And a lamp—I don't want any of them to break their neck in that corridor."

After a few minutes searching, they were able to produce both. Bea went over to the cell to unlock it. She placed her hand on the metal door, screamed, and jumped away.

"Iron," she said, looking at her hand. Her palm was red; luckily she'd pulled her hand away before it had the chance to do anything more than scald her. She should have felt the warning tingle—a stupid mistake caused no doubt by her mounting exhaustion. "Whoever's doing this must have been worried they'd be found out. There must be gloves somewhere…"

Alternately blowing on and shaking her hand, Bea turned back to the larder to search for some heavy gloves when she heard a creak behind her.

Mistasinon was helping the women out. He had one hand on the door, keeping it open, holding his other hand out to each of the women, making sure they noticed the little step that the bottom bar created.

Bea chewed her lip, watching him.

And then she went over and helped him get the women out of the cell, being careful not to touch the iron bars herself.

"Pass me that lamp," she said, once the women were all safely out of the cell. "If I take this one and you take the other one, we can sort of ferry them in the middle."

Mistasinon rubbed his neck. "I think I can smell some others," he said. "Why don't you take these ones back, and I'll go and see?"

"But we need you to keep the brown suits away."

His lips twitched in a smile. "Bea, you're going to be walking through the Academy with ten Redacted characters. I don't think I'd be much help if a brown suit were to stumble upon you. Just be careful. Do you remember the way back?"

"I think so, but—"

"I have to go and check. We can't leave any behind. Go on, you'll be fine."

Bea wanted to ask him to come with her, but she couldn't think of any reason convincing enough. It never occurred to her to just say she didn't want him to leave her.

"Alright," she said.

"Alright," he said.

"See you in a bit, then."

"Be careful," he replied. "And... I'm sorry, all of me, about what happened between us."

"What do you mean—"

But he'd already gone, darting through the door on the far side of the room. Bea stood for a moment, staring at the door. Shaking her head, she took the lamp and said to the women, "Follow me."

"if you like."

"if you like."

"if you like."

"if you like."

"if you like."

"if you likc."

"if you like."

"if you like."

"if you like."

"if you like."

F. D. Lee

Bea led them back through the corridor, the lamp making the journey much easier.

"Gosh, look at those smiles," Chokey said, once the women were safely out the other side. "You know, they rather remind me of someone…"

"Your friends," Hemmings said. "Fake smiles."

Chokey peered at the closest Redacted woman. "Oh, yes! You're right! I shouldn't be surprised if I can never look at them again, now you've pointed it out."

"Let's get them back to our room," Bea said, privately thinking if Chokey never spoke to those bullies again, it would be no bad thing. "I'll open the pathway to Melly's Mirror, and then you two can take them through."

"Aren't you coming too, darling?"

Bea looked back at the corridor. "Mistasinon thinks there are more. I'm going to come back here and help him."

She wasn't in all honesty sure when she'd decided that, but the moment she said it she knew it was the right thing to do.

❄

Hidden in the darkness, the ghost of Isabella watched as they led the other ghosts away. From somewhere in her broken mind, the thought came:

Wait.

❄

There was a crash from upstairs.

Melly had known this moment would come—that the Plotter would betray them. Perhaps that was why she'd decided, a few days ago, to leave her Mirror uncovered. Perhaps she was ready to let it all go.

Perhaps.

Or perhaps it was time to follow in her husband's footsteps, in Bea and Joan's footsteps, and to fight back.

312

Picking up a bat, she got up cautiously and followed the sound. She dropped it when she saw what was happening on her upstairs landing.

"Hullo there! You must be Melly? You wouldn't mind helping, would you? Only I should think it a terrible shame if one of them fell down the stairs and broke their neck, given all the trouble we've gone to get them here."

On the landing at the top of her stairs was a blonde dwarf with rosy cheeks and her hair in bunches, helping a female character through her Mirror.

"What in the five hells is going on? Who are you?" Melly demanded, pulling herself up to her full height, her green eyes narrowing.

For the second time in her life, it had absolutely no effect.

"What? Oh, yes, sorry," Chokey said, helping another woman through the Mirror. "I'm Dea'dora Kilumal Ogrechoker, but you can call me Chokey. Pleased to meet you—Buttercup said you're a witch, is that true? I've never met a witch before, can you believe it? My brother is going to be a villain, though I shouldn't think they'll make him a witch. He's a boy," Chokey clarified unnecessarily. "I don't think they do boy witches. Isn't that strange? I shouldn't have thought there was any reason why boys can't be witches, but there you go."

"Wait, you know Bea?" Melly asked, grasping at this lifebelt of familiarity in the tempestuous waters of Chokey's patter.

"Oh, yes, darling! How else would we be here if we didn't? Gosh, that would be funny, wouldn't it? Imagine, us just turning up randomly in your house with ten Redacted characters!"

"Ten what?"

"These women, darling. Now, I hate to be a bore, but do you think you might lend a hand, only we're getting a bit chocka up here and as I said, I don't trust them on the stairs."

Half an hour later and the Redacted women had been divided between Melly's bedroom and her spare room. She was now sitting in her living room, smoking, as the blonde dwarf and a really very intense elf with red streaks in his hair were telling her an impossible story.

Except, of course, she knew it was all true.

What she couldn't believe was that Bea had managed to get herself caught up in it all.

Again.

"…And then her Plotter rolled up, and he helped us get the characters out. Buttercup and he are getting some more now," Chokey finished.

"Her Plotter? Damn him. He swore he wouldn't involve her."

"Oh, he didn't," Chokey said. "We heard the whole thing from the bathroom. I think Buttercup rather hounded him, actually. They're terribly sweet, aren't they? All that nervous tension! So romantic! Gosh, Hemmings, doesn't it remind you of that summer with Edgar and the teeth?"

Hemmings nodded his head sagely. "Love does tend to promote strange behaviour. I might make it the focus of my next journal."

"What a wonderful idea!" Chokey said, patting his knee happily. "I should think that would do you the worlds of good, darling. Love is such a nice thing to think about."

"Yes," Hemmings mused. "There is madness in love, but there is also love in madness. Oh *yes*. Of course, I would have to also consider obsession and pain, and what it truly, really means to embrace one's desires." His eyes were alight. "Gosh…"

"Oh. Well, yes… that too," Chokey replied. She was still patting his knee, but it had lost some of its enthusiasm. She turned back to Melly. "Anyway, darling, there you have it."

"There you have it," Melly repeated weakly.

"We'd better make a start on moving these characters on to this Ana character Buttercup talked about. I don't know what's keeping her and her Plotter."

Melly stood up. "I dare say whatever Bea is doing, she knows what she's about. There'll be no talking her out of it, anyway, even if she doesn't."

"So you'll help us?" Chokey asked.

Melly thought about the ten Redacted women now in situ in her cottage. "I don't think I've got much choice, have I? Come on, let's get them to Ana."

And then I think I'd better do something about all this, Melly added to herself.

XLVII

Bea made her way back to the room with the cell in it. She wasn't surprised when she found it empty.

You shouldn't have left without him. You should have stayed, or made him come with you.

She pushed the thought aside. What she needed to think about now was what to do next. She put the lamp down, carefully turning off the flame. And then she walked to the opposite door and opened it.

Beyond was another room, this one full of... equipment. It was the only word she could think of.

Two long tables sat parallel to each other, their surface covered with strange metal and glass objects. There was a clockwork wheel, spinning slowly to the sound of clicking machinery. Sticking out from the wheel were glass vials filled with a dirty white liquid. As the clockwork wheel spun, the liquid in the vials moved in a heavy, viscous way that reminded Bea of oil.

In addition to the spinning wheel, there were glass bulbs and tubes that twisted and turned in crazed patterns, the same thick liquid flowing through the tubes to drip into the bulbs, and things that were something like hurricane lamps, but with the glass tops filled with yet more of the thick white liquid, bubbling away as they were heated by small flames below.

That's the same stuff I found before, Bea thought, looking at the liquid. *And it was in Dionne's room, I'm sure of it. It must be what Mistasinon saw—no, smelled.*

She walked between the two tables, the click-clack of the clockwork and the bubbling pops of the thick liquid the only sounds, other than her footsteps. At the end of the room was another door. Bea opened it.

The door flew away from her grip, caught in the vicious wind. Snow flew around her, taking advantage of the opportunity to get into the relative warm of the woodshed. Bea braced herself against the frame and heaved the door shut.

And that was it. There was nowhere else to go, except where she'd come from.

Where was he?

Bea was about to turn around when her eye caught something in the floor. A metal ring. She reached out for it and then pulled her hand back. More carefully, she hovered her hand above the ring. Sure enough, she felt the tingle of iron against her skin.

Bea pursed her lips.

Right then.

So of all the places Mistasinon could possibly be, he's going to be down there, isn't he?

Of course he is.

Bea went back to the cell room and searched the larder for something to cover her hand with. Having found a rag and wrapped it carefully around her hand, she returned to the equipment room and, after a few false starts, managed the get the trapdoor open. A definite success for fairy ingenuity, she felt. A staircase unwound beneath her.

She could hear voices now.

Mistasinon... and West? It had to be. Bea was pretty sure she'd recognise that deep, husky voice anywhere. She made her way down the stairs, following the sound of their voices.

Behind her, the ghost of Isabella detached itself, unnoticed, from the shadows.

Mistasinon had found West in the basement of the woodshed. She was sitting at a desk, surrounded by empty bottles.

In the centre of the room was a large leather chair. It was tilted slightly so that if you sat in it, you would lean backwards. There were straps hanging down from its sides, positioned in such a way that they would reach over the sitter's chest, hips, legs and head.

"You came to me," West said, jumping up from her seat. "I didn't know... I didn't know... But you came. I hoped you would."

Mistasinon looked around the room. "You Redact them here?"

"What? Oh, yes. You call it that too?"

Mistasinon turned his attention back to West. "What else would it be called?"

"Letheination."

Mistasinon frowned.

Could she have said…?

But no…

That was impossible.

But she had…

No…

Yes…

"Letheination. Letheinate. I named it for the river," West explained, seeing the confusion on his face. "I assumed that's where the stones come from."

Mistasinon rubbed his neck. "Wait," he said. "I can't…" He concentrated, trying to find the right thought. "You're talking about the Lethe?"

West perched on the edge of her desk, smiling apologetically. "I'm sorry, this is my fault. I go too quickly, I know. I forget sometimes to give people time to catch up. Yes, I'm talking about the Lethe. The river of forgetfulness. Of course, you were chained by the River Styx. I saw you there. I mean, I saw you there with my eyes, not with my vision."

Whatever it was that Mistasinon had thought he was going to do once he found the Redaction room, it fell away from him in that moment.

The Styx.

The river that led into the Shadow Land, where the Shadow Master ruled.

He felt the weight inside him begin to tug.

"How do you know about the Styx?" he asked.

"I know it all. I know it all," West replied, her rich voice soothing. "You're the Cerberus. You're a victim of Hades, just as I am a victim of Apollo. We're the same, and now we're both here, together. The music brought me, led me here, the music that ties the universe together. The music that hums in the centre of the tree, that flows through its branches and feeds its fruit. Do you know about the tree? Have you seen it? You will. I think. It's hard to tell with you."

Mistasinon wasn't listening. All he could hear was a roar, the sounds of his hims screaming together, their confusion for once united.

How does she know...?
Does it matter...?
The Shadow Land...
The Shadow Master...
And the screams, the screams, the screams...

He collapsed onto the Redaction chair, the weight in his centre suddenly so strong his legs could no longer support him.

"Who are you?"

"We're from the same world, you and I. We're the same," West repeated gently. "But it was Apollo who ruined me, who raped me. He put them all inside me. I didn't have three heads. None of it was divided. You don't know how lucky you were, Cerberus. Three heads, all separate, no second thoughts, no second-guesses... And a voice to tell you what to do. It must have been like death... peaceful."

He felt sick, suddenly. Giddy as a leaf in a hurricane, weightless as a falling body. Seizing their moment, the other hims whined and roared, clamouring for control, to speak to West, to kill her, to beg her to look after them. The one that might be Mistasinon sought for purchase.

"You don't... How can you...?"

"You're afraid. You've been afraid for so very, very long. I know fear, Cerberus. I know the fear of having no control, of having no power. Just as I understand what it is that's happening to you, now."

"Understand?"

"Oh, yes, I understand. When Apollo gave me the visions, he meant to punish me. And what a punishment it was. Can you imagine? Everyone's futures in my head, and no room for me. Isn't that how you feel now?"

"I... yes..." Mistasinon shook his head, trying to clear it, trying to shake off the memories West had invoked.

It was such a struggle to stay above the roaring shadows, the incessant barking of his hims…

And with each second that passed, the weight was pulling him down.

"Who are you?" he repeated.

"You know who I am," West said. "I am the one who denied the God Apollo his way with me and was punished for my rebellion, my refusal. I am the one who sees the future, and yet no one believes me when I tell them what is to come. I am the one who foresaw the murder of her family and could do nothing about it. I am the one who saw the war, and no one believed me. They thought I was mad, and then they murdered me."

She made her way over to him. "My tragedy was told and retold throughout our homeland, a warning to anyone who would refuse the Gods their petty pleasures. And I am the one who knows what you are and where you come from."

She pressed her hand against his face. "You know who I am. Say my name."

Mistasinon swallowed. It was impossible. She had to be lying. She was mad. He could smell the chalky scent of Redaction on her breath, the reek of it clawing its way out of the empty bottles on her desk.

"Say my name," West repeated.

No…

Yes…

This is her.

She knows us.

"Say my name."

Mistasinon shook his head, his thoughts racing.

She's lying. We're alone. She'll leave us. She'll—

And then, before he knew what was happening, West had pushed him back on the chair. He screamed, and the third one went to slash her with his claws—

—Where are our claws—fingernails, neat, trimmed you keep them neat, so careful, so meticulous—no claws, never again—

West grabbed the strap and locked the heavy buckle over his chest. She tied the other strap over his hips and then two more, one around each of his legs. He struggled, but the leather was thick and strong, and he was on his back, with nothing to get purchase against.

"Tell me you believe me, Cerberus," she demanded. "Tell me who I am."

Mistasinon strained, lifting his head as much as he was able so that he could look at her.

"Cassandra," he said. "The woman who was cursed with perfect prophesy, cursed to be ignored and spoken over, to be disbelieved. You're Cassandra."

West burst into tears.

XLVIII

Ana, Royal Adviser to King John of Llanotterly, didn't have cynical moments in the same way that fish don't have wet moments.

She eyed the latest invention warily. With all the unwanted brilliance of sunlight through drawn curtains on a hangover, it was dawning on her that someone in the armoury was getting a lot of extracurricular experience out of John's injury.

This new contraption involved a chair attached to the bannisters of the grand staircase via a series of pipes and rails. Although the word 'attached' did very little to encompass the sight now before her.

The grand staircase of Llanotterly Castle certainly lived up to its name. It was huge, curving around the main hall in the centre of the 'H' shaped castle, doing more than simply joining both the upper and lower floors and each of the four wings. The grand staircase *made* the castle.

Llanotterly Castle had been in John's family for generations, and each of his forebears had taken a perverse and extraordinarily scattered approach to maintaining it.

The south wing had been decorated by his grandfather, George, in the Penqioan style, and as such was resplendent in jade and gold, with delicately painted wall murals and red pillars. Cut across the central keep to the Throne Room, and you would find yourself surrounded by carved wooden walls and trophy heads, to the taste of his father, Edward. His great-grandmother, Queen Margaret, had had a penchant for gilt and velvet, along with a rather more alarming fondness for beheadings and hangings.

Even his great-great-grand uncle, who had only served as Prince Regent for three months before being deposed by 'Red Meg', had managed to stamp his personality on the place, bequeathing the rulers of Llanotterly with vast friezes of birds carved into the stone ceilings of almost every room, regardless of whether they actually matched.

Nothing was ever replaced, either. This was one of the few things shared by both the extremely poor and the extraordinarily rich: things didn't get thrown away. Of course, the reasons behind such frugality were very far from equal, and certainly, by the time King John came to the throne, all the money had been frittered away by his forebears. But even so, he hadn't yet managed to bring himself to sell any of the castle's furniture or art.

For the rulers of Llanotterly, a bird in the hand was worth two in the bush, even if that bird was a ceiling mounted stone flamingo.

And all these varied attempts at interior design converged in the Grand Hall, its huge, wide staircase serving as a bridge to both the different areas of the castle and the different tastes of its owners.

It was now covered in lengths of bronze, brass and iron pipework, interspersed with valves whistling and hissing as they burped out white clouds of scalding steam. The whole thing looked to Ana like a death trap designed by the kind of person who solves maths problems for fun.

"I say, this is all pretty ripping, isn't it?" John exclaimed. "So how does it work?"

"Well, m'lord, in theory, all you've gotta do is get yourself into the chair, there, and pull that lever, there, and the chair'll carry you down the stairs."

Ana fixed Harold with her sludgy green gaze. "In theory?"

"Ah, well, m'lady, we're pretty sure we've got all the kinks worked out. The last test gave us some really good results."

John beamed. "Splendid!"

"Define 'good'," Ana said, not taking her eyes off Harold.

Harold thought for a moment about what to say. Ana waited. She may have only been Royal Adviser for six months, but she had quickly worked out how to handle some of John's more antiquated staff.

"Well," Harold said, hooking his thumbs in his overall pockets, "That depends on what framework you're using."

"Go on," Ana said icily.

"You see, the old Adviser, beggin' your presence, m'lady, he was often of the opinion that as long as things got done, they were good."

"The last Adviser was an enemy of the crown who attacked the King."

"Now, now," John said, a note of warning in his voice. "There's no need to go raking up muck."

Ana folded her arms. "Fine. Let's just say that my definition of a 'good result' is probably quite different from the previous Adviser's. And that my advice to you, Harold, is to tell me what happened the last time anyone—"

"—thing, m'lady—"

"Any*thing* used this moving chair."

Harold glanced at the King. "Well, m'lord, you know that bit of back bacon you had for breakfast three days past? And that stew the night afore last? And those sausages?"

"Damn right I do. Three days of pork," John said, smiling at the memory. And then he frowned. "I say, you're not suggesting that…?"

"It's quite common to use pigs when testing new machinery, m'lord," Harold said. "And we reckon we've got the problem fixed now. The last one didn't even singe."

"What *did* happen to it?" Ana asked.

Harold glanced up. John and Ana's gaze followed.

High above them, almost imperceptible in the stone fresco of birds, was the outline of what looked, now they came to concentrate on it, very much like that of a pig, caught in mid-flight.

"Well, I'll be buggered," John said.

"It is rather something, isn't it?" Ana replied.

"I never did like that eagle, mind you," John added, still looking up. "Hardly a chummy fellow, I always thought. He had a beak that always seemed to be staring at one."

"Not any longer, I think."

"No, I rather suspect not."

Ana pulled her gaze from the porcine predicament. "Right," she said to Harold. "I think that my advice is that his Highness go nowhere near this… thing… until we have had a least one successful journey from the top to the bottom of the stairs."

Harold nodded his head sagely and reached for his paper and pencil. "No problem, m'lady—"

"And I don't mean successful in the sense that whatever it is that goes wrong is slightly less wrong that whatever it was that went wrong before. I expect to see a pig get on the chair at the top and come off it again at the bottom. In fact, while we're at it, can you not find another way to test this blasted thing? I doubt the birds would survive another go, to say nothing of the morality of flinging pigs around."

Ana and John left Harold muttering under his breath about the job opportunities available to him in one of the other Four Kingdoms.

John pushed himself along the corridor in his wheeled chair, grunting occasionally as it caught on an uneven piece of floor. Ana made a note in her head wherever he came into difficulty to get the floors planed or the carpets refitted.

When he'd first started using the wheeled chair she'd offered to push him over the difficult bits. It was one of the few times she'd ever seen John truly lose his temper. He had to get used to it, he'd said, and he couldn't do that with her fussin' over him like a nanny. Ana had stormed off, angry with him for his stubbornness and with herself for her thoughtlessness—but most of all, angry at the situation for its heartlessness.

They were getting better at it now. John had moments when his frustration would get the better of him, but Ana had also learnt that he was incredibly resilient. More so than she suspected she would be in the same situation. And John was beginning to understand that she didn't know what to do or say around him, and so sometimes she got it wrong. They were, as he was fond of saying, 'muddling along as best they could, given the circs'.

"Blasted nuisance not having the steamer chair-lift up and running," he said as they made their way to his study.

"It'll be fine," Ana said.

"Now I'm thinking about it, all I can smell is bacon."

"It'll be fine," Ana said.

"There are worse smells, I suppose."

"It'll be fine," Ana said.

John put the brakes on and looked up at Ana. "Will you stop saying everything's going to be fine? It's very far from being fine, from where I'm sitting. We're about to start a war, and I can't even get down the bloody stairs."

Ana stopped as well. "What do you want me to say?"

"What you're paid to say, madam."

"The truth, then? This plan is almost impossible. If it goes wrong, it'll be a disaster. But if it works... We could end it all. Added to that, none of the other counties or fiefdoms have been willing to do business with us. We need to get you out and seen, your Majesty. People need to know you're alive."

John looked down at his legs. "Alive and kicking," he said.

"Quite."

"Righto," John said, flicking the brake off his wheels and pushing himself forward. "Let's show 'em just how much fight we've got in us, eh? Put our shoulders to the wheel, what?"

Ana allowed herself a smile. "Roll with the punches, your Majesty?"

"Atta gel," John said, grinning. "We can't just wait around, spinning our wheels."

"Exactly," she said. "A rolling stone gathers no moss."

"We've set the wheels in motion now."

"And it's the squeaky wheel that gets the grease."

John burst out laughing.

Ana joined him. She couldn't remember who had first started the game, but that didn't matter. It was theirs now. And it helped to face things head on. She remembered her mother, when she wasn't struck down with her nerves, used to say that it was better to light a candle than curse the darkness.

Ana didn't agree with that. She thought it was better to set the whole damn building ablaze and eradicate the darkness completely. She and John parted ways, and Ana made her way back to her office.

In the centre of the room was the witch, Melly, flanked by ten smiling women.

Bea stood, frozen in shock, on the stairwell.

Mistasinon was the Beast?

No... He couldn't be. The Beast was a three-headed, dog-like monster. Mistasinon was a tall, slender Plotter with large, gentle brown eyes and a smile that made you sad and happy all at once.

But even as she tried to convince herself of this, her memories threw up things he'd said, things he'd done, things that told her *yes*.

He was powerful, strong and fast. He'd fought a troll and won. He'd called off the witchlein at the Ball, and they'd obeyed him. He could smell things no one else could... Mortal gods, he'd always known when she was close by.

Bea's stomach lurched.

He'd never been frightened of the GenAm, or the Beast. He'd told her things no one should know. He'd spoken about faraway places and distant times. He'd touched the iron, and it hadn't burned him.

No wonder he didn't resemble any tribe. He wasn't one of the fae.

She sank down onto the steps, listening to them talking, knowing that it was true.

Mistasinon was the Beast.

He had overseen the Great Redaction. He had helped the Teller imprison them all in a cage they couldn't even see. He had hunted so many fae, delivering them to the Redactionists. He was the thing that people feared. He was the thing that chased, that never stopped, that never let them escape.

Mistasinon was the Beast. West was the Redactionist.

They were together, while she was here, all alone.

And she had to stop them.

⁕

The ghost of Isabella hovered at the top of the stairs, by the trapdoor. She could hear her. That deep voice.

She was alive...

A day in the park, the sun shining on her face. An argument, loud and angry, and she cried herself to sleep.

She was alive...

But there were others down there, too.

The ghost of Isabella hesitated. And then she drifted over to the door and watched the hole in the floor.

XLIX

W est wiped her eyes.

"I can help you. If you help me," she said. She disappeared from his field of vision and then came back, a fresh bottle of Letheinate in her hand. "You drink it. Drink it down, and it takes it away. It makes it silent... normal... How I remember it used to be, before he, before he..."

Mistasinon let his head fall back against the chair, no longer able to stand looking at the turmoil on West's face.

"I know what happened to you," he said, the words coming from a long way away. It was easier now he was tied down. There was a comfort to it. The one that he thought might be him recoiled at the notion, but the second one whispered, *yes, yes, this is what we need*. "It shouldn't have. I'm sorry."

West took a sip of her medicine, her eyes regaining some of their focus.

"Thank you," she said. "It was... it was unfortunate. Bad luck, perhaps. I always remember it differently. Sometimes I don't remember it at all."

"How... how did you end up here? In Thaiana?"

West shrugged, taking another sip. "I was murdered, you know that part of the story?"

"Yes."

"So, of course, I went to Hades. That's when I first saw you. You were bigger, then. Well... of course you were. You were terrifying. But I understand you better now. Oh... yes. I died, and I was taken to the field of punishment." She gripped the bottle of Letheinate so tightly her knuckles whitened. "The field of punishment! After everything that had happened to me. Everything they did to me, the Gods decided *I* had committed a crime against *them*."

Mistasinon blinked, his eyes stinging. He realised he was crying.

"I'd suffered all my life, and I was expected to suffer in death as well?" West fumed, throwing the empty bottle to the floor and grabbing another. "And then, I don't know when, Hades sent you away. I had my chance. There was no guard, no one patrolling the Styx. I didn't know what would happen—I couldn't see the future there, in the Underworld, but it didn't matter. What else could happen to me? So I escaped. I went to find Elysium—"

"The field of the worthy, for those who had lived virtuous lives," Mistasinon said, his voice stained by the shadows inside him. West had tied him to the weight, and it was pulling him down, too far down, and the shadows were rising up, immersing him.

His other hims were panicking, drowning in the darkness. They screamed, clawing at his mind, trying to stay ahead of the rising shadows.

Something was wrong... There were no colours now... Only shadows. He couldn't think. He was a broken mirror, fractured; a snowflake, melting; a memory, fading; a ghost, waning.

"Yes," West said, the sound of her deep voice the only solid thing in the world. "But I got lost. And then I heard the music. I followed it. I travelled for months. Or maybe hours. Or years. Time doesn't work there, does it? Not really. Hades has seasons, but not time. I travelled, and it got darker and darker, but I kept on. Do you know where the music led me?"

"Tartarus," he whispered.

"Yes. The world below the Underworld. The final world—well, no, we know better than that, don't we? There, the music was louder, deafening. But still I followed it. I couldn't stop, couldn't stop, couldn't stop. I saw the tree and all the colours... And this one, this world... The colour was so warm... I couldn't see, couldn't see, couldn't see..."

She took another gulp of Letheinate, pausing for a moment with her eyes closed. And then she continued, "The tree brought me here, to Thaiana. I chose this world. You chose the one filled with nymphs and satyrs. The fae, or so they call themselves. Why?"

"I don't remember. I was afraid, I wanted the Shadow Master—"

"Hades," West interrupted. "Call him by his name and spit in his eye."

Mistasinon shook his head in frantic refusal. "I can't. I'm not allowed to name the Gods. The Shadow Master," he repeated, trying to blink away his tears. "I wanted to find him. I needed him.

But I was lost. I was lost, and I tried to find him, to track him, but it was all wrong."

"Tell me what happened to you," West commanded. "Tell me the truth. I know it, anyway, but you need to say it. We need to free each other, and then we can escape."

He swallowed, the commanding tone of her voice reaching into him, flicking a switch he'd hoped had been buried deep in the shadows. But they were rising now, weren't they? Taking him over.

"The hero killed my brother... And that was the deal, that was what I'd been promised. I gave up my life so that my brother could have one. But the hero killed him like he was a monster, but he wasn't. He was just... he was big, and he looked different, and he was in the way. But the hero just cut him down, and the Shadow Master let him. He let my brother die."

He could hear the pain and panic in his voice, but he couldn't stop talking. His weakness exposed him, shamed him. He was *bad*.

Perhaps, if he'd still been separate, he might have been stronger? But then, he'd always felt this way...

Memories frothed across the boiling surface of the rising shadows, roiling, popping bubbles of things he'd spent years forgetting, now burning away whatever it was he had been changed into, leaving him blistered and raw.

"Tell me what happened next," West urged. "That's the only part I can't see. Did you go back? Is that why I can't see it? *Did you go back?*"

"The Shadow Master... he was my world. He was my master, he was supposed to... And he gave me to the hero. He gave me to the hero, gave me away to the one who killed my brother," Mistasinon sobbed. "They made a bargain, and the Shadow Master sent me away, and I... and I..."

He faltered, consumed by shame and the darkness. His other hims were silent now. He was lost and alone.

"I understand," West whispered, drawing close to him, sipping her drink. "Despite it all, every betrayal, every abuse, you wanted to go back. You needed to go back."

Mistasinon's chest rose and fell, rose and fell, pressing against the belt holding him down.

"Yes, yes, please, I'm so sorry. I'm so sorry. I escaped the hero, I ran, I ran, I found the entrance to the Shadow Land, but I... I don't know... I was lost... Nothing was right... And then I heard the music, and I was in the Land of the Fae. But it was the same. Gods, only they called themselves fae, playing with the lives of people," he said. "And I wanted it to stop. No more Gods, no more games. The Teller.... The Teller cared about me, and he had a plan. He had a vision. He said he could stop it. Stop the Gods, steal their fire."

He took a heaving breath. "I did awful things. Wicked things. But I couldn't let it happen again, no more war, no more death. No more heroes. And the Teller was my new master. He cared about me... He told me I was worth caring about."

West reached out, brushing away his tears. "And now here you are, caught between the monster and the man," she said gently. "You can't take three minds and press them into one. You can't... you can't..." Another gulp of Letheinate. "It's too much to carry. I have a thousand minds in mine, Cerberus. They all came back when I arrived here. Futures aren't set, they're choices... So many futures. That's what I carry with me. All those minds in my mind. I know your burden. And I can help you."

Mistasinon nuzzled into her hand, desperate for the certainty she was offering.

"We're not like them," West continued. "The Gods or the mortals here. We're different. Letheination... I found a way to distil it, to make it work differently. For me, it quietens the other minds. It pushes them away, for a time. But for you... If I give you the right amount, it will balance them. There would be just one. One mind, one master. You. You could be your master. If you help me."

She took her hand away, and he whined for its loss.

"What? What do you want me to do?"

"I want you to take me back to Hades," she said. "I don't care where I end up, which field. I just want to go back. There, I was only one. I can't die here, there's no guarantee where I'll go if I die here."

331

"But I... I don't know how..." he cried. "I don't know how! I wanted to go back, I tried, for years and years. I'm sorry, I'm sorry. Please, please. Help me. Please."

The shadows were high now, seeping into his mouth, crawling up his nose, worming their way into his eyes, his ears, drowning him. He could feel himself, himself, himself... Who was drowning...? He didn't know what was happening. Something had broken... Something had let the shadows out...

He screamed, thrashing uselessly against the heavy bonds.

"I don't know what's left of me. Which one am I? Did I die? Did I die? Which one... I don't... Please... I'm frightened... Please..."

"Take me back to Hades."

"I don't... I can't... I don't know how..."

"Then you're no good to me."

"Please... Please... I'm sorry... Please..."

West turned away from him in disgust. That was when she saw Bea, standing in the doorway.

L

"Ah, the fairy. I know what you do," West said.

Bea folded her arms. "No one knows what anyone will do."

West sighed. "Of course, you don't believe me. Let me ask you another question then. What were you doing?"

Bea glanced at the Beast, tied to the chair, sobbing. She didn't even know if he knew she was here.

"Listening," she said. "And thinking."

West took a sip from the bottle in her hand. The... what had she called it...? Letheinate? The Redaction drink.

"Would you like to know what happens to you?"

"No, thank you," Bea said. "From what I gather, knowing the future isn't all it's cracked up to be."

"What does it matter, if you don't believe me, anyway?" West replied. "Here, let me give you one for free: if the time comes, he won't choose you. He'll choose himself. He'll never think you really—"

Bea screamed and charged at West. But the woman ducked to the side, and she crashed into her desk. Empty bottles clattered to the floor.

"I knew you would do that," West sighed. "You can't fight me. Now ask me why I altered all those women. You ask me, and I tell you. So ask me."

"Fine," Bea snapped, glaring at her. "Why did you do it?"

"I, what's the word you like? Ah, yes. I 'Redacted' those women because I was asked to. You, your kind, you can't touch the stones, can you? But I can, and so I did. A year or so ago, after the Cerberus changed, your senate—your General Administration— was looking for a replacement, and that was my chance. I knew where to go, who to find, and I explained what I could do. It was easy to work the stones into the Letheination. I'd already seen what I do, so I did it." West laughed. "I tricked the God! I said I wanted status in return for the Letheination process. But it was always for the Cerberus. I only ever wanted the Cerberus."

Bea frowned, trying to untangle the chain of events. She was so tired, the painkillers were wearing off, and her head hurt; her hands and legs were sore from her encounter with Barret. West was talking in riddles... And, tied to the table, shivering, covered in sweat and tears, was the Beast.

And yet, no more than a couple of hours ago, that same creature had lain on her bed, curled up small...

She shook her head, needing to concentrate on what was happening now. "So a year ago, someone from the GenAm made a deal with you to Redact humans in return for fae gifts. But in actual fact, you did it because you wanted to get hold of the Beast?"

"Yes, yes. That's what I said."

Bea looked over at the Beast. He'd quietened, but every now and again he shuddered. "You wanted the Beast because you want him to take you home? You're both from the same place?"

West nodded her head. "Now ask me about you. Ask why you're so important."

"What about me?"

"Nothing about you! You aren't important at all. It was always about him. I needed him here, and you were the way that he came. You were, at best, a delivery method. Hermes incarnate."

Bea pressed her lips together. A word surfaced: deuteragonist. She'd assumed everything was about her, but she wasn't the centre of it, not at all.

"Huh," she said, shrugging. "I don't know who Hermes is, but I dare say I've been called worse. And now—"

"And now you're going to threaten me, but it won't work. I know what you're going to do. I *see* you. I saw you cause Barret to fall, do you know that? If it makes you feel better, I did warn him. He didn't believe me, either."

Ignoring West, Bea glanced at the Beast. He'd gone very still.

"You go to him, I don't stop you," West said, drinking her drink.

Bea hesitated. And then she walked over to him. His eyes were blank, staring up at something only he could see, his skin shiny with sweat and the silvery trails of his tears. He was breathing, but only just. She waved her hand over his face. He didn't react.

"What's wrong with him?"

"I'd say he's dying. Possibly. If you were listening, you'd know I can't see his future. I'd hoped he would take me back, but he says he can't. I thought he'd *want* to come with me, that he just needed to remember, to accept what he was," she added, sounding for once uncertain. "So I opened him up. I think… I think I got it wrong. I always do what I see myself doing, but with him, I didn't know what I do, so I did what I did."

Bea fisted her hair, oddly grateful for the pain the action caused, trying to make sense of what was happening. "How can he be dying? You were just talking to him."

"I would guess his mind is collapsing. The Cerberus isn't one head, is he? Three minds pushed into one. He was never meant to be, not as he is now. Whoever made him made a mistake."

Yes, Bea thought, *someone had very definitely made a mistake.* The Beast was a monster, but it was an effective one. Why would anyone want to hide it away in the body of a man? Had they been trying to punish it?

She looked down at the Beast, the thing in the body of Mistasinon.

If they had wanted to punish it, they'd found a brilliant way to do so. Bea had enough difficulty knowing what to do, working out what she thought and why she did things, and it was just her in her head.

She frowned.

Was it really just her in her head? She didn't always agree with herself, the mortal gods knew, and there were things that she wished she hadn't done, things she wished she had. How many hers did she have in her head, when you really thought about it?

But I've had practice arguing with myself. I didn't just wake up one morning with all my own thoughts jammed in my head. I know, right at the bottom, in the deepest part of me, which one I really am.

West came and stood next to her, still calmly sipping her Letheinate. "You don't stop me," she said, conversationally. "I know you don't. I don't know whether you don't because I tell you that you don't, though. I've never got the hang of that."

Bea ignored her.

"But I can't tell you what happens next," West said.

"Because of your 'Letheinate', I suppose?" Bea replied sourly.

"Partly. Now, yes, I can't see. But I watched this meeting or versions of it. I know what you'll do when you're acting on your own, and I knew if he came here, you would follow. But for the Cerberus, I can never tell. That's why I don't know if he'll die."

Bea looked down at him, trying to think.

What is a person? Memories. Actions. Choices. All bundled up. A walking ghost house, filled with the spirits of old decisions. But that couldn't be all there was to it, otherwise how could anything ever change? There has to be a point when you own up to what you've done, too. You can't blame everything on ghosts.

The Beast wheezed, his chest fluttering.

Bea chewed her nail. Could she let him die?

And if she didn't, did she know what she would be saving?

He was the Beast. He was a monster and an enabler of monsters. But she'd heard what he'd said. She'd heard the fear and shame and sorrow in his voice. And, really, what was he now? Had the Beast died when he'd changed, or simply been buried?

Bea reached out and pressed her hand to his cheek. He didn't react. His skin was boiling hot.

She thought about the person she knew, not the Beast. The man she'd met at the Plot Department. The one who'd lied, but the same one who'd tried to make things better, without hurting anyone. The one who thought people deserved a chance, no matter who they were.

She listened to her thoughts, and then she listened to herself.

She made a choice.

"Give Mistasinon the Redaction water. If you're from the same place, it'll do the same thing to him as it does to you."

"Clever," West said. "But no."

Bea turned on her. "What do you mean, 'no'? I thought that was the whole point of this? Give it to him."

West shook her head. "Let the Cerberus suffer and die here in this wretched world like he's letting me. It deserves it, anyway—

isn't that what you've always wanted? A future without the 'Beast' in it? Besides, if I can't see his future, maybe it's because he hasn't got one."

Bea flexed her hands into fists.

"Uh-ah," West cautioned, waving the Letheinate at her. "Don't move, or else I'll throw this all over you. I'm going to leave now. You won't... don't... follow me." She glanced at the bottle in her hand. "Too much. And still, it'll wear off. You know, I used to feel pity for all of you? I used to think you were all trapped, locked into your futures. But you're not. I'm the one who's trapped." She reached the staircase. "You still don't believe me, do you?"

Bea glared at her, hating her more than any person she'd ever met.

"No. I don't believe you."

"I didn't think so," West said, shaking her head sadly. "Never mind. You'll regret not asking me when you see the tree."

And with that, she left.

Bea stood, torn between chasing after her and staying with Mistasinon. She wiped her face, trying to think.

If she let West go...

If she let Mistasinon die...

Bea tried to work it all out, all the possible ramifications of whatever choice she might make. But she couldn't know, could she? She just had to do what felt right, at this moment, and hope that it was the best choice. Because, really, wasn't that what it all amounted to?

She stayed with Mistasinon.

His chest was still, and it was only because she could hear his breath, very faintly, that she knew he was still alive.

Bea undid the belts tying him down and brushed his hair back from his burning forehead.

And then she waited for him to die.

"I expect you've got questions," Melly said.

They were back in Ana's office, having found somewhere safe for the Redacted women.

"You're damn right I do. What happened to those women? It's grotesque. They just do whatever you ask them to do."

Ana was the kind of person for whom the idea of doing what she was told was only palatable if it happened to be what she had intended to do anyway.

"You remember the dead girl, the one with—"

"I remember," Ana said shortly.

"We did that to her. The fae. And we've found a way to do it to more people too, without them ever complaining, ever refusing us."

Melly told Ana about the Redacted characters.

"You're not fairies or pixies or whatever," Ana said when Melly had finished. "You're monsters."

"Yes. But I need your help finding a bigger monster."

For a moment, Melly thought Ana was going to hit her. But the human managed to rein in her temper.

"Go on," Ana said through gritted teeth.

"I want your help to find the old Adviser, Seven."

"What makes you think I can help you?"

Melly paused, and then said, "Because I suspect you want to find him, too. It's what I would do if I were in your position."

Ana stood, face still, her eyes narrowed. And then she took a seat. "Alright. I'm listening."

Melly sat down and pulled a cigarette from her case. Ana made a face but didn't stop her. "The creature you call Seven is a genie."

If Melly had expected Ana to gasp in surprise, she was disappointed.

"Well, I knew he wasn't human," Ana said. "We don't tend to turn into giant frost monsters and disappear into thin air, kidnapping neighbouring royalty. At least, not the first two things," she conceded, remembering her history. "Why do you think we're looking for him?"

"Because, as you just said, you saw how powerful he is. And you're trying to avoid a war with the Baron, the one in Cerne Bralksteld."

Ana threaded her fingers together and brought them to her lips.

Melly waited.

"Yes. You're right," Ana said at last. "We want to find him. How do you fit into all this?"

"I want to help you find him. And then I want you to give him to me."

Ana laughed. "Why would I do that?"

"Because without him, you and your kind are in serious danger from us. The GenAm—that is, our Lords and Ladies—have resorted to Redacting the characters because we lost the genie. And without him, we'll continue Redacting you. We know it can be done now."

Ana leaned back in her chair, thinking. And then she said, "You brought me ten women in a state I would never wish to see anyone in, ever again. But what you don't understand is that the Baron is taking hundreds, maybe thousands, of people prisoner, forcing them into slavery. With Seven, we might have a chance of stopping him. Perhaps losing a few to the fae is a worthwhile loss if it means we can stop the Baron."

"It probably would be, if it would stop there. But it won't. I know my kind, and what we're capable of. You're nothing to us, Ana. Characters—humans—are less than toys. Children love their toys, and we don't love you. You're like those things, the metal things with teeth that eat the water…"

"You mean the steam engines?"

"Yes. For a long time, we didn't know how to use you, and it didn't matter because we had the genies. But if we've found a way to make you behave the way we want you to, we'll take it. That's why we're more dangerous to you than this Baron is. We're stronger than you, faster than you, we live longer than you. Imagine if we had complete access to your world. Nothing holding us back, except our imaginations."

Ana paled. But when she spoke next, her voice was steady. "Why would you want to stop that, though? It sounds like a good deal, from your end."

"Because it's been too long, and there are too many of us now. It would be the end of us, too. Not in the same way as what would face you, but an end nevertheless."

F. D. Lee

"Say I agree with you, what about the Baron? Even if he is less of a threat to us than your kind, he's still a threat. People die in his manufactories, and I won't have it continue while I can stop it."

"I think I can give you something to help you with the Baron if you let me take the genie. It's not as strong as him, I admit. But it's stronger than you, and has fae power."

"Enough riddles. What are you offering?"

Melly stubbed her cigarette out.

"Me," she said.

LI

Mistasinon's breath stuttered on his lips.

Bea turned her head, not wanting to see it when it happened.

And then she spotted it. On the floor, with all the bottles that had been knocked from the desk. A finger, maybe two, of the Letheinate, lying thickly in the bottom of the bottle.

Bea tumbled across the floor, grabbed it, dashed back to Mistasinon, and pressed the bottle to his lips. The Letheinate crawled slowly towards the lip, and then landed heavily against Mistasinon's mouth.

He wasn't drinking it.

Panicking, Bea did something that, had she been thinking clearly, even she might not have done.

In one hand, she grabbed his cheeks and forced his mouth open, while the thick, dirty white liquid slowly made its way from his lips, down his face. With her other hand, she held the bottle upright, pouring the last of it into his mouth.

Her eyes darted between the contents of the bottle, slowly sliding into his mouth, and the Letheinate that was inching down his chin, ever closer to her hand.

She waited.

She waited.

She waited.

Just as the Letheinate was a hair's breadth from her skin, she pulled away.

That was it.

There was nothing else she could do.

Mistasinon's eyes fluttered, and his chest expanded. Bea watched, chewing her nails, as he started to breathe again.

"Am I alive?" he managed, his voice rasping.

Bea laughed. "I think so. I have no idea what in the five hells you are, but I think you're alive."

The ghost of Isabella watched as the monster climbed out of the trapdoor.

She leapt forward, grabbing West.

The monster screamed and struggled, but the ghost of Isabella held on tight, pulling her towards the woodshed door, the one she had opened.

Into the cold, into the snow, the ghost of Isabella dragged the monster. The storm snapped at her, sharp-toothed snowflakes, biting, biting, biting. But Isabella didn't exist anymore, and the pain was distant. Her hands in the monster's hair, dragging her further away from the building, out into the ghastly nothingness.

"I couldn't see you, I couldn't see you," West screamed, clawing at the ghost of Isabella.

She was alive...

A bright sunny morning in the church, and her family around her... I do, and her heart swelling with joy. A bedside and a last breath, the end of one cycle. A cry, as old as time, and the beginning of a new cycle.

She was alive...

Guilt. She'd stolen something and they'd found out, and they were angry with her. She didn't know if she was guilty for stealing or guilty for being caught.

She was alive...

Sadness. Shame. Guilt. Joy. Happiness. Pain. Love. Boredom. Fear. All these things spiralled inside the ghost of Isabella. Half-formed, half-understood, dancing across the gaps in her half-Redacted mind.

The ghost of Isabella began to slow down, to feel tired, cold. The monster wasn't struggling anymore. Old, thin skin, the monster's black dress growing heavier as the snow froze her, her head, caught at the scalp in the grip of the ghost of Isabella's hand, had stopped moving. Stopped wailing. Stopped begging.

She was...

She was...

The monster was dead.

The ghost of Isabella dropped the monster, and lay down in the snow, the cold numbing the torn and jagged edges of her thoughts. She looked up at the sky, the storm churning, endlessly slicing up the heavens.

The ghost of Isabella drifted off to sleep, her mind finally stilled.

Bea very carefully propped Mistasinon up against the wall, back in the Academy. She wasn't exactly confident about leaving him on his own, but there was something she had to do. Grabbing the lamp, she took a minute to reassure him she would be back—a reassurance which he seemed almost entirely oblivious to—and made her back down the hidden passageway, to the woodshed.

She set the lamp down in the little larder by the cell and went into the room with all the bottles and equipment. It took longer than she would have liked, but eventually, she found what she was looking for: a bottle of clear, oily liquid that nearly took the top of her head off when she tentatively sniffed it.

Next, she went back downstairs to West's Letheination room, her eyes skidding away from the chair in the centre of the floor, and quickly checked there were no Redacted women she'd missed. She knew there wasn't, but equally, she knew she'd never stop worrying about it if she didn't check.

Once she was sure the room was empty, she poured half the bottle of clear liquid over the chair and West's desk, saturating her notebooks. She then repeated the same processes in the two rooms upstairs, making sure to douse anything that looked flammable.

Finally, standing in the relative safety of the stone passageway, she threw the lamp back into the woodshed, waiting only to make sure the flames caught.

LII

It wasn't until they reached the assembly room that the uproar began. Brown suits were running to and fro frantically, while a crowd of students milled around, getting underfoot and gossiping in huddles. Dafi was standing in the centre of a group of Masters, lecturing them on the problems of West's management and how he'd known all along something like this would happen.

You don't know the half of it, Bea thought to herself.

Having a pretty good idea what it was that was causing all the trouble—after all, she was the one who'd fallen through the glass ceiling—Bea sidled past the hubbub as best she could, trying not to draw attention to herself. Mistasinon didn't make it very easy, shaking and shivering, his blue suit drawing attention. But thankfully, the brown suits were either too busy trying to find West or Barret or trying to keep the other recruits out of the assembly room to do more than frown at her as she made her way back to her room.

She managed to get her bedroom door open through the judicious use of a good kick, ignoring the stiffness in her leg as she did so. Mistasinon looked up, confused, and then drifted away again.

"Darling, have you seen—oh, my!" Chokey exclaimed, taking in the sight of them. "Here, let me help. Hemmings!"

Hemmings jumped up and took Mistasinon from Bea, carefully depositing him on her bed. The Plotter mumbled something which might have been a thank you or might have just been nonsense.

"What happened to him? Gosh, West didn't Redact him, did she?" Chokey said in her not-really-a-whisper.

Bea shook her head. "No. I did."

Chokey and Hemmings stared at her. For the first time since she'd met them, they were both completely lost for words.

Yawning, Bea considered resting against the wall and then realised what a stupid idea that was. She looked longingly at her bed, where Mistasinon was now sitting, gazing at his hands.

All she wanted to do was crawl into bed and sleep for a week. She'd even take the nightmares. Every part of her hurt, her head was pounding, her eyes stinging with tiredness.

Hemmings and Chokey were sharing confused glances, their eyes darting between each other, Bea and, finally, Mistasinon. Sighing, Bea went to her bag, still packed from the day of her meeting with West, and fished out some more birch leaf and devil's claw. Ignoring Chokey and Hemmings, she went into the bathroom, closed the door, and very slowly, very methodically, made herself another herbal infusion.

She sat on the toilet and sipped her drink, taking her time. There were a thousand things she needed to think about, but right now she was happy to just concentrate on the pungent, green tonic.

There was a knock on the door.

"Hi," Bea said.

Chokey pushed the door open. "Darling? We've given Mistasinon a blanket. I offered him some rum, but he didn't answer. He's stopped shaking, though. There's some more rum if you like?"

Bea smiled but declined. "I don't think my head could take it right now. Maybe later." She swallowed the last of her drink, and they re-joined Hemmings.

Mistasinon had indeed stopped shaking. He was wrapped up in Chokey's quilt, the jolly pink and white patchwork at odds with his sickly pallor.

Kneeling down next to him, Bea rested her hand on his thigh. "Mistasinon?"

He looked up, blinking.

"I'm just going to step outside, with Chokey and Hemmings. Will you be alright?"

A beat, and then he nodded. "... Yes. It's just so quiet. I feel empty."

Bea pressed her lips together. She didn't really know how to respond, so she just squeezed his leg in what she hoped was a comforting manner. Standing, she signalled to Chokey and Hemmings to follow her.

As soon as the door was closed, Hemmings turned on her.

"What in the five hells do you mean, you Redacted him?" he demanded, furious. "How *dare* you? Redaction's the epitome of everything wrong with it all! How can you possibly justify—"

Chokey rested a hand on his arm, silencing him. "Darling, do calm down. Let her explain."

"Honestly, I'm not sure I can," Bea said, trying to keep the exhaustion out of her voice. "West... did something to him. He was dying. I had to make a choice, and there wasn't any time to think it through. I gave him some of the Letheinate—"

"The what, darling?"

"Oh. That's what West called her Redaction drink. She had this whole room set up with bottles and jars and machinery. I don't know how she did it, but she found a way to turn the Erasers into this weird drink. That's what she must have used on the women. Anyway. What was I saying?"

"That there wasn't any time," Chokey prompted. "So you gave him some of this Redaction stuff."

"Oh, yes. Right." Bea pinched the bridge of her nose. "Yes. So, West left. I don't know what happened to her. But he was dying, and it was the only thing I could think of, other than letting him die, I mean."

Hemmings' shoulders relaxed. "Oh. Well, that makes more sense. It's only in moments of extremity that we truly behave as ourselves. It sounds like you did very well," he added.

Bea wondered if he'd still think that if he knew she'd saved the life of the Beast. Aloud, she asked, "What about Melly and the Redacted women?"

Chokey filled her in, and then explained that she and Hemmings had returned to find the whole Academy in absolute pandemonium. They'd debated going back to the room with the secret passageway but had decided that they were probably more likely to draw the brown suits there, what with them running around, looking for West and Barret. So they'd come back to their room and waited, growing ever more anxious.

"It'll be worse when they realise West isn't here," Chokey finished.

Stifling another yawn, Bea was about to answer when someone shoved her from behind.

346

"This is your fault, isn't it?"

Carol was shaking with anger, her golden eyes narrow slits.

"Oh, do shut up, Althaus," Chokey said.

"Go get lost down a mine, Ogrechoker, I'm not talking to you."

Hemmings drew himself up to his full height, stepping in front of Chokey and Bea. "Don't you speak to my sister like that, you nasty little bully."

Carol opened her mouth to scream at Hemmings.

"Just… Just stop it, all of you," Bea said, putting her hands up. "Right. Carol. Yes, whatever is happening, I can absolutely promise you it's my fault, cross my heart and really, seriously, hope to die—at least that way I might finally get some rest. Now, please, what exactly is it I've done? Everyone knows about the assembly room," she added, in the hope of speeding things along. "That was definitely me."

It was almost worth everything that had happened to see the expression on Carol's face. The little imp seemed entirely thrown.

"You haven't heard?"

Bea wondered for a moment if they'd found West's Letheination workshop but quickly dismissed the idea. It was way out in the storm, in a stone building; the fire she'd set wouldn't be noticeable from the Academy, and she doubted anyone else even knew the building existed.

"Heard what?"

"They're closing the Academy. West's missing, her troll too. The assembly room is ruined, and the storm's getting in. The Content Department's coming in the morning to take us all back. It's over."

Bea tried very hard to hide her relief, not wanting to set Carol off again. "What will happen to all the recruits?"

"I don't know. I expect their lot will be alright," Carol huffed, glaring at Chokey and Hemmings. "Mummy and Daddy will see to that. But I'll never be an FME now, and I know you've got something to do with it. They never should have let a fairy in. You've literally destroyed the place. And everyone saw you, fawning over your Plotter, bold as brass, so I expect you'll get away with it too."

Chokey shook her head. "But they can't close it down. Mama's traded for our place here, she'll be absolutely furious."

347

F. D. Lee

"Good," Carol said. "It's nice to see one of you lot suffer for once." She turned to Bea, pointing a finger in her face. "And I'll get you, cabbage mother, you see if I don't."

Carol spun on her heel and marched off, leaving the three of them standing in the hallway.

"Well, that was fun," Bea said. "I actually think I might be warming to Carol. At least she's consistent."

She glanced at the door to their room. Hemmings and Chokey followed her gaze.

"Do you want us to come back in with you?" Hemmings asked.

For a moment, Bea considered it. Hemmings and Chokey could watch Mistasinon, and she could go to bed. But of course, she knew that wasn't what was going to happen—she didn't need West's curse to see this particular future.

"Better not," she said. "I'm sorry. Is there somewhere you can go?"

"Oh yes, darling, of course," Chokey answered, taking Hemmings by the hand. "I dare say Tiff's got room. Besides, I want to find out what's happening. Mama really will be *frite-fully* cross if we are being turfed out. Come on, Hemmings."

Bea watched them go, took a deep breath, and stepped back into the bedroom, closing the door softly behind her.

LIII

Mistasinon was still on her bed, but he'd taken off Chokey's quilt and folded it neatly on the floor. He looked up when Bea came in, and then quickly looked away. At least he seemed more compos mentis, now. She noticed the glass of rum Chokey had offered him was empty.

"How are you feeling?" Bea asked him.

"Oh. Um. Yes. Better."

"Good."

Bea dithered for a moment and then joined him on the bed, more out of sheer exhaustion than anything else. Or, rather, anything she was prepared to admit to.

They sat for a long while, watching the wall. Bea kicked her legs up in front of her, so they were sticking out from the bed.

"So," she said, concentrating on her boots. "You knew West, before all this?"

Next to her, she heard Mistasinon draw in a deep breath.

"Yes. I mean, not personally. But her story was… it was quite famous."

"What happened to her? I caught bits of it. Someone—a mortal god?—punished her for something by making her see the future?"

"Yes, but no one would believe her prophecies. They all thought she was mad, that she was making it up. They even blamed her for what happened to her; you don't deny the Gods, not unless you're asking to be punished."

Bea kept her eyes on her feet, kicking them up and down. The rhythm was comforting, in a strange way. "And that's what happened to you when you were in the other world? The one you're really from?"

It seemed like Mistasinon wasn't going to answer. But then he said, very quietly, "You know what I am?"

"I heard," Bea said, still not looking at him.

"So you know I'm the—"

349

"I know what you *were*," Bea interrupted. "I'm not sure yet what you are."

She could feel his confusion, radiating off him like heat. She desperately wanted to look at him, but she knew it would be harder if she did. "What happened to you, I mean before you came to the Land?"

"I made a deal to guard the Shadow Land, so that my brother, Orthrus, could live a normal life," Mistasinon said. "Or as close to normal as he could, given what he was. But a hero killed him, and he ended up in the Shadow Land anyway."

"But he was with you?"

"Yes. But he shouldn't have been. The Shadow Land was... It wasn't a good place. I didn't want him there, but I accepted it as my master's choice," Mistasinon continued, his voice distant. "I *was* angry, though. The Shadow Master knew it, I think. He didn't break his word often. He was proud, honest, and I suppose... I think my anger shamed him."

Bea wanted to interrupt him, then. She wanted to tell him that from what she could gather, this 'Shadow Master' had shamed himself, but she held her tongue, letting Mistasinon continue.

"Anyway, sometime later—time was strange there, it didn't always make sense—but sometime later, the hero who murdered my brother arrived in the Shadow Land. He wasn't dead, he snuck in. And I thought then... I thought my master was going to make it right. I thought he would punish the hero. I remember... I remember watching them talk, all three of me certain that it was going to work out."

"But it didn't?"

Mistasinon let out a bitter laugh. "No. The Shadow Master bargained us away. He let the hero take us, a trophy to give to someone else. We, I, couldn't understand what we'd done wrong. I'd never misbehaved. Never been disloyal. Only angry... Angry he let my brother die."

Bea stole a glance at him. His hands were gripping his knees, his knuckles white, his head bowed.

"But I went. I went with the hero because that's what the Shadow Master wanted me to do. I was always good. Until I escaped. We ran away from the hero. I tried to find my way back," Mistasinon said, a sudden urgency in his voice. "I don't think the Shadow Master meant to give me away. I think it was a mistake. But when we tried to find our way back, I couldn't. The Shadow Land's confusing, even for me. We wandered, I don't know how long, in the Underworld, and then we heard the music, followed it…"

"Music?"

"Yes, a kind of drumming… Deep, almost inside you, but outside you, too. It's hard to explain. I followed it until it was so loud, it overwhelmed us. And then…. And then we were in the Land of the Fae. West said she chose Thaiana when she came through. I don't remember if I chose the Land, or if we just ended up there."

Mistasinon stopped, swallowed.

"But the Land, Ænathlin, the ruins of the other cities, it was similar, in a way. Perhaps that's why I ended up there. All the fae, playing Gods, telling their stories. No rules. No boundaries. I hated it, but still… It was familiar. Then the Teller found us and told me his plan. And it made sense. If I helped him, all that cruelty would stop."

Then he said, more quietly, "And it was… nice… to have someone telling us what to do again, even if it was hurting people. To have a master."

Sighing, Bea finally forced herself to turn and face him. "How do you feel now?"

Mistasinon was still staring at his hands, his hair falling across his face. "The Letheinate… It did something to me. Am I… Am I alone?"

Bea pressed her lips together. She'd been thinking about that. It could be that the Letheination process had Redacted something in him, that was true. But she wasn't entirely certain that he hadn't died on that table.

Something had been uncovered in West's basement, and maybe it had needed to be so that it *could* die.

"I don't know which me I am," Mistasinon mumbled. "I don't know who I am."

"Look at me," Bea instructed. He did so. "You're you—all of you. No one is just one thing. That's just… how it is."

She remembered what Hemmings had said about everyone being a leaf, but also being part of the tree.

"It's easier, I think, if you're honest with yourself. If you face up to who you are and where you come from... It's confusing sometimes, and sometimes it isn't. But ultimately, we have to make the best choices we can, when we get the chance to make them."

"I never had to make a choice before I was changed. I just... I did what my master told me to do. I was good. The Teller Cared About Me and—"

"Enough of that," Bea snapped. "I don't imagine I'll ever really understand what it was like for you, but now you have to make your own decisions, for yourself, based on what *you* think is right. And you have to be prepared to answer for them, and how your choices affect the world."

"But I tried to. I was trying to be better, to make everything right. I know I'm a monster."

"You're not a monster," Bea said, more gently. "The Beast was, yes, and you're going to have to make that right, somehow. But it sounds to me like the... the Cerberus was a victim of some very bad men. And now you're Mistasinon. That's who I saved."

Outside the snow fell against the window, insulating them from the world. The wind battered the walls of the Academy, but it couldn't find a way in. Mistasinon cocked his head, listening to it.

"Thank you. For saving me," he said.

"Mmm. Thank me by being a good person. It's all going to get very messy if anyone ever finds out what you used to be." A yawn escaped her. "Sorry. I'm not bored, I promise."

For the first time since she came into the room, he looked at her properly.

"Are you alright?"

"I'm just tired. It's been a long day. Hells, it's been a long six months. And I haven't been sleeping well."

Mistasinon got up from the bed. "I'll go, let you get some sleep."

"You can stay here," Bea heard herself say. "If you want to," she added.

"I don't..."

"Or go. Your choice. But I'm going to sleep, whether you're here or not. I honestly don't think I could stay awake, even if I wanted to."

Only pausing to kick her boots off, Bea lay down on her bed and pulled the covers over her. She could feel her heart beating and decided not to examine the reason why too closely.

One, two, three, four… She counted in her head, trying to distract herself.

And then she felt a weight on the mattress. She lifted her head up. Mistasinon was sitting at her feet. He took his jacket and shoes off and started to settle himself at the foot of the bed. She moved over slightly and lifted up the covers. After a moment's hesitation, he crawled up the bed, settling in next to her.

Bea closed her eyes, listening to the wind and the soft sound of Mistasinon breathing, his body warming her.

And for the first time in months, she slept soundly.

The story continues in *The Princess And The Orrery*

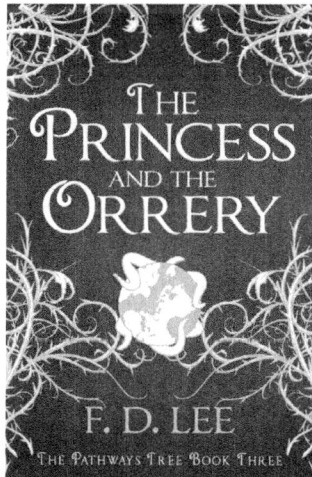

Seven, the last surviving genie, is out for revenge.

Betrayed by the woman he loves, kidnapped, tortured, and separated from the source of his power, Seven's only goal is to punish the people who have wronged him.

That is until he's forced to work with Amelia.

Amelia is bright, precocious and does *not* have time for his vendetta. She is working on a machine designed to map the planets, an orrery, and has been promised a permanent home with the Sisterhood of Cultivators if she succeeds. The only problem is, the orrery is a lot more than a simple machine—it is also a doorway. And when a door is left open, anything might come through...

When Seven realises what it is Amelia is building and the danger it presents, he must make a choice—the hardest choice he has ever faced: to act selflessly.

Can Seven put aside his own wishes in order to play the hero and save the world?

And, more importantly, does he even want to?

Get your copy today!
Available in ebook, paperback, and audiobook

https://www.bklnk.com/B07L4ND1Q8
(this link will redirect to your local Amazon store)

Thank you for reading. If you have a minute to leave an honest review, that would be very much appreciated. Your review will help others decide if they want to read this book—it need only be a line or two, and makes a big difference!

https://www.bklnk.com/review/B01LZ0XIWC
(Link will auto-direct to your local Amazon store)

Sign up for my newsletter to get access to bonus unpublished material and deleted scenes, early access to new titles, and information about special offers. As a subscriber, you can also join our secret Facebook group.

http://eepurl.com/dvj-fv

Author's Note

The numerical system that Bea is forced to memorise while studying at the Academy is based on a real thing. Originally designed by Antti Aarne, the codex was later modified by Stith Thompson and, most recently, by Hans-Jörg Uther. The ATU, as it is known, is an amazing feat, and is well worth a wiki-binge. Having said that, I can see why Bea was less than impressed by having to commit such a system to memory.

Equally, the plot and character types that Dafi insists she learns are inspired by Joseph Campbell's work on mythologies and monomyths. The study of 'story' is a vast and complex field and again is well worth delving into. I particularly recommend Jonathan Gottschall's 'The Storytelling Animal', if you're interested.

Finally, in The Academy, I use the acronym ETPs for my Empty Protagonists. This was actually a lot trickier to settle on than it might at first appear. The actual name given to empty protagonists (at least on TV Tropes) is Empty Shell Protagonists, which for The Academy would abbreviate to ESPs. However, as ESP also stands for Extra-Sensory Perception—and I suspect is more commonly recognised as such—I decided to rejig the name to avoid people making the wrong inference.

I did consider using EVP, Empty Vessel Protagonists, but on researching it, I discovered that EVP also already exists and is actually a common term in ghost hunting circles (Electronic Voice Phenomenon). While I did consider EVP for nothing else but the sheer bliss of being *that* meta, in the end, I thought it might confuse things.

Thanks

Again, I'd like to take a moment to thank the following people for helping me through the process of writing this book.

Big thanks must firstly go to Jon, who helped me work out the storyline and how certain things would work (or not!) in terms of this book and future instalments. I am especially indebted to him for his knowledge of the classics and his patience in teaching me.

Equally, I am hugely indebted to Nina and Miranda for reading numerous drafts and making very sound comments, all of which greatly improved the book. Also huge thanks to Miranda and Alex for putting up with me banging on about this book when all they really wanted to do was get drunk and listen to Donovan. A truly noble sacrifice, and one for which I am eternally grateful.

Much thanks go to Kat and Tim, who both waded through the first complete draft, and were on point with their comments and critiques. Thanks also to Tim for designing the beautiful GenAm posters and the images of Bea and Seven—they are absolutely stunning. I also want to thank my husband, James, for once again supporting me throughout, and for putting up with long periods of 'widowhood' while I wrote.

I made the mistake of thinking writing a second book would be easier—it wasn't! But a difficult task was made infinitely more bearable thanks to these wonderful people.

Thanks too to Liz Rippington for her proofreading, comments and enthusiasm, all of which were very gratefully received! Thanks also to Jane Dixon-Smith for my beautiful cover—another classic.

My most humble thanks also to everyone who read The Fairy's Tale (in all its forms). Your enthusiasm and engagement with Bea and her misadventures is what has made this book possible. Thank you so much for taking the time to read it, and for following me on

Facebook and Twitter, liking, commenting and generally talking to me!

Writing is a very fun but very arduous process; knowing that it has a purpose and that people want to read your work is what makes it worthwhile. In that vein, I'd like to shout out to a few people especially: Emelia, Pam, Teddy, Jo, James, C.J., Glen, Lucinda, Linda, Mark, Paul, Penny, Roz, Sara, Lee, and Nick.

And finally, thank you for reading!

Printed in Great Britain
by Amazon

37147543R00205